THE
COBBLER'S
DAUGHTER

The Cobbler's Daughter by G. S. Singer

Copyright © 2019 G. S. Singer

Interior design by Jacqueline Cook
Front cover design by Mad Designs
Edited by Karissa Harlow and Ellen Schlossberg

ISBN: 978-1-61179-349-9 (Paperback)

ISBN: 978-1-61179-350-5 (e-book)

BISAC Subject Headings:
FIC002000 FICTION / Action & Adventure
FIC027170 FICTION / Romance / Historical / Victorian

Address all correspondence to:
Fireship Press, LLC
P.O. Box 68412
Tucson, AZ 85737

Visit our website at:
www.fireshippress.com

THE
COBBLER'S
DAUGHTER

G. S. SINGER

FIRESHIP
PRESS

Chapter One

Brittan Salter craved revenge. Not because he missed the joy girls at Fatima's on Rue des Soeurs, and not because he couldn't bet on the camel races. He didn't blame the prison sergeant for stealing his clothes and giving him rags, and he wasn't upset that his meals, when he got them, tasted like sawdust soaked in brine. Being sentenced without a trial two months ago by what passed for a judge in this country was not the reason he was angry, nor was it because he'd only managed to insult the Khedive of Egypt, Isma'il the Magnificent, twice before being thrown to the ground and arrested. Even his appointment today at sunrise to be shot through the heart by twelve, under-trained riflemen did not raise his ire to the point of revenge. The whippings, however, did.

How they yearned to hear him whimper as they tied him to the post. Longed for him to scream when the lash ripped skin from flesh. Ached to see him tremble in the pause between each strike when fire burned through his nerves and blood coursed down his back.

By God, they could cut the meat from his bones inch by inch and he would not give them satisfaction. For the thousandth time, he uttered the vow that kept him alive.

"The Khedive will pay for every stripe."

The cadence of boot steps and the click of rifles echoed from the courtyard. Britt struggled to his feet. Daybreak. The firing squad was moving into position.

Like every morning since his incarceration, he pushed his way through the stink and filth of a hundred sleeping men, over rat holes and around piles of excrement. When he reached the wall, his fingers found the ancient handholds and, despite his wounds, he climbed the centuries-old block. High above the floor, light from a small window pierced the hazy air. He pressed his cheeks to the bars.

Dawn lit the rooftops of Alexandria. Farther out, the Mediterranean glistened. Clippers and steamships crowded the harbor, their stacks and rigging silhouetted against a clear, red sky. Egypt was beautiful; he'd give it that. But with the Confederacy gone now seven years, and the world hungry for cotton, a flood of gold had turned the Khedive from monarch to tyrant.

"...pay for every stripe."

Beneath him in the cell, keys jangled and hinges squealed. The soldiers had come for him. How long did he have? One minute? Two? Britt closed his eyes and waited.

Laughter broke the stillness. His eyes opened. In the square below the prison, children ran between the tents and stalls of the marketplace. They stole figs from a woman in black, who bit her forefinger and swore. Turbaned Bedouins grinned. In open doorways, old men puffed their pipes and nodded.

Britt smiled. Even under a despot's thumb, life goes on. When the rifles were aimed at his chest, and the blindfold tied over his eyes, he would peer into the blackness and see these images: the children, the figs, the woman, the Bedouins, the doorways, the old men.

His gaze returned to the doorways. Near the middle of the square, that door off by itself, why had it been painted blue? As he pondered, the blue door opened, and a man in a gray burnoose stepped into the street.

Britt squinted into the rising sun. The man was taller than most Egyptians and crossed the square with a purposeful stride. When he reached a large, one-wheeled barrow, he flipped a coin to a boy who stood guard. The boy ran off as the man in the gray burnoose adjusted something amid the sacks piled six or seven high in the barrow.

The barrow seemed unusually heavy for one filled only with sacks of grain, and the man had great difficulty lifting the handles and maneuvering it across the rutted street. When man and barrow had traveled no farther than the prison wall, the barrow wobbled and fell, and the sacks tumbled against the stones.

Oddly, the man in the gray burnoose made no effort to lift the sacks or even right the barrow. Instead, he turned and hurried away. Halfway across the street, a lock of blond flashed from under his hood. And there, a boot shined black beneath the hem of his burnoose. At the blue door, the man stopped and faced the prison. He raised a single index finger high above his head, held it a moment, then disappeared inside.

Britt eyed the still open blue door and wondered what he had witnessed. His gaze shifted to the barrow tipped against the prison wall. Faint against the early light, smoke rose from the sacks of grain.

Counting quietly, he climbed to the floor. Excitement and apprehension filled his heart, pounding hard in time with the seconds passing over his lips. *Eight, nine, ten…* Across the cell, the sergeant and two soldiers were searching for him, rousting the prisoners one by one.

Britt bent low and weaved between the murderers and thieves, awake now and arguing amongst themselves. Whispering numbers through the teens, he tore off bits of cloth from the tatters that covered his body and stuffed them into his ears. By the time he counted to twenty-one, he'd arrived at the farthest end of the cell.

A fleshy prisoner studied him from the corner. "To possess such muscles, your mother must have bred with a camel." He spat into the dirt. "What do you want, giant?"

Britt barely heard him through the wadding in his ears. He knew the man as an informer. "I want that corner."

Two, lean, bare-chested men rose from the floor and stood. The informer pointed toward the soldiers working their way closer, examining each prisoner's face. "Leave, son of a whore, before I call to the sergeant."

Britt clenched his fists and tried to keep the numbers in his head. *Thirty. Thirty-one.* "The men you betrayed await you in hell."

The informer swung. Britt dodged and drove his knuckles into the man's face. The informer's head crashed back into the wall. *Thirty-five.* Britt wrapped his arm around the man's neck and threw him from the corner. *Thirty-seven.* The informer's companions sprang. Britt kneed one in the gut and elbowed the other in the throat. They fell away as the informer returned, fists swinging, blood streaming from his nose. *Forty-two.*

A line of prisoners gathered to watch. They cheered when Britt blocked the informer's punches and hit him in the stomach. *Forty-seven.* The man doubled over. Britt caught him by the waist and spun him around. *Fifty.* He locked the man's flailing arms behind his back. *Fifty-three.* He pulled the informer down on top of him where floor and walls met. *Fifty-six. Fifty-seven.* The sergeant and his soldiers had reached the barricade of shouting prisoners. *Fifty-nine.* Britt closed his eyes and spoke the last number aloud. *"Sixty."*

Nothing happened.

"Damnation!" Britt cursed and kept counting. *Sixty-one, sixty-two.* Still nothing. *Sixty-three, Sixty-four.*

The informer fought to get free. Britt strengthened his grip. *Something was wrong. His timing was off, or he'd miscounted. A single finger meant one minute. Sixty seconds. Working in coal mines, he'd counted it a thousand times.*

Sixty-six. Sixty-seven. Britt cracked one eyelid. The soldiers had punched through the ring of prisoners. Pistol aimed, the sergeant shouted for him to surrender. *Seventy. Seventy-one.* The informer stopped fighting and began to laugh.

The numbers in Britt's head vanished. *The man in the burnoose... His face was in shadow... but the blond hair, the index finger...*

The informer laughed louder. Prisoners joined in. The sergeant's pistol cracked. Britt jerked forward. Chips flew from the stones behind his head.

The sacks, the smoke, the boot, the barrow, the man in the burnoose... Had it all been a mistake? Had everything he'd seen been the fantasy of a doomed man?

The far wall exploded in a deafening boom. Smoke and debris filled the cell with darkness. Something heavy struck the informer's gut making him convulse and shake. Britt held tight and savored the smell of the detonation.

The informer shuddered then relaxed. When the ring of the blast dissipated, Britt pulled the cloth from his ears and listened. Cries and moans were all he heard.

He pushed the informer's body to the floor. Pulverized masonry saturated the air like silt in muddy water. Brown sunlight streamed through a jagged, wagon-sized hole. The concussion had knocked everyone down; sergeant, soldiers, and prisoners lay scattered about.

Slowly, stunned inmates began to rise and stumble toward the gaping light. Britt crawled over shattered stones and injured men. At the edge of the hole, he stretched his body over the rubble and opened his eyes in a dead man's stare. Dust-covered prisoners staggered past him. They climbed out the hole, gathered in the ruined marketplace, and gazed numbly at the open sky.

Britt didn't flinch at the staccato bang of the Gatling gun high above him on the prison wall, nor wince as inmates spun to earth, flesh torn away in chunks, rags red with gore. From his corpse-like pose, he watched the prisoners in the marketplace wake from their trance and run. He lay perfectly still as twenty more soldiers entered the cell, raced past him and fanned from the wall's breach like hornets from a punctured hive. He saw their boots trample tents and stalls and heard their rifles snap. He watched them chase prisoners through screaming crowds, down the streets and out beyond the marketplace.

When the soldiers had gone, and the melee calmed to a scene of sobbing women and cursing merchants, Britt leaped through the hole and dashed toward the open blue door. At the threshold, two arms jerked him inside.

Britt embraced his old friend. "Damn your bones, Lockie. Did you have to wait until the last second?"

"I couldnae act until the Khedive left and his soldiers relaxed."

Britt pulled away, eyes keen. "How long has the bastard been gone?"

The Scotsman swept a gray robe from a hook. "His Blasted Magnificence left on the royal yacht day before yesterday. We've got to hurry. I've tickets on a paddle steamer with a load of cotton. She's a fast boat and, with the king stopping in Italy and Great Britain, we'll beat him to New York by a month."

Teeth clenched against the pain, Britt shrugged off his filthy rags. He felt Lockie's eyes linger on the ooze and scabs that striped his back.

"Villains cut you good, didn't they, lad?"

Britt shook on the robe. "That they did, Lockie. And when we reach New York, king or not, the Khedive will pay for every stripe."

Chapter Two

A stranger pointed me to the Broadway Omnibus. Ten minutes later, the spire of Trinity Church emerged from the fog like an accusing finger. Stained glass blurred against brick, and the hands of the clock aligned north and south. As we rumbled past Liberty Street, the bells began a woeful peal. Six o' clock. I was late for work.

The conductor swayed toward me down the crowded aisle. "Wall Street," he shouted above the tolling bells, "next stop." He bent close and touched the bill of his cap. "Don't I know you?"

His liquored breath wrinkled my nose. Eager to disembark, I gathered my bag and portfolio.

"You're Miss Crispin," he announced, "Miss Duncan's new friend."

Several riders stared. "Yes," I said, hoping the bells muted my voice. "Jennifer Crispin."

His gaze passed over the crowded car then returned. "Where is Miss Duncan? Not ill, I trust."

Despite his inebriation, I wondered if he might help. Cleo Duncan, my roommate, had not been seen since yesterday before lunch, nor had her bed been slept in last night. Although an emancipated woman is obliged to seek no one's permission, Cleo was much too considerate to vanish without a word.

I stood as the sixth and final bell faded. "No, not ill. She—"

The omnibus lurched to a halt. Departing passengers shoved me toward the exit. I had barely lifted the hem of my dress and stepped to the pavement before they pushed me aside. Counting clerks and stock traders, by the look of their ties and vests, they rushed down Wall Street toward the rising sun.

I raced after them, imagining the disapproving stare of my new employer when I offered my excuse. Without Cleo to guide me through the maze of omnibus stops, intersections, and unyielding hacks, my solitary journey from Dey Street had been both maddening and miraculous. Surely, arriving a few minutes past the hour on my third day of work would not result in dismissal.

Street sweepers tended a mountain of manure near the old Customs House. I pinched my nose and crossed to Broad Street careful to keep my black, practical boots free from stain. Directions had never come easily to me and, although up until now my attempt to recall the street corners and turns had been inadequate, from this point on I was certain of my course.

With my destination not fifty feet ahead, a mighty cheer startled me. Drumbeats followed, so loud they overwhelmed not only the shuffle of shoe leather on pavement but also the clatter of carriage wheels on cobblestone. The clerks and stock traders around me scarcely took notice, nor did the shopkeepers, who were busy sweeping yesterday's dirt from their stores. I was not surprised. Nothing, I suspect, could turn a New Yorker's head, not even bloody murder on the sidewalk. *Murder!* Cleo's warnings came back to me. Killers stalked the city, sexual deviants, even white slavers. As the cheers and drumbeats grew louder, I weaved and bobbed among the foot traffic, praying the commotion ahead bore no relation to her disappearance.

Arriving at the storefront that housed my workplace, I pushed through a throng of onlookers and saw several war veterans in Union blue beating furiously on drums. Behind them, a mob shook placards and waved flags. A gentleman with red and white ribbons on his coat offered leaflets to passersby. In front of all, two women in black bonnets and machine-made dresses carried a "NO VOTES FOR

WOMEN" sign.

Anti-suffragettes! I should have known. With the upcoming presidential election, their kind would be chanting on every corner. Disgusted, I stepped up to the office door, but, as I searched my bag for the key, three protesters bent their arms and threw.

I arched backward. The projectiles passed within an inch of my face and smacked against the window beside me. A splatter of white eggshell and yellow ooze ran from the words: *Talmadge's Weekly Newspaper*.

The mob bellowed a great hurrah. Drumbeats reverberated off buildings. Signs shook. Flags waved. Catcalls filled the air.

The tumult died. I stood up straight. My corset, ever an ill-fitting foundation, pinched me severely. Tugging at it through my dress, I noticed a banner painted with my employer's portrait newly stretched across the bricks. Beside her face, bold letters spelled out: *Glorianna Talmadge, President for 1872.*

These demonstrators, I realized, had not chosen this location by chance. They came to protest the lady on the banner, well-known, newspaper publisher, champion of feminine rights, my employer, and now, apparently, the first woman to run for president. Fearing further assault, I lodged my portfolio under my arm and pushed the key into the lock.

While I strove to make the rusty lock turn, a solitary policeman arrived. He pointed his club at the three women who threw the eggs, but they paid him no mind. One of them shook her fist at me. Anticipating the worst, I wiggled the key harder.

"*Fornicator!*" the lady screamed, hurling the insult like an anarchist's bomb. She and her companions hefted more eggs. Never one to retreat, I glared at them and stuck out my tongue. The women threw again. I held up my portfolio and ducked. Yolk and shell exploded across Glorianna's likeness.

Goodness, I thought, still cowed behind my shield. The whoops and hollers from the crowd sounded more like rowdies at a street fight than civilized men and women. These people were dangerous and getting bolder with each passing minute. What would they throw five days hence, on November fifth, the day of the presidential election?

Cabbages? Rocks? Beer bottles full of flaming lamp oil? I rose to full height. If Glorianna Talmadge had the fortitude to announce herself the first female candidate for president, then I had the pluck to arrive at work despite a gang of malcontent demonstrators.

The tweet of the policeman's whistle interrupted my thoughts. Arms extended, the officer attempted to shoo the troublemakers to the edge of the sidewalk, but, emboldened by the accuracy of their eggs, the mob shouted louder, chanting:

"Stay in the kitchen!
No votes for women!
Stay in the kitchen!
No votes for women!"

The drumbeats rose in frequency and volume. *"Harlots!"* someone yelled. *"Sodomites!"* cried another. *"No Free Love! No woman president!"*

I wrenched the key hard, lurched into the office, and locked the door.

Surrounded by heavy file cabinets and layout tables, immersed in the smell of gaslights and newsprint, I finally felt safe. Seeing that neither Glorianna nor the other office girls had arrived, I slid quietly behind my desk, opened my portfolio, and wet my pen. As any aspiring journalist would, I began to write about the morning's events. With not a full page completed, the lock clicked, the door burst open, and Violet Obermyer stumbled inside.

Egg white glistened in her hair. Yolk dripped off her nose. Bits of eggshell accented the tortoise buttons of her tan serge suit. She turned the lock then wobbled toward me, portly in her size six shoes.

At my desk, she wiped her cheek with the meat of her thumb and gave her wrist a flick. Yellow dots burst across my paper. "Where is she?" Violet asked in the drab tone of a battle-stunned soldier.

Her concern for my roommate gave me heart. "Cleo vanished yesterday. I fear she's been kidnapped—or worse."

Violet snapped from her daze and huffed a bead of yolk off her nose. "Not Cleo. Glorianna." Before I could answer, she dropped into a chair by Cleo's empty desk and shook her head. "Never mind. It doesn't matter. For twenty years I've worked to change this wretched planet, and what has it gotten me? Eggs!"

Violet was *Talmadge's Weekly's* top writer. By *working to change the world* she referred, of course, to her essays on contraception, birth control, and woman's suffrage. But provocative as those writings were, her most forbidden articles professed the doctrine of Free Love, the notion that women could have sexual relations with whomever they wished, whenever they wished. If men could act like rutting beasts, she wrote, why not women? Intellectually, I accepted the premise, although the thought of such promiscuous behavior made my cheeks tint and my legs weak.

I shook a handkerchief from my purse and wiped at her cheeks. "Violet, go home and wash up. Have some hot tea. These lunatics will go away after the election, you'll see."

"Horse spit!" She snatched the handkerchief from my hand and dabbed at her dress. "Anthony Comstock and his lackeys are scouring the city. Whisper the words contraceptive or Free Love and his Society for the Prevention of Vice will track you down and drag you off to jail. Presidential election be damned; I'm marrying John."

I almost burst my corset. "The crapper salesman?"

Violet stopped dabbing and looked up. "Sanitary appliances."

I contemplated the term momentarily. "But your articles? Your followers? You can't become a…a…housewife."

Violet's back straightened. Her face glowed. Her eyes shined. "Can and will. I'll bake pies. I'll dust shelves. I'll make beds. I may even produce offspring."

I was horror-struck. "But Violet, what about Free Love?"

Wistful sorrow befell Violet's splattered face. She gave back my handkerchief then cupped my cheeks with chubby hands. "Jenny," she sighed, "sweet, innocent Jenny. I had hoped we could become closer, but I'm afraid it's not meant to be."

Uncomfortable with this intimacy, I tried to pull away, but her eyes flared and she seized my lapels.

"And when I'm married, and when John is flopping about on top of me like a beached mullet, when he's snorting and grunting like a hog, I'll close my eyes and think of you."

I froze in place. What the devil was Violet talking about?

"Listen," she said, yanking me even closer, breath hot on my face. "The fight isn't over. You'll pick up the banner. You'll carry it for me, for Glorianna, and for all the oppressed women of the world."

Still distraught over Cleo's disappearance, the enormity of Violet's words crushed me. "All oppressed women?" I squeaked. "But I'm only the filing clerk. Besides, Glorianna won't even look at my writing."

Violet released my jacket. As I fell back against my seat, she wedged a pair of reading glasses on her nose and swept up my egg-splattered papers. Her pupils marched left to right across the article with military precision and, despite her deepening frown, my spirits soared. Halfway down the page, she dropped the paper on the desk.

"Well," she said, taking off her glasses and waving them back and forth, "you say you're a writer and that's good enough for me. But if you want to be famous, you'll need more confidence, more exposure, and most importantly, some assistance."

I was confused. "But I don't want to be famous. I just want to better the world."

Violet smiled as though I were ten. "Young lady," she cooed, "fame is paramount. Without fame there are no readers, and without readers there is no change. If you wish to better the world, fame is essential."

Becoming a writer was more complex than I thought. "Then how do I achieve fame?"

She slipped her glasses into her purse. "Simple. You need just one article published, only one. Then, when the world sees how wonderful you write, they'll clamor for your work. They'll howl for your work. You'll be like Cinderella at the ball."

The words *By Jennifer Crispin* printed in twenty-point, bold-face type, suddenly materialized in my head.

Damn it, if fame is what a writer needed to change the world, then so be it. But as every writer knew, getting that first article published was always the hardest part. No editor in the city would consider the work of a complete unknown. Yet, as I gazed at Violet's face—the smear of egg now dried and cracking on her cheek—my resolve weakened.

"You'd actually help me?"

Violet gave a sly smile. "Well, I wanted it to be a surprise, but, if you must know, your career has already launched."

"What?"

"Done," she said, dusting her palms together as if brushing away my troubles. "Finished. Over. You will be published in the next *Weekly*, the very issue due out this afternoon."

"This afternoon? But how? You've only just read my article—and it's not even finished."

Violet swung her hand this way and that. "I know, I know." She leaned close, her voice a whisper. "I've signed your name to one of *my* articles."

I jumped from my chair. "One of *your* articles?"

"Can't you see it?" Violet asked, gently pulling me to my seat. "Your name will be on the front page. It doesn't matter who really wrote the article or even what it's about. It only matters that you get published. Once in print, everyone will just assume you're a good writer, and the offers will pour in."

I contemplated this notion with furrowed brow.

Maybe Violet was right. Her heart-felt cause was feminine suffrage and equality. Wouldn't she want to help a struggling member of her own sex? Hadn't she gone out of her way to read my writing and give me advice? In fact, the more I thought about it, the more I was convinced of Violet's good intentions. Still, shouldn't the woman have at least asked before signing my name to one of her own articles?

"I don't know if this is such a good idea."

Violet stood. "Don't be silly." She smoothed her dress. "Anyway, the article isn't much, just a little exposé."

"An exposé?"

Violet's eyes locked mine. "You want fame, don't you?" She shoved a folded paper into my hand. "When Glorianna arrives, give her this note. It's from Molly." She bent down, kissed me on the lips then hurried out the door.

I dragged my sleeve across my mouth. Through the window, I saw several eggs explode on her back as she scurried across the street with three women in pursuit. When she vanished around the corner, I tucked her note in my pocket then picked up my pen and touched it to my tongue. What on earth made Violet suddenly decide to help me?

Chapter Three

"Saint Michael, the archangel, defend us in battle. Be our protection against the wickedness and snares of the devil..."

Britt opened his eyes in the darkened room to see Lockie wrapped in a blanket like an Aberdeen Blackfriar, hands clasped in benediction, knees on the floorboards.

"May God rebuke him, we humbly pray; and do thou, O Prince of the heavenly host, by the power of God..."

"Lockie," Britt grumbled, digging the sleep from his eyes, "what the devil are you mumbling about?"

Lockie's features tightened. *"...cast into Hell, Satan, and all the evil spirits..."*

Britt glanced at the window shade ringed with light. "Damnation," he barked. "The sun's already up. Why didn't you wake me?"

Lockie slapped his hands on his thighs. "Can a man nae finish his prayers without your blaspheming?"

Britt cast off his covers and sat on the bed. The room was cold. He was hungry too. "You've never prayed a day in your life."

"Have so."

"When?"

"Once a year."

"What is today then—your birthday?"

Lockie gave a snort and clasped his hands again. "It's All Hallow's Eve."

"All Hallow's Eve? You're scared of ghosts?"

"Lord strike me, Britt, will you let me finish my prayer or nae?"

Britt got up and opened the shade. Sunrise washed the stained walls and worn furniture. He rinsed his face in the basin while Lockie continued. "...*who prowl throughout the world seeking the ruin of souls. Amen!*" The Scottsman cast Britt a damning squint then stood

"Now that you've made us late with your incantations," Britt said, shaking out his hands, "we must be off. His Majesty's ship arrives this morning, and I want to see for myself that no one has pushed the weasel overboard en route."

"A prayer is nae an incantation. "You're either too young or too dumb to understand tonight's danger. My second wife did nae believe either, and Satan took her in the throes of passion, All Hallow's Eve, 1857.

Britt stopped hopping into his pant leg. "She died in your arms?"

"Ach!" Lockie grunted. "Nae mine, her lover's. He died, too, poor bastard."

"Well," Britt said, stepping into the other leg, "tonight holds danger, I'll grant you that, but it won't come from the Dark One, his minions, or jealous lovers." He buttoned his pants then picked up his Hopkins & Allen pocket pistol from the table and spun the cylinder.

Lockie eyed the weapon and frowned. "I'd be ashamed to carry that wee pea popper."

Britt dropped the gun in his pocket. "I've more than enough steel in my pants, thank you."

Lockie pulled a large Smith and Wesson revolver halfway out of his shoulder holster then slammed it back down. "Maybe for the ladies."

Shrugging into their jackets, Britt and Lockie stepped lightly down the stairs, past the Gabler piano in the sitting room, and through the hallway hung with photographs. In the haberdashery below, they crept between tables packed with rows of brightly colored shirts. Loud snores behind an unmarked door seemed to rattle the gas lamps. Britt muted the bell over the front door with his hand, and the two men stepped into the cool of morning.

Clouds streaked the sky above silent cobblestones and dark brick. Wagons rattled and clattered. Britt rapped his knuckles on the side of a hansom parked at the curb. "Fulton Street Market."

The cabbie studied Britt a moment. "Two bits extra."

"What for," Britt asked, "disturbing your rest?"

The cabbie drew back, indignant. "A great hulking gent like yourself might give my Josie a limp."

Britt grabbed the roof rack and tipped the cab toward him off its wheels. "A great hulking gent like myself might give *you* a limp." Released, the carriage clunked to the pavement. He climbed inside.

Seated next to him, Lockie chuckled. "Great hulking gent…"

Britt held his tongue. Men of his height and muscular build were not common, but he'd be damned if some cabbie charged him extra for it.

At the market, Lockie tossed the driver a coin, and they walked north beside vacant oyster stands and shuttered crab shacks. Fish bones crunched beneath their feet. Men in rubber boots wheeled barrows of iced cod and haddock. Britt pinched his nose. "Smells worse here than that awful soup you savor."

Lockie wet his lips. "Aye, cullen skink. My first wife made it best."

At a shanty papered with posters soliciting money for the Great Whaling Disaster, they bought braised sardines and bottles of ginger beer. Breakfast in hand, the men walked down the wharf alongside Slip Twenty-three. Lockie found some crates for them to sit on, and side-by-side they ate.

Britt watched the sun rise through the clouds above Long Island. He hadn't seen a proper daybreak since he and Lockie arrived in New York a month ago. At least it seemed that way. Never mind the reek of garbage, the immensity of the view thrilled him. A hell of a sight better than staring into a wall of dirt while sweat dripped down your neck. All the view lacked was a mile of sheening water, but low fog obscured the entire East River.

Ship's bells and steam whistles were the only evidence the water

21

existed—that and the twin stone towers of Roebling's suspension bridge. Across the river, the Gothic arches of the Brooklyn tower barely peeked above the fog, while just a few hundred yards from where he sat, the Manhattan tower pierced its shroud like a New World Gibraltar.

Britt tried to envision the finished structure as he'd seen it drawn in the *Times*. Once completed, the two granite towers, each almost three hundred feet high, would support four steel cables thick as a man's waist. Smaller cables would suspend a causeway of steel and wood connecting Manhattan to Brooklyn. Separate lanes on the eighty-five-foot wide thoroughfare would carry trains, wagon traffic, and pedestrians.

By God, if men could hang a mile-long road a hundred feet above the water, they could build anything. What miracle would be wrought next? Lighter than air clipper ships? The proposed canal across Panama? There had even been speculation of a speaking telegraph and some manner of incandescence in a jar.

He and Lockie had spent four years in Egypt working on the Suez Canal, and during that short time, the wounds of war had all but healed. Commerce had so changed America, that their Egyptian adventure seemed little more than a pictorial in *Frank Leslie's Illustrated Newspaper*—except for the scars on his back, which pained him nightly. Now, after a month of hard labor, their task was finished. Today would be his brightest day, even if Lockie considered Halloween his darkest.

A long whistle blast drew a nudge from Lockie. The fog parted for a purple prow adorned with golden swirls and a sphinx figurehead. Indifferent to scattered bottles, wood, and debris, the ship divided the dark water as steam tugs nudged it alongside the wharf.

When the vessel was tied off, sailors in dress purple rolled tarpaulins off the hold. A steam derrick set atop iron girders dropped its hook into the abyss and birthed a dazzling purple coach. After bringing it weightlessly to the wharf, footmen led twin black Arabians down the gangplank and hitched them to the coach. With a blast of the ship's whistle, six guards wearing purple fezes and black frock coats marched from the ship's cabin and surrounded the fairytale coach.

To better see the spectacle, Britt and Lockie wandered down among a group of spectators gathered across from the ship. Mostly sailors, fishmongers, and newspapermen, their laughter and chitchat set Britt's senses on edge. Something was wrong. The Khedive never showed himself in public. But with the coach door open, and his escorts in place, it seemed as if the king might actually stroll down the gangplank unescorted.

Maybe democracy had gone to the fool's head. Could the monarch be so enamored with American freedom that he might expose himself to mortal threat as he never would in Egypt? In Alexandria, countless revolutionaries, outraged an Albanian overlord ruled Egypt, would gladly trade death by torture for a chance to thrust a dagger into the king's black heart. And yet, as Britt watched, here came the Khedive down the gangplank to his coach like Figaro waltzing to his barbering cart, smiling and waving to the citizenry of New York.

Something dark flushed over Britt, an emotion he hadn't felt since the lash had ignited his flesh like a burning fuse. Hate was the name for it. Hatred unbound. Hatred for a brutal despot gleefully aloof to the suffering and death he caused.

Blind, numb to his own actions, Britt reached into his pocket and wrapped his fingers around the butt of his pocket pistol. He drew out the weapon, aimed, and pulled the trigger.

Lockie's hand jammed the hammer as it dropped. Eyes creased with the pain, he eased the mechanism off his flesh. "Put that pea popper away," he whispered, pulling Britt toward him by the lapel. "Now is nae the time. We've worked too hard to throw it all aside."

Britt resisted then nodded, gaze downcast, embarrassed by his loss of control. He slipped the pistol into his pocket, and Lockie led him to shore end of the wharf.

The Khedive's coach rumbled toward them. Tassels and coattails flapping, guards hung from the running boards, roof, and trunk. As the carriage veered past, wind and dust shut Britt's eyes. Blinking away the grit, he watched the rig turn on South Street then make a quick jog onto Fletcher.

Britt raised his hand. A cab pulled from a line and stopped beside them. The Scotsman opened the door.

"Follow the Khedive," Britt said. "You'll catch him when his coach slows for traffic. Make sure he deposits his money in Bulwark Bank. I'll get our explosives. What's the gentleman's name?"

"Dandy Johnny." Lockie stepped into the carriage. "Yesterday, his gang, the Whyos, killed two guards at Bronx Station and stole a case of nitro. You'll find him on Mulberry at a bar called The Morgue."

"Meet me at Molly's," Britt shouted as the cab pulled away.

Chapter Four

I was still pondering Violet's sudden generosity when once again the lock clicked, the door opened, and the rest of the office girls rushed inside. All had been hit by eggs.

Abigail slammed the door and locked it. She patted the egg stains on her dress with shaky fingers. "What are we going to do?"

Laura reached for the knob. "I'm going home."

Mavis pushed her aside and threw an iron bolt on the door. "No one's going anywhere. It's too dangerous."

A cabbage hit the window and exploded. Everyone jumped. Through egg and bits of green, I saw that more protesters had joined the demonstration. A second policeman had arrived, but the two officers seemed unable to control the crowd.

"Glorianna should have been here by now," Abigail said, voice trembling.

Mavis huffed. "She won't come to work with those mad fools outside."

Tears wet Laura's eyes. "Glorianna's presidential campaign is the very reason those people want to break in and kill us."

I had heard enough. "Quiet, all of you. They don't want to kill us." Stares assaulted me. "And no one is breaking in, either."

Three loud bangs resounded off the front door.

"Here they come!" Laura yelled.

"Dear Lord," Abigail gasped.

Mavis snatched the poker from the coal stove and waved it over her head. "Let them try."

Knocks rang out again, louder. The women bundled close. I pried myself away and inched toward the sound. Abigail, Laura, and Mavis shuffled behind.

I stopped at the door. "Who is it?"

"It's me, damn it. Open up. Who threw the bolt?"

We vented a collective sigh. I withdrew the bolt and Glorianna Talmadge—feminist, birth control advocate, Free Lover, suffragette, vegetarian, communist, publisher, spiritualist, and, as of late, presidential candidate—burst into the room like a locomotive from a tunnel.

She wore Cuban heel boots, a frock coat, a white bow tie, and her trademark, of course—scandalous long pants. Her face was smooth, her hair jet black, her nose straight, and her cheekbones high. At thirty-four, she was still quite beautiful, with fiery eyes and a commanding voice.

She leaned an egg-splattered parasol against the wall. "Abigail, why aren't you at your desk? Mavis, has the paper arrived from the printers? Laura, what about the monthly figures?" The women fell in line at my back as I followed Glorianna across the room. She glanced behind. "Has anyone seen Violet?"

I summoned my strength and delivered the bad news. "Violet quit."

Glorianna braked to a halt. "Violet what?"

I stopped short. The girls bumped into me one after another. "Quit," I said, recovering from their impact. "A few minutes ago. She's had enough."

Glorianna looked up, eyes focused on a microscopic pinpoint a short distance from her nose. Gears and shafts seemed to turn in her head.

"Violet's getting married," I said.

Glorianna's trance broke. "The crapper salesman?"

I nodded. "Sanitary appliances."

Instantly, the storefront window shattered with a crash. Abigail screamed. Glass and cabbage sparkled in a cool rush of air. A rock clattered across my desk, skipped over Laura's ledgers, ricocheted off the top of the potbellied stove, and knocked the flue from its connection. Soot poured from the broken pipe, filling the office with a dismal haze.

Like a general standing amid the smoke of cannon fire, Glorianna turned a slow, cold eye on the demonstrators outside. They were jumping up and down, fists high, cheering wildly, the beat of their drums rumbling through the hole in the glass where the word *Weekly* used to be.

Another rock sailed through the window, this time taking out the word *Talmadge's*. It twirled across my desk and spun to a stop at the tip of Glorianna's unflinching Cuban heel boot. The candidate stared down at the projectile for a second then raised her head slowly, eyes bright, inspiration undimmed by smoke, smell, or broken glass. "Ladies, it's time to retreat. The Commodore is waiting in the alley."

Glorianna herded us to the back room and opened the rear door with her key. Two bays hitched to an indigo landau stamped the cobblestones. As I entered the carriage, my gaze fell first upon a pair of red, Moroccan slippers, then on the man himself. The Commodore uncrossed his legs and turned toward me.

Forehead high, hair curly white, cheeks carpeted with great muttonchops, he sat comfortably erect, head stiff, eyes keen, cigar fumes circling his great cauliflower face. I imagined him a bust on the dollar bill, the face of American capitalism. By owning six major railroads, four steamship lines, two senators, three congressmen, and the Secretary of Commerce, Commodore Cornelius Vanderbilt was, after all, the richest man in the world.

The carriage was small but plush, upholstered in white leather. Fresh flowers poked from glass vases by the doors. I sat across from the Commodore, who flicked his cigar out the window and grinned. "Delighted," he said bowing. He kissed my hand. Was that a lick? My skin was wet, slimy. Disgusted, I wiped it on the seat.

Abigail slid in next to me, then Mavis, then Laura. Glorianna entered last. With all the seats taken, she sat on the Commodore's lap. He wrapped his arm around her waist.

"My, my," the Commodore said, "so many beautiful ladies. I'm reminded of my last visit to Molly de Ford's brothel. In fact, I feel a growing urge to hurry there now."

Hearing Molly's name jarred my memory. I took the note from my pocket and handed it to Glorianna. "Violet asked me to give you this."

She opened the note, read it, and smiled.

The Commodore's left eyebrow rose. "The Khedive? I was told he deposited two million dollars in gold certificates at Bulwark Bank this morning."

Glorianna tucked the note into her breast pocket. "His Egyptian Highness is at Molly's right now, squandering his country's wealth on ladies of joy."

"Well," the Commodore said, rubbing his palms, "then we must route the royal passions to a more financial track."

"Exactly," Glorianna said. "Your Erie railroad stock comes to mind."

"And I'm eager to sell that worthless paper—at the right price, of course." The Commodore looked at me and winked.

I blushed at this unseemly attention and glanced away. The other girls peered nervously out the carriage windows, wary, no doubt, of angry protesters. When I looked again, Glorianna was jabbing the Commodore's gold cravat with her forefinger. "Do you remember Black Friday?"

The Commodore snatched up Glorianna's finger and kissed it. "How could I forget?"

"Indeed," Glorianna said, "but while others lost fortunes, you made one, didn't you?"

"Thanks to your help, my dumpling."

"Quite a wicked sum, too," Glorianna added.

"Of which you took half." The Commodore drew his tongue down Glorianna's finger. She glanced sidelong at me as if to flaunt the tycoon's interest. "But why waste all that money running for president?" the Commodore asked in a puzzled tone. When Glorianna did not respond, he bit her fingertip.

Glorianna jerked her digit from his mouth and examined it. Finding no injury she said, "You have your indulgences, too, Commodore, but I'll wager more profit will come of mine."

"I may not live to see that wager pay," the Commodore said with a grin. His demeanor darkened. "Then you'll help arrange the sale of my Erie stock?"

"Just as I helped you on Black Friday."

The Commodore stroked Glorianna's thigh. "And when our business is concluded?"

Glorianna smiled demurely and covered his hand with hers. "We'll see."

I listened with eyes wide. Cleo had mentioned that Glorianna and the Commodore were business associates, but this stimulating display made it seem like they were so much more. I'd never seen this side of Glorianna, never seen her act the temptress. Maybe she really believed in Free Love.

"May we go now?" Abigail pleaded.

The Commodore took a speaking tube from its hook and blew. A low whistle sounded somewhere outside. Remembering my portfolio and article lying on the desk, I jumped up and squeezed my way toward the door.

The Commodore touched my ankle and slid his leathery fingers up my calf. "Where are you going, my plum?"

Embarrassed and alarmed, I brushed away his hand. "I— I've forgotten something."

Glorianna shot me a stare. "Jenny. We've tarried too long."

"I'll only be a moment," I said. Once outside, I rushed across the alley and through the back door.

Acrid smoke filled the office. I held my nose and crunched across the glass-strewn floor. More glass covered the open portfolio lying on my desk. I raked the jagged pieces aside with my purse and lifted my papers. They hung like rags. Looking past the ruined pages and out the broken window, a shard-framed image burned into my mind.

The protester's numbers had swelled to fifty or sixty. Signs and flags jostled above their heads. Ten or twelve more policemen had arrived.

They stood like a human chain, holding hands, bowing outward against the pressure of the mob. An officer on horseback trotted back and forth in the street. Drumbeats and chants split the air.

"No Free Love!
No Free Love!
No Free Love!"

Dread filled me. I stuffed the papers into their leather case then backed away from the shattered window. Anxiety nipped as I hurried between the desks and pushed open the back door.

The Commodore's carriage was gone.

Stunned, I stepped inside and closed the door. After a moment, I opened the door and looked again. The carriage was unmistakably gone.

My senses reeled. Where did they go? Why had they left? Couldn't they wait? I'd only been a minute. I stepped a few paces into the alley and looked in both directions.

The corridor wasn't long. As I remembered, one end opened on Exchange Place, the other on Broad Street. Standing in the alley, I had no idea which street was which. Directions had never come easily to me.

Hugging my portfolio, I stepped into the office, closed the door, and slumped in the chair by Mavis' desk. My choices were few. I could leave by the back door, drift the streets rudderless until I recognized my location, or I could run out the front door, face the screaming crowd with its cabbages, eggs, and rocks, and keep running until I reached Dey Street.

Oddly, the latter ordeal appealed to me more.

The police were out front, and I had been taught to always trust a lawman. If a rock struck my head, knocking me bleeding and unconscious to the pavement, I could only believe that, true to their oath, a bluecoat would summon an ambulance wagon to carry me to City Hospital. Alone in the alleys, I could be knifed, beaten, or God knew what else. Maybe even kidnapped by a slavery ring and sold into the harem of an Indian rajah or Berber prince.

I stood immediately. Once I made a decision, I rarely faltered. Marching purposely across the room, I opened the front door and stepped outside holding my leather portfolio in front of me. The scene confronted me in lightning flashes: screaming women, shouting men, placards, police, bystanders. Eggs whizzed from the crowd. I ducked and twisted. One whacked against the door. Another hit my portfolio.

Cheers broke from the crowd, which propelled itself forward against the policemen's clasped hands. Angry arms stretched and groped, reaching, grabbing, trying to get me, to assault me, to rip me limb from limb.

Terrified by the insanity in the protester's faces, I flattened myself against the door. What did these people want? I wasn't Glorianna Talmadge. I wasn't running for president. I was only the filing clerk, for heaven's—

The chain of policemen broke like a waterlogged dike. The crowd gushed forth, a tidal swell of indignant moralists bent on quenching the fires of birth control, women's suffrage, communism, vegetarianism, and the evils of Free Love before it consumed the very foundation of their beloved society.

Chapter Five

I ran back through the smoke-filled office, past my despoiled desk, past Laura's ledgers, past the broken stovepipe and out the rear door with no concern whatsoever for murderers, rape artists, rajahs, or Berber princes. Protesters streamed into the alley behind me, screaming, shouting slogans, and hurling insults. Drumbeats echoed off the brick as I sped toward the alley's end, lungs straining against laces and whalebone. But as the protesters' heavy steps drew close and I braced myself for a thrashing, a curious incident occurred.

A shadow fell over the entire alley. Drumbeats ebbed and died. Shouts trickled away to nothing, and my pursuers and I staggered to a halt. The event reminded me of a past event that to this day remains vivid in my mind.

Sometimes at dusk, when twilight invades the sky, I can still hear my mother wail, still see her drop to her knees and pray for Lord Jesus to deliver us. I was a child of twelve. My father stood beside me gazing upwards, an unfinished shoe in his calloused hands. Men from the blacksmith's shop and livery stable wandered into the dusty street beside us. They stared into the sky and trembled, as if facing, not only their own death but the death of the entire universe.

The eerie gloom did not scare me, however. I knew the cause exactly.

I'd read about solar eclipses in *Scientific American*. The moon moving in front of the sun was a perfectly natural astronomical occurrence.

But that day, standing in the street at noon and listening to my mother weep, for the first time in my life I realized that, even at my tender age, I understood more about the workings of the world than most adults.

Now, as darkness consumed the alley, I expected to see the lunar orb obscuring the morning sun. Instead, a tremendous gray, net-covered ball hovered above the rooftops. A wicker basket hung below the sphere. Trailing from the basket, a line of flags and pennants snapped in the breeze like the tail of some colossal kite. *It's an aerial engine,* I thought, similar to the one I'd read about in Jules Verne's book—*Five Weeks in a Balloon.*

Within the minute, the sun reappeared in a blaze of light. Squinting against the glare, I looked behind me. The protesters and pursuers stared upward, shading their brows, still enthralled by the wonderful craft. Safe for the moment, I looked skyward again.

Fully illuminated by sunlight, the balloon drifted across the morning blue. Spread across the sphere, a banner read: *Professor Lowe's Transatlantic Flight.* A man waved vigorously from the basket's rim as if he was the monarch of the air, and we were his earthbound subjects. Envy filled my heart. What I would have given at that moment to be aloft in that wonderful ship high above the sordid turmoil of New York City.

Then, as quickly as he arrived, Professor Lowe and his balloon disappeared beyond the rooftops. Seizing the opportunity, I ran from the alley and lost myself among the shuffling New Yorkers. After a full minute, I looked behind. The alley had melted into the featureless brick walls that lined the street. I had no idea where I was. *Talmadge's Weekly* was the farthest south I'd ever been, and I'd never been north of *Hundschlanger's Lodging for Girls.*

Our Pottsville neighbor, Mrs. Steinmetz, had recommended the establishment. "*Mein liebe*, Hilda, stay there," she told me in fractured English. "Hilda *ist* such a *gute* girl." Well, having grown up with Hilda, I can assure you she was most definitely not a *gute* girl. In fact, rumors now circulated Mrs. Hundschlanger's that since being evicted, the *gute* girl was working as an actress. Cleo had informed me what that meant.

I slowed to a fast walk. Not far away, hacks and wagons rolled through an intersection. Men in coats and women in shawls dodged traffic and manure. Surely, up ahead I could find a street name.

Halfway there, I passed a tobacconist's shop. The air outside had a pleasant aroma, and I found myself enjoying the bouquet of Cavendish, Burley, and, my father's favorite, Perique. The fragrance returned me to his workshop, the smoke of his pipe, the smell of glue, of dye, and the tang of hides. Strange, but I could almost hear the tap of his hammer on shoe soles. Caught in my reverie, I failed to notice a youth sprinting toward me until the last moment. The lad, a telegraph runner judging by his hat and pouch, bumped my shoulder hard. As I spun to keep from falling, his hand reached out and squeezed my bosom.

I swung my portfolio with both hands. The roughie ducked, and I landed only a glancing blow on his side. Finding my balance, I heard him laugh as he hurried away.

Scoundrel! I had forgotten Cleo's admonition to be ever vigilant against sexual deviants. I pinched my dress at my waist and wiggled my corset into place. If given the chance, I would flatten one of these rogues with a strong right hook.

"You hurt?"

The man's voice startled me. I turned too fast, almost losing my balance again. His eel skin shoes attracted me first. Eroded and frayed, they seemed so worn not even my father could have saved them. Above the shoes, he wore a pair of yellow-and-black-checkered pants, and, above those, a yellow jacket. His pocked cheeks bore a scuffed, street-worn look. A smoking cigar fidgeted nervously between his odd, flat lips.

"You hurt?" the man asked again.

"Yes," I replied, dusting off my dress. "I mean, no. I'm quite fine."

The man took off his yellow derby and patted his black pomaded hair. "You ever hear of Anthony Comstock?"

The question took me aback. Vaguely, I knew the name. Violet had mentioned it along with something about lackeys dragging you off to jail. "Some sort of fanatic, isn't he?"

"Fanatic?" the man repeated. "Yes, Comstock's a fanatic, and thank God for him. This city would be worse than Sodom and Gomorrah if it wasn't for his *society*."

I supposed the man would next ask for a donation. Besides volunteers collecting for different calamities, New York seemed full of people begging money for various *societies*. Aside from collecting for charitable causes like the Great Whaling Disaster, most promoted some Utopian settlement or doomsday colony. "Sir," I said, hoping to calm the gentleman, "I'm sure you represent a worthwhile cause, but at present my funds are short."

"I'm talking about The Society for the Suppression of Vice," the fellow responded in the holy tones of a Methodist preacher. A glint of recognition lit his eyes. "You're Cleo Duncan's friend."

I stepped backward. The gentleman scared me now. How did he know Cleo's name?

He grasped his lapel and pulled. Silver gleamed from a star pinned to his shirt. The hilt of a pistol protruded from his belt. "Special Detective McCauley," he said, letting the fabric go. "You started working for Mrs. Talmadge a few days ago."

My muscles relaxed. He was a policeman. Thank God. "I'm Jenny Crispin," I said, feeling no longer afraid. "Her new filing clerk."

McCauley stepped forward and, in one deft motion, batted my portfolio to the ground, seized my arms, and clapped a set of manacles on my wrists. "Miss Crispin, you're under arrest for the possession of indecent articles, for distributing obscene materials, and for inciting a riot."

He pulled me forward by the chain. I tripped and almost fell. "But I'm only the filing clerk."

McCauley jerked the chain tighter. "You've also knowingly aided in the distribution of birth control literature."

"But I just file papers," I pleaded. "Newspaper clippings, bills, receipts, things like that."

"Tell it to the magistrate."

The magistrate? I'd never been arrested in my life. What would happen to me? A fine? A night in jail? Prison?

McCauley started down the sidewalk, leading me by the chain. I stepped lively to keep the pressure and pain off my wrists. On the left, the alley behind *Talmadge's Weekly* came into view. When we reached the opening, McCauley stopped. "You seem like a decent girl; Jennifer is it?"

The protesters had gone. Books and chairs smoldered on the cobblestones. Newspapers blew in the wind. "Everyone calls me, Jenny," I said.

"Jenny, huh. Nice name." McCauley's tongue fidgeted around the end of his cigar. "You know, Jenny, the women's jail is an awful place, lots of bad ladies in there: whores, thieves, murderers. Those dames stick a shiv between your ribs just the same as they was saying hello."

"A shiv?"

"It's a crude knife. Jailbirds make 'em out of anything they can, a tin can or a bed iron. Scrape 'em on the floor till they're sharp as a razor. Got nothing better to do than stab each other in the gut. And the guards, they're worse than the prisoners. Be a real shame for a girl like you to spend a year or two in jail. They don't call it the Tombs for nothing."

The Tombs? Was this weasel trying to scare me or let me go? Did he want me to fawn? Beg? Sweet-talk? I could do that. I could sweet-talk. In a man's world, what woman couldn't? I smiled my best "I'm-really-a-good-girl" smile and tried to imagine I was standing in the presence of Saint Jude.

"Honestly, Officer McCauley, I had no idea any of those things were crimes. I just file papers. I'll be good from now on; I promise. I'm not from New York; I'm from Pottsville."

"Pottsville?" McCauley asked. "Pennsylvania? I popped another girl from Pottsville, yesterday. Plied her trade on Barclay Street near Bulwark Bank. Hilda, her name was."

The detective pulled me into the alley and backed me into a doorway. He dropped the manacle chain and began to stroke my fingers. "You know, Jenny, I could do you a favor."

His skin felt greasy. I wanted to jerk my hands away. Truthfully, I wanted to knee him in the groin. That's what mother had taught me to do if any man touched me—that, and poke out his eyes, preferably with something sharp.

McCauley pressed closer. I saw his face clearly now. A thousand tiny craters scarred his flesh, like an engraving of the moon I'd seen in *Harper's Weekly*. With a grin, he slithered his hand up my arm and touched my breast. The other hand bunched up my skirt.

Remembering the deviant telegraph runner, I clasped my manacled hands together and slugged him with my best right hook. McCauley pitched backward, hands to his face, good eye swirling with anger.

I pushed off the wall and slammed into his shoulder. As he tumbled to the ground, I broke into a run. Not the silly run of a lady, but a hard, steady, leg pumping, boy catching run I'd used effectively in the schoolyard. The wrist irons, however, didn't help.

At alley's end, I arced left and raced around the corner, clasped hands moving side to side, manacle chain rattling, and purse bouncing against my back like a saddlebag on a pony. Women stopped as I passed. Men gawked, excited no doubt by my kicking legs, flying skirt, and stockinged calves. I turned left again at the next corner and ran into the intersection.

A dappled horse reared. Hooves beat the air. The driver of the wagon cursed as he fought to control his charge. Behind me, a water wagon thundered by only a foot away. When it passed, I hurried toward the sidewalk. Ten feet from the curb, a hansom cut me off in a storm of dust. Manure splattered my black practical boots. I reached the sidewalk coughing and gagging.

Slow down, I thought, hands on knees, heart pounding, chest heaving, corset digging into my armpits. *You could have been killed. Thank God, you've lost McCauley.* I straightened up and looked around, hoping I was right.

Bulwark Bank stood on the corner. Above its roof, the steeple of Trinity Church pointed skyward. The area looked familiar. I'd passed here this morning on the Broadway Omnibus. If I could make it to Trinity Church, I was sure I could find my way to my room on Dey Street.

I walked briskly down the sidewalk, smoothed my hair as best I could, and stomped the manure from my boots. Despite the cool weather, my skin burned and itched beneath my clothes.

The business district disappeared behind me. Here, once opulent homes faced the sidewalk—older mansions with leaning gates and unkempt yards. Leaves blew across my path. Shoeless children played in the street. At the end of the block, I turned and looked. There was McCauley, loping toward me in those yellow-and-black-checkered pants.

Chapter Six

Britt walked up South Street still troubled by his foolish assassination attempt. One day, the Scotsman would not be there to save him, and his emotions would get him killed. Memories of the lash returned and the muscles on his back twitched. He'd come close to death in Egypt. Just how much longer Lockie's loyalty would last before he realized his imagined debt had been paid Britt did not know. But whatever misguided allegiance made the Scotsman stay, he was thankful for it.

South Street ended in a row of wooden barricades. He jumped over and cut through several blocks of rubble, the remnants of demolished warehouses and tenements brought down to make room for the entrance to the new bridge to Brooklyn. Workmen loading bricks into a huge wagon paid him little attention.

Emerging from the smell and dust of shattered buildings, he brushed off his jacket and walked north on Bowery Street then west on Worth. At the corner of Mulberry, the odor of baked bread drifted in the air. Handcarts laden with potatoes, cabbage, and fresh meat lined one side of the street. Wagons heaped with sacks of flour and barrels of milk lined the other. Housewives in scarves haggled over the price of everything from zucchini to cuts of lamb. Others picked through bins of onions, garlic bulbs and herbs tied with strings. Beyond the mill of sellers and buyers, girls on the sidewalk jumped rope while boys played hoop. Men in black coats, derbies, and ties loitered in open doorways. Above them, old women watched from iron balconies.

Reminded of Alexandria, Britt pushed through the crowd. A short distance past the market, he stopped an elderly gentleman and inquired about The Morgue. The man guided him further up Mulberry Street. When they came to a hand-lettered sign above a large, sooty window, the gent stopped and held out his palm. Britt pressed a coin into his bent fingers.

The smell of mold and beer wafted through the open door. Inside, crude benches and chairs were arranged in no particular order. As he entered, a man seated near the door rapped his bottle on the wood.

"Is Johnny Dolan about?" Britt asked.

The man pointed the neck of the bottle toward the bar. Behind it, an aproned barkeep polished a glass with a rag. "Dandy Johnny ain't here," he said without looking up.

Britt crossed to the bar. He pulled the cloth from the barkeep's hand and threw it aside. "Tell him a man with money is waiting."

The barkeep looked Britt in the eye then disappeared through a curtain. A minute later, he returned with a short, well-dressed man smoking a cigarette.

"Johnny Dolan?" Britt asked.

"Who's asking?"

Dolan seemed young to be the boss of such a notorious gang. "I'm here for nitro."

The Whyos leader squinted against the cigarette smoke in his eyes. "Safe to crack?"

"Revenge," Britt answered.

Johnny plucked the cigarette from his lips and grinned with crooked teeth. "Won't be no trace of the fella left then."

"None."

Johnny's smile withered. "One hundred a bottle. Lay it on the bar."

"I'll give you fifty."

Johnny crushed his cigarette into the bar top. "Pricey bit that nitro. But revenge is sweet. That's what they say, ain't it? This is the good stuff.

Not watered down. Hard to get. One hundred. Show it now."

Although he felt like dragging the little man over the bar and teaching him a few manners, Britt said only, "When I get a taste."

Johnny frowned. He motioned to the barkeep who started through the curtains. "And be careful," Johnny called after him. "Bump that soup too hard and we'll be toasting Satan." He turned back to Britt and leaned close. "A job like that needs protection. Cut us in."

"There is no job, only revenge."

"And you aim to punish him good, else why not slit his throat. We'll take what's left. You get away clean."

The barkeep returned and, with great care, placed a small, brown, stoppered bottle on the bar. Britt reached for it, but Johnny blocked his hand. "Show me the one."

When five twenty-dollar notes from his billfold were on the bar, Britt tipped the bottle sideways, twisted out the cork, and touched it to his tongue. Frowning, he replaced the cork then picked up his money. "This stuff wouldn't blow the bloomers off your granny."

Johnny snatched a revolver from his coat and leveled it at Britt's chest. "My granny don't wear bloomers. Good or bad, the deal is done. Hand me the one, or I shoot."

Britt threw the twenties in the air. As Johnny looked, Britt wrenched the gun from his hand and swung it toward the barkeep who had pulled a pepperbox from his apron. Britt fired. The barkeep crumpled, squeezing off a shot as he did. By the front door, the man in the sweater leaped to his feet drawing a shotgun from beside his chair. Britt fired again and the man collapsed. He swung the pistol toward Johnny, but the little Whyo had already ducked through the back curtains and was gone.

Britt gathered his money. He walked behind the bar. On the other side of the curtains, he found a cramped kitchen. An open door led to a damp alley strewn with broken bottles and crates. Seeing no trace of Johnny, Britt shoved the pistol in his belt then closed the door and locked it.

The kitchen contained a stove, a sink, empty shelves, and an icebox. He opened the icebox, hoping to find more nitro, but saw only a single crock of milk. He lifted the lid, sniffed, then drank. As he placed the milk back in the icebox, voices and shouts echoed from the alley.

Returning to the bar, the bottle of nitro caught his attention. He'd lied to Johnny. Although old and weak, the nitro still had about a quarter of its kick left, not enough for his purposes but enough to make Johnny think twice about coming after him. The last thing he needed was the Whyos gang chasing him the rest of the day.

Britt crushed his eyes shut and gave the bottle four shakes. For good measure, he gave it one more. He placed the bottle on the bar. Happy to still have his hands, he ran to the kitchen and unlocked the door to the alley. The shouts grew louder. He raced through the bar and jumped over the dead man lying athwart the front door. Outside, he squatted by the large window and aimed Johnny's pistol through the glass at the bottle of nitroglycerin.

With a crash, six thugs swarmed into the bar from the curtained doorway and rushed around the room waving their guns. Johnny entered last. Apparently livid at not finding Britt, he swept a row of glasses from a shelf and cursed.

Britt ignored the Whyos' leader and concentrated on the bottle. He hoped Johnny's pistol was accurate. Only a bullseye would make the nitro explode. A near miss wouldn't do. Satisfied with his aim, he squeezed the trigger.

The room exploded in a splintering boom. Britt rolled into a ball as fire and debris shattered the window and blew into the street. Without containment, the weakened nitro didn't have its full force but was still powerful enough to knock down everything and everyone in the room.

Britt stood and brushed bits of glass and wood from his hair and jacket. The pistol shot had been perfect. He turned the gun in his hand. What an extraordinary weapon. The grip felt comfortable, and the balance was marvelous. He read the words stamped on the side: Webley's RIC. An English brand, as he remembered. He slipped the revolver into his coat pocket and walked into the smoky bar.

Tables and chairs lay at odd angles. Gang members moaned and rolled about the floor, clothes singed. He found Johnny behind the bar, grabbed him by the collar, and slapped him into consciousness.

"That nitro was at least six months old," he shouted. "Where's the good stuff?" Stunned by the blast, Johnny just blinked at him. "Where?" Britt shouted again.

"Red Scarves," Johnny choked. "They snatched my shipment."

Britt dragged Johnny closer. "When?"

"Yesterday."

Johnny's eyes closed, but Britt shook him awake. "Where can I find the Red Scarves?"

"Tenth Street, Atlas Brewing."

Britt dropped Johnny to the floor. He reached into the man's coat, unbuckled his holster, and stripped it out. The strap contained a dozen or more loops filled with cartridges. He fastened the leather around his shoulder and holstered the Webley. On the way to the door, he tossed his old pocket pistol to the barroom floor. A crowd parted as he emerged from the smoking building.

Back at the market, he nodded politely to the men in black coats, tipped his hat to the housewives, and waved to the children on the sidewalk. Nobody cared. They seemed more interested in the police whistles rising in volume from all directions.

At Worth Street, he hailed a hansom. Wind cooled the flush in his face but his heart still pounded. A bit of pleasure would take the edge off. He popped the lid of his watch. Ten o'clock. Just enough time before his meeting with Lockie. The Scotsman would not be pleased he'd failed to secure their explosives.

Twenty minutes later, Britt stepped from the carriage, paid the driver, then climbed the porch steps to de Ford's brothel. Molly met him at the door. "What's on your lip?"

Britt wiped his mouth and looked at his hand. "Dried milk."

"How about something stronger?"

"I need it," he said, following her into the parlor. "A meeting with a scoundrel named Johnny Dolan has left my throat parched."

Molly stopped at a sideboard set with cakes, crackers, and decanters of liquor. "Dandy Johnny of the Whyos? I hope you didn't cross him. He's known to carry a grudge." She offered him three fingers of whiskey in cut crystal.

Britt knocked back the drink and Molly refilled his glass. Britt threw that back as well. "I doubt Mr. Dolan will feel like bothering anyone for a few days."

"Go upstairs," Molly said, taking the glass from his hand. "I'll send a girl. Anyone in particular?"

Lately, Rebecca was his favorite. Fresh, lively, and well proportioned, she possessed all the attributes one sought in a working girl. "Rebecca will do nicely."

"Rebecca is visiting her mother in Queens, but I've a new girl taking her place. Trained her myself."

"I prefer someone with experience."

Molly placed her hand on his chest. "You might be pleasantly surprised."

Resigned to the new girl, he picked up a copy of the *New York Times* from the sideboard and carried it upstairs. The room he favored was larger than the others, decorated with floral wallpaper and furnished with only an iron bed and a nightstand. He draped his shoulder holster and jacket over the bedpost, took off the rest of his clothes, climbed under the covers, and began to read.

The front page carried the usual sagas: political and economic problems in the Southern states, Berber slavers trading in young white girls, more progress on the bridge. The second page featured presidential endorsements. Below articles on Grant and Greeley, he could scarcely believe what he saw. A newspaperwoman, suffragette, and Free Lover named Glorianna Talmadge had entered the race for president. A cartoon depicted her as Satan holding a card printed with the words "Be saved by Free Love." The caption under the cartoon read "Get thee behind me, Mrs. Satan." A woman president of all things. Unbelievable. Apparently, not every change in America had been for the better.

Beginning to feel the alcohol's effects, he folded back the page and came across an article on Archer Gideon, the Confederate Cavalry General, well known during the war for his lightning fast hit-and-run tactics. Gideon had come to the city to rail against the government's policies toward the South. The Grant administration, Gideon proclaimed in an exclusive interview, was punishing the Southern people unfairly and setting back their economy a hundred years.

Further down, he saw mention of a large Halloween gathering tonight in City Hall Park and a masquerade ball for the city elite at the Astor House. Better not tell Lockie about any Halloween festivities. He was spooked enough.

Britt laid the newspaper on the nightstand and stared at the door. Lockie would arrive any minute. What was keeping this new girl? Punctuality was essential for a proper business relationship. And having grown up in a brothel, Britt understood well that prostitution was a business, a noble profession, akin to laundering, barbering, or doctoring. The girls provided a service, and men gladly paid. Compensation, like every other occupation, was commensurate with experience and skill. He knew nothing about this new girl, but Rebecca was not only experienced and skilled, she also enjoyed her work and took pride in a job well done—at least with him.

Britt liked to suppose her special considerations grew from personal affection—an affection he did not return other than pleasant friendship, of course. It wouldn't do to get emotionally attached to a professional. He'd crossed that line long ago with a working girl, and the emotional scars still pained him. But the harsh lessons of the past did not mean he couldn't enjoy Rebecca's special favors in the present.

Still, it was possible her affections might be genuinely pure. He wasn't entirely without charm. True, he could be crude and loud, and he was certainly not the most attractive of men. But if a lady of joy went beyond her duty to give him that extra bit of pleasure, he was not averse to returning the favor by bestowing some additional pleasure as well. After all, spending the first sixteen years of his life in a brothel had taught him more than a few ways to please a woman.

Yes, Rebecca was an excellent practitioner of her craft. Well taught. Maybe by Molly herself. He'd never had the pleasure of bedding the Madame de Ford, either before his foray to Egypt or since his return. Her mattress days were behind her now, anyway, but he'd heard rumors. If this new girl was as good as Rebecca, taught by Molly herself as she had claimed, then maybe he was in for a sensual experience unlike any other.

Chapter Seven

Eager to escape McCauley, I cut between the houses along an iron fence, hiding the manacles behind crossed arms. I emerged on the next block, alongside a freshly painted porch attached to a columned mansion. Near the street, a modest sign declared the name *de Ford's* in flowing cursive letters. Parked at the curb stood a purple carriage trimmed in gold.

A thunder of footsteps inside the mansion drew my attention, and I crouched behind a hedge of boxwood. The front door opened, spilling out a half dozen men in black frock coats and purple, tasseled fezes. As if they'd done it a thousand times, the men formed a semi-circle.

Peering between their pant legs, I glimpsed a pair of curious purple and gold pointed shoes facing someone on the threshold—a lady wearing unusual high-heeled brocade boots barely visible beneath a satin gown. As I strained to decipher their indistinct voices, the woman's hand swung down and cupped the man's crotch. If that action wasn't brazen enough, the woman began patting the bulge much as a mother might pat a boy's head when sending him off to school.

With a final squeeze, the goodbye was complete. The men in purple fezes closed around their charge like a velvet case around an amethyst. They crossed the porch together, descended the steps, and discharged the mysterious man into the ornate carriage. Seconds later, the carriage drawn by two black steeds rolled away with men in fezes hanging from every corner.

Stunned by the spectacle, my gaze returned to the sign: *de Ford's*. Commodore Vanderbilt had mentioned the name this morning. Glorianna, too.

The house, the yard, the intimate behavior: this was Molly de Ford's establishment. Molly de Ford, the infamous Madame. Molly was Glorianna's good friend. I'd been told they took tea together. Surely, as a brothel owner, Molly held no love for the police. If anyone could help me in my predicament, couldn't Molly?

I skirted the edge of the porch then climbed the stairs. Instead of knocking, I placed my manacled hands on the knob, quietly opened the door, and tiptoed in.

The foyer was large, filled with luxurious blue chairs and a blue velvet couch. Perfume hung in the air. On a sideboard, crackers and cakes filled plates beside liquor bottles and glasses. The melodious tones of a music box resounded from a hallway. A stairway ascended under a large curtained window. Classical paintings hung from the red striped wallpaper—nudes mostly, plump women, reclining about, eating fruit from golden platters. Urgent footsteps thumped on the porch, and I dove behind the couch.

The front door opened. Heavy breathing rasped above the music box. Lighter footsteps sounded next, in the direction of the hall. The footsteps stopped short.

"McCauley," a woman said, irritated. "What are you doing here? Haven't I already paid you this month?"

I peeked around the corner of the couch. Yellow-and-black-checkered pants above eel skin shoes stood less than five feet away. Nearby, a satin gown rippled over high brocade heels.

"Shut your yap, Molly," McCauley said. "I chased a girl in here. Where'd she go?"

"No girls here but my girls."

"This dolly-mop ain't one of yours. I saw her come in the front door. Five-eight, blond hair, blue outfit."

47

"Who socked your peeper?"

"Never mind. Lock the door. I'm searching the house."

I heard a key rattle in the lock then the checkered legs stomped off toward the hallway with the satin gown flouncing after them. I hesitated a second then beat it up the carpeted stairs. The steps ended in a garish red hallway lined with green doors. I picked one at random and pushed it open.

A lady wearing nothing but black boots and a western style hat sat astride a man's belly while he arched his back and rose on all fours. Oddly, she faced backward of all things, hands on his knees, legs spread, bouncing like a trick rider on a stallion. Eyes closed, faces contorted as if in pain, both man and woman appeared in the throes of some cathartic seizure. Just as I thought to shout for help, their bodies grew agonizingly stiff, whereupon they collapsed to the bed in perfect calm. I closed the door and opened another across the hall.

Above the rumpled sheets on a brass bed, a fat, naked man hung from a hook in the ceiling, wrists tied by a velvet rope. Head drooping on triple chins, his swollen limbs sprouted from a bloated body in a way that reminded me of an immense, white sausage—stuffed, tied, and hung in the butcher's window.

Beside the bed, dressed in a red corset, red knee boots and nothing else, a lady with voluminous hair and breasts flicked a tasseled whip against the man's scarlet buttocks. "You're a penny short," the woman shouted, hand on hip. "Count the money again." She whipped his dimpled flesh once more. His body tightened and convulsed. "You're a penny short. Count it again."

Realizing they were not alone, both lady and man stared at me like actors startled by a cabbage thrown from the audience. I backed slowly out of the room and closed the door. Shouts and bellows reverberated from the first floor. Terror struck, I ran down the hall, opened another door, stepped inside, and slammed it.

Propped against the headboard of a large iron bed, his face turned in profile, a man sat reading a newspaper, the bedcovers pulled to his waist. Large hands, powerful arms, broad shoulders, the fellow bristled with masculinity. Had he worn tights, I would have guessed his occupation as carnival strong man or maybe prizefighter. His bare muscles, however, had the hardened sheen of a laborer.

But workmen rarely have such a contemplative look. No laborer, he. Despite his muscled frame, this man held the thoughtful aspect of a professor. He lowered the paper and peered at me.

Brown eyes, small mouth over tremendous jaw, his clean-shaven chin hinted black, the same color as his hair, shorn only an inch long against all modern convention. I smiled uneasily and wished I could see his boots. Some say the eyes are windows to the soul, but father always said you could tell more from a person's shoes.

His gaze fell to my wrist irons. "Well, well," he said, sitting up higher, "Molly was right; this is a pleasant surprise."

Heavy footfalls rang from the hall. Frantic, I rushed to his side and dropped to the floor to conceal myself beneath the bed. Low boards made that impossible. I stood immediately. The windowless room was bare except for bed and nightstand. Loud knocks boomed at the door. With my pulse pounding and nowhere else to hide, I tore back the covers.

"Good Lord," I gasped. "You're naked!"

Chapter Eight

I'd always considered myself morally superior to those silly girls who leered wide-eyed at muscle-bound ditch-diggers then fanned their heated cheeks and panted. Mother said a virtuous woman must rise above the animal attraction of sweat-soaked shirts—even if pressed against burly necks, flexing forearms, and strapping shoulders.

But Mother never mentioned anything like *this* magnificent fellow. I couldn't stop ogling his body. As a specimen, he was superb: his brawny chest, his rippled stomach, the dark hair that trailed down to... to... I clamped my hand over my eyes.

"Do you approve?" the naked man asked, amused, as if being examined nude occurred every day.

"Yes," I said. "I mean, no. I mean—you're naked."

Heavy knocks sounded at the door again. The doorknob turned.

Eyes averted, conscience torn between sin and survival, having nowhere else to hide, I jumped into his bed and tried to curl into nothingness. As the door swung open, I pulled the blanket over my head and buried my face in the pillow.

"Blast it, Britt," a thick Scottish voice boomed. "I spend all morning chasing after the Khedive while you lounge about with a chippie."

I uncovered my head and looked. The Scotsman appeared to be in his mid-forties, my height, medium build with dun-colored hair and a gap-toothed smile. He wore a bright blue shirt and dull brown pants. Relieved he wasn't McCauley, I endeavored to scramble from the bed. Before I could escape, however, my bunkmate seized my waist.

His laughter shook the bed. "Patience, Lockie. Molly has a girl for you, too, but first, tell me about the Khedive."

Fighting to escape the stranger's grasp, I arched my back and kicked my legs, but the rogue moved his hand to my head, jammed my face into the feather pillow, and the two men continued their conversation as if I didn't exist.

"I followed the king as you asked," the Scotsman said. "Surrounded by his blackguards, he went straight to Bulwark Bank. They opened early just for him. He entered carrying a leather case and came out empty-handed. Then he marched across the street and rented the entire third floor of the Astor House. After that, I followed him here."

"The Khedive, here?" Britt asked. "At Molly's? Right under my nose? The bastard always was insatiable."

Barely hearing them, I kicked my legs and jangled my wrist irons desperate to get free.

"Feisty one you've got there," the Scotsman remarked. "Reminds me of my third wife. She loved the manacles, as well." His tone changed. "The king and his purple minions left here only minutes ago. If you got the soup from Johnny Dolan, the deed is done whenever you give the word."

"Dandy Johnny did not come through," Britt growled.

"Without that juice, our whole plan is for naught."

"Calm yourself, Lockie. Midnight hasn't arrived, and I've other leads. We'll get that juice, don't worry. Now, go see Molly about a lass."

Juice, soup—were these men chefs? Hoping to beg the Scotsman for help, I worked my head free. I'd just opened my mouth when Britt placed his hand on the crown of my head and pushed, driving my face back into the pillow.

The door clicked shut.

Had I not been trapped between the pillow and this strongman's hand, I should have realized that the gentleman they referred to was the

King of Egypt—the same fellow Glorianna and the Commodore had discussed in the carriage, and none other than the man in purple shoes I'd seen earlier on the porch. Fear, however, had worked its spidery legs into my mind, and while I was sure my bedmate believed my struggles to be a whore's playful fun, I feared for my safety and my virtue.

When the pressure of his hand eased, I lifted my head. "Let me go," I pleaded softly, afraid to raise my voice lest McCauley hear me. "I am not the woman you think. I only sought refuge in this brothel to escape a pervert."

He laughed again, harder. "Yes, of course, you did. How dreadful. Let me help you out of these clothes."

He threw back the bed cover. As one hand held the manacles above my head, the other worked swiftly through the buttons on the side of my skirt. I twisted and kicked but the strength of this giant was too great.

"You don't understand," I implored as he stripped the skirt off my bloomered legs. "I'm not a woman of ill morals, but an innocent girl trapped by extraordinary circumstances."

He slapped my behind hard. "And the most articulate strumpet I've ever met. You must earn big tips."

Chuckling at some private joke, he opened my jacket and unfastened the buttons of my blouse. Anger replaced my fear. "Damn you," I cursed, struggling to keep my voice low, jerking this way and that. "I'm telling the truth. Release me this instant."

A gasp ripped from my throat as he reached under my blouse and released the laces on my corset. I divulge that after struggling so hard, losing that constrictive appliance felt wonderful.

He pulled out the corset, threw it to the floor, then slid my blouse and jacket over my head and up my arms until they stopped at my wrist chains. When he released my hands, I dropped immediately to the bed and began to strike his chest.

A great smile erupted on his face. "You're quite an actress."

With that, he pulled the bed covers over us both, dragged me on top of him and started caressing my chemise-clad body in a manner that I imagine some wanton women might consider pleasant.

Cloaked by the bed cover, desperate to get away, I pushed against his flesh and worked my way down his chest, but my palms lost their grip on his moist skin, and down I fell face first into his groin. My fingers, desperate for purchase, locked around something enormous.

Good Lord!

Urgent knocks filled the room. The door clicked, and the knob rattled. I froze instantly, trembling fingers still clenched around my discovery.

"Seen a girl come in here, five-eight, blond hair, dark clothes?"

McCauley! I would have recognized that voice anywhere. My body tightened like a knot, and with it, my grip.

Britt's muscles stiffened from the pressure of my clasp. He poked his head from the covers and spoke, his voice painfully tense. "Can't you see I'm busy? Who the devil are you?"

"Special Detective McCauley."

I squeezed harder.

Britt's back arched, raising me and the covers off the bed. "No one like that here," he grunted. "Now get the hell out."

The silence lasted hours.

"Well?" Britt asked, voice tight, body strained against my grip. "If you don't mind, I'm... occupied."

The door slammed.

My fingers relaxed, but before Britt's body dropped to the bed, his hands were everywhere: lifting my chemise, feeling my thighs, pulling at my bloomers. My eyes opened wide. This was it. I was going to be raped like a Sabine wench.

And what should I expect? After all, I was in a naked man's bed, squeezing his most private parts. What else could he take me for, but a harlot, a hooker, or a peddlesnatch?

The thread of my thoughts snapped.

His hands were touching, rubbing, caressing. I blush to say, it felt good, so good. My lids sank low. My mouth fell open. Was this was what Glorianna and Violet were preaching? Was this their revolution, their freedom, their emancipation? Was this their *Free Love*?

I didn't know. My head swirled; my senses churned. My body

spun like a tornado, a whirlpool, an intense, irrevocable, undeniable maelstrom of, of, of…

His voice in my ear wrenched me to my senses. "Clever idea, these wrist irons. Innocent victim, indeed."

Damn it, trapped between McCauley and a sexual maniac. "No," I managed to say, "you don't understand."

"Oh, yes, I do."

He smothered his lips against mine.

I struggled to push away his mouth and speak. I wanted to tell him I wasn't a woman of low morals, that I'd been forced into extraordinary circumstances by a corrupt policeman, but his kissing and sucking and biting made it impossible. Muzzled and muted by his lips, I jerked and jumped and tried to get free, but it only seemed to excite him.

He pulled away. "Lockie was right. You are a feisty one."

Before I could speak, he latched onto my ankles and spread my legs wide. I grabbed the bed sheets in shaking fists and prepared for the worst: to be plundered, ravaged, and God knew what else by this sex-crazed Goliath. All options spent, I did the only thing I could. I closed my eyes and screamed.

The door banged open.

"What the hell's going on here? You're not my new girl."

Britt released my ankles. I slid from the covers and clunked to the floor at the side of the bed.

My eyes jerked open. An upside down woman stood in an upside down doorway clutching the doorknob of an upside down door. The bed springs squeaked and suddenly an upside down Britt stood dangling over me.

"Molly, are you mad? If she's not your new girl, who the hell am I paying for?"

The upside down woman pointed. "That's the girl McCauley was looking for."

They both stared down at me. I smiled and stood. Clad only in chemise, bloomers, and my black practical boots, I tried to untangle my blouse and jacket from the wrist irons. Giving up, I clutched the clothes against my body. "It was a mistake. I didn't do anything. I was—"

"I know you," Molly said cutting me off. "You work for Glorianna."

I slumped. My knees knocked. "I'm the filing clerk."

Britt glared at Molly. His big jaw dropped. "Wait a minute; you're serious. She really doesn't work for you?"

"She works for Glorianna Talmadge. You know, Mrs. Satan."

"The suffragette?"

"That's right, the woman who's running for president."

He pointed a thumb toward me. "Then she's not a professional?"

"Not yet."

"Well, she sure acts like a professional."

Molly shrugged and backed halfway out the door. "Comes natural to some girls. You two finish your little slap and tickle. The Khedive paid me well. I've turned a neat wage in spite of McCauley's visit." She looked at me. "But clear out quick, sweetie. I don't need that pervert around here any more than once a month."

The door closed.

Britt's face reddened; his chest shook. Other parts shook too. "Damn it, you could have told me you weren't one of Molly's girls."

"I did, you ox. If your mind hadn't been clouded by lust, you would have heard me. Or do you enjoy forcing yourself upon helpless virgins?"

"You're a virgin?" he shouted.

"Of course, I'm a virgin. What of it?"

Britt exploded in a torrent of muttering and cursing. He stomped around the room waving his hands before stopping abruptly. "What the devil are you trying to do to me?"

"To you?" I asked. "I believe *you* were attempting to deflower *me*."

"Deflower? You're insane."

Britt snatched a bright red shirt from the nightstand and pulled it over his chest.

The intense color of his shirt distracted me momentarily. "Hey, you're not leaving are you?"

He finished buttoning his shirt and started hopping into a pair of black pants. "That's exactly what I'm doing."

At least his pants were of normal color. "You can't leave. I need your help."

Britt sat on the bed and pulled on a sock. "Help yourself."

I pushed my blouse and jacket off the manacles, up my arms, and over my head. I grabbed my corset off the floor and tried to fasten it around my waist. The wrist irons weren't helping. "A gentleman would help a lady get dressed."

"Gentlemen do not deflower virgins," he said, pulling on the other sock.

"An emancipated woman may choose any sexual partner she sees fit," I said loudly.

He rose from the bed in a huff. "Not this partner."

Teeth clenched, I yanked the corset from my body. Damn it, the manacles made dressing impossible. Exasperated, I shook my fists and rattled the chain in the air.

Britt seized my hands. He whipped a piece of metal from his breast pocket, shoved it into the manacles and pulled. With a snap, the irons banged to the floor.

I rubbed my wrists and stared at him in amazement. "How did you do that?"

Britt grunted and pulled on his boots—half Wellington's, old, but well cared for. A second later, jacket over his arm, buttoning his pants, he was out the door. I gathered up my bag and hurried after him, arms heaped with clothes, corset flapping. How I hated that blasted thing.

I danced into my skirt in the garish hallway, then chased Britt down the stairs while he put on his jacket. Music tinkled in the foyer. "Wait," I called, following him out the door, corset clutched under my arm, fingers fumbling with my buttons. "Wait," I yelled again.

Stumbling across the porch, I buttoned my blouse and tugged on my jacket. He was already past the sign marked *de Ford's* and entering a hackney parked at the curb. Halfway down the steps, my corset caught on a boxwood branch and fell from my grip. I rushed back, picked it up then turned around. Britt had just shut the carriage door and was calling to the driver.

"Wait," I cried, standing on the walkway, voice desperate, shirttail out, bloomers drooping, skirt half buttoned, corset dangling from one hand. "Britt, please, don't leave me. I need your help."

Someone grabbed my shoulder and spun me around. I wobbled to stay upright. My purse and corset fell to the walk.

McCauley stood in front of me, pants checkered, skin pocked, his left eye circled in a blue-black ring. He grabbed my wrist and bent my arm behind my back. "Gotcha, bitch."

Chapter Nine

I doubled over in pain.

McCauley leaned toward me, gloating and smirking, the heat of his cigar almost burning my ear. "Thought you could get the best of Badger McCauley, did you?" He wrenched my arm. Muscles twisted, and my eyes teared.

"You should have given me what I wanted," he sneered. "Now instead of going to the Tombs, I may stick a shiv in your gut, myself." His free hand pushed hard between my shoulders and propelled me toward the curb.

All at once, Britt stood beside me. He ripped McCauley's hand from my arm and lifted him effortlessly off the ground by his wrist. Seeming to enjoy the detective's ruined shoes beat the air, Britt held the man aloft for a moment, before dropping him on the porch.

McCauley rubbed his wrist. "Salter," he growled. "That was you upstairs, wasn't it?"

"Can't leave the ladies alone, can you, McCauley?"

"The tables have turned, big man. You're the one in trouble now. I represent The Society for the—"

McCauley never finished. Britt popped him with an expert right jab. The detective's head snapped back and he collapsed at the top of the stairs. Dead or unconscious, his limp body slid slowly down the steps, head bumping each tread with a hollow thump, thump, thump.

Britt picked up my purse and handed it to me. He took my elbow and walked me to the carriage. A minute later, I sat beside him on the brown leather seat. "Did you kill him?"

Britt rapped the ceiling. "I should have."

The rig jerked forward. Molly de Ford's establishment slipped from view and with it the image of Detective McCauley, head resting peacefully on the last step, arms spread across the walkway, my hated corset lying beside him.

A great anxiety left me. Maybe it was the rattle of horse and carriage or the leisurely way the decrepit mansions drifted past. Maybe it was sitting quietly encased in the pleasant musk of soft leather. Maybe it was just having a gentleman close by, but whatever the reason, for the first time since leaving my room this morning, I felt at peace.

"Brittan."

"Beg pardon?" I said, turning from the window.

"Brittan Salter," my rescuer said, smiling. "Britt, to most people."

"Jennifer Crispin," I said. "My friends call me, Jenny."

I offered my hand. His fingers were huge, and I wondered if digit girth and length might have some relation to the size of men's other appendages. Releasing my hand, his gaze dropped to my chest. Embarrassed, I half-turned in my seat, unbuttoned my blouse, and began to button it correctly. Why I should act so modestly with a man who'd practically raped me, I didn't know.

"Where do you live?" Britt asked.

"*Mrs. Hundschlanger's Lodging for Girls*. It's on Dey Street, two blocks from City Hall. Could you take me there?"

Britt twisted sideways, opened a small window behind his head, and spoke my address to the driver, whose eyes grew large at the sight of my still open blouse. Britt slid the window shut. "How old are you, Jenny?"

The question was blunt and having been recently jilted by my fiancé mere days before our wedding, I debated whether or not to tell him. What business was it of his even if he had saved my life? "Twenty-six," I said defensively. "And you?"

"Thirty-two. Molly said you work for who?"

I finished with the buttons and began tucking in my blouse. "I'm a filing clerk for Glorianna Talmadge, the feminist."

"Oh, yes, Mrs. Satan."

The nickname irked me. "Her name is Glorianna. She says all prophets are misunderstood in their own time."

"So," he said in an enlightened tone, "Glorianna is a prophet as well as a suffragette?"

I glanced over my shoulder. "Glorianna says she brings the gospel of universal suffrage to all women." As an ignorant male, I felt obliged to educate him in modern feminist views.

"I don't know any suffragettes," he said.

I finished tucking in my blouse and faced him. "Well, maybe you ought to, Mr. Salter."

"Britt," he said.

"Britt." I smiled; he wasn't so bad.

He returned the smile. "Knowing *one* suffragette is enough."

"Don't you want women to vote?" I asked.

"As long as women are more interested in their hair than politics, I doubt men will ever voluntarily give them the vote."

My hands flew to my head. My hair. I'd completely forgotten about my hair. Frantic, I took the mirror from my purse. What a mess. I prodded here, pushed there, but it made no difference.

"What did I tell you?"

Peeved, I looked at him over the top of my mirror. "Tell me what?"

"Your hair."

I jammed the mirror into my purse. "I know all about politics, thank you."

"I'm sure," he said. "Which candidate is the most handsome. Who has the best-trimmed beard. What color their eyes are. Like I said, women will never get the right to vote."

"Well, Mr. Salter, for your information, Glorianna says women *already* have the right to vote. It's written in the constitution."

"Oh?"

"She says the 14th and 15th amendments not only freed the slaves, they guaranteed the vote to *all citizens*. Women are citizens too, you know."

"I'm afraid the government doesn't see it that way."

"Glorianna says the government needs a change. She says in five days not only will the women of America rise up, push their way into the voting booths, and cast their votes for her, but that every reasoning adult male will do the same."

"Every reasoning adult male?" Britt asked. "Are you sure of that?"

"Absolutely," I said. "Who else would they reasonably vote for?"

He offered an open palm. "They could reelect General Grant."

"Haven't you heard of the *Credit Mobilier* scandal?"

"Credit what?"

"*Mobilier*," I said. "It's French. For a man who reads the newspaper, you seem very ill-informed."

"I could read more if I wasn't interrupted by ladies in wrist irons," Britt said under his breath.

"Either way," I said, building upon my victory, "it is *you* who knows little about politics. Grant's administration let the Union Pacific Railroad steal millions from the American taxpayer through a fraudulent company called *Credit Mobilier,* and so far the president has done little if anything about it."

"So Grant is out," he conceded. "What about Horace Greeley?"

"Greeley?" I asked, stunned that anyone would consider such a preposterous choice. "Don't make me laugh. What is his platform? Go west young man? He bailed the Confederate President, Jefferson Davis, out of jail for heaven's sake. Greeley's a well-meaning fool. Everyone knows newspapermen make terrible politicians."

His head cocked. "Doesn't Mrs. Satan publish a newspaper?"

"That's different," I said. "Glorianna is a newspaper*woman*."

Britt gazed out the window. The carriage turned north as I struggled on. "Anyway, Glorianna says the right to vote is just one tiny part of the women's movement."

He seemed more occupied with a passing omnibus than women's issues. I tried a new tack. "Glorianna believes in other doctrines as well:

spiritualism, vegetarianism, Free Love…"

"Forget about Mrs. Satan," Britt said swinging back from the window. "Surely, you believe in something besides what Glorianna Talmadge tells you."

My mind went blank. I stared at his face and blinked. He had beautiful eyes, deep and brown, piercing in their way.

The carriage hit a bump. "Well?" he asked.

I cleared my throat. "I believe in universal suffrage, women's rights, and, oh yes, communism. Workers should own the means of production. The masses are tired of being exploited by greedy capitalists."

"Miss Crispin," he said slowly, "very few masses have financed a railroad."

I thought a minute before remembering my Marx. "A central committee would decide how and where such projects would be built."

Britt examined the ceiling.

I frowned, realizing my student was getting bored. "I tried vegetarianism once. It gave me gas."

Britt wrinkled his nose.

"As for spiritualism," I ventured, "the whole notion of deceased spirits floating about seems a bit unsettling."

"You realize tonight is Halloween?"

I laughed nervously. "Oh, yes, and I believe in Free Love. A woman should be able to use her body in any way she pleases. I mean, in any way that pleases her."

His gaze connected swiftly to mine. "You mean women should be allowed to whore around like men?"

"Mr. Salter," I exclaimed, "You put it very indelicately."

"Britt," he said, grinning.

I shifted uncomfortably in my seat. "If a woman wishes to know a man—in the biblical sense—why should that be anybody's business but hers?"

"Well," he said, crossing his arms, "you weren't so thrilled with Free Love back at Molly's."

My cheeks burned. "Really, sir, I scarcely know you."

Britt eyed me with suspicion. "You mean had you known me better you might have…" He cleared his throat and pulled at his lapels. "Let's put Free Love aside. Tell me what made McCauley so mad at you."

Thankful for the change of subject, I answered eagerly. "He wanted to arrest Glorianna, but all he got was me. Later, he offered to release me in exchange for—taking liberties."

"Did you give him that shiner?"

I lowered my head and nodded. "I'm sorry I dragged you into my troubles, Britt."

"McCauley needed a good walloping."

I looked up. "He knew your name."

"I met him in the war. Best tracker in the Army. He could find a platoon, a patrol, or a single man. Badger McCauley, we called him. Single-minded bastard. Never gives up."

"What happened between you two?"

Britt's mouth tightened as if reliving an unpleasant memory. "McCauley always did his tracking alone, but rumors started drifting in so, one day, I followed him. I caught him in a farmhouse defiling two girls. The youngest was only a child. Found out he'd been doing that sort of thing for half the war."

I made a pistol of my hand. "You should have shot him where he stood."

"Had I known the commander wouldn't prosecute, I would have."

"You mean the Army didn't arrest him?"

Britt shook his head. "Transferred him to a different unit. Said things like that happened all the time. Said the Army couldn't afford to lose a valuable man like McCauley."

"And now he's a vice detective."

"Still a valuable man."

I peered at Britt. "What about you? You don't know much about current events. Have you been away?"

Britt's expression grew dark. "Egypt," he said curtly.

Sand dunes and camels appeared in my mind, palm trees set against crumbling pyramids, bearded statues, shattered temples, the Sphinx. Wonder colored my voice. "You've really been to Egypt?"

"Worked there as a mercenary."

"You? A soldier of fortune? Trading courage for gold? Selling victory to the highest bidder?"

Britt laughed. "You make it sound like a penny dreadful. The work was hot and sweaty and paid little."

"Why did you do it?"

"Employment was scarce after the war. Lockie and I signed on under Colonel Thaddeus Mott. We trained the Khedive's men to use explosives."

"Whatever for?"

"To dig their new canal."

"The Suez Canal," I said, remembering pictures I'd seen in *Frank Leslie's Illustrated Newspaper.*

"That's right," he said. "Experts called it impossible. The Khedive figured differently. Smart man—ruthless, too."

I trembled with excitement. "You *met* the Khedive?"

"Only a few times. Mostly Lockie and I dealt with his ministers. But I'll never forget the banquets and balls the Khedive threw. Ras El Tin palace gleamed like a brass bowl: German orchestras, French food, Swiss pastries. A thousand guests attended each event, men decked out like Beau Brummell, women like Cinderella. Princes and emperors common as beggars at a free lunch. Cost the Khedive a barrel of gold for every party."

"So now you're in New York. A man of your skills must be a military engineer or a defense consultant."

Britt chuckled. "No, just a salesman."

"Yes, of course," I said, squaring my shoulders. "Dynamite. Gun cotton. Artillery."

"Patent medicine."

I slumped. "You're not serious."

"Serious as the gout. Lockie and I are tired of working hard, sweating, blowing things up, and beating ourselves to death. From now on we're using our brains. We're cashing in and making a fortune."

"I don't understand. There can't be much money in patent medicine."

"Certainly there is," he said. "Look, the country is changing. People are buying all manner of things—products they're called. Companies are selling these products to the entire nation at once: breakfast cereal, biscuit mix, crackers, wire fencing, firearms… They call it marketing."

"So patent medicine is the *product* you're *marketing*?"

"That's right, and a damn good product it is."

Britt reached into his jacket, extracted a corked blue bottle, and displayed it on the muscle of his crooked arm. "*Doctor Sekhmet's Magnetic Vegetable Compound*: wild yam, sarsaparilla, licorice, yucca, and saw palmetto, blended according to an ancient Egyptian recipe discovered chiseled on stone tablets in the temple at Karnak. Bonded and patented." He pulled the cork. "Ninety percent alcohol. Like a taste?"

A mix of shock and disappointment filled me. Never in a hundred years could I have imagined Britt as a patent medicine salesman. And yet, sitting there holding a bottle in his giant hand, jaw twisted into a satisfied smile, he seemed the perfect pitchman for the curative powers of *Doctor Sekhmet's Magnetic Vegetable Compound*, guaranteed to eliminate the symptoms of neuritis, neuralgia, dropsy, consumption, and the bloody flux. I wrinkled my nose. "No, thank you."

He corked the bottle and pushed it into my hand. "Have a free sample."

I slipped the bottle into my purse. "How many have you sold?"

"Ten."

"Cases?"

"Bottles. To friends mostly. But business will pick up. A good product sells itself."

I sighed. "This Sekhmet fellow was a friend of yours?"

"*She* wasn't a fellow. She was the physician to the pharaoh himself."

"Which pharaoh?"

"Doesn't matter, but she was so good that Ra—"

"The Sun-God."

Britt gave me a smile. "—elevated her to the status of daughter, whereupon she promptly punished mankind for mocking her father."

"Never anger a woman," I said.

"That's why you gave McCauley a black eye."

"I told you, he tried to take liberties with my person."

"Miss Crispin?"

"Jenny," I corrected.

"Jenny, you're obviously not from New York. You must have come here for a reason."

I clasped my hands together in my lap. "I realize now it was a hasty decision."

"What decision?"

"Leaving Pottsville."

"Beau trouble?" he asked, sounding fatherly.

His acuity shocked me. "A disagreement about my beliefs."

"Imagine that," Britt said. "The cad."

"Dorian De Greer. His family owns Pottsville Bank and Trust among several other banks. In Pottsville, that's the same as royalty. Which makes Dorian—"

"Prince of Pots?" he said, cutting me off.

I stared at him cryptically then grinned. "Prince or not, no man tells Jenny Crispin what to do."

Britt yawned. "So you said."

I slapped my palm on the seat to wake him. "I'll not be a man's slave. I want to do things, see things. I want to be a writer. I want to change the world. I want to go places: London, Paris, Rome—"

"Egypt?"

"Exactly," I said. "I want to climb the Sphinx, explore the pyramids— not just look at pictures in *Frank Leslie's Illustrated Newspaper.*"

"But for the time being you work for Mrs. Satan."

That name infuriated me. I crossed my arms and looked out the window. The spire of Saint Paul's Church rose above the buildings. Mrs. Hundschlanger's was only a block away. I turned and faced Britt squarely. "Her name is Glorianna Talmadge, *not* Mrs. Satan."

"Well," Britt said, "*Glorianna* and her preaching have gotten you in trouble with the law, haven't they? So what now?"

What now? I repeated. Escaping McCauley had consumed all my effort. I hadn't given the future any thought. What *was* I going to do when I returned to Mrs. Hundschlanger's? I couldn't go back to

Talmadge's Weekly, at least not until after the election, not with Special Detective Badger McCauley prowling about. And then there was Cleo.

"I must find my roommate, Cleo," I whispered. "She left work at lunchtime yesterday and never came back."

Mrs. Hundschlanger's building came into view. The hackney stopped across the street. Britt took hold of the door latch. "This Cleo of yours probably spent the night at a friend's. She's most likely waiting for you inside."

He turned the knob, stepped out, and offered his hand. I took it and descended to the street. "I pray you're right, Mr. Salter."

"Britt," he corrected.

"Britt," I said, smiling. "Will I see you again?"

He kissed my hand. "That will be impossible. I'm leaving town this evening."

"Not because of any trouble I've caused?" I asked, suddenly worried for him.

"No, Lockie and I are making a big sale tonight after which it will be much safer if we're far, far away. And if I were you, Jenny Crispin, I'd go far, far away too. That little tap I gave McCauley won't stop him. He'll be back on your trail within the hour."

With that, he climbed into the carriage. As it rattled off, I hurried toward my building hoping to find Cleo waiting for me.

Chapter Ten

Britt opened the hackney's window and spoke to the driver. "Atlas Brewing, Tenth Street." He glanced behind. Jenny was rushing up the steps into her building. The girl did have a certain allure. Lively, young, fresh, well proportioned, as perfect in many ways as Rebecca. Still, how could he have been fooled into thinking she was a working girl? So completely and utterly fooled?

He closed the window and settled back in the seat. It was the wrist irons, of course. They'd thrown off his judgment. He wasn't sure why her chains had been so exciting. Something out of the ordinary, he supposed. He needed that, needed change, stimulation. He hadn't received those things at Molly's, not today, not sexually anyway.

Yet, once he and Jenny had gotten over the initial misunderstanding of their meeting, he'd had fun in a wholesome sort of way, the rapid banter of their conversation, the innuendo, the excitement in her eyes, the genuine interest she showed in him without the need for monetary reward. He found their time together quite pleasant. Out of the ordinary, really, different from the paid women he usually came in contact with.

Britt opened the window once more. *Mrs. Hundschlanger's Lodging for Girls* was barely visible against the background of brownstones and apartment houses. He supposed there was no way he would ever see the young lady again. When his *big sale* was over, he wouldn't be able to return to New York for a long, long time. Maybe never. And if she didn't leave town like he'd suggested, McCauley would track her down and arrest her. Regardless, a girl like that, a virgin of all things, would surely have no interest in a soldier of fortune who grew up in a brothel and spent his time jumping from one adventure to the next—when he wasn't dallying in a bawdy house.

No, a young lady like Jenny would have no more than a passing interest in a man like him. Living in a residence for girls, she would more likely meet her mate at some church social. He'd be a clerk at Macy's or a bank teller. A thin, bandy fellow, a virgin like her. Probably top each other under the covers in the dark of night, quiet as mice—with all their clothes on. The whole act would take less than a minute. Pity, she might never find someone to teach her the finer points of pleasure, as he had been taught in his youth.

Then again, a girl who wanted to travel the world and see the pyramids might not be satisfied with a bank teller or a clerk from Macy's. Maybe locked up inside that prim virgin beat the heart of a hooker.

Too bad he wouldn't get the chance to find out—and now that he thought about it, he really didn't want to. Until some brave knight relieved that girl of her vestal burden—and it wouldn't be him—she was still a virgin, and virgins, he had always heard, were a messy lot, crying, clinging, and confused.

Half a block from Atlas Brewing, Britt rapped on the roof of the hackney. The rig pulled to the curb and stopped. Abandoned buildings and empty warehouses gave the area a rundown look. As the hackney wheeled away, Britt pulled the Webley from his shoulder holster and set the hammer to half cock. He opened the loading gate and spun the cylinder until the spent round he'd used on the bottle of nitro at Johnny Dolan's appeared. After ejecting it, he inserted a fresh cartridge from the loops on the belt. The Webley was a fine piece and it couldn't have come at a better time. He pushed the weapon into its holster. Even Lockie, the consummate firearms expert, would be impressed when he saw it.

Chiseled stone letters identified the ornate but crumbling building as the Atlas Brewing Company. *Only the Finest Hops Used* bespoke an artfully painted, although peeling, sign. Fallen from the facade, bricks littered the ground at the boarded entrance. Britt walked around back. A tall wooden fence stretched for at least half a block. He climbed through a section of missing slats and found himself in an overgrown field. Decrepit wagons, also bearing the name "Atlas Brewing Co.," lined up as if awaiting their drivers for the last ten years. Out of place, horses grazed near a jumble of rotting barrels. As he turned to face the building, a voice called out behind him: "Look what we have here, Billy, a trespasser."

Britt turned. Two men in black coats and red scarves came toward him. One man, no older than mid-twenties, had a nest of unruly red hair and grinned beneath a broken nose. The other wore a short beard, a large belly, and held a gun.

"Good afternoon, sir," said the man, pointing the gun. "Billy," he said to his companion, "see if this gentleman carries a weapon." Billy reached in Britt's coat, extracted the Webley, and stuffed it into his belt.

Dismayed at the loss of his weapon, Britt said, "Take me to your boss."

"Well," said the fat man with mock sadness, "my boss, as you call him, is very busy and therefore employs Billy and me to keep trespassers like you from taking up his valuable time."

"He's expecting me," Britt said. "I've an important message."

"A clever ruse," the fat man said, "but you must be more exact. I have found that people facing death tell all manner of outrageous mendacities. Please be quick, though, as my inclination is to shoot you now."

"For a man with a gun," Britt said, "you speak most eloquently; however, when your boss asks whether I've arrived and then finds out you have killed me, had you five times the eloquence it would not save you from death."

"And you, sir," said the fat man, smiling, "are no less a man of eloquence. Now I must discern whether you employ your verbiage to

70

deceive, or do, in fact, have an urgent message."

After a moment's reflection, he motioned with his gun toward a rear door. Inside, they passed through a dark, cavernous room. Footsteps echoed over enormous copper pipes and vessels. The air smelled of hops and yeast. At the back wall, Billy opened a door, and Britt entered what could have been a brightly lit drawing room in an alderman's house.

Four armed people stood around a table: an older man dressed in simple country clothes, a younger man in a short jacket and white shirt, and two black-suited gentlemen. It didn't appear possible, but one of the gentlemen, a tall, gaunt man with a narrow goatee and bony face, bore a distinct resemblance to the engraving of General Archer Gideon Britt had seen in the *Times* not an hour earlier.

The interruption appeared to disturb the four men. The fat man apologized, saying they'd brought the stranger only because he claimed to have an important message. Britt detected in the well-dressed men an arrogance he'd seen in many officers he'd served under during the war, the attitude that lesser men were expendable.

The man resembling General Gideon leaned forward, resting his hands on the table. "Sir," he said with a strong Tennessee accent, "if you have a name, say it. If you have a message, speak it."

Boldness, Britt decided, was his best plan. "My name is Brittan Salter, and you, I presume, are General Gideon."

The general scrutinized him. If impressed or alarmed to be recognized, he gave no sign. "What is your message?"

"A case of Albany explosives has recently come into your possession. I need one bottle of nitroglycerin from that case. I'll pay double the going price."

General Gideon glanced at the two men beside him. "Why, may I ask, do you desire this one bottle of nitroglycerin?" he asked Britt

Britt kept his gaze level on General Gideon. "A stump, sir. I have a tree stump I wish to remove."

"A stump?"

"Yes, sir. A large, troublesome stump. Let me also add, that should you need an expert in the field of explosives, I offer my services."

"I see. Then may I ask you, Mr. Salter, do your sympathies lie with the South or with the North?"

Britt knew the answer Gideon sought, but a man of the general's caliber could not be easily fooled—and Britt had never been a good liar. Again he played it bold. "My sympathies lie with the men who pay me."

"Would you travel wherever necessary for those men?"

"For the right pay."

"Would you destroy whatever and whoever you are called upon to destroy?"

"For the right pay."

The general straightened. "Mr. Salter, I, too, have a message, one of far-reaching consequences, which I will soon deliver to the Union. For that, I need all the nitroglycerin in my possession. A man like you, who sells his allegiance to the highest bidder, is a man who cannot be trusted. I would sooner hang a mercenary than fight beside him."

So much for boldness. The fat man and Billy took Britt by the arms and marched him out the door, through the brewery, and into the overgrown yard.

"Your message did not please the general," the fat man said. "Billy, bring up one of those wheelbarrows."

"What message of far-reaching consequences is General Gideon talking about?" Britt asked after Billy disappeared around the corner

"I admire your curiosity in the face of death, Mr. Salter, but I cannot divulge any more than to say, men of vainglorious character, such as General Gideon, do not take defeat lightly."

"Why not elaborate?" Britt asked. "I'll be dead in a few minutes. You're a member of the Red Scarves. Do you take orders from Gideon?"

The fat man smiled. "Despite what the general said about mercenaries, until his gold runs out, the Red Scarves are his paid soldiers."

"Surely," Britt said with feigned astonishment, "you wouldn't have me believe General Gideon is a hypocri—"

Britt spun swiftly and punched the fat man in the head so hard and so suddenly he flew through the air several feet. The pistol fell from his hand and clanked to the ground. Britt picked up the weapon and turned it over in his hands. Army Colt, .44 caliber, dirty and worn badly. He'd be surprised if it even fired.

After setting the hammer to half-cock, Britt turned the cylinder to the best looking cap, then cocked the hammer. He walked along the side of the warehouse after Billy. Peeking around the corner, he saw the young man struggling with a wheelbarrow, presumably to move Britt's dead body on. When Billy rounded the building, Britt pressed the Colt into his ribs.

Billy dropped the handles of the barrow and raised his arms. Britt took his Webley from Billy's belt and shoved it under his chin.

"What is General Gideon's bold message?"

"I don't know; I swear."

"When will it be delivered?"

"Tonight," Billy said, quivering.

Britt pushed the Webley harder into the soft flesh between Billy's jawbones. "What time tonight?"

Billy rose on tiptoes. "I don't know."

"Where, then?"

"I don't know that, either. Please, sir, don't kill me. I'm not a Red Scarf. I'm just here to earn some extra money. I have a son."

The fear in Billy's eyes showed he was telling the truth, so Britt smacked him on the head with the butt of the Colt, and he collapsed. Taking Billy's arm, Britt dragged him to the entrance of the warehouse and dropped his body next to the fat man. After opening the warehouse door, he pointed the Colt at the ground and pulled the trigger. Nothing.

Damn weapon hadn't been fired in years. Had the fat man really intended to kill him with it? Apparently not. More likely he used the weapon as a club to knock people over the head. Britt cocked the hammer and pulled the trigger again. Nothing. After the fourth pull, the gun discharged. He dropped the Colt on the fat man's chest, hurried inside the brewery, and hid behind a vat.

General Gideon and the three men came idly out of their drawing room. They walked to the open door and looked down at the fat man and Billy. "Mr. Salter has killed them both," General Gideon said in a matter-of-fact tone.

Britt fired his Webley from behind the vat forcing Gideon and his men out the door to look for cover in the field. Gideon took a position behind a wagon and returned fire while the other three men gathered the horses. Britt advanced to the open door and shot sparingly. His goal was to drive Gideon and his men from the location, not kill them. He hoped the nitro was stored somewhere in the building. All he needed was one bottle. They could have the rest of the explosive to carry out whatever nefarious plan they had devised.

The four men mounted their horses and fled, escaping through a far gate in the fence. Britt ejected the spent casings in the Webley and reloaded the chambers. Gideon and his men would return shortly, but not before they regrouped. He had ten to fifteen minutes.

The drawing room was just as they had left it except the table was now devoid of papers. None of the men had carried anything with them when they had escaped so they must have locked the papers up before coming outside. Not that he cared; he only wanted the nitro.

A door off the drawing room led to a smaller room containing shelves of rifles and pistols, as well as boxes of ammunition. In the corner stood an icebox. This had to be where the nitro was stored. But when he looked inside, the icebox held only a tin of half-eaten apple cobbler. He dipped in his finger and licked it. Not bad, but he'd tasted better.

Returning to the drawing room, he noticed a drawer in the side of the table. A tug on the handle proved the drawer locked, but a deft twist of his knife rendered the lock worthless. Inside the drawer, he found a three-page speech written in tight handwriting lambasting Grant for his reconstruction policies toward the South. Under the speech were receipts from Foster's Mercantile Exchange for several clocks and small firearms. Folded and tied with a ribbon were letters to friends and relatives in Tennessee. Beside the letters was an advertisement for the Viking Ice Company on Water Street.

Disappointed, and with no time to search the entire premises, Britt left the drawing room and exited the brewery. In the yard, the fat man and Billy moaned. To the clatter of approaching horseshoes on cobblestone, Britt walked across the overgrown yard and slipped out through the missing slats in the fence. From the window of a half-demolished cooperage across the street, he watched the general arrive with several new men on horseback. While they galloped about the brewery yard, Britt hurried down a narrow alley filled with puddles and trash until, three blocks later, he found an idle hackney driver who demanded cash in hand before taking him to his shop on Barclay Street.

The inside air smelled of damp earth. Glass rattled as Britt closed the door. Sunlight shining through a hundred blue medicine bottles stacked in the window cast the room in azure squares. Lockie sat in one of two chairs against the wall, his face a blue chessboard.

"Where's the Khedive," Britt asked before Lockie could speak.

"Bryant's Opera House."

"Absorbing Western culture? Let me guess: *Silver Demon*."

Lockie smiled and shook his head. "Closed last week. *The Bohemian Girl* is playing now."

"Never heard of it."

"You've nae heard such caterwauling, either. And the story is worse. A baby raised by gypsies discovers she's of noble birth."

"You don't believe it could happen?"

"Ach! There isn't a noble alive who wouldn't slaughter every last gypsy in his kingdom. I walked out during the first act. I'll nae return till it's over. What about the nitro?"

Britt shook his head. "It's so close, I can smell it."

"But you couldnae steal us a wee bottle?"

"General Gideon has it hidden somewhere."

Lockie leaned forward in his chair. "Archer Gideon, the Confederate general? What's he doing in town?"

Britt sat down beside him. "Apparently, still fighting the war."

"He'll nae win any battles in New York City."

"Gideon is planning to deliver some sort of far-reaching message tonight using the nitro. Exactly where and when, I don't know."

"His message had better nae involve the Khedive."

Britt laughed. "Wouldn't that be a cruel joke."

"On us or the Khedive? Without that nitro, we've nothing. A month's work gone for naught. The Khedive will return to Egypt richer than ever, and we'll be paupers. It's tonight or never. I told you Hallow's Eve was bad luck. How long do we have?"

Britt fished out his watch and rubbed his thumb over the gold hunter case. He'd bought the timepiece from a stranded sailor for two dollars. He popped the lid. "Thirteen hours."

Lockie took out his own pocket watch and held it conspicuously at arm's length. Britt had seen the timepiece many times, a Kullberg astronomical, open-face, chronometer. When it came to mechanisms, the Scotsman always had to have the best.

"Intermission is over," Lockie said, making a show of winding the Kullberg's stem. He slipped the chronometer back into his pocket. "I've got to get to the theater. Nae telling where his highness will go next, but I'm betting on the Blackenstoe's Circus in Central Park. The advertisements describe a lady trapeze artist who hangs by her hair." He grinned. "Nae Scotsman worth his sporran would miss that."

Britt rose from his chair as Lockie hurried out the door. Thirteen hours left and he hadn't a clue where to get a bottle of nitro.

Chapter Eleven

After searching the building for Cleo, I sat in Mrs. Hundschlanger's lobby, imagining the horrors she might be facing. The other boarders seated around me prattled on about fashion and food. None of them knew of Cleo's whereabouts, nor did they seem to care. Outraged by their apathy, I was just forming a plan to find my friend when Abigail came down the stairs with her suitcase.

"Jenny," she said, sitting beside me, "thank goodness you're safe. I begged Glorianna to wait for you, but she would hear none of it." For the first time, Abigail seemed to notice my disheveled appearance. "You look...distraught."

"I'm fine," I said, rubbing my wrists. "Have you seen Cleo?"

"Not since yesterday morning."

Her answer was expected. "After you abandoned me, a Detective McCauley from The Society for the Suppression of Vice arrested me."

Abigail, always dramatic, clutched her heart. "Goodness. Why you?"

"Because the man is a pervert who wants to jail everyone at *Talmadge's Weekly.*"

"Everyone?"

"Including you."

Abigail's eyes grew large and moist. "But I'm only the copy girl."

"And I'm just a filing clerk. But you, me, Mavis, Laura, and especially Glorianna are in grave danger. McCauley wants all of us in jail for the singular crime of daring to believe we are men's equal."

"But he let you go," she said.

"No, I escaped. However, now that I think about it," I said in a lowered voice, "McCauley may have nabbed Cleo. I'm going to the police station to find out."

Her fear shifted to alarm. "But McCauley will capture you."

"I still have to go."

"Alone?"

"How else?"

"This is serious," Abigail said, wiping her eyes. "I don't trust the police. You could be arrested or killed—even worse."

"Abigail, what could be worse than being killed?"

She raised her chin defiantly. "Being kidnapped and sold into slavery."

I cocked my head. "Don't you think people are exaggerating the dangers of kidnapping just a little?"

Abigail stood. "No," she said, loud enough to draw the notice of the girls around us. "And what if McCauley isn't working alone? What if there are scores of detectives scouring the city for you and me and Cleo?"

Mindful of our lodge mates' curiosity, I stood as well. "McCauley works alone. A friend told me."

"Well," Abigail said, stamping her six-eyelet lace boot, "no vice detective is going to arrest me. Father will be here any minute to take me home to Brooklyn."

The words *vice detective* and *arrest* ignited an explosion of conversation and questions from the other girls. Wishing to avoid attention, I hurried upstairs to my room. Once inside, I tipped some water from the pitcher to the washbowl then stripped off my dirty clothes. As my soapy hands caressed my breasts and belly, my encounter in Britt's bed crept into my mind. Despite the frigid water, my skin flushed, my breath deepened, and my pulse quickened. Baffled as to why my own fingers should evoke mental images of Britt's naked form, let alone affect the internal workings of my physiology, I hastily rinsed and dried. But an ill-defined craving still lingered within me.

With none of my usual undergarments dry from an earlier washing, I shimmied into my new silk chemise—the something blue Dorian had given me to wear beneath my wedding dress. I combed my hair then put on a freshly pressed, full length, black dress that fit me without my awful corset. Lastly, I scrubbed the grime from my boots and rubbed them down with father's special polish. After retrieving my map and the two dollars I kept hidden under the bed springs, I returned downstairs. Only one or two of the girls met my gaze. Abigail and her suitcase were gone. Pleased for her safety, but feeling apprehensive about my upcoming quest, I left the building and walked east toward City Hall.

Bright, late morning sunshine, and unseasonable warmth for the last day of October, made my walk pleasant. Pigeons fluttered from the sidewalk in front of me. Leaves swirled. Peddlers touted meat pies and roast chicken legs, but lunch was still two hours away. After crossing Broadway, I stopped at the fountain in City Hall Park, rested on its edge, and consulted my map.

One block north and three blocks east, 49 Beekman Street to be exact, was the closest police station. Built of red brick and white stone, police officers in long blue coats came and went through its large double doors flanked by round, white lights on brass pedestals.

What would Britt do? I asked myself, wavering where I stood. Simple. He'd storm inside, grab McCauley by the collar, punch him on the chin, and demand to know where Cleo was. The image of such a scene brought a smile to my lips.

A policeman tipped his hat as he passed. My smile withered. I was in a dangerous place. In spite of my fear, I called out to him. "Officer?"

He turned around.

Dressed in sturdy, well-shined, walking shoes, the policeman was tall and wide but not in a muscular way. Unlike Britt's small, tight waist, this fellow carried a large belly. Still, it was easy to see that one blow from his meaty paws could send a hoodlum to the street unconscious.

He walked closer. "Yes, Missy, will you be needing some assistance?"

The policeman was Irish, of course, and I had no problem acting meek and frightened in his presence. "Excuse me, Officer, are you familiar with *Mrs. Hundschlanger's Lodging for Girls?*"

"Certainly," he said, seizing the chance to help a young lady in need. "Just down from the Astor House on Dey Street."

"Mrs. Hundschlanger sent me to inquire about one of her lodgers. She's gone missing."

"Missing, you say? How long?"

"Since yesterday noon."

He took my elbow. "You'd better speak to the sergeant."

I hesitated.

"No need to be afraid, now. We'll help you find your lost girl. I've a daughter myself almost your age."

Inside the station, the sergeant busied himself behind a large desk covered in paperwork. Notices and wanted posters plastered the wall behind him. Thankfully, none bore any resemblance to me.

"Who's this, Quinn? Lady of the evening?"

"Show some respect, Doyle. The Missy's trying to find a friend. Lives at old lady Hundschlanger's. Been gone since yesterday noon."

The sergeant, a red-nosed man with sunken cheeks, regarded me suspiciously. "Name?"

"Cleopatra Duncan," I said.

He pulled a tattered ledger from a drawer, opened it, and ran his finger down a line of cursive entries. "We've no Duncans," he said, looking up, "not today and not yesterday. She'll show up. Found a beau, most likely."

Whether by worry, fear, or desperation, I managed to conjure a tear for Officer Quinn. He frowned and turned to Sergeant Doyle. "Doyle, now you know them girls never gives their real name. How's about letting Missy here have a look in the chicken coop?"

Doyle slammed the book shut and tossed it in the drawer. "Take her if you want. But you'll mop the floor if she loses her breakfast."

Quinn guided me through a paint worn door. The smell of human filth overwhelmed me, but, frankly, I'd smelled worse in Arden's Embalmery back home. Inside a ten-by-ten cell, five women dressed from tawdry to shabby sat on a bench. One of them, obviously drunk, shouted when she saw us. "Here you go, ladies. Now we've enough girls to open our own knock shop. What do you say, Quinn? We'll split with you. Twice what you make now."

Quinn cleared his throat ominously then bent low to my ear. "Any of these *ladies* your missing girl?"

Most wore shabby boots. Three of the women, although late thirties like Cleo, carried the seasoned look of the street. The fourth, a girl of no more than fourteen, wore a pair of expensive eight button, velvet top shoes. The last girl sat on the end of the bench with her face turned against the wall and her shoes hidden from view. I walked to the side of the cell for a better look.

"Hilda? Hilda Steinmetz, is that you?"

Unmasked, Hilda rushed to the bars, her face inches from mine. "Jenny, please don't tell the other girls. It's not what you think."

One of the women laughed. Fearful that Hilda would speak my full name aloud, I held a finger to my lips and shushed.

"I was minding my own business," Hilda said, "when a detective arrested me like a common peddlesnatch."

"Who are you calling common?" the drunk woman scorned.

"Black and yellow pants?" I asked.

"How did you know?"

"McCauley," growled another woman. "Popped us all. On some kind of a tear, he is."

Hilda's eyes betrayed her fear. "Don't tell anyone, please. Father cut off my funds last month so when I lost my job at the Mercantile Exchange, what was I to do? I had no food, no lodging."

She started to weep. The women quieted. "Hilda," I asked, "have you seen Cleo Duncan? McCauley is after her as well. Has she been through here?"

Hilda nodded through tears. "McCauley said Cleo tried to resist when he arrested her. He said she was injured."

I pressed my body against the bars. "How bad was she hurt?"

"I don't know," Hilda said, "but McCauley had her taken to City Hospital."

Back outside, Officer Quinn gave me directions to City Hospital—six blocks north on Broadway between Worth and Duane—then wished me luck.

Four stories tall and separated from Broadway by a large tree-filled lawn, the steeple-topped structure resembled a country manor more than a place of medicine. As I approached the entrance, my fear of arrest vanished, replaced wholly by concern for Cleo.

A middle-aged nurse seated at a receiving desk, greeted me as I entered. "Visiting a patient?"

"I'm here to see Cleo Duncan."

Just like the sergeant before her, she consulted a ledger. "When was she admitted?"

"Yesterday, I presume. She was injured."

"Brought in by ambulance wagon then?"

"Yes. Maybe. I'm not sure."

She opened a different ledger and read. "I'm sorry, we have no Cleo Duncan listed."

"But she has to be here."

The nurse gestured to a bench. "There's one other possibility. Please take a seat. Someone will be out to talk to you."

I had no more taken my seat when a door banged opened, and a gentleman with a bandage on his knee hopped to the middle of the room, followed by a nurse holding a crutch. The nurse tried to push the crutch into man's hand, but he knocked it away and began cursing loudly. A bearded gentleman, well dressed in a black suit and calfskin shoes, entered the room next, accompanied by an orderly pushing a wicker chair on wheels. After a brief struggle, the orderly bound the man into the chair with straps, and the bearded gentleman walked over to me.

"My name is Doctor Horton. You are?"

"Jennifer Crispin," I said, standing. "I'm looking for Cleo Duncan. She was brought here yesterday with an injury."

Doctor Horton nodded mournfully. "Come with me, please."

I followed him through white corridors, aware he might be leading me straight into McCauley's hands, but so great was my concern for

Cleo's health that I did not care. After guiding me through several wards, he stopped at a plain, black door.

"Miss Crispin, this door is unmarked for a reason."

His grave tone gave me unease.

"Three kinds of patients arrive at City Hospital," he continued. "The first have easily repaired injuries, broken bones or lacerations."

"Like the gentleman with the bad knee."

"Precisely. The second have ailments about which medical science knows little, the sugar sickness or cancer, for example. With these diseases, we treat the symptoms as best we can and pray for God's intervention."

My unease grew to dread.

"And some patients, I'm afraid, arrive here already at peace with the Maker."

He pushed open the door and the hospital's sparkling white gave way to stark brick and an iron stairway. Twenty steps down, the air carried an odor of camphor mixed with decay. At the bottom, I saw twelve tables lined up against a far wall, each draped with a sheet.

Doctor Horton walked me closer. "The deceased who arrive by ambulance wagon are not logged in by the receiving nurse but proceed directly to the morgue. Sometimes we know their names, other times we do not. Your Cleo may be among these lost souls."

The first table contained a gray-faced man in his thirties. The second, an aged woman. The third held a lady in her early forties. Death so changes a person's appearance that I stared at the woman's face, unsure of whether she was Cleo. But the bow of her lips and her black hair soon convinced me she was not.

And so we continued down the line of bodies, Doctor Horton lifting each sheet as I studied the corpse's face only to shake my head. At the last one, I paused. "If this isn't Cleo, I shall be at a loss."

"When there is hope, there is never loss," the doctor said. With that, he lifted the sheet.

Shock pervaded me like a chill. Merciful God, it couldn't be. The dead woman wasn't Cleo, but *Laura*, Glorianna's accountant.

Doctor Horton caught me as I fell and carried me to a chair.

I sat stunned. An orderly came over and spoke to Doctor Horton. The doctor touched my shoulder. He offered a few words of condolence and apology then hurried off. Before long, the orderly left too.

McCauley had killed Laura, I was sure of it. And if nothing were done, Glorianna, Violet, Cleo, and I would be next.

Britt was right. I needed to get far, far away. But as I rose from the chair, the sound of weeping filtered into my thoughts.

A smart girl would have run straight to Bulwark Bank, withdrawn her funds, and bought a ticket on the next train to Pottsville. But something familiar in the crier's voice compelled me to follow the sound through an open door into a small office. Inside, seated in a chair, I found Cleo.

Her clothes were torn, and her face was bruised. I rushed toward her. Emotion, pent up since her disappearance, gushed forth and I fell to my knees hugging her to my chest. Then the door to the office slammed shut.

McCauley stepped from behind it. "Trackers have a saying: When you lose the track, you bait a trap."

I threw myself at him, but a well-aimed fist knocked me to the floor. He withdrew the revolver from inside his coat and pointed it at me. "Maybe you'd prefer lying under a sheet."

I stood slowly. "You killed Laura."

"She resisted arrest," McCauley said, teeth clamped on his cigar. "I had no choice."

My jaw burned where he'd struck it, but I refused to show pain. "You set up the whole thing, didn't you?"

"I couldn't take a chance on you escaping again."

"So you lied to Hilda about Cleo."

Cigar still tight, McCauley grinned from one side of his mouth. "Worked damn well, don't you think?"

"Are you going to kill us too?" I asked.

"You're too useful to kill."

"What are you talking about?"

He plucked the cigar from his mouth and blew a puff of smoke. "You're going to lead me to Mrs. Satan."

"I'll never betray Glorianna."

"No?" he asked, as if amused. "Then your friend, Cleo, will end up on a slab next to Laura."

Had his gun been in my hand, I would have shot him in the heart. "What in hell's name are you talking about?"

"Simple," he said, jerking the pistol toward Cleo. "I'm taking your friend here to Ludlow Street Jail, and if you don't lead me to Glorianna Talmadge by twelve o'clock tonight, she'll be transferred to the Tombs where a nice little lady I know will gut her like a pig."

Chapter Twelve

For me, the path of life has always been narrow and my direction upon it straight. But rain had now washed the path completely away, and I drifted in a swollen river swept along by currents I could not control.

Gut her like a pig.

McCauley had played me for a fool. Worse than that, he'd forced me into the devil's choice. I couldn't abandon Cleo, but neither could I betray Glorianna. The forces that drove people mad instantly seemed clear.

Brain swirling, I walked to Broadway and ambled south toward City Hall. In front of Colgan's Brewery, an elderly gentleman watched me from an omnibus stop. I sat on the bench beside him. My nerves were strained to breaking. As I longed for a way to steady them, something Britt said in the carriage came to mind: *Ninety percent alcohol. Like a drink?* The bottle was still in my pocket. Without a thought, I pulled the cork and gulped.

My throat burned. My eyes watered. I coughed uncontrollably. The elderly man got up and left. Several passersby stared. Suppressing a gag, I read the bottle's label.

Doctor Sekhmet's Magnetic Vegetable Compound.

Blended According to an Ancient Egyptian Recipe Chiseled on Stone Tablets in the Temple at Karnak.

Effective Against the Rigors of Weak Nerves, Weak Heart, Malaria, Cholera, Colds, Catarrh, Grip, Rheumatism & Female Complaints.

Bonded and Patented 1872.

At the bottom in small letters, I saw an address:
3 Barclay Street, New York City, New York.

I took off at a run. Barclay Street was but two blocks away. I knew that because Bulwark Bank stood on the corner of Broadway and Barclay. Britt's shop must be right around the corner. He'd helped me once; maybe he'd do it again.

Out of breath, I turned right at Barclay and slowed to a walk. Just past Bulwark Bank stood a narrow storefront, its single window filled from top to bottom with blue bottles. Above the window, a signboard hung on iron rods: *Doctor Sekhmet's Magnetic Vegetable Compound.*

This was Britt's shop. It had to be. With any luck, he was inside preparing for his big dangerous sale. I tried the door. I rattled the doorknob. I rapped on the window. No one answered. Desperate, I cupped my hands against the glass and looked. Blue bottles blocked everything. As I turned to leave, Britt opened the door.

"What are *you* doing here?"

I threw my arms around his waist and buried my head in his chest.

He sniffed at my face. "Have you been drinking?"

I held out the empty medicine bottle then related my quest to find Cleo and the subsequent confrontation with McCauley.

Without a word, he walked me to Broadway and a waiting hackney. "Don't send me away," I pleaded, bracing myself against the frame of the carriage's open door.

"I'm not sending you away," he said, pushing me inside. "I'm hungry. We're going to eat."

Embarrassed, I sat, eyes downcast. "Britt, your boots are filthy."

He stomped his boots. Fresh dirt fell to the carriage floor. "I was in the basement when you knocked. The floor is dirt."

"Basement floors are usually hard. You should have yours packed." I took the egg-stained handkerchief from my purse and wiped at his boots. "Father used to say, 'take care of your shoes, and they'll take care of you.'"

Finished, I held the dirty cloth by the corner unsure of what to do with it. Britt plucked it from my fingers and tossed it out the window.

"Hey," I cried, "that was my handkerchief."

"Your filthy handkerchief."

I faced forward, arms crossed. "Yes, well I could have laundered it."

After a moderate drive, the carriage pulled to the curb in front of a tavern named Kelley's Paddock. Britt helped me out, and we entered the establishment to the hum of talk and laughter.

The interior was dim, illuminated only by a few small windows that lined the front. Shadowy bridles and dull saddles adorned the walls. Horseshoes hung between. Pipe smoke, thick as low clouds, mixed with the smell of tanned leather and soured beer; the odor gave me a headache. A walnut bar filled one wall where men in dusty jackets stuffed their faces and slurped their beers. Above their heads hung a campaign poster of President Grant and his running mate, Henry Wilson. In the picture, both candidates wore leather aprons. A banner declared Henry Wilson the Natick Shoemaker.

As our presence became known, patrons stopped eating. Forks clanged to their plates and mugs slammed on the bar. The tavern's chatter quieted until the only sound heard was the buzz of flies over buckets of beer and half-eaten sausages.

"This ain't a bawdy house," an angry voice called. "We don't allow no women in here."

My heart stopped.

A bear of a man stepped forward, thickset, robust, his great curly beard connecting black eyes to belly. Britt swept me behind him. "Then who let *you* in?"

The bear sucked up his gut. "At Kelly's, we keep our codwinkers in the honky tonk."

"Then run to the alley," Britt answered coldly, "you've got customers waiting."

The bear's teeth clenched. Spittle flew from his mouth and he threw a punch. Britt ducked and stepped aside. Momentum carried the bear lumbering forward. As he passed, Britt laid his foot on the man's rump and pushed him head first into the bar. The clientèle cheered. Beer splashed from buckets. Glasses fell to the floor and shattered.

The man staggered back. Blood oozed from his forehead but he recovered quickly. Crouched low, arms moving in slow circles, he approached Britt like a wrestler.

Britt positioned his fists in a classic boxing stance. He feinted, jabbed, missed, then jabbed again. The creature swung a roundhouse, which connected with Britt's chin. His head jerked sideways. A yellow grin erupted in the bear's beard. "There's an Irish welcome to you and your whore."

Britt rubbed his jaw. "After I teach you some manners, I'll tie you down and let your boys have at your arse."

The big man brayed a rough laugh. "It'll be the best the lads ever had." He ducked his head and, charging like a crazed bull, caught Britt in the gut. The two men tumbled into a table, which shattered into firewood. Laughing, the big man rolled off Britt and onto his feet. Ringed by cheering men, he turned a slow circle, pounded his fists against his chest like an ape, and howled at the ceiling. "Who's the best of the 1st New York Volunteers? Who's the best of Serrel's Engineers?"

Britt struggled to his hands and knees amid the celebrating patrons. The bear man, still basking in his companion's cheers, clapped his arm around Britt's waist and helped him to his feet. "Salter, you old bastard, where have you been these past four years?"

Britt wiped a smear of blood from his lip. "Egypt."

The bear man didn't seem to care and roared to the crowd, "Britt is home, lads."

The *lads* crowded round, shaking Britt's hand and slapping his back.

Standing against the wall, I observed the commotion pondering what had just transpired. Mr. Darwin aside, I wondered if men might be a different species than women, some breed of baboon or wild ox.

The bear man bulled his way through the crowd and thrust his bloodied face in mine. "Sorry to offend you, Miss. It was only a joke. I meant no harm. Any girlie of Britt's is welcome here. A fine man, he is, a crackerjack with the fulminate."

Girlie, indeed. The man was a clod. I managed a sneer.

Amid further backslapping and hugging, Britt returned with two beers and a plate of boiled eggs with dried fish. He led me to a scarred table beneath a painting of a horse. After surviving that masculine encounter, I needed a drink, so I snatched up the beer and gulped. It tasted good.

"Would you like a beer?" Britt said, eyebrows raised.

I laughed and wiped the foam from my lip. "Father taught me. The taste reminds me of him. He was a cobbler."

"The cobbler's daughter has no shoes."

"I've heard that all my life," I said, remembering my father's face. "One pair of boots is all you need, he always said. One pair of black, practical boots."

"He's gone now, isn't he?"

There was something about Britt I liked, a tender side he tried to hide. "Yes, but not from my heart."

"The war?"

I nodded.

"And your mother?"

I fought the knot in my throat. "Gone too. The doctor called it phrenitis. Others had a crueler name. Mother's death was the real reason I left Pottsville."

Britt said nothing. I pushed the memories away and motioned toward the men still lively at the bar. "What about you? Do all your old friends greet you so...affectionately?"

"These fellows do. I was in their unit for a time, the 1st New York Volunteers."

"The bear as well?"

Britt shook his head and smiled. "Sergeant Tillison. Loves a fight, doesn't he?"

"He called you a crackerjack with the fumigate."

"Fulminate. A compound of mercury we used to detonate explosives."

"Yes," I said, recalling our conversation in the carriage. "Before you merchandised products, you were an explosives expert."

The light caught Britt's eyes. He smiled faintly and looked past my shoulder as if someone he hadn't seen in years stood behind me. "In the war, we destroyed anything and everything: bridges, buildings, fortifications, railroad tracks. Blew up whatever they ordered us to. I learned about blasting in the Pennsylvania coal mines."

"*You* were a coal miner—in Pennsylvania?"

His focus returned to my face. "Until the war."

"I grew up in a coal town, too."

"So you mentioned—Pottsville."

I paused. "Britt, will you help me save Cleo?"

He took my hand. "Jenny, you need to get on a train and get the hell out of New York."

I pulled my fingers away. "I can't leave Cleo. McCauley will kill her."

Britt's empty hand became a pointing finger. "McCauley will kill you."

"No," I said loudly, "I must help Cleo."

"Jenny," Britt said, voice low and stern. "Listen to me. There's nothing you can do. This is too big. You've got to leave—now."

I shook my head and pushed back from the table. What silly idea had led me to think this stranger would help me? I was a suffragette, for God's sake—a feminist, a communist, and, to him, that meant a silly girl with silly ideas. He'd rather be with his backslapping, head-banging, jaw-busting, simian friends. Nothing would probably please him more than to see me walk out that front door and never return.

"I'd better go. You've done too much for me already."

I hurried toward the door. The workmen had finished their lunch and were leaving, too, donning their coats and downing their last few drops of beer. I fought my way through them, pushing forward until the musk of work and sweat and unwashed clothes surrounded me. And then I was standing in front of the tavern, blinded by sunlight. Bodies pushed me from behind, into the city, into the traffic, into the great collection of indifferent humanity that was New York. Noise and motion assailed me. Omnibuses trundled by on the street, carts rumbled, wagons thundered, cabbies shouted. I bolted headlong down the sidewalk. After running two blocks, my footsteps slowed. Winded, I found a bench and collapsed.

My head ached. It ached from the smell of the tavern, from the city's boom, from McCauley, and from Britt—callous Britt who was too busy merchandising to care about me, my troubles, women's suffrage, communism, or even Free Love.

Chin against chest, I cupped my hands over my ears and closed my eyes.

The ballroom spun around me in a smear of white. *Perpetual Motion* by Strauss: the tune was my favorite. Soaring violins and swooning cellos filled the crepe papered room—every corner, every niche, bright and uplifting. I was twirling, swirling, dizzy with the music's beat. Dorian smiled, and my heart melted.

How handsome he looked, how dashing.

Aquiline nose, pale eyes, full lips, brilliant teeth—he threw back his head and laughed. Tall and athletic, he was dressed in white: shirt, coat, square-toed, tie shoes. His gloved hands held mine as we circled the hall, the tail of his cutaway coat chasing my gown across the floor.

Did he like the way I looked? Was he pleased?

The last song of the last ball of the season ended and, as we whirled to a stop, I noticed George Arden, the undertaker's son, standing by the wall. He must have arrived late. How curious to see him at a party. His doleful eyes caught mine. I looked away.

Dorian dropped my hands. He walked through the double doors and onto the veranda. I lifted my hem from the floor and hurried after him, worried someone might see my practical black boots. My friend, Sally Van Helton, stood in a green dress alone by a column. Was that jealousy in her eyes?

Outside, the air was cool and smelled of honeysuckle. Strauss still waltzing in my head, I rose on tiptoes to kiss Dorian's lips. He looked away and focused on the stars and waning moon. I sank to my heels, thinking of Mother's last moments of lucidity. "Men find engagements difficult," she'd told me. "Be patient, play up to a man. Be what he needs. Do what he wants. It's a wife's role."

"I'll no longer be working at my uncle's bank."

"Oh?" I asked, attentive to Dorian's voice.

"Father has returned from England. He's taking a new position. He's promised me a job."

I took Dorian's hand. "You'll excel at whatever position he offers."

"I'll earn twice what I'm making now and receive commissions as well."

"Someday you'll head your own bank."

Dorian looked toward the ballroom. "That won't come soon enough."

I saw his face in profile, almost regal in its shape, and it struck me how lucky I was.

I was pretty, of course, but not beautiful, not like Sally Van Helton. I wasn't rich like Julia Wheeler, either. I'd come from a modest home. A cobbler's daughter would never be wealthy. I had no illusions. Marriage was a bargain, and, as bargains went, I offered little except a sharp mind and a strong will, qualities that, in a woman, meant little when families joined.

In the doorway, a rustling curtain caught my eye; a green hem slipped from view.

Dorian took my hand and pulled me toward him. His face glowed from within, pallid in the moonlight. "My father has spoken to me on the matter of our engagement."

Apprehension touched me. "You didn't mention my mother's condition, did you?"

He released a weary sigh. "How could I not? Father would have found out soon enough. Everyone in Pottsville knows your mother is mad."

The awful word made me snap. I flung down his hand. "She's not mad. She has phrenitis."

"Phrenitis, then. Why will you not commit her to the state asylum?"

93

"Mrs. Steinmetz takes care of her."

"But every penny you earn goes to keep up your mother. And it's not like she'd know where she was. Her mind is feeble, for God's sake."

A tense silence passed between us. I counted the seconds as Dorian pulled uneasily at his cuffs.

"Your mother's condition isn't the problem anyway. Bankers are a serious lot—conservative, set in their ways. Do you understand what I'm saying?"

I struggled to sound pleasant. "From what you've told me, there is no one more serious than your father."

"His blessing is paramount."

"Of course."

"Jenny, he holds my future in his hands. I cannot afford to mislead him. I've told him about your…views."

"My views?"

Dorian looked again to the stars. "He says you're too outspoken."

"About what? Abolition? Surely, he opposed slavery."

"It's not that," Dorian said. "You say things, talk to women about the vote, about feminine rights, even about controlling the conception of children."

"This is America, Dorian. Everyone is allowed an opinion."

He pulled off a white glove and patted his forehead. "Jenny, listen. Two days ago, Frank Sosebee came to me unable to make the payment on his new gelding. He said you stirred up his wife, that she'd taken half their money and hid it because she didn't want him squandering it on horses."

The incident was fresh in my mind. "I merely told Mary that since she worked just as hard on the farm as he did, the money they earned was rightfully half hers."

Dorian pulled off his other glove. "And two days before that, Josephine Wilson marched into the bank and ordered the teller to open an account in her name separate from her husband's. Can you imagine? Her own separate bank account?"

"What's wrong with a woman having her own money?" I asked.

"Nothing is wrong with women having a few dollars, but wives should keep their pennies and nickels in kitchen crockery or under the mattress, not in the bank."

"The bank ought to welcome their money."

"Jenny," Dorian said, shaking his gloves at me, "big city banks may do that, but here in Pottsville people will talk if unescorted women parade in and out of the bank depositing money."

I thrust my hand onto my hip. "It wouldn't matter to me one jot what people said."

"That's not the worst. Yesterday, Mrs. Bratten informed me that three ladies, including her niece, Elmira Johnston, insisted their husbands stop visiting Madame Andrew's establishment."

"Those men have wives," I said. "Why should they seek satisfaction elsewhere?"

"It's only natural for men to release their baser urges outside the home."

"What about the ladies?" I demanded. "What about Mrs. Johnston? She has baser urges, too."

Dorian stepped backward. "She most certainly does not," he said, voice indignant. "No proper woman does."

"Are you quite sure of that?"

Dorian paused to mop his brow again. "It doesn't matter what I'm sure of. It's Father."

"Your father's an educated man," I said, squaring my shoulders. "Surely he believes a woman may speak her mind. Your mother must express herself to him on occasions."

"It's different when a wife chastises a man for a household offense, when he disrupts a woman's schedule, when he breaks a dish, or soils her carpet. But you preach that women should enter men's sovereign domain. You want women to compete with men in business, politics, and God knows what else. Your ideas are too radical, Jenny Crispin. He won't let them stand."

I crossed my arms. "Then he objects to a woman having a mind."

"He believes women should stay in the home, in the kitchen, in the nursery, and in their place."

I turned my back to him. In the ballroom, guests were making their final goodbyes. The orchestra was packing up. "Then," I said coldly, "you must make a choice."

Wind rustled the trees. Branches rattled against the windows above the veranda. In the ballroom, I saw Sally Van Helton, a delicate china doll in a perfect, conical green dress standing silently, hands clasped at her waist.

"The choice has already been made, Jenny. Father says I'll never get this promotion as long as we remain betrothed. My future is with the bank. Without it, I'm nothing."

I spun around. "You mean you're nothing without your father."

He started toward the door then turned. "There will be no engagement and no marriage. Mark my words, Jenny. Nothing good will come of your views. If you're ever to be happy, you must stop preaching and writing and stirring up trouble. Women's emancipation is a dream. You must take your place in the kitchen, bear children, and become a good, obedient wife."

Chapter Thirteen

"Stop!" Britt yelled. The hackney rolled to a halt. He opened the door and stood on the running board. That girl sitting on the bench at the omnibus stop... Slender, dressed in black... No, Jenny's hair was blond. He closed the door and fell into the seat. How long had he been searching? *Why* had he been searching? Virgins!

He slipped his watch from its pocket and popped the cover. Twelve hours left. Through the window, he saw masts and rigging above the buildings. The East River was only a block away. Viking Ice Company—wasn't it around here? Water Street, if he remembered correctly.

Five minutes later, Britt stood in front of a two-story wooden warehouse resembling an enormous planked box resting in a puddle of water—even though it hadn't rained in days. Parked in the puddle, ice wagons lined up under a canvas awning. At regular intervals, blocks of ice slid down a long chute and slammed into each other with a crunch. Men in boots used pointed tongs to pick up the heavy blocks and heave them into the wagons.

Britt sidestepped through the standing water and went inside. Mist floated in the air. A short man wearing a fur cap and fur coat sat behind a desk. "How many ton?" he asked, absorbed in his paperwork.

"I'm inquiring about an order," Britt responded.

"Yes, sir," the man said, still occupied by papers on his desk. "How many ton?"

"A gentleman named Archer Gideon ordered some ice. Yesterday, I believe."

The man stared at Britt. "You're not here to buy ice?"

"No, I'm asking about ice ordered by Archer Gideon."

The man came around his desk. "Was it not delivered? Viking Ice prides itself on fast delivery."

"Yes," Britt said, "it was delivered. At least I assume it was delivered."

"What was the man's name?"

"Archer Gideon."

"And the order was placed when?"

"Yesterday, most likely."

The man in the fur hat walked behind his desk and began to lift bills off a spindle, examining them one by one. After emptying the spindle, he slammed the whole lot down. "I'm afraid we've made no deliveries to anyone named Archer Gideon. Do you know where the delivery was made?"

"I had hoped you could tell me."

"We make a great many deliveries each day. Without a location, I cannot be of assistance."

Britt frowned. This was not what he wanted to hear. The only thing he could do now was go back to the Atlas Brewing Company and see if Gideon was still there.

The man in the fur hat came around his desk and stood before Britt. "It takes muscles to deliver ice."

"The blocks look quite heavy," Britt said, wondering if he should bring Lockie with him in case Gideon had more men.

"Yes, quite heavy." The man patted Britt's shoulders. "You look very strong. Do you need a job? I pay my drivers well."

"No, thank you," Britt said, shaking his head. Of course, there was no guarantee that Gideon would still be there. In fact—

"I lost a driver this morning," the man said, interrupting Britt's thoughts. "My sister's son, Billy Riley."

Britt took sudden notice. "Does Billy have red hair?"

"Oh, yes. A big Irish lad."

"And a broken nose?"

"Yes, that's Billy. Slipped in a puddle out front and fell on his face. Happened last year. Not very bright, Billy. Easily persuaded. I fear someone's talked him into doing things he shouldn't be doing. It's happened before. He'll come back, though. I'm sure of it. What do you say? The job takes a strong body more than any skill. Of course, you must know horses. Ice wagons are heavy."

Britt stepped forward. "Would you mind if I talked with Billy? Maybe I can persuade him to return to work. Where does he live?"

Less than two blocks away, Billy's tenement was an older building, judging by the lack of ornamentation. Britt tried the front door and found it locked. Likely only the occupants had a key. Rather than pick the lock, he walked beside the building, down a narrow packed-dirt path, into a large, grassy yard. Several children played near the rear steps of the building. Clotheslines crisscrossed the air above him. Privies stood along a fence where a gate was open. Deep ruts led from the street to a weathered shed. Red water puddled under the shed door.

This does not look good, Britt thought. He unhooked the rope on the shed door and pulled it open. Illuminated by a wedge of daylight, Billy lay on the dirt floor, head resting in a pool of water and blood, the sharp end of a pair of ice tongs thrust deep into his skull.

The wound appeared fresh; he'd been killed less than thirty minutes ago. Britt searched Billy's pockets and found a few coins and a key ring. Outside in the sunlight, he closed the shed door and walked around to the tenement's entrance. The key worked after a few jiggles, and he went inside.

The lobby smelled of leeks. Stair treads creaked underfoot as he climbed to the second floor. Muted words echoed down a long hallway, foreign tongues: German and something else—Russian maybe. Britt pushed the second key into a door marked twenty-three, Billy's apartment according to the man at Viking Ice. Hand on the grip of his Webley, finger on the trigger, he pushed open the door.

Bed. Table. Chairs. Sink. Nobody home. Britt returned his pistol to its holster, walked in, and shut the door. A small fireplace stunk of damp ashes. He moved to the window and looked down into the yard behind the building. Children chased each other across the yard. Everything seemed calm. Billy's body had not been discovered.

Britt opened a cabinet above the sink, finding a few cans of condensed milk and a tin of crackers. Under the sink, a wooden box contained white cloths. A rumple of blankets on the floor, a lantern on the table, several dishes: Billy owned few possessions, that much was obvious. Against the wall beside the bed, Britt came across something unexpected—a cheap suitcase containing several dresses and a pair of lady's shoes. Interesting. Did Billy have a wife? Britt heard a noise and turned.

"Don't move, Mr. Salter."

One of General Gideon's associates from the drawing room at Atlas Brewing stood ten feet away, pistol in hand.

"Who are you?" Britt asked.

"Colonel Warder. Why are you so interested in General Gideon's activities?"

"General Gideon's activities do not concern me. I only want one bottle of nitroglycerin."

"And why is that?"

"As I told you. I have a large tree stump I wish to remove. You have stolen an entire case of nitro. Why not sell one bottle. I would pay handsomely."

"You expect me to believe you tracked down the stolen case of nitroglycerin, invaded the thieves meeting, fought two men, and engaged in gunfire all to remove a stump? Sir, I call you a liar to your face."

"What can be so important that you will miss one bottle of nitro?"

"Tonight, General Gideon and I will send the Union a powerful statement that will not be misunderstood."

"An act of revenge? The war is over, Colonel Warder."

"This is no act of revenge, but a bold strategy to save the South."

"Is that why you killed Billy, to save the South?"

"He knew too much. As do you."

Something moved in the corner of Britt's eye. Colonel Warder spun toward the movement. Britt drew the Webley and shot. The colonel fell backward and thumped to the floor, still clutching his gun. Britt whirled and aimed his pistol at the movement.

Tears welling in his tiny eyes, a small brown-haired child stood on a pile of blankets. He wore a dingy shirt and a diaper. Britt had entirely missed him. He must have been burrowed under his blanket fast asleep. The child was little more than a baby, a boy from what Britt could tell, a boy who had just saved his life. Dear Lord, was this Billy's child?

Britt walked around the bed for a better look. How old was the lad? He called up his knowledge of children, which wasn't much. The boy walked, so that meant he was over one year old. He also carried a small India rubber cup, which meant his mother, if he still had a mother, had weaned him.

Realizing he was pointing the Webley at the child, Britt slipped the gun into its holster then squatted. How does one talk to a child? Do they understand simple words, commands? "Here, boy," he said, speaking as he would to a dog. The boy toddled immediately to Britt and hugged him.

Britt felt a sudden rush of vertigo, not unlike the taste of strong nitro. The tiny arms around his chest, the boy's plump cheek against his, the unconditional trust, the warmth of his little body—it took Britt's breath away. Recovering, he picked the boy up.

A fine looking lad he was, complete in all his extremities, small yet perfectly formed. His eyes were clear and sharp, his lips full with four bright teeth behind them. Britt carried him to the table and stood him on it. Stepping back, Britt realized his hand and the front of his coat were damp.

"Well," Britt said, shaking his hand, "you've pissed yourself—and me."

The boy giggled.

His laugh was infectious and Britt laughed too. "You think that's funny, do you? I suppose you would."

Britt laid the boy on the table and examined his diaper. The construction seemed simple enough, a few folds of cloth secured by curious metal pins. He unclipped the pins, but as he opened the diaper a stream of pee shot into the air. Britt leaped to the side. The boy laughed again. So did Britt.

With a new cloth from the box under the sink, Britt used the old diaper as a guide and soon had a reasonably well-fastened diaper on the boy. He wrapped the child in the blanket off the bed, carried him into the hall and knocked on the closest door. A short, exhausted lady wearing a man's black coat answered. Two small children held fast to her legs.

"Do you know Billy Riley who lives next door?" Britt asked, hoping she wouldn't inquire about the gunshot.

"Billy, ja," the woman replied, nose wrinkled as if smelling something unpleasant.

"Billy will be gone for awhile and needs someone to watch his child."

The woman's displeasure turned to alarm. "No, no. No more children." She waved her hand. "No vatch."

She tried to shut the door, but Britt rested his hand against the wood. "Does Billy have a wife or a lady friend?"

After a moment of pushing at the door the woman gave up and dropped her arms to her side. "Ja. Tillie. She vork at Madame Georgia's. She ist voman of sin. Billie ist sinful. Boy ist sinful."

Britt released the door and the woman slammed it.

Back in Billy's room, Britt walked around the dead colonel and took a can of condensed milk from the cabinet. He holed the top with his knife and mixed it with some water in the boy's cup. While the boy drank, Britt took the remaining diapers from under the sink and stuffed them into his coat pockets along with the extra cans of milk. Feeling like a nursemaid, he carried the boy, still wrapped in the blanket, downstairs and out the front door. In the street, he hailed a hack and asked the driver to carry him to Madame Georgia's. "You're taking a baby to a whorehouse?" the driver asked.

Settled against the hack's seat leather, Britt watched the boy drink.

When the cup was empty, the boy fell asleep in the crook of his arm. Britt wondered if the lad would remember his father. Probably not. Britt couldn't remember his father—if he'd ever had one for longer than fifteen minutes—or even his mother. He remembered little of his early life, just a vague succession of painted women. His memories only really started at age six or seven. That's when his chores had began: emptying the spittoons, sweeping the floors, burning the trash, even boiling the laundry. He'd learned soon enough that keeping to the shadows was his best chance for survival. Still, there had always been trouble and Madame Becker, the tough brunette who owned the brothel and carried a parasol gun, had been his ready protectress, there to save him—mostly from do-gooders.

Church groups and child protection societies had tried to take him away several times. Madame Becker had met them on the porch, her parasol cocked and loaded with twenty-aught buckshot. By the time Britt was fourteen, six feet tall, his virginity long gone, the Samaritans considered him a lost cause.

It wasn't a bad upbringing. He'd eaten relatively well, never lacked for company, and learned how to please a woman. He'd even found love, briefly, and with disastrous consequences. Madame Becker had said nothing ruined happiness faster than love.

The hack stopped in front of a clap-sided house set off the street. The porch sagged and the roof—missing a good many shingles—looked as if a stiff wind might blow it off. Britt climbed out and paid the driver. Angry words drifted from the house next door where two men argued in the front yard. With the boy in his arms, Britt stepped over a drunk passed out on the sidewalk, climbed the stairs to the porch, and opened the front door. A middle-aged woman in red bonnet and bustle dress met him. "You can't bring a baby in here."

"Madame Georgia? The owner?" Britt asked.

"Yes," the woman said, attention focused on the child.

Britt thought a moment. "Then I suppose I must tell you."

"Tell me what?"

Britt pushed past Madame Georgia. He stopped in the receiving room and faced her. "I'm Doctor Salter with the Public Health

Division, and I bear ill tidings. It's Tillie. The Turkish Crotch Blisters she consulted with me about last week have spread to her child." Britt gave a nodding glance to the boy sleeping in his arms.

Madame Georgia's eyelids fluttered. She lost her balance. Britt caught her with his free hand and guided her to a divan. "Which room is Tillie's?"

"Room three," the woman sputtered.

Still carrying the boy, Britt walked down the hall and opened Tillie's door. On a cast iron bed, a girl in a blue corset straddled a man wearing red long johns pulled down to his knees. Britt grabbed the girl's arm with his free hand, dragged her off, and pressed the boy into her arms. Cursing, the man leaped from the bed and began tugging up his underwear. Before he could raise the garment to his waist, Britt pinned the man's wrists behind his back, planted his foot on the man's bare rump and pushed him toward the open doorway. Legs trapped by the half-down long johns, the man fell and rolled into the hall. Britt shut and locked the door.

"What in Hell's name are you doing," Tillie screamed.

The girl's shrill voice and the sound of man's fists beating on the door upset the boy, who started crying. Britt took the boy from her and placed him on the bed.

"Billy has been murdered," Britt said, facing the girl, voice cold. "Your son was alone. I've brought him to you."

Tillie shook her finger. "Jeffery is not my son. He was on his way to the orphanage when Billy rescued him. What about my suitcase? My clothes and shoes were inside. Did you bring it?"

Fury rose in Britt. He'd seen her kind before, grown up with women like her. She was the worst kind of prostitute, selfish and uncaring. Whether born that way or forced into it by society, he didn't know and didn't care. He would not allow her to hurt this little boy. Britt picked the girl up by the neck and lifted her off the floor.

After counting to five, he dropped her into a love seat. Tillie gasped for air. Tears streamed down her face. "You could have killed me."

Britt made the meanest face he could muster. "Are you sure Billy was not the father?"

"Jeffery's father was a sailor," Tillie sobbed, "frozen to death in the Great Whaling Disaster. Thirty-three ships caught in the ice above Alaska."

"And the mother?"

Tillie stared at Britt for a moment. "Only God knows."

Britt didn't believe a word of it. "Who wanted Billy dead?"

"Billy was mixed up with the Red Scarves. He bragged he was going to make a fortune. He was supposed to steal an ice wagon from his uncle and deliver it to them."

"Deliver it where?"

"Athena Stable on Franklin Street. I don't know the address."

"What time?"

"He wanted me to come to his apartment at four to watch Jeffery, so it must have been after that."

Britt made a claw of his hand. "Do you know any of these people's names?"

Tillie clutched her throat. "I don't know anything more, I promise."

She started shaking and crying. It was time to go. When he opened the door, the man he'd thrown from the room—his long johns now up and fastened—lunged at him. Britt picked him up over his head and threw him into the love seat next to Tillie. As Britt started to leave, he found Jeffery wrapped around his leg.

He lifted the boy. "I suppose you're right, Jeffery. You can't stay here, can you?"

Britt carried Jeffery down the hall and into the receiving room. Madame Georgia reclined in the divan, fanning herself. "Will she live, Doctor?"

Britt paused by the front door. "It's serious," he said, solemnly. "But if you apply a poultice of mustard powder with a pinch of salt and gunpowder to her womanly parts twice a day, she'll be fine."

Outside, the same hack he'd arrived in waited at the curb. The driver tipped his hat. "Did the lad have a good time?"

"Splendid," Britt answered, smiling. "Viking Ice Company."

Workers stood idly beside their ice wagons, smoking pipes and talking. Britt drew only a few odd stares as he stepped from the hack holding a small child. The office was quiet and appeared empty. A door led into a warehouse filled from floor to the ceiling with thousands of translucent blocks of glimmering ice. The temperature felt like mid-winter. He wrapped the blanket tightly around Jeffery. A workman in a thick coat and gloves walked toward him over the wet, plank floor.

"You looking for Mr. Delaney?" the workman asked, white vapor blowing from his mouth.

"Is he the boss?" Britt asked. "Where can I find him?"

The workman studied Britt warily. "Gone for the rest of the day. His nephew, Billy, been murdered. Now you here holding Billy's son."

The chill of the warehouse seemed to penetrate Britt's clothes. He hadn't counted on Billy's body being discovered so quickly, or that Billy's son would be recognized. He could easily be arrested for murder and kidnapping. Coming back to the ice company had not been wise. Now he had no choice but to trust this man.

"I found Billy with ice tongs through his head. The boy was alone in Billy's room. I had hoped to leave him with his uncle."

The workman seemed to weigh Britt's words. He cradled the boy's cheek. "Mr. Delaney don't want nothing to do with this boy. Neither did Billy's aunt. Billy took Jeffery in and cared for him. He was like that. Had a good heart but no good sense. That's why he started up with those Red Scarves. I knew it would come to a bad end."

"Can you take the boy?" Britt asked, holding Jeffery out to him.

The workman held up his hands. "Got too many mouths of my own."

Britt drew Jeffery back to his chest.

"Tell me the truth," the workman said. "You kill Billy?"

Britt met the workman's gaze. "A man named Colonel Warder killed Billy. He's lying on the floor in Billy's apartment with a bullet in his heart."

The workman nodded, understanding.

Britt hurried back across the warehouse, through the office and into the sunlight. A policeman had arrived and was questioning a group of workers. The officer saw Britt with the boy and started toward him. Britt stepped into the still waiting hack and slapped his palm on the ceiling. "Away. Hurry!"

The rig lurched forward. Through the rear window, Britt saw the policeman hesitate then return to the group of workers.

He turned forward and relaxed. Jeffery was smiling at him.

Britt smiled too. "You've nerves of steel, Jeffery."

Jeffery laughed.

"But what to do with you?" he said, tickling the boy's belly between diaper and shirt. "Your father is dead. If Tillie is your mother, you're better off without her. Your uncle doesn't want you, nor does your aunt. I suppose you're mine."

Britt gave the driver an address then settled into the seat. Even if he'd been free of tonight's events, he wasn't prepared to care for an orphan, not mentally, physically, or spiritually. A child did not need a cranky bachelor, prone to drinking and whoring, for a protector. A child needed loving parents. His own youth was proof of that. Not that he had turned out badly, but there'd been pain—more pain than he liked to remember.

Chapter Fourteen

Unlike the aroma of baking bread, Christmas cookies, and Thanksgiving ham, the childhood memories that drifted from the black tunnels of Britt's mind were filled with the odor of sweaty men, cheap perfume, and even cheaper liquor. Even so, he cherished those memories, and he cherished the pain they brought. His most painful were those of Penelope.

He could still see the shape of her breasts beneath her nightgown and her perfect toes, golden and smooth, as she climbed the steps and sat beside him on the back porch of Madame Becker's brothel.

"You are Brittan?"

Britt closed the book he was reading and pushed it under his thigh. Aileen was right when she said the new girl's accent was musical. Cajun, she called it. "Yes, I'm Brittan."

"Do you always read books while you work? What if I do that? Who would pay me?"

Britt laughed. He glanced at the pot on the fire in the backyard to make sure the boiling water was still above the linens. "You won't tell Madame Becker, will you?"

Sweat glistened above her lip and her body smelled of damp sheets. She was younger than the other girls at the brothel, maybe only a few years older than he was.

"I can keep a secret," she purred, "but Madame Becker already knows, yes? Did she tell you my name?"

The girl's hair fell in dollar-sized curls around her oval face. Chiseled nose and full lips, her deep brown eyes and honey skin reminded him of a postcard he'd seen of Sara Bernhardt, the famous actress, mostly because of her striking beauty more than any resemblance. "Madame Becker called you Penelope. When I heard your name, I got very excited."

Penelope's brows rose. Her eyes sparkled in the sunlight. "Usually, it takes more than my name to excite a man."

Britt laughed a second time. "Penelope is the name of a character in a book I'm reading."

Penelope pouted theatrically, back arched, arms on hips. "Who is this person that steal my name?"

Britt's gaze was drawn again to her breasts pressed against soft cloth. "Penelope was Ulysses' wife."

Her demeanor shifted to surprise. "Ulysses? Like President Grant? In this book I am married to the president?"

"This Ulysses is not the president," Britt said, his gaze rising to her face, "but the king of an island called Ithaca. One day, he sailed away and his faithful wife, Penelope, waited twenty years for him to return."

Penelope shook her head. "No wife is faithful to a husband who leaves for twenty years."

Britt thought she was probably right. "It's just a myth."

"What is a myth?"

"A story so old no one knows whether it is true or false"

Penelope's full lips curved to a smile. "I can tell you this myth is false. If President Ulysses leaves for twenty years, his wife will need many lovers to keep her satisfied while he is gone."

Britt picked up a wooden pole leaning against the porch and walked down the steps to the fire. "Not president," he called back to her, "king. Maybe Penelope loved Ulysses a great deal, and maybe he loved her."

"Balderdash!" Penelope answered. "If King Ulysses love Penelope so much, why do he leave in the first place? For another woman?"

"To fight a war," Britt said, stirring the linens in the pot.

"Oh, fighting wars," Penelope said knowingly. "War is the only thing men love more than a woman's pokie."

Britt pushed the linens under the water. "But on the way home from the war, Ulysses got lost and battled a one-eyed giant."

"I too have battled one-eyed giants," Penelope said, grinning, "a great many."

"Not only that," Britt added, "he was kidnapped for seven years by a woman named Calypso who wanted to marry him."

"Ulysses is a pig," Penelope said. "He made up the giant to fool Penelope about why he is gone so long." She hoisted her nightgown, walked down the steps onto the sparse grass, and stood beside him.

"Then why didn't he just stay with Calypso?" Britt asked.

Her fingers touched him between the shoulders. "If men do not grow tired of the same woman, I would have no job."

"Well," he said, swirling the linens round and round, "whatever the reason, Ulysses returned home."

She traced her fingers down his spine. "Penelope is a better lover than Calypso. That is the reason he came back."

Britt stopped stirring. "But Ulysses returned disguised as a beggar."

Penelope hit Britt's shoulder with the flat of her hand. "Of course, he did. Penelope is so mad he leave for twenty years, she kill him if he show his face."

Britt withdrew the stick from the tub and walked her to the steps. "When Ulysses finally arrived home, he found a hundred men waiting to marry Penelope."

Penelope sat and shook her finger. "I told you she has many lovers, did I?"

Britt jabbed the pole like a spear. "Ulysses killed them all."

Penelope winced. She patted the step beside her. "Did they hang him for murder?"

"You forgot," Britt said as he sat. "Ulysses was the king of the island."

"A good lawyer doesn't hurt either."

He leaned the pole against the porch. "Maybe."

"But now," Penelope said, "at least we know why Ulysses' wife wait for him all those years—he is rich. And I suppose they live happily ever after?"

"Of course."

Penelope grabbed Britt's arm and pulled him close. "You won't leave me to fight a war, will you, Brittan?"

"If I do, will you take many lovers while I'm gone?"

Penelope made a mock frown. "I have to, it's my job. But I only think of you." She drew her fingertips along the inside of his thigh.

Britt was used to being teased by the girls but Penelope's touch felt different. "Aren't you worried I'll murder your lovers?"

Penelope pressed her hand to his crotch, squeezed momentarily then released. "My lovers never stay more than thirty minutes. Besides, I won't need any lovers if you know how to satisfy me."

"Women," Britt said, frowning, "can never be satisfied."

Penelope's eyes flared. "Who told you this lie—the fools who come here and pay for pleasure?"

"Tell me then," he asked, "how does one satisfy a woman?"

"Ah," she said, pressing her face close to his, touching his lips with her fingertip. "That is something that cannot be told, nor read of in books. Someone must teach you."

"Who would teach me?" he whispered.

Britt closed his eyes and his lessons arose from the shafts and pits of his mind where he'd hidden them. His sweet, sweet lessons. Every week after that, Penelope taught him something new: the secret places that made a woman moan, the caresses that made her gasp, the special touches that made her cry out. Penelope even taught him about his own body by doing things to him that gave him more pleasure than he ever knew possible.

One day, as they lie in bed, passion spent, her breasts against his chest, she rubbed her leg on his and asked a question. "Will you teach me to read, Brittan?"

Britt gave her a long appraising look. "I thought you could already read."

She rolled away. "A girl learns to fool people. I never go to school."

"Why not?"

"My family live in Pointe Coupee, along the river. Papa say the river teach us all we need to know."

"What did the river teach you?"

"Mosquitoes, opossums, snakes." She laughed and covered her mouth.

"Is that why you left?"

She pulled the sheets over them both and curled into a ball with her back against his chest. "Papa marry me to a man down in Baton Rouge. The man beat me so I run away."

Britt touched her side. "How long ago was that?"

"Not long." She rolled over and faced him. "A year more or less."

Britt kissed her forefinger. "Baton Rouge is a long way from Wilkes-Barre."

Penelope tucked her head beneath his chin. "One day my husband leave for the market. I sneak out of the house and go downtown. A big steamboat is at the dock. Someone tell me the ship's name is Natchez. The captain walks the deck. He wears a little cap and a big beard. He watches me admiring his boat. He invites me on board. Inside, I never see anything so beautiful, all polished wood and brass. The captain seat me at a big table and feed me beefsteak and potatoes. We drink wine and laugh and talk. That afternoon, my husband come looking for me. I know he will beat me if he find me. I don't want to go back so I ask the captain to hide me. My husband know I am on that boat. Maybe someone tell him. The captain take out his pistol. He tell my husband to get off his boat, or he will kill him. I never had a man fight for me, no.

"That evening the steamboat float up the river like a dream. The engines beat, the band play, people dance and eat. I meet rich gentlemen. They drink and gamble and treat me like a lady. They take me to their rooms. I make them happy, and they give me money. Even when I give half to the captain, I still have more money than I ever know. The gentlemen ask me to come with them to their fancy houses up North. But I don't need no master. I stay on the boat and drink and dance and make gentlemen happy until we reach Cincinnati."

Her cool hands took his, and she stared into his eyes. "Brittan, you never see buildings so big in that town. It is like a dream. The captain want me to stay on his boat, but I take my money and sneak away again. I work on George Street at Madame Clark's house for a while, then I take the train here." Penelope kissed him on the lips. "You teach me to read, Britt. We start tomorrow. Now you go. If I don't make money, Madame Becker throw me out."

Britt kissed her. He put on his clothes and left to sit on the porch. The setting sun shined golden through the trees. Carriages moved up the street to Madame Becker's and the other establishments in the neighborhood. Men got out, some well dressed, others in work shirts and plain brown pants. As they climbed the steps and went inside, Britt dreamed of Penelope, her honey-toned body, her brilliant smile, her musical voice, and her simple wisdom.

Madame Becker wouldn't like him leaving. Who would boil the linens and sweep the floors? But he couldn't stay. He had to find a real job. A man couldn't support a wife on what he earned—which was nothing but room and board. He needed more than that. They could not live on Penelope's earnings either. A woman using her body to support herself was understandable when she had no man, but once they were married, all that would stop.

The front door opened and Madame Becker, bejeweled and elegant, her hair rolled and pinned, stepped onto the porch. "Brittan," she said, voice sharp, "I've been looking for you all over the house. Get off the porch. Three girls need fresh linen."

Britt rose and followed the Madame inside. Several men sat in the lobby listening to Ailene sing and play the piano. At the cabinet by the pantry, he took out three sets of bed linens and carried them down the chestnut paneled hallway. Laughter and indelicate sounds came from behind closed doors. Esther, arms crossed, doused in rouge and wearing only a corset, stood by the door to her room. "I've been waiting ten minutes."

He slid off a set of linen but held it out of reach. "Esther, always angry. That little thing of yours needs a rest, anyway." Esther wrinkled her nose. She snatched the linen from his hand, went inside, and slammed the door.

Sissie sat at the vanity in her room combing her hair. She stood when Britt entered. "Spending time with Penelope again?" She winked a dark blue eye.

Britt winked back. "Not all of it,"

Sissie slapped his rump. "Some of us feel neglected, you know."

Britt smiled. He liked Sissie's sense of humor. She was fun in bed, too, but wanted him finished and out quickly.

Penelope's room was next. The door was slightly open. Britt heard a man speaking with a Cajun lilt. He stood close and listened.

"Damn it, girl, I have to bring you home. By man and God, he is your husband. He own you. You can't run away."

"You only come because that jackass pay you. You don't care about me. You want that money he give you when you bring me to him. You nothing but a bounty man."

"That ain't it. That ain't it at all. You disgrace our family working here."

"Disgrace, fie. You don't know what is disgrace, Jed. Our papa disgrace me for years and you do nothing. He sell me to a man who beat me and you do nothing. Now you come here because that jackass give you gold. You bring disgrace, not me."

"Talk that way to me, no. You always have a mouth on you. That is why you husband beat you. You run around on him. You want that strange. You call me a bounty man, I call you whore. That is what you are, whore. Our mother cry for you in her grave. I sooner you dead than sell that *galette* to any man who pay you."

Britt heard furniture move and Penelope scream. He rushed into the room. Jed held a knife to her throat. He was small and wiry. Britt outweighed him by at least seventy-five pounds. Jed spun when he saw Britt. "You stay away, *peeshwank*. Dead or alive, she going home to her husband."

Britt held the linen like a shield. "Put away the knife. She's not leaving."

Jed threw Penelope to the bed. He faced Britt, knife drawing angry

114

circles in the air. "This between kin."

Britt felt a surge of strength. "She's mine."

"You die for this whore, *peeshwank*?" Jed laughed. "How stupid, you?"

Jed lunged. Britt threw the linen in his face. Jed swatted it away and swung his knife. Britt twisted. The knife missed his body but slashed his arm. He didn't care. With the knife on its downward swing, Britt dove at Jed. They hit the floor. The knife slashed wildly, but Britt grabbed Jed's wrists. He turned the blade and plunged it into Jed's chest.

Blood welled in Jed's mouth. He coughed and gurgled and spat. His body jerked. His limbs quivered, and then, with a final shake, he died. Britt stood. The knife fell from his hand and clunked to the floor.

"What you do?" Penelope cried. "You kill him. You kill my brother." She dropped to her knees, lifted Jed's head and pressed it to her chest. "Jed, oh, Jed. What he do? You don't die. I love you."

Britt stepped back. His breaths came short and shallow. The other girls and their customers crowded into the room. Men whispered among themselves. Girls wept.

Penelope snatched up Jed's knife. She climbed to her feet and faced Britt. Blood stained her hands and nightgown. "You kill my brother. You murder my Jed."

"I had to," Britt pleaded. "His knife was at your throat. He would have killed you."

Penelope crossed the room. She raised the knife over her head with both hands. "You kill my brother."

Britt stepped backward. "I saved your life. You'd be dead if I hadn't stopped him."

She screamed and brought the knife down hard toward his chest. Britt grabbed her hand and twisted away the knife. "What the hell are you doing? I thought you loved me."

"Love." She spat the word like a curse. "I hate you, pig. You are only in my bed because Madame Becker pay me."

Britt threw Penelope to the floor next to her brother. She seemed to weigh nothing. He flung the knife against the wall then turned and pushed his way past the crowd. Aileen and Sissie stood in the hall.

They followed him to the other side of the house and Madame Becker's room. Britt slammed open the door. "Did you pay Penelope to bed me?"

Madame Becker sat at her desk, body straight, shoulders square, silent.

"Answer me," Britt yelled, tears in his eyes. "Did you pay her?"

"Yes," the woman said.

Britt made his way to her bed and sat, head in hands. The story of Jed's death spilled from him. Madame Becker stood. She spoke briefly with Aileen and Sissie in the hall, then returned to the room and closed the door.

Britt wept. Madame Becker spread the bloody edges of the wound on his arm. From the sewing kit in her desk, she took a needle and threaded it. She wet the towel from her washbowl then sat beside him on the bed. "This will hurt."

The needle piercing flesh was minor compared to the pain in his heart. "Why did you do it?"

Madame Becker tied off the final knot and bit the thread in two. "I sell pleasure to men, but they never think of the woman. A woman needs pleasure, too. I wanted you to learn that. I wanted you to learn how to please a woman."

"Why didn't you tell me? Why did you let me fall in love?"

"That wasn't supposed to happen."

"But it did, and now Penelope's brother is dead."

"Yes," Madame Becker said, standing. She laid the bloody towel and needle beside the washbowl. "And soon the police will knock on my door. Before they do, you must leave."

Britt looked at her for the first time since entering her room. "But he tried to kill me."

"That doesn't matter," she said, eyes harder than he'd ever seen them. "We can't take the chance. You must go. The police are corrupt. They might arrest you to blackmail me. The girls and I will cover for you."

"Penelope?"

"She'll say nothing; I promise. Now hurry."

116

And then he was on the street, walking east, carrying his few belongings in a carpet bag, his pocket heavy with the sixteen silver dollars Madame Becker had given him, one for every year of his life. He slept that night in the Viceroy Hotel for thirty cents and went looking for a job the next morning. Experience sweeping floors, washing laundry, and cleaning spittoons was no help. Hard labor was the only work available. That afternoon, he signed at the Apex Smokeless Coal Mine as a miner.

In the darkest hole of the mine, throwing his pickaxe against black walls in the glow of a candle, Penelope haunted him. The money Madame Becker had paid her was nothing. She loved him. She had to. The way her sweet arms had held him, the way her brown eyes had caressed him, the way she'd smiled—no one could feign love like that, no one.

A month into his employment, the shotsman, an Irishman with one eye, blew himself up igniting explosives in a borehole on the lowest level of the mine. The last three shotsmen had killed themselves in similar ways. Britt volunteered to take over the job, which paid twice his current wages of two dollars a week. The concentration and danger, he hoped, would keep his mind off of Penelope. And if he died, it would be no great loss.

Britt soon found he enjoyed detonating explosives. The mine owner loaned him a book on the subject, which he devoured. He developed his own techniques for blasting anthracite from the ground. Carelessness and ignorance, he discovered, were the only dangers. Soon, the miners respected the safety of his blasts.

On his one hundredth successful shot, in celebration of his survival more than anything else, several of his friends packed him into an ore wagon and rode together to town for a night at Del Brady's Tavern. Whiskey after whiskey followed and by ten o'clock, drunk, Britt fell fast asleep in his chair. He awoke in the wagon outside Madame Becker's brothel, head still swimming.

Music drifted into the street. Aileen was at the piano. He recognized the tune: "Ah! May the Red Rose Live Away." She'd always loved songs by Stephen Foster.

He climbed out the wagon and tottered up the walkway to the front steps. Shadows flickered behind the curtains. Laughter and the song's chorus drifted into the night.

Ah! May the red rose live away, To smile upon earth and sky! Why should the beautiful ever weep? Why should the beautiful die?

Inside the house, his friends—clothes and faces dark with coal dust—stood in a circle around Aileen at the piano. They cheered when they saw him at the open front door then broke ranks and dragged him into the lobby. His features also covered in black, Aileen gave no sign she recognized him.

Presently, the other girls, cheeks powdered and rouged, sashayed into the room: Sissie, Esther, Jane, Bella, Moll, and finally Penelope. Britt stood to one side as the miners whistled and shouted. He watched Penelope's brown eyes play over the men. Honey skin, brown hair, sharp nose, full lips—in the year since he'd fled Madame Becker's, her beauty had only grown.

When her gaze reached him, his breath caught. Eyes locked on his, she stepped forward, grabbed the closest miner, and threw her arms around his neck. The miner swung her like a child. As her bare feet touched the carpet, she looked at Britt long and hard then led her client down the hall.

Sissie appeared in front of him. She lifted his chin. "Brittan? I thought that was you." she tugged him toward the hall. "C'mon, let's go. You know, I've missed you."

He slipped his fingers from hers and walked out the front door.

A week later, on a sunny Saturday morning, scrubbed of most of the coal dust and wearing his best clothes, he returned. Aileen answered his knock. She let him in without a word. He walked down the hall to Penelope's room. The door was open. The bed was made, but Penelope's belongings were gone.

Panicked, Britt rushed across the house the way he had after killing Penelope's brother. Madame Becker was at her desk. She saw him sway on the threshold. "Penelope is gone," she said, swiveling from her ledger. "Her husband sent two men to fetch her. They arrived day before yesterday and took her back to Baton Rouge."

Britt did not move. Love was what he'd hoped for. Rejection was what he'd feared. That she might be gone, he had not even considered.

He entered the room and for the first time in his life, kissed Madame Becker on the forehead. She stood and the two embraced. "Remember, Brittan," the Madame said, laying a palm upon his cheek. "You're better off without love. But if you must play the game, keep your heart close lest others see what it holds and use it against you."

Britt nodded and, without a word, left the room. In the lobby, Aileen played "Annie My Own" on the piano. He opened the front door and walked down the steps. Once in the street, he turned in the direction of Del Brady's Tavern.

Chapter Fifteen

The carriage stopped in front of a modest brownstone. Britt paid the driver then carried Jeffery up the steps. Red paint peeled from the door and rust flaked from the knocker. The place seemed to be falling apart. He'd have to speak to the landlord about maintaining the house better. He wasn't paying good money for the man to collect rent and do nothing in return. The key turned smoothly in the lock. As the door opened, he called out, "Madame, are you home?"

A woman's voice returned from beyond the arched foyer. "Brittan! Merciful heaven, is that you?"

"Yes, it's me. I've brought a friend. His name is Jeffery. Can you receive visitors?"

The woman's voice grew nearer. "Yes, of course."

An elderly woman appeared in the foyer arch. Once tall but now stooped, she still dressed in risqué elegance, gray hair curled, jewels hanging about her plunging neckline, makeup more tasteful than in her active days. She stopped upon seeing Jeffery. "Is he yours, Brittan?"

"For the time being, I am his protector. Or he mine, rather. Jeffery saved my life."

Madame Becker took Jeffery from Britt's arms and carried him to the kitchen. "Brittan, his diaper is wet."

"He's already pissed on me once." Britt took the diapers and milk from his pockets and set them on the table.

Madame Becker unpinned Jeffery's diaper. "Has he eaten?"

"I gave him some milk."

"What about you? Are you hungry? It's past noon." She took off the wet diaper and dropped it into the sink.

Britt stepped back. "Be alert. He's well-armed and fires at will."

Madame Becker busied herself wetting a cloth. "Where are his parents?"

"His father was murdered. His mother is too busy earning a living on her back to care about him. Tell me if you've heard this story."

"Stop complaining," she said, wringing out the cloth. "Your mother loved you more than you know."

Britt rolled his eyes. "She left with a traveling apothecary when I was six months old."

The woman swabbed Jeffery's bottom with the cloth then deftly folded a diaper and pinned it in place. "Your mother's heart overflowed with love for her fellow man."

Britt frowned. "My mother could take on four of her fellow men at a time and frequently did."

Madame Becker pinned the diaper at the corners. "All the money she earned went to you."

"She spent every cent on laudanum and liquor."

Hands on hips, the woman turned and faced Britt. "How do you know all this if she left when you were six months old?"

"You told me."

Madame Becker dismissed him with a wave. "Never mind about your mother." She picked up Jeffery. "What about you, Brittan? Have you found yourself a woman yet, respectable or otherwise?"

"No," Britt said, following her into the sitting room, "but a woman has found me."

Madame Becker placed Jeffery on the Turkish carpet. She sat on the couch while he tottered about the room. "Who is this brave girl?"

Britt joined her on the couch. "A virgin. One minute, she hates me. The next, she demands I pluck her flower."

"Let her have fun. She'll only be a virgin once."

"Really?" Britt laughed. "You renewed several of your girls virginity nightly. Sometimes twice a night."

"A little pig's blood was the secret."

"And charged highly for it too."

Madame Becker pointed her crooked finger at Britt. "You won't see acting like that at Gideon's Opera House."

Britt shook his head. "Jenny is no actress."

"An emancipated woman, then."

"Precisely! A suffragette."

"And she scares you to your boots," the Madame said, smiling.

"No, she petrifies me. What shall I do?"

Madame Becker put her arm around Britt and drew him close. "Be wary, Brittan. This Jenny is not as emancipated as she thinks."

"So I thought."

The Madame pushed him away. "Nor are you the Titan you believe yourself to be."

Britt grumbled.

"However," the woman continued, "she may be just what you need."

"Well," Britt said, voice forlorn, "she's gone now anyway. Run off, too head strong to listen to common sense."

"More likely, too headstrong to obey your orders." Madame Becker rubbed his bristled hair. "She'll come back. Meanwhile, I'll take care of your waif."

Britt stood. "Promise me you'll find Jeffery a good family."

She took his hand. "Why don't you stay? You never told me if you were hungry."

"Thank you," he said, feeling guilty, "but there's no time."

He kissed Madame Becker on the forehead then slipped out the front door before Jeffery could realize he was gone. He found himself on an empty sidewalk without a hansom or hackney in sight. He should have paid the driver to wait for him. No matter, Broadway was only a couple of blocks away. He checked his watch: 1:10PM, less than eleven hours left to find a bottle of nitro. As he walked, he tried to order the events in his mind.

Billy was to take the ice wagon to the Athena Stable on Franklin Street some time after four o'clock. General Gideon sent Colonel Warder to retrieve the wagon early and kill Billy to keep him quiet. The wagon contained the nitro because the only safe way to transport nitro was to cool it below forty degrees. But what did General Gideon have planned for it? What was he going to destroy? What was his bold statement to be?

Not that it mattered. He and Lockie had their own bold statement to worry about. He didn't have time for men still fighting the rebellion. His war was over—at least, it would be. After tonight, the Khedive's debt would be paid in full, and he and Lockie could go on with their lives. *If* they could find a bottle of nitro.

Arriving at Broadway, Britt waited at the omnibus stop behind a mother with a baby. When it arrived, he found the lower, inside seats filled, so he followed the woman with the baby up the outside spiral stairs to the open, top level and sat across from her on the bench that ran along the rail.

He hadn't ridden on top of an omnibus in so long; he'd forgotten how pleasant it was. Up here, the air seemed cleaner, devoid of the usual smell of horse piss and manure. Rolling along on top of the world, it appeared to Britt he had the best seat in the house for the best show in New York. As if Broadway and its chaos of horses, hacks, and pedestrians were a twenty-cent matinee with him in the balcony.

The omnibus rolled to a stop and rocked side to side as more passengers boarded. Below him, a young lady about Jenny's age bought a ticket and ascended the stairs. Blond, confident, and curvaceous, when she reached the top level he realized it was Rebecca, his favorite girl from Molly's brothel. Seeing him, she lifted her lavender dress above her boots and stepped his way. "A strong fellow such as yourself wouldn't mind a lady's company, would he?"

Britt chuckled as he stood. "Molly said you were visiting your mother."

"Is that what she told you?"

The vehicle jerked forward, throwing her into Britt's arms. The scent of jasmine and the crush of her bosom against his chest awakened his loins, ungratified from the morning. The lady with the baby frowned at them. When the omnibus steadied, he offered Rebecca a seat. She lingered in his embrace a moment then settled onto the bench. He sat beside her and asked, "Are you moving to another establishment?"

She smiled with even, white teeth. "A girl can't live off her charms forever. I plan to open my own house."

"Here in Manhattan?"

"The Barbary Coast. I've already secured a ticket west, rented an apartment, and sent my belongings ahead."

The idea of Rebecca alone on the Barbary Coast disturbed him. That section of San Francisco was well known for its cutthroats, and opium dens. "Are you sure that's wise?"

Rebecca's eyes blazed. "And New York is safe? At least vice detectives won't be knocking on my door every day."

Britt had not meant to offend her. "You'll need plenty of money to open your own house."

She smiled. "On the coast, a street girl can make a hundred dollars a day, and even beggars pay in gold."

Foolish decisions. First Jenny, now Rebecca. "Working the crowd is dangerous business. How will you protect yourself?"

Rebecca flicked a speck off her knee. "Have a keen eye for hooligans, of course. But if a man gets rough, I'm prepared." She lifted the hem of her dress to reveal a holstered pepperbox strapped to her ankle. "Five shots, that one. I've another six shot in my bag and a blackjack in my pocket. I won't be working the docks or back alleys, if that's what you think. Besides, I've already put plenty in the bank; it won't be long before there's enough for my own establishment."

Britt hoped that was true. Regardless, he admired her pluck.

Her tongue touched her upper lip. "What say you, Britt? I'm not leaving until morning. Have you time to wish me a naughty *bon voyage?*"

Their past pleasures tripped through his mind. So far the day *had* been irksome. He fingered his watch through the fabric of his vest. "Nothing would suit me better," he said, sighing, "but today, time is short. However, as we ride, maybe you could lend me some insight."

Rebecca reared back as if to see him better. "You? Seeking insight from me? Insight into what?"

Britt rubbed his thighs and cleared his throat. "Women."

She laughed, most unladylike. "Aren't you a rare one. Well, Mother taught me never to lend, and knowledge like that comes dear."

Lockie was right. Rebecca did have an eye for profit. Britt smiled and took out his wallet. "How dear?"

She pinched her lower lip and feigned contemplation. "One dollar."

"Done." Britt thumbed a bill into her hand as the woman with the baby, now awake and crying, stared disapprovingly. He waited while Rebecca pushed the money into her bodice. "Here is my first question. Who is the more emancipated—streetwalker or feminist?"

"Streetwalker," Rebecca said instantly, as if the speed of her answer counted.

"Why is that?" Britt asked.

Her mouth opened in astonishment. "All feminists do is preach and march and beg men to give them this so-called right or that basic freedom. I don't beg men for anything. They beg me."

"What about Free Love?"

The woman bouncing the crying baby froze when she heard the words. Her eyes widened, and the baby began crying louder.

"Free Love is my stock and trade," Rebecca said, smiling sweetly at the shocked woman. "Feminists give lip service to Free Love but blush if asked to provide it."

Some do more than blush, Britt thought, remembering Jenny's outrage at Molly's. "But feminists want equal wages."

The baby cried louder and Rebecca leaned close, her bosom almost touching his chest. "Equal wages? Lord, I earn ten times what most men make. I've even invested in a stock ticker device invented by a fellow named Edison." She put her mouth close to his ear and whispered, "The man's a genius. One day, he'll make me rich."

More bad decisions, Britt thought. "All inventors claim to make their investors thousands. Tell me about virgins."

"Tell you what?" she asked, pulling back.

"Are they mad?"

Rebecca's eyes blinked. She seemed at a loss. "I was a virgin once," she said finally.

"How long ago was that?" he asked, laughing.

She glanced at her hands folded in her lap. "On my wedding night."

Britt felt his cheeks warm. "You were married?"

"To my childhood sweetheart." Rebecca smiled at the baby, a pacifier now pumping between her lips. The woman with the child smiled back. A bump shook the omnibus and Rebecca's eyes drifted to the wagons and carriages below them. "Robert was killed at the Battle of Bull Run. We'd only been married six weeks."

Britt took her hands and held them. "Didn't you have family to return to?"

Tears glistened in her eyes. "Every moment I spent with them reminded me of Robert. I had to make a new start, so I moved to New York. One job led to another and here I am, a woman of means."

She sniffed then offered a smile as the omnibus stopped again. "I cannot speak for other girls, but my memories of Robert, the church wedding, our first night together, and losing my virginity will always be my fondest." She kissed Britt on the cheek. "And you, Mr. Salter, will always be my favorite customer. Thank you for reminding me of memories I had pushed away."

Britt released her hands. If any girl could do well in San Francisco, Rebecca could.

She stood and shook out her dress. "Come visit me on the coast. We'd make excellent business partners."

Britt stood as well. He watched the incoming passengers jump to the side as Rebecca sashayed to the rear of the omnibus and descended the stairs. Once on the sidewalk, she approached a short, well-dressed man in a beaver hat. The two locked arms as the omnibus pulled forward.

Not far away, Britt noticed something. Down there on the bench, that girl sitting alone, head down, melancholy—was that Jenny?

"Jenny!" he called out, cupping his hands around his mouth. "Jenny!"

126

The girl on the bench took no notice and she faded into the monotony of the city's texture as the omnibus pulled away. He tried to remember the details of her surroundings, the advertisements, the signs, the buildings, the very bench she sat on. With that picture in his mind, he pushed past the lady with the baby and the passengers standing in the aisle.

The spiral staircase at the rear of the omnibus was packed. Britt worked his way down the first few steps then gave up, climbed over the handrail, and let himself down the outside of the stairway hand over hand. When his boot tips dragged the cobblestones, he let go and trotted alongside the carriage holding on to the handrail for balance. After a few feet, he tripped and fell. The omnibus continued on, leaving him face down in the street. He curled to a sitting position and looked up. A team of draft horses bore down on him only yards away.

Chapter Sixteen

I sat on the bench for what seemed like hours, ears covered and eyes shut tight. I wanted to blame someone for being homeless, jobless and thrust into an impossible situation. I wanted to blame Dorian and his bank-owning family. I wanted to blame McCauley and Britt and my poor dead mother—especially my mother for trying to push me into marriage and for going mad.

I wanted to blame my father too. I wanted to blame him for getting killed in the war and leaving me alone to care for a mother descending back through childhood into infancy. I wanted to blame the whole damned world, blame it for being cold and cruel and heartless. But I couldn't. I couldn't blame anyone except myself.

Something tugged my sleeve. A one-legged man dressed in a torn Union soldier's jacket wobbled before me, hair greasy, eyes sunken, bony fingers locked around a homemade crutch, filthy toes punched through a broken military boot. Saliva and meaningless sounds dribbled from his toothless mouth. He tugged my sleeve again and rattled a cup.

I forced the pain to my mind's darkest corner and lifted myself from the bench. Babbling and smiling, the beggar shook the cup again. I searched my bag for my coin purse. A dollar and seventy-five cents— it was all the money I possessed. I dropped the coins in his cup with a clink. He limped away, bowing and nodding, his indecipherable patter blending with the traffic's rumble.

And that was that. My money was gone. Giving it away was stupid, but there were worse things than being homeless and penniless. I stepped from the bench and brushed at my dress. Nothing would get the best of me, nothing. Not this city, not McCauley, not Dorian, not even Britt.

"Damn it, Jenny, where have you been?"

Britt stood in front of me, coat dusty like he'd nearly been run over by a team of horses. His face looked red with exertion and his finger wagged at me like an irate teacher.

"Of all the stupid, idiotic, addle-brained…"

Once again I threw my arms around his waist—and this time I couldn't blame alcohol.

"…dumb, thick-headed, reckless, fool-hardy…"

He waved and a hackney pulled to the curb. His fingers disengaged my hands and pointed. "Get in."

I crossed my arms "Not until you promise to help Cleo."

He sighed. "Get in; we'll talk."

Smiling, I climbed inside and sat. Britt gave the driver an address then took a seat opposite me. He seemed relieved to sit down, as if he'd been through some sort of ordeal. "Tell me about Cleo," he said reluctantly.

I brushed at his clothes. "McCauley will kill her if I don't deliver Glorianna to him."

"I'm not worried about Glorianna; she can take care of herself. Where is Cleo now?"

"Ludlow Street Jail," I said. "She'll be there until McCauley has her transferred to the Tombs where a lady in his employ will, quote, 'gut her like a pig.'"

"I wouldn't put it past him," he admitted.

"But I can't betray Glorianna."

"Maybe you won't have to."

My spirits buoyed. "Then you'll help me get Cleo out of jail?"

"Maybe."

"But how?"

"The less you know the better," he said. "Trust me; I've had experience in jail breaking."

For some reason, I believed him. "Are we going there now?"

"No, Cleo will have to wait until after my big sale. Right now we're going to my lodging."

Proper women did not go to men's *lodgings*. I knew that, of course, but Britt had done more for me than any other living man. He had literally saved my life. And yet I knew nothing about him except that beneath his muscled chest beat a heart warm enough to come not only to my rescue but Cleo's as well.

"Britt?" I asked timidly.

The afternoon sunlight sent a hard shadow across his jaw, accenting his tiny lips and the bridge of his nose. As he turned, one eye sparkled golden.

"Britt?" I asked again. "Thank you for helping me."

He crossed his arms and frowned. "Someone had to."

I smiled, knowing how hard it was for him to take credit or compliment. "I'm glad it was you."

Vaguely, he smiled back. "Me too."

I switched sides and sat next to him. City Hall Park came into view. Workmen were building some sort of raised platform or stage on the lawn. Further east, workers tore down shops and houses to make room for the entrance causeway to the new bridge. The rumble of heavy wagons shook the carriage. Drays filled with broken planks and debris moved past the window.

I rested my hand on his. "Britt, you never told me why you left Egypt."

"It's a dull story," he said, still watching the ballet of construction and destruction. "After we finished our work on the Suez Canal, there wasn't much for us to do. Let's just say my relationship with the Khedive deteriorated. Lockie and I left Egypt on less than friendly terms."

My mind returned to the man in purple shoes and his bodyguards. "This morning at Madame de Ford's, that was the Khedive, wasn't it?"

Britt faced me. "The Khedive will stay a few months. He'll sample the ladies and invest in some railroads then he'll return to Egypt thinking himself a worldly modern ruler."

"But you're not going back?"

Britt laughed. "No future for me in Egypt, that's certain."

"What then?"

"Have you ever looked around to see what's happening in the United States?"

"You mean like products and merchandising?"

"That's part of it, but I'm talking about bigger things. It's obvious when you return from overseas. Industry is moving in this country like no other place on Earth. The Khedive sees it. That's why he's investing here. America is booming: the transcontinental railroad, the transatlantic telegraph cable, the bridge to Brooklyn."

The hackney stopped at a glass-fronted store on Clinton Street. Britt eased through the carriage door, held out his hand, and guided me down the steps. As Britt pulled out a money clip and paid the driver, I read the lettering on the window: *Mendlebaum's Haberdashery.*

I plucked at his red shirt. "You live in a men's clothing store?"

He stuffed the clip in his pocket. "Lockie and I rent rooms above the shop. Marm's a good landlord. She doesn't ask questions like 'Who's that girl?' and 'Are you two married?'"

A bell tinkled when he opened the door. I walked past him into the store. Hundreds of colorful shirts lay folded on oak tables. More shirts hung from wooden hangers. Piano music drifted in from beyond a curtained alcove. I picked up a purple shirt from a rack and held it by the hook. The cloth looked like it hadn't been touched in years; dust lined the fabric where it folded over the hanger. "Marm doesn't sell many shirts here, does she?"

"The store is a front. Marm runs a fencing operation."

I wasn't quite clear why someone who installed fences needed a front.

The piano music increased in volume. An enormous woman wearing a green frock and red lace shoes appeared at the open curtain. Tall as Britt and just as wide, shelves shook and tables quaked as she approached. Gas lamps rattled and flickered.

She took the shirt from my hand and blew off the dust. Her lips parted to an amber smile. "You like my shirts?" she asked in a thick German accent.

I backed up against Britt. Her face displayed a manly cast despite rouged cheeks, scarlet lips, and a voluminous black wig. "They're very colorful," I said.

Marm hung the shirt in its place then scowled, "I vouldn't know."

Britt pushed me forward. "Marm, this is Jenny Crispin, a friend. She'll be staying with me for a while."

Without acknowledgment, Marm swept me aside. She rested a large hand on Britt's chest and smiled coyly. "Britt, darlink, dat shirt look so nice on you. Vat color is it?"

"Red."

"Britt, you look so good in red."

Britt eased Marm's hand from his chest. "Thank you, Marm."

The woman moved closer. "Britt," she whispered, loud enough for me to hear, "darlink, vat you vant mit skinny *shiksa*? Better you should have real voman." She clamped her fingers behind his head, pulled his cheek against her lips, and released him with an audible smack. In return, Britt whacked her posterior.

Marm squealed. "You devil. Come mit me tonight. You and I, ve drink. No one know. Not even little *shiksa*."

"We'll see. Is Lockie in?"

Marm threw her hands in the air. "Are you deaf? All day long he is banging dat piano, banging and banging and banging. Britt, I go insane. Make him stop."

I followed Britt through the curtain and down a dim hall hung with photographs of dreary people—Marm's associates, Britt explained. The hall opened to a large sitting room where Lockie, the Scotsman I'd seen at Molly's brothel, sat playing the piano.

He lifted his hands from the keyboard when he saw me. "Well, if it isn't the wee, feisty chippie. She must have been very good."

"Lockie, this is Jenny, and she's most definitely not a chippie."

Lockie wiped the sandy hair from his eyes and stood immediately. "Sorry, lass." He took my hand and kissed it. "Pleasure to meet you."

"Get ready," Britt said to Lockie. You and I are leaving as soon as I show Jenny our room."

Lockie swiveled around and touched his fingers to the keys. A pleasant jig filled the room. "I'll be right here, lad."

Britt led me up a narrow stairway. The music faded as we climbed, replaced by the hollow tap of our shoe soles. As we neared the top, I felt breathless, but not from exertion.

I looked behind. Two steps below, Britt's eyes were at last level with mine. Those eyes hid something painful, something I knew Britt didn't want to share. In a strange way, I felt closer to Britt in that stairway than I had half-naked in his bed. I guess everyone bears some kind of sorrow.

Distracted, I stumbled at the top of the stairs. Britt caught my waist. The climb was short so I don't know why, but by the time we stood in front of his door, I thought my heart would jump from my chest.

Inside his room, a dresser was positioned against the wall. Beside it stood a table. On opposite walls, neatly made beds faced each other. The room looked clean and orderly except for the hundreds of medicine bottles on the window ledge, the washstand, the table, and even the floor. Wooden cases containing more lay stacked against the wall. I picked up a bottle. Britt eased it gently from my hand and placed it on the table.

The touch of his fingers, his body so close, alone with him in his room I found myself light headed. Driven by some baser urge, I latched onto his shoulders and hauled myself up on tiptoes. He resisted at first then conceded. I bit his lip and pushed my tongue against his teeth. To my surprise, his mouth opened.

His tongue found mine. Heat flooded down my neck, over my breasts, and into my thighs. A splendid delirium came over me. I seemed at once blind and deaf and mute, unable to sense anything but the sweet taste of his lips and mouth.

He disengaged my hands from his head. "What was that for?"

"For finding me."

His face wrinkled uncomfortably. He walked me backward and sat me on the edge of one bed. "Next time, I may not be there."

I hoped that would never be true.

"Now, wait here," he said. "I'll help Cleo if I can, but Lockie and I have business first. I'll come back around six."

Bottles tinkled as he left the room and closed the door. His Wellingtons clicked down the stairs. A few seconds later, the piano music stopped.

I watched out the window. After exchanging a few words on the sidewalk, Britt and Lockie walked away from the haberdashery and joined the other pedestrians.

Alone in the room, a thousand blue bottles stared at me. The idea of Britt selling potions door to door seemed preposterous. Nothing else added up either: Marm and her colorful shirts, the fight at the bar, Britt and Lockie returning from Egypt, their interest in the Khedive.

I plucked a bottle off the windowsill and twisted it in my hand. Sunlight glinted blue through the glass. I didn't want to stay in this room. McCauley was out there somewhere. What if he followed me here? I looked back out the window. Britt and Lockie were halfway down the block.

I set the bottle with its brothers, grabbed my purse, and raced out the door. My boots skipped rapidly down the stairs. So what if I tagged along? Britt wouldn't even know. I'd stay a short distance behind, out of sight, hiding behind pedestrians and street vendors.

And if there were any real trouble, I could always scream. Britt would come running. He'd come before, hadn't he?

Marm looked up as I passed through the haberdashery. The bell over the door rang and then I was outside in the sunlight, following Britt and Lockie down the busy sidewalk, keeping my head low, watching them from the corner of my eye. They crossed the street at the next intersection and turned right. An endless parade of hacks and hansoms made it impossible for me to follow them. The afternoon rush home had begun. I waited for an opening in traffic then fled to the opposite side of the street.

Luckily, Britt's tall stature and short hair made him easy to pick from the crowd. Halfway down the next block, the two men stopped.

I waited by a newspaper stand while Lockie gestured as if making some important point. Britt shook his head in disagreement.

While they argued, I glanced over the rows of newspapers and read the headlines. "Greeley this." "Grant that." "Bridge Cable Arrives." "Transatlantic Balloon Flight." "Egyptian King…" A man in a knit cap cut the string from a bundle of newspapers. When he ripped off the wrinkled top copy, I saw *Talmadge's Weekly* in thick lettering and remembered Violet's article—the one with my name on it.

As I moved forward to read the front page, a medieval jester stepped in my way. I jerked backward. How rude! Did they not have proper manners in the twelfth century? The jester stopped at the pavement's edge. His belled hat and shoes jingled as he flagged down a hansom. People pointed and laughed. The jester's rig arrived and, as the carriage pulled away, I puzzled on his appearance.

Of course. This was Halloween. There'd be parties, balls, celebrations. People would dress in costume. Tonight, kings and queens would promenade the sidewalks. Barn animals would sing and mythic creatures would stalk the night.

Cleo had said the tradition had grown in recent years, and she was hoping to attend the Banker's Masquerade at the Astor House. Dreaming of costumes, I looked casually back up the sidewalk.

Britt and Lockie were gone.

I raced up the block, weaving among the pedestrians and bumping people aside. Hoping to see above the crowd, I climbed the front steps of a tenement and shaded my brow. I spotted him half a block away, his unmistakable head bobbing above the throng.

Down the steps I fled and pushed through the crowd. A man cursed as I brushed by him. Another man gave a coarse whistle. A mother carrying a basket clutched her child to her legs. I had to catch Britt, and catch him soon. If he reached the next intersection, there was no telling which way he might turn.

I jumped to see over the masses. There he was, twenty feet ahead. I jumped again. His cropped, dark head was moving among the bonnets and derbies. Anxious, I ran hard. When he was right in front of me, I grabbed his arm and spun him around.

Angry eyes glared above a narrow hooked nose. The man wasn't Britt.

I gasped an apology. The stranger jerked his arm free and hurried away as if I carried cholera. Hands on knees, I struggled to catch my wind. After a minute or so, I straightened and scrutinized my surroundings. Damn it, where was Britt? More importantly, where was I?

Chapter Seventeen

"The lass must go," Lockie said as they walked east on Grand Street into a group of suffragettes. "She's bad luck."

Britt dodged a woman handing out "VOTES FOR WOMEN" leaflets. "I can't turn Jenny out just yet."

"Why not?" Lockie asked. "You've nae fallen in love, have you?"

A man beating a drum passed between them. Britt wondered if the fellow had a real job to return to after the election. "She has nowhere to go."

"So I thought," Lockie said. "You *have* fallen in love."

A man in a soldier's jacket blew a bugle in Britt's ear. He snatched the horn from the man's mouth, threw it to the sidewalk, and kept walking. "Damn it, I haven't fallen in love. McCauley will arrest her—or worse."

The suffragettes passed behind them. "That's nae our concern." Lockie said. "What's more important? The Khedive or the girl?"

Britt stopped suddenly. "Do you want to call it quits? Is that it?"

"Ach," Lockie exclaimed, "we don't even have any nitro and there's only nine hours left."

Britt forced himself to calm. He laid his hand on Lockie's shoulder. "We'll get the nitro. The girl is nothing."

Lockie raised an eyebrow. "Glad to hear you say it."

But Britt feared this would not be the end of it. Jenny was a hopeless cause. He knew that. He also knew it wasn't his job to save every lost virgin in New York City. He'd warned her twice to leave town and she'd ignored him. Still, he'd promised to help, in a manner of speaking. Right now, however, he didn't have time to think about it. "How far is Franklin Street?"

Lockie raised his hand and signaled a hansom. "Too far to walk."

Fifteen minutes later, they got out at the intersection of Franklin and Centre Street. A fruit vendor gave them directions to the Athena Stable. Once there, Lockie went inside to inquire about renting a buggy while Britt waited around the corner.

Ten minutes later, Lockie returned. "The owner says all his buggies are rented, but I clearly saw two gigs lying idle and three horses in their stalls. The ice wagon is inside too, hitched to a mule and ready to go."

Britt nodded. None of this was unexpected. "How many men?"

"Not counting the two stable hands, there were three. Their leader was a tall, middle-aged man with a beard and a narrow face."

Britt gazed up and down the street. Traffic was light; hopefully, there would be little notice if shooting started. "Sounds like General Gideon."

"He had the bearing of a general."

"And the other two?"

"An older fellow, haggard and rough. He sat at a table polishing a Vetterli repeater."

Britt's ears perked. "A Vetterli bolt action? Are you sure?"

"With a telescopic sight along the length of the barrel."

"A sharpshooter, then."

Lockie eyed Britt intently. "If I didn't know better, I'd say he was Jack Hinson."

The name triggered Britt's memory. "Union troops tracked Hinson down and killed him."

"They tried, but he slipped away."

"Hinson was General Gideon's guide during the assault on the Union supply center in Johnsonville."

"And up to nae good in Gideon's company again, I'll wager."

Britt tried to fit Hinson's presence with the other facts. General Gideon had assembled a Confederate sharpshooter armed with a Vetterli repeating rifle together with a case of nitro. Exactly what was he up to? "And the last man?"

"An ordinary gent. Average height, black jacket, derby, minding his own business, setting the time on a wind-up alarm clock."

General Gideon, a sharpshooter, and an unknown third man. Whatever they were scheming, Britt couldn't let them interfere with their plans. "The nitro is what we're after. Let's not forget it."

"What's our next move?"

Britt spoke without hesitation. "The Barryville Strategy."

Lockie shook his head "The Barryville Strategy will never work."

"Why not?"

"It did nae work in Barryville, did it?"

"Only because we didn't execute it properly."

"What makes you think we'll do better now?"

"Because I know what went wrong," Britt said, confident.

"Which was?"

"You were not indignant enough."

"Are you daft? I could have played the Strand. What about the sharpshooter?"

Britt shrugged. "Hinson's Vetterli will be useless in such close quarters."

"Who distracts?" Lockie asked, still unsure.

"You could have played the Strand, remember?"

Clearly not overjoyed, Lockie took out his Smith & Wesson revolver, broke it open, and checked the cartridges. Britt slipped his Webley from its holster, eager to show it off. Lockie saw the pistol and winced. "Ach. Where did you get that pig iron?"

Britt turned the gun right and left as if he'd missed some glaring defect. "Webley is one of the finest pistols on the planet. This one was a personal gift from Dandy Johnny Dolan, leader of the Whyos gang. I thought you'd like it."

Lockie shook his head. "Finest pistol indeed. You'll be lucky to hit a bull's ass at five feet."

Britt couldn't believe what he heard. "Now *you've* gone daft. We're talking about a Webley RIC. I hit a bottle of nitro at fifty feet."

Lockie massaged his forehead. "RIC stands for Royal Irish Constabulary. It's a blasted police pistol. The firearm might be average at best if it was the long barreled model, but you've got the wee short barrel. Absolutely worthless. That shot you made was pure luck, one in a million. You couldnae repeat that it if your life depended on it." He pulled out his Kullberg chronometer. "2:20PM. The drama starts at 2:30, agreed?"

Shaking his head, Lockie walked up the sidewalk toward the street entrance to the stable. Britt worked his way to the entrance in the alley. When he got to the large double door at the rear, he waited out of sight and listened.

"I've been cheated," Lockie's outraged voice called from inside the stable. "You've two perfectly fine buggies right there. Why will you nae rent me one?"

Britt peeked around the corner of the door. One of the stablemen, the owner by his boots and leather apron, rushed to calm Lockie. "Now see here," Lockie said loudly, "does a Scotsman's money nae spend? Will you nae take a Scotsman's dollars because he's nae a fine Southern gentleman?"

Lockie peeled several bills from a bundle in his pocket and threw them in General Gideon's direction. The general appeared on the verge of losing his temper. Hinson seemed more preoccupied with his Vetterli repeater than the disagreement at the far end of the stable. The man with the clock watched Lockie's performance with apparent curiosity.

Britt saw his chance. Pistol drawn, he crept in and seized General Gideon. He pinned the general's arms behind his back and pressed the Webley into his ear where the other men could clearly see it. Lockie already had his Smith & Wesson out and trained on the sharpshooter.

"Mr. Salter," Gideon said through clenched teeth, "again you disturb me. You are a particularly annoying man."

Britt kept Gideon's body between him and the sharpshooter. "You should have sold me the nitro when I asked for it, General. Your associate, Colonel Warder, murdered young Billy for no good reason. I killed him, and I will kill you unless I get the nitro I am after."

Keeping his pistol on the sharpshooter, Lockie opened the rear door of the ice wagon and looked inside. "It's here, Britt, a whole case of Albany Explosives Nitroglycerin."

"Take out one bottle and let's leave these gentlemen to their worst."

The general squirmed. "By depriving us of a single bottle you reduce the chances of our success by one sixth. I can't afford to take that risk."

Britt pushed the pistol hard into the general's ear, bending his head to one side. "You don't have a choice. Lockie, get the bottle."

Lockie climbed into the ice wagon. With Lockie out of sight, Hinson peered into his scope and pointed his rifle toward Britt. "I could send a bullet straight through both General Gideon and you, Mr. Salter."

Britt shoved General Gideon a step closer to Hinson. "Your sharpshooter doesn't seem to have a high regard for your life, General."

Grinning like a opossum, teeth yellow and black, Hinson fired. The bullet struck the barrel of Britt's Webley and knocked it out of his hand. Alerted by the rifle's report, Lockie jumped from the wagon and fired three shots at the sharpshooter. Driven to the floor by the volley from Lockie's Smith & Wesson, Hinson managed to aim his weapon just as Lockie and Britt dove behind a watering trough.

A thunder of bullets struck the trough. When the fusillade stopped, Lockie ejected his spent cartridges. "I told you the Barryville Strategy wouldnae work."

"It seemed like a good idea," Britt said. Two bullets zinged over their heads. "Did you get the nitro?"

Lockie pushed in three fresh cartridges, popped up, fired twice, and dropped down. "Of course I did nae get the nitro. I was busy saving your life."

Britt heard the Vetterli crack. He and Lockie ducked as a hole appeared in the trough. Water spewed out in a stream. "Damn it," Britt said. "I need a pistol."

Lockie pulled up his pants leg, reached into a holster, and extracted another, smaller Smith & Wesson. "Try to hold on to this one a wee bit harder."

Both men popped up and fired. General Gideon, Hinson, and the man with the clock were in the ice wagon. They returned fire. The man with the clock sat in the driver's seat. He snapped the reins and the mule bolted for the open door. Britt and Lockie shot back. As the wagon passed, the man flipped a clock device at them. Britt pushed Lockie behind the trough and fell on top of him just as the device exploded, pulverizing the trough in a shower of water and splinters.

Recovering, Britt and Lockie climbed to their feet and scrambled out the front door. The ice wagon was halfway down the street, its back doors open. Hidden behind blocks of ice, Hinson fired his Vetterli out the rear. The wooden doorframe shattered near Britt's head. He fired back knowing it was almost impossible for any pistol to hit a moving target that far away. When the wagon disappeared around a corner, he and Lockie returned to the stable.

"That man in the derby," Britt said, shaking the water from his jacket. "I recognized him too late. John Maxwell is his name. He blew up a barge of munitions at City Point, Virginia when I was stationed there in '64. Used a clockwork bomb. Came to see his handiwork the next day and a guard recognized him. He was arrested but later escaped."

Lockie took out a handkerchief and rubbed the water off his pistol. "So Gideon has a case of nitro, a sharpshooter, and a man who builds clockwork bombs."

"Maxwell isn't just a man who builds clockwork bombs. He was a member of the Confederate Secret Service."

"A spy, you mean."

"Exactly."

Although famished from all the activity, Britt forced himself to examine the stable for any clue that might lead to the nitro. The two stablemen had run off when the shooting started, but he seriously doubted they knew anything about Gideon's plans.

In the straw near where Hinson had sat, he found a crumpled piece of paper. On the paper was a crude drawing of what appeared to be the new bridge to Brooklyn. Three groups of double arrows pointed at the

Manhattan tower. Whoever had drawn the picture lacked any trace of artistic ability. Written beside the picture was an address close to where Lockie and he had eaten breakfast that morning. Next to the address, someone had scrawled 10:00PM. Whether the drawing, the time, and the address were related to each other or to Gideon and the nitro, Britt had no way of knowing. He folded the paper and put it in his pocket.

Not far away, his Webley lay on the ground. Britt spun the cylinder and worked the hammer. Except for a small nick on the barrel, the pistol appeared completely functional.

Across the stable, Lockie finished hitching a horse to the last of the two buggies. Britt offered him his Smith & Wesson, but Lockie held up his hands. "Are you sure you wouldn't rather keep it? You'd be lucky to hit a nail with the butt of that Webley, let alone a target with a bullet."

Britt shook the Smith. "Take your weapon. The Webley is a perfectly fine pistol."

"You're as hard headed as my fourth wife. Silly woman divorced me and married a stockbroker. Poor dear lives in a mansion now—with five servants."

Lockie took the Smith and slipped it into his leg holster. He handed Britt a whip with instructions to lose the stolen buggy as soon as he could. Britt agreed and the two men climbed into their rigs.

Police whistles blew as Britt snapped the reins and followed Lockie's buggy out the stable door into the alley. At Lafayette, they turned south. When they reached City Hall Park, Lockie turned toward Marm's.

Britt continued down Broadway. A hansom in front of him stopped short. Distracted, he pulled the reins hard to avoid a collision. The drawing of the bridge tower was on his mind. Three groups of double arrows—one for each bottle of nitro—six arrows in total, all pointing at the Manhattan bridge tower. If General Gideon truly wanted to send a powerful message to the North, there would be no better way than to blow up the symbol of Yankee wealth and prosperity—the new bridge to Brooklyn.

Every newspaper in the country would carry the headlines. The general would claim responsibility and demand Grant change his policies toward the South lest more vital structures be destroyed. With the press and public screaming, the government would seem powerless. Britt had to stop Gideon, but it wasn't the destruction of the bridge tower he feared. He worried the general would waste all the nitro and leave nothing for him.

Chapter Eighteen

I turned in a slow circle. Brick buildings, cobblestones, people, carriages: why did all parts of the city look the same? After losing Britt and Lockie, I had no idea where I was. But unlike earlier, this time I was prepared. My map was in my purse.

I'd given my last dollar to the cripple and whether Britt continued to help me or not, I needed money. Satisfied I knew where I was, and confident that nothing bad could happen as long as I kept to the main streets, I began my journey.

Mother's mind, never completely sound, had deteriorated steadily after my father's death. Within the year, I'd hired Mrs. Steinmetz to look after her. The woman's wages, combined with my room and board, had forced me to work ten hours a day keeping ledgers, writing letters, and filing papers for Arden Dry Goods, Arden Livery, Arden Coal Shaft Number Three, and Arden Embalmery. All were vital business interests of Pottsville mortician, J. Thomas Arden.

Like most embalmists, Mr. Arden had prospered during the war. But unlike most, he'd invested his profits wisely. Short of stature and highly opinionated, he was an arrogant man who cut a comical figure strutting up and down Main Street in his long coat and tall beaver hat. His son, George, however, was the complete opposite.

I'd grown up with George. We all had: Dorian, Sally Helton, Julia Wheeler, and I. In school, the boy had suffered cruelly from the other children's taunts and jeers. "Where'd your father dig *you* up?" "Nice clothes, whose corpse did you rob?" "Go gnaw a bone."

Life wasn't easy for the undertaker's son.

Somehow, despite the abuse, George survived. When he was old enough, his father taught him the family trade and, like most sons and daughters, he became a useful member of our little town. In many ways, however, George remained withdrawn. I can still smell the chemical odor that preceded his arrival each day to my office, still see him standing in the doorway, staring at me through those thick glasses, wringing his red-gloved hands and scraping the floor with the toe of his blood-splattered boot. Thank God he was too shy to talk to me in public. Not that I disliked him personally, but the thought of all the bodies he'd eviscerated and drained made me uneasy.

Having traversed eighteen blocks west and twelve blocks south lost in my memories, I now proudly stood at the corner of Barclay and Broadway, just west of City Hall Park. The disposal of mother's estate—mostly housewares, clothes, and small furnishings—had netted me a modest amount. I'd used the money to finance my move from Pottsville to New York. The remaining funds—still a considerable sum—now rested in Bulwark Bank, the building directly in front of me.

At the door, a rotund bank guard wearing a red jacket and cap stopped me. "On your heels, girlie, you'll find no customers here."

With my sternest expression, I reached into my bag, extracted my savings book, and waved it in his face. The man snatched up the book and thumbed its pages. He handed it back and, with a tip of his cap, opened the door.

A low hum filled the building: telegraph keys, jingling silver, and thumbs counting currency. Rectangular shafts of sunlight illuminated the marble floor. Golden chandeliers hung on iron chains. From the far wall, I picked out one of the twenty or so tellers in green eye shades and walked toward him. Another guard approached me suspiciously, hand resting on the pearl hilt of a holstered Colt. "May I help?"

I held up my book and motioned toward the line of tellers. The guard nodded and I continued on.

The teller, a bald elderly man wearing bifocals, counted money with ink-stained fingertips. I waited patiently until he finished, then spoke. "I'd like to close my account."

The teller peered at me through his green eyeshade. "Are you sure, young lady? A penny saved is a penny earned."

"Yes, I'm sure."

He took my book and opened it. "Withdraw all twenty-three dollars?" he asked in a high voice.

"Yes."

Without looking up, he consulted a sheet of paper. "You are Jennifer Crispin?"

"Yes."

"One minute."

The teller hung a closed sign at his window then disappeared through a maze of desks and clerks. While I waited, I thought of Dorian working somewhere in the bowels of Pottsville Bank and Trust, pouring over contracts, examining clauses, and inserting addendums. I thought about the mansion he would have bought me and the staff of servants needed to run it. I tried to imagine myself a lady of society gossiping over afternoon teas and fussing at the maids for improperly cleaning the silver. I pictured large dinners and nights at the theater. I saw myself wearing the finest clothes and riding in a large carriage. It would have been an envious life.

And where was I now?

Slinking about the street, chased by police, accosted by men, staying over a haberdashery with a gentleman I barely knew, and withdrawing my life savings just to survive.

"Miss Crispin?"

The old teller stood beside me. "There's a slight problem with your account."

My interest adjusted to a fine focus. "Problem? What kind of problem?"

"Come with me, please."

I followed the teller across the marble floor, through the squares of afternoon light and under the golden chandeliers. We entered a walnut door in a walnut wall, and the lobby's hum stilled to the quiet of green carpet and pale wallpaper.

Open doors lined a long hall hung with paintings of geese and swamps. Through one of the open doors, I saw leather chairs behind wide desks. Tall hats hung beside wool coats and silver canes. Men in striped suits and silk cravats looked up as we passed. At the end of the hall, the teller pointed to a white bench beside a door marked with two words: *Stock Acquisitions*. I sat and waited as the teller scurried away.

In the muffled quiet, I heard a youthful but angry voice from inside the office. Driven to curiosity by boredom, I cocked my head and listened.

"The plain truth is that the railroads are overbuilt. They've borrowed to the limit while Grant's incompetent administration hoards the money supply instead of increasing it. The bubble will burst. Mark my words, within a month there'll be a panic worse than '57. Stocks will fall and the already rock bottom price of Erie will plummet to nothing. The time to sell is now."

"I understand your point," another voice said, *"but as of late, Erie Railroad shares have been rising steadily. Only a fool would sell rising stock."*

"Only a fool would watch his investments decrease tenfold in as many hours. I assure you, the rise is only temporary. The bank is too heavily invested in Erie stock, and our cash reserves are dangerously low. The time to sell is now, especially with the Khedive a willing buyer and his gold certificates resting in our vault. We have enough Erie stock to satisfy the Khedive's thirst for American steam. Did you forget how much we lost three years ago on Black Friday?"

"Black Friday. Must you bring that up? Not only did Fisk sell us that worthless Erie stock, but we've never completely recovered from his underhanded gold manipulations. If Stokes hadn't killed him over that whore, I would have."

"Let us face facts. The bank is wavering on the edge of insolvency. If the market ripples, we'll be begging on the street. This is our chance to refill

the coffers. Remember, if the Khedive doesn't buy from us, he'll buy from Vanderbilt. Why let that rascal take all the profit?"

"I admit your point is good. You're no fool. Send our proposal to the Khedive. He's staying at the Astor House. He can give us his decision tonight at the masquerade ball."

The room went quiet.

My gaze drifted across the hall to a painting of rolling hills, running dogs, and hunters in high black boots. I imagined the men behind the oak door shaking hands and toasting their fiscal guile with fifty-year-old scotch. Hunters: that's what they were, aristocracy on a foxhunt. Only instead of fox, they chased the wily dollar. That's what capitalists did, didn't they? Chase the dollar by exploiting the labors of the common man—and woman. Why else would they take an innocent girl's savings, her last twenty-three dollars? Damn it, I needed that money. What could be wrong with my account? And why did I have to see the bank president?

"Jenny?"

I recognized that criticizing, superior voice immediately. "Dorian?"

Dressed in white from shirt to shoes, Dorian peered down his long nose, eyes sparkling like wet glass—almost as if he were pleased to see me.

He spread his arms. "This is my promotion, the one I mentioned. I'm stock acquisition manager here at Bulwark Bank."

My ire burst forth. "Well, Bulwark Bank has stolen my life savings."

"Stolen? I hardly think my father needs..."

"Your father?"

"My father, Theobald de Greer, he's the new president of Bulwark Bank. I told you he'd accepted an out of town position."

"And also that he disapproved of my views," I said, remembering the terrible talk we'd had on the veranda.

"Yes," Dorian said uneasily. He sat down beside me. "Well, you'll be pleased to know he's not feeling well and has been hiding in his office ever since the newspapers arrived today."

"I take no pleasure in your father's illness," I said, "but do tell me how you and Sally like the city."

"New York is a filthy place," Dorian said, distracted.

"Sally isn't happy here?" I asked, confused by his answer. "Maybe you could find accommodations further out. Brooklyn, perhaps. When the new bridge is finished."

"She refused come to here with me," Dorian said, looking down at his folded hands.

"You mean she's still in Pottsville?"

Dorian seemed to shrivel like a salted slug. "Sally left me for George."

I tried to make sense of his words. "George Arden? Thomas Arden's son?"

Dorian nodded woefully.

"The embalmist?" I asked, unable to contain my glee.

He nodded again.

"All in two weeks? But that smell?"

Dorian slumped into the seat so far his white suit seemed to merge with the bench. "Sally married the stinking son of the worm doctor."

I so squirmed with delight that my twenty-three dollars seemed entirely insignificant. This news was beyond price. Dorian De Greer, Lord of Loans, Prince of Pots—dumped for the undertaker's son.

"I suppose it only natural that Sally should leave me," Dorian said, "depressed as I was after you ran out on me."

"After I ran out on *you*?"

"That night at the ball when you told me you were leaving me, when you said you couldn't be cooped up looking after a house and servants. I was devastated, flattened. Don't you remember?"

I jumped to my feet. "Of all the twisted, lying, dishonest…. I never said I was leaving. You dumped me."

He examined his fingernails. "Either way, it doesn't matter. I've met someone new." He looked up. "Hilda Steinmetz, do you remember her?"

"Hilda? From Pottsville?"

"I chanced to meet her the other day, right here on Barclay Street. Quite a coincidence, if I may say. She's an actress now. I find that terribly exciting."

I thought about Hilda locked up for prostitution. "Yes, it's terribly exciting."

"We're going to the Banker's Masquerade tonight."

"Well," I said, "you'd better get over to the Second Ward Police Station with some bail—"

"Jennifer Crispin?"

I swung around. Standing by an open door marked *PRESIDENT* stood a man with a belly so large I was sure he hadn't seen his French cut buckle shoes in years. Face grim, he stepped forward, "Miss Crispin, I'd like a word with you."

I recognized him immediately—not as Theobald de Greer, Dorian's father and bank president but as a bloated, triple chinned, mottled blue sausage.

Could I ever expunge that memory? Dorian's father, Theobald de Greer, newly installed president of Bulwark Bank, was none other than the red buttocked man I'd seen hanging naked from a hook at Madame de Ford's.

The bank president returned to his office and called sharply, "Miss Crispin, come here and take a seat."

I wavered on my feet. Dorian rose beside me. "Jenny? You look pale? Are you well?" He pressed something into my hand. "Here, take my card. I'm staying at the Astor House. Perhaps we could have lunch?"

He turned and walked away. I let the card slip from my grasp and flutter to the carpet.

"Miss Crispin," the president called. "Come in here immediately. It's nearly four-thirty. The bank will close soon."

He held the door as I scooted past and collapsed into a round back chair. The office reeked of wealth and high connections. Accommodations and testimonials hung between shelves of ledgers. Names embellished brass plaques: Morality Board, Temperance League, Woman's Domestic Organization, The Society for the Suppression of Vice. On the corner of a desk—broad as a railroad car—stood a daguerreotype of the bank president flanked by twenty policemen. On the opposite corner rested a bronze statuette of a woman, baby in one arm, sword in the other. Cast into the base were the words: *Feminine Virtue*.

Amidst this display, Dorian's father sat like a king in his royal vestments: black wool coat with linen lapels, a pearl buttoned vest, English collared shirt with necktie of Peking silk.

"Jennifer Crispin."

I jerked to numb attention in my chair.

"You work for Glorianna Talmadge, don't you?"

I focused on his face trying to shut out the hideous naked sausages intruding into my mind. "Ah..."

"And you write articles for *Talmadge's Weekly*?"

"Ah..."

The sausage man nodded at me, his triple chin expanding and contracting with each movement of his head. His eyes spoke loud and clear—*Don't lie to me!* Grunting, he reached out a sausage arm and flopped a newspaper on the desk with a bang. "Did you write this article?"

Still trying to dispose of his horrible image, I puzzled over the question. Article? What did an article have to do with anything?

Like sewage from a broken pipe, my encounter with Violet seeped up from a forgotten corner of my mind. I leaned forward and moved the newspaper closer. It was the latest edition of *Talmadge's Weekly*, freshly printed and released. A headline blazed in large letters across the top:

BANKER'S BIZARRE BEHAVIOR AT BROTHEL

Printed beneath it in twenty point bold-face type:

By Jennifer Crispin

I gasped aloud and fell back into the chair. The sausage man snatched up the newspaper. He waddled around the desk and stood over me, face red, chins jiggling, newspaper shaking in his fist.

"Exactly what kind of man-hating she-demon are you, Miss Crispin? Have you any idea the damage this article will do to my bank? To my reputation?"

My mouth moved mutely. I wanted to explain that I didn't write that article, that I'd been duped by a scheming reporter whose intentions

I mistook for honorable. My throat, however, was paralyzed.

The president loomed closer. "Miss Crispin, the real world is vastly different from the idealized, emancipated planet you fantasize about. Although you may not realize it, men are not the same as women. We require services most wives are unwilling to perform. Do you understand that, Miss Crispin? Do you?"

I nodded dumbly.

"And sneaking about, spying on a gentleman's private activities and then reporting those activities in a newspaper for the whole world to see… Why, it's contemptible. It's despicable. It's appalling. When the rest of the city reads this, I'll be a laughing stock."

I swallowed hard and called up my last iota of courage. "Mr. De Greer, about my money…"

The sausage man's blotched skin turned instantly red, his cheeks puffed, and his ears flushed a deep shade of scarlet. "Your money?" he boomed.

Barely able to control his rage, the president fumbled his way around the desk and dropped into his chair. Books and ledgers crashed to the floor. The statue of *Feminine Virtue* trembled in its place as his fingers fought to lodge a pair of pince-nez glasses on his nose. He thumbed angrily through an open ledger then bent low and read. He looked up in shock.

"You say you want your money? You say you want your entire twenty-three dollars? Miss Crispin, the damage you've done to this bank and my reputation will cost thousands, possibly tens of thousands of dollars. Let me tell you exactly what you're getting from this bank."

He took off the glasses and slammed the ledger shut. His eyes closed, and he inhaled deeply. Calm seemed to color his face and hope flickered in my bosom.

Maybe the ranting was over. Maybe he'd come to his senses. The article was Violet's fault, not mine. I wanted to tell him that. I wanted to say that Violet had used my name without permission, and not out of any altruism either, but rather to keep the Society for the Suppression of Vice from tracking her down, arresting her, and locking her up in the Tombs with shiv toting lunatics.

Dorian's father opened his eyes. I smiled my best I'm-really-a-good-girl smile.

"Miss Crispin," he said, voice firm and resolute, "you're not getting one dime from this bank. And what's more, I've instructed my son, Dorian, to summon my personal friend, Detective McCauley of the Society for the Suppression of Vice. He's probably walking through the front door this very moment."

Chapter Nineteen

My chair crashed backward to the floor as I jumped to my feet and bolted for the door. The sausage man sprang from behind the desk with remarkable speed. He grabbed my arm and held on tight. "Where do you think you're going?"

I fought against his grip, but he was an Everest of flesh, vast and immobile.

"You're staying right here until McCauley arrives."

I jerked again, prying at his pudgy fingers. Desperate, I searched the room for any means of escape.

A victorious grin spread across the president's lips. "Thought you could run, didn't you, Miss Crispin? In a few minutes you'll be on your way to the Tombs. I'm pressing charges for slander, libel, and character assassination."

Driven by thoughts of cold stone walls and demented inmates, my mind raced like a cornered rat. Images hurtled through my brain: the president's bloated face, his fingers clamped to my wrist, the photographs of policemen, the statuette on the desk, the plaques on the walls. My gaze shot back to the statuette. The little bronze woman seemed to look directly at me. Words leaped from the base like divine inspiration: *Feminine Virtue.*

I snatched up the statuette and slammed it against the president's head.

The impact sent a shock wave undulating across his fat cheeks, through his triple chins and down his neck. He fell backward, crashed into the wall, and collapsed in the corner. A testimonial plaque dropped on his head and broke.

"Help," he cried, his booming voice now a whimper. "Help. She struck me."

Two clerks in visors appeared at the door, mouths open at the sight of their president in pain on the floor. They looked from the reddish bump swelling on the president's temple to the statuette in my hand.

I stared at the statuette too. My God, what had I done? I'd attacked the man, assaulted and bloodied him.

"Stop her," the bank president squeaked.

The clerks came at me. I swung the bronze in a wild arch. "Stand back. I'm armed."

The men leaped into the hall. The foxhunting picture teetered and fell. I stepped out of the office pointing the statuette like a gun then turned and raced down the green carpet.

At the end of the hall, I threw my body against the walnut door. A sharp bang echoed through the lobby like a gunshot. Tellers paused mid-count. Customers stopped and listened. The guard reached for his Colt.

The still echoing boom masked the sound of my practical boots clattering over the marble floor. I ran through the rectangular shafts of light and under the golden chandeliers. The red-coated door guard tipped his cap and swung open the door. Outside, in the late afternoon sun, I found myself skipping down the steps toward the sidewalk.

Whistle tweets blew behind me. I shoved the statuette into my purse and mixed swiftly with the foot traffic. At the end of the bank building, I turned the corner and stopped to gather my strength.

I peeked toward the bank. Police swarmed the steps like ants on honey. Conspicuous among them was Badger McCauley and his yellow-and-black-checkered pants. I pulled back my head and pressed my hand over my heart. So close, so very close. How much longer would my luck hold out?

Feminine Virtue felt like a lead weight in my purse. I shifted the strap to my other shoulder and walked a short distance down Barclay Street. Something blue caught my eye. A massive display filled a store's window beneath a swinging sign: *Dr. Sekhmet's Magnetic Vegetable Compound.* I was at Britt's shop.

Angry voices shouted from Broadway. McCauley and his men were almost to the corner. I grabbed the doorknob and turned. It was unlocked but I hesitated before entering. Britt told me to stay in his room. Wouldn't he be mad if I suddenly showed up?

My back straightened. What if he did? I was a grown woman—a wanted woman, but a grown woman. No one could tell me what to do, least of all a man.

I jerked open the door, stepped inside, and locked it behind me. Breath ragged, I crouched by the window and waited.

A policeman hurtled past, his shape distorted by the wall of bottles. Seconds later, two more distorted policemen followed. Then came a fourth man who stopped at the window, cupped his hands and looked into the glass.

I slid farther into the shadows and watched. Face disfigured by medicine bottles, derby outlined in blue, cigar shifting across his mouth—even in this grotesque form I recognized McCauley instantly.

He vanished in a flash of light.

Relieved, I stood and surveyed the room. Dirt covered the floor. Shovels and picks leaned against the wall. As a place of merchandising, Britt's storefront lacked much. I seriously doubted whether any proper customer would ever set foot in a store so filthy.

Curious, stepping lightly to keep my boots free from dirt, I entered the next room dimly lit by a gas lamp. I turned the valve and, in the brightened light, saw to my surprise mounds of brown earth completely filled the room from floor to ceiling.

Just how all this dirt squared with *merchandising products* I didn't understand.

I ventured no further into the store. After thirty minutes or so passed, I dusted the soil from my boots and left the shop.

Once again on Broadway, seeing no sign of McCauley or the police, I lowered my head and walked east with a purposeful stride. Thoughts of Violet—sneaking, underhanded, deceitful Violet—consumed my mind. *They'll clamor for your work. They'll howl for your work. You'll be like Cinderella at the ball.* As fairy godmother, Violet had failed miserably. What the woman needed was a serious lesson in *Feminine Virtue.* Twenty minutes later I stood in front of *Talmadge's Weekly.*

Boards crisscrossed the shattered window. The banner announcing Glorianna's candidacy hung in tatters, her image defaced with devil horns and a goatee. I opened the door with my key and looked inside. The air smelled of smoke. Broken glass and wood scraps littered the floor. Shelves, chairs, books—the mob had destroyed almost everything. Only the heavy desks were left unscathed, although some of the drawers were gone. Mavis stood by the coal stove, feeding what papers remained into the fire. She gazed up as I entered. "Jenny, you look as if Satan himself is after you."

I shut the door and locked it. "Laura is dead and they've arrested Cleo."

Mavis cinched her mouth and shook her head.

"Have you heard from Violet?" I asked, contemplating revenge.

"Not a word," Mavis said. She threw a bundle of letters into the fire. "I suppose she's run off with her crapper salesman."

"Sanitary appliances," I corrected without thinking.

Mavis gave me a knowing look. "Violet certainly saw the handwriting on the wall."

She certainly did. "What about you, Mavis? Will you be safe?"

"Oh, they won't arrest me," Mavis said. "My brother-in-law is the police commissioner, Simon Westerfield. Maybe you've heard of him."

I shook my head. "Well, the police have tried to arrest *me.*"

Mavis prodded the burning letters with a poker. "I'm sorry, Jenny. I wish I could help."

"Is Glorianna safe?" I asked.

"She's hiding at the Commodore's home on Washington Place, preparing for tonight's rally."

I had entirely forgotten about the rally. "That's tonight?"

Mavis picked up another stack of letters. "At Apollo Hall, just off Broadway."

"Glorianna won't show up, will she?"

Mavis pushed more letters into the stove. "If she doesn't, she'll be branded a coward."

"But the police will lock her up in the Tombs if they catch her."

"The police wouldn't dare," Mavis said, stomping a few glowing embers that had fallen from the open stove door.

"What do you mean?"

Mavis closed the stove door and faced me. "You don't think three thousand loyal constituents will stand idly by while policemen drag Glorianna from the stage in chains, do you? There'd be a massacre."

"A massacre for whom?"

"For everyone involved."

Three thousand constituents or not, knowing what I knew of McCauley I could not believe he would allow Glorianna to speak tonight unhindered. "What time is the rally?"

"It starts at 9:00PM. Glorianna comes on a short time later."

Alarm bells rang in my head. "My goodness, what time is it now?"

Mavis pointed to the clock hanging lopsided on the wall. "5:45."

I rushed out the door. I had fifteen minutes to get back to Marm's place before Britt arrived—and it looked like rain.

At 6:10, droplets started to fall. I entered the haberdashery, thankful to have beaten the rain and that Marm wasn't inside scowling and fussing over her shirts. On the walk over, I'd thought of an excuse to tell Britt. I'd say I'd only stepped out for a bit of fresh air. The room was stuffy, and I was bored. Surely, he would understand.

Inside the haberdashery, somber piano music blended with the patter of rain. Traversing the dark hall under the stony, photographic watch of Marm's associates, I imagined Britt waiting for me, stern faced and angry, his half Wellington boot tapping impatiently while Lockie hammered dirges on the keyboard.

But when I entered the sitting room, Lockie was alone at the piano—which more resembled a dining table than a musical instrument—his head thrust forward, concentration fixed upon a sheet of music. I sat beside him on the bench. "Has Britt returned?"

Lockie's concentration broke, and he assumed a more relaxed style of playing. "He'll be along any minute."

I'd always been fascinated how some people could talk while playing piano. I could scarcely talk while tying my shoes.

Lockie's playing grew vigorous. "You like?"

"Very spritely."

"Bought it today," he said above the music. "It's called, 'Up in a Balloon.'"

I read the title and the words beneath it: *written by A. Shuman.* "Did you see the observation balloon over the city?"

The music diminished to almost nothing. "What observation balloon?"

"This morning, floating over the city. It was big and gray with a basket hanging below it and a man inside."

Lockie shrugged. His hands resumed their energetic dance and the room once again filled with notes.

Assuming the conversation was over, I rose from the bench, pondering the coincidence of music and balloon. I felt sure Lockie was toying with me. He must have seen the balloon. What a couple of larks these two men were. And what did patent medicine have to do with dirt? Really! My thoughts shifted back to Britt.

I sat back down and laid my hands over Lockie's. The music died in a sour tinkle. "Lockie, tell me about Britt."

Lockie swung his feet around the bench and faced the sitting room. "I've been waiting for this. You've nae fallen for him, have you?"

"Nae. I mean no. I mean, I like him."

The rain's clatter filled the room. After a pause, Lockie cracked his knuckles. "I wouldn't invest too much time in Britt. He's nae much for settling down. That's why he prefers the professional lasses. Nae broken hearts when it's time to move on."

"Has he ever had a steady girl?"

"A few have tried to nail his boot to the floor, but none have succeeded."

"You two have a special bond, don't you?"

Lockie nested his fingers. "You ever hear of the Battle of the Crater?"
I shook my head.

"Didn't think so. The victors don't generally celebrate their defeats. It was late June, 1864, and hotter than hell. I was with the 48th Pennsylvania Volunteers outside Petersburg, Virginia. For months, we'd been exchanging fire with the Rebs nae one hundred thirty feet apart. General Burnside, incompetent at anything but growing whiskers, convened a meeting to ask his officers for advice. Only Colonel Pleasants, our commander and a mining engineer, offered a solution—dig a tunnel under the enemy fortifications, fill it with explosives, and blow a hole in the Confederate lines. We worked by candlelight in that damned hole, inhaling foul air, stooped over, backs aching, clothes filthy. That's how I met Britt."

Lockie paused a moment to examine his fingertips. Outside, the rain leveled to a steady rumble.

"Britt came from another company—the 1st New York, I think. He'd heard we needed miners and signed on to help. Within a month, Britt and I and fifty or so other men had dug five hundred eleven feet through clay and rock. At the end of the shaft we chiseled a cavity directly beneath the Confederate fortifications. For two days we packed the hole with four tons of black powder. Captain Pleasants himself lit the long fuse, but something went wrong. Forty-five minutes later it still had nae exploded. Britt and I volunteered to see why.

"Our candles were useless. The burning fuse had filled the tunnel with thick white smoke. We felt our way blindly, crawling on hands and knees, counting our steps, trying to measure as best we could how far into the shaft we'd gone. By luck we found the problem. The fuse had parted fifty feet from the charge. I struck a Lucifer, touched the fuse, and we raced like hell through the dark."

Outside, a thunderclap startled me. "You were lucky to get out alive."

"Luckier than you know. Britt and I were still in the tunnel when the charge ignited."

"With four tons of powder, you should have been blown to dust."

"I do nae remember the tunnel collapsing," Lockie said, voice

161

breaking. "I woke up in an army field hospital with two broken legs and a half dozen cracked ribs. The doctor said everyone had given us both up for dead. But buried down in that hole, Britt made a bargain. If Fate would let us live, the next time death knocked on the door, he'd let him in without a fight. It took four hours for him to dig us both out."

"Four and a half."

Britt filled the doorway, red shirt dirty, jacket soaked. Anger dripped from his face, and the air in the sitting room vibrated with tension. As if well familiar with Britt's wrath, Lockie swung quietly to the keyboard and soft notes filled the air.

I feared little. Britt's fury was mostly bluster—at least with me. I stood and brushed at his shirt. "Merchandise any products today?"

Ignoring the question, he jerked his head toward the stairs. "I want to talk with you."

In his room, I sat on the bed. Bottles clinked ominously as he closed the door. "You were in my shop, weren't you? Don't lie. Your boot prints were everywhere."

My fabricated excuse dissolved and I fell back on the truth. "Surely you didn't expect me to stay *here*."

"I expected you to do as I asked. The streets are dangerous. You're a wanted woman."

"I went to the bank."

"Then what were you doing in my shop?"

"I hid there. I was being chased."

He whipped off his jacket and flung it against the wall. "Do you want to wind up in a jail cell?"

I didn't answer his question. "Just what are you and Lockie up to?"

He bent over and pointed a thick finger in my face. "I told you, we sell patent medicine."

Angry now, too, I pointed my finger back at him. "I wasn't born last week. If you two sell patent medicine, I'm the Queen Mum."

"Maybe you are," he said, straightening up, "but I told you to stay here."

"Listen, Mr. Salter, despite our almost sharing carnal intimacy,

162

we're not married and I haven't promised to obey."

A wave of rigidity solidified his neck. It flowed down his arms and into his fists. He swung stiffly to the washstand, tugged out his shirttail, and pulled the shirt over his head, exposing his bare back, broad and wide as a wagon's wheel.

It was a crude display but, unwilling to give him the satisfaction of a comment, I bit my tongue. Whether he meant the exhibit as an insult, I could not say. Our encounter at Madame de Ford's had taught me that prancing around without clothes affected Britt no more than an average man going without a hat. This sudden abundance of male flesh, however, made the temperature of my womanly parts rise nearly to the point of combustion.

Try as I might, I couldn't stop ogling the hard spheres of his buttocks against his trousers as he bent over the washbasin, nor could I contain the secret thrill I received watching water splash onto his hair, run down the tree trunk of his neck, and trickle across the massive V of his back. The ugly scars I saw, visibly spanning the width of his blades, however, soon quenched my fire.

"Those scars," I asked. "How did you get them?"

Britt spun around and caught me staring. "A keepsake from Egypt."

He lifted a towel off its hook and rubbed it leisurely through his hair, flexing his muscles and taunting me with his naked chest, as if daring me to react. But I didn't. I just stared at him boldly, again mesmerized by his arms, his chest, the curve of his breasts, and the dark circles of his tiny nipples. How would it have felt, I wondered, had he used me to quench his lust?

He dragged the towel across his back and under his arms.

The idea of being conquered and physically penetrated by a man repulsed me, of course. But in some strange way, against everything my mother had taught me, the notion sent tingling moisture into my loins.

And why should that bother me? After all, these *were* modern times. Glorianna and Violet had written over and over that using men for pleasure was perfectly permissible, even proper. Didn't Free Love mean that sexual release was no longer men's private domain? I couldn't deny that part of me wanted to melt against his flesh and feel the measure of his vitality.

He drew the cloth over his stomach and up his side.

Men were animals; I knew that, every woman did. Had Madame de Ford not answered my scream, he would have ravaged me like a beast.

But if I were an emancipated woman, if I were truly liberated, if I really believed in Free Love, then where else could I find a more fitting specimen to steal my maidenhood and make a woman of me?

Excited and frightened, my stomach twisted in knots, I rose from the bed, resolved to learn more about lust and love and this mysterious man. As I approached, eyes gleaming, he stepped backward and held the towel across his chest. "What the devil are you doing?"

Doing? I didn't quite know what I was doing.

I brushed the towel aside and laid my hands flat on the musculature of his stomach.

He jumped at my touch. His skin was hot and taut, his flesh hard. I slid my fingers down his sides and stroked his inner thigh like a teamster feels a horse's flank. By the way he jerked, you would have thought the tables had turned from this morning. Then, driven by some inexplicable urge, I bit his nipple.

He caught my wrists and yanked me away. His voice cracked. "What the hell are you up to?"

My body went limp. "I wanted… I thought you'd like… I was curious about…"

"Curious?" he asked. "Are all suffragettes this randy?"

"Randy?" I jerked my hands free. My cheeks burned. "What's that supposed to mean?"

He dropped the towel, opened the dresser drawer, and snatched out a bright green shirt. Unnaturally modest, he turned away and pushed his arms in the sleeves. "Never mind what it means."

"But I thought you liked me," I said.

"I do," he said over his shoulder, "but not that way, and certainly not now."

"Then when?"

"Never."

"Never?" I repeated. "Is there something wrong with me?"

He tucked in his shirttail then turned around. "Yes, there are three things wrong with you: one, you're a virgin; two, I don't have time to get involved; three, you're a virgin."

I was beginning to hate my chastity.

"And what were you doing at the bank?" he asked.

"If you must know," I said, "I have an account there."

"Which bank?"

"Bulwark Bank."

"*You* have an account at Bulwark Bank? What on Earth for?"

"The usual things," I said, "rent, clothes, food." The mention of food made my stomach churn. Except for a few sips of beer, I had gone all day without nourishment.

He cinched his belt hard, features thick with irritation. Except for the eyes. I saw it now, his golden eyes glimmered and betrayed him. They shined like a clear, winter sunrise.

My stomach discharged a wave of pain. "Let's forget about it," I said, more concerned now with food. "Could you at least buy me dinner?"

His mood lightened. He fastened his collar and then made a tug at the bulge in his crotch. "You should buy *me* dinner."

"What?" I asked, distracted by his bulge.

"Dinner," he repeated. "It is you who should buy dinner for me."

"Why should I pay?" I asked, startled.

"You're emancipated aren't you?"

"Yes, of course."

"Well, why should men always buy dinner?" he asked. "You say the sexes are equal. Prove it."

"But I haven't any money."

"You went to the bank, didn't you?"

I related the incident of the sausage man and *Feminine Virtue* and why I had no money.

Britt chuckled at my story. "If only I'd have been there."

I grinned. "What about Delmonico's? I could pay you back."

"I hate Delmonico's," he said. "Too crowded. How about Chinese?"
"Chinese what?"

Chapter Twenty

Before he left, Britt gave Lockie instructions to meet him at the newspaper stand near Chatham Square at 7:30PM. I assumed the meeting involved their big sale. Although curious, I asked nothing, knowing I would receive no answer.

Outside Marm's, the setting sun lit the heavens deep crimson. The rooftops, like castle parapets, separated sky from city. Below, brick walls lay in shadow, while in the street, still wet from the rain, paving stones glowed like nested rubies.

Britt hailed a hack. We climbed inside and rode south on Clinton Street. Bare trees and sidewalks passed us. Turning west on Grand, I spied a man wearing a red and gold robe, his head topped by a king's crown. On the opposite side of the street, Britt pointed to a bearded Mercury complete with feathered hat and winged shoes. The demigod stood on the corner looking confused, as if wondering which way to Olympus.

I read the passing street signs: Essex, Allen, Eldridge. After a few intersections, the brick buildings changed to clapboard shacks. On Chrystie Street we turned south again. The sun's remnants dimmed and died. Rundown storefronts and houses faded into darkness, and soon I saw nothing save coal-grimed windows floating in black. I slid close to Britt and held his hand. In time, the carriage turned again and eventually stopped. Britt escorted me out. Vague, angular shapes towered beneath a star filled night. Somewhere, a dog barked.

"Where are we?" I asked, pressing close.

"Hester Street."

I repeated the name silently, wondering if I'd ever seen it on my map. "Why?"

Britt pressed a coin into the driver's gloved hand. "We're at a friend's place."

As the hack clattered away, I recalled Britt's other friends, the ones who liked to fight. Tapping my boot for someplace to step, I followed Britt onto a boardwalk under the leaning roof of a ramshackle building. Shadows moved behind dirty glass. Wonderful smells drifted through the air: roasting meat and frying vegetables. My stomach grumbled as Britt opened a door.

Warm air rushed out, thick with the aromas of tobacco, food, incense, and spice. Alien words accosted my ears: broken syllables, words twisted and torn, chopped in bits and put back together. The chattering stopped as we entered.

The interior was dim. Paper globes hung in mist. Faces, flat and round and luminescent, looked up beneath lanterned tables. One of the faces approached us.

I'd never seen anyone from China this close. Short yet broad of shoulder, the man wore a white shirt and black skullcap. Smoke curled from a long clay pipe in his hand. Was that a pigtail on his shoulder?

"Mista Britt. Long time, aye. This you woman?"

Britt shook the Chinaman's hand. "Good to see you, Shen. This is Miss Crispin, a friend. She's never eaten Chinese food."

The Chinaman bowed. "Food good here. You taste. You like. Come. Sit."

He barked quick syllables and several men left a nearby table. Britt held my chair. The furniture was crude, little more than boards nailed together. My forefinger traced pictures and symbols whittled into the wood. "Curious figures these."

The disjointed chitchat returned to the room. "Chinese writing,"

Britt said. "I've never mastered but a few of the characters."

Shen returned with cups of tea. "Britt, you finally back from Egypt, aye?"

Britt nodded.

"Khedive bastard. Treat you bad, aye. Lucky I get out."

Britt motioned with his hand. "You've a nice place here, Shen."

The Chinaman slipped some sticks from his apron and laid them on the table. "Rent too damn high. What you do now, Britt?"

Britt took a bottle from his pocket and held it. "I sell medicine."

Shen plucked the bottle from Britt's hand and squinted at the label. He uncorked it and sniffed.

Britt brought his rolled fingers to his mouth. "Drink."

Shen pressed the bottle to his lips and drank. He wiped his mouth with a white sleeve. His eyes disappeared and a black smile cracked his face. "That good brew, aye."

"Keep it," Britt said, "I've more."

Shen took two more slugs then left. I turned to Britt. "You knew Shen in Egypt?"

"The Khedive loved Chinese food. Shen was his personal chef."

"But Shen didn't like the Khedive?"

"Once, after a big dinner, the Khedive got ill in front of his guests. He accused Shen of trying to poison him."

"Did he?"

"Maybe," Britt said. "Despots have a way of angering people."

"So Shen had to leave."

"Escape is a better word."

"With a little of your help?" I asked.

Britt winked. "Just a little."

Shen came back with three glasses and a bottle. "This Shen's medicine."

He gave us each a glass then took the last one for himself. "Fortune!"

Britt repeated the toast. He and Shen each downed the liquid in a single gulp. Finished, they focused expectant eyes on me.

The glass shook in my hands. I brought it to my nose and sniffed. It smelled like turpentine.

I searched the room. Every Chinaman in the place watched me, each smiling like a man who'd just handed out an exploding cigar. I touched the glass to my lips and gulped.

A warm sensation invaded my tongue, a silky and soothing heat. The liquor had little taste other than the alcohol. I licked my lips. With the afterglow of the first swig still tingling my palate, I took an even bigger gulp.

A bomb exploded in my mouth. My eyes watered. My nose ran. Fire seared my throat from teeth to gut. I stuck out my tongue and blew, wondering if they'd given me acid. Then I heard laughter. The dingy restaurant shook, a rolling sea of convulsing faces.

Shen eyed me keenly. "Good, aye? You like Shen's medicine?"

Mouth open, hacking dry coughs, I clutched my throat and nodded dumbly. Shen apparently took this as a good sign and wandered off through the chuckling customers, beaming like a new father.

Britt suppressed a snicker. "You're quite a girl, Jenny Crispin."

I waved my hand in front of my mouth. "You could have warned me."

"Where's the fun in that?"

I kicked his shin under the table. "I could have warned you of that, too."

Britt's face scrunched to a ball.

I savored his agony. After all my frustration, giving him an ounce of pain seemed well worth drinking Shen's rotgut liquor. Frankly, I felt like having another gulp of the swill just to prove I was the better man—so to speak.

I refilled my glass, toasted Britt, then drank. Amazingly, the stuff didn't burn as bad the third time, sliding down my gullet merely like hot coals instead of molten steel, a fact I attributed to the deadening of my flesh beyond sensation.

Several gulps later, Britt started to look silly with his ridiculous short hair, his over-sized jaw, and his brown, puppy-dog eyes. What was he thinking about? Why was he smiling and, come to think of it, what was I doing here in this establishment, surrounded by jabbering Chinamen in black skullcaps and pigtails?

Contentment pervaded my body like a warm bath. I felt at home and at ease as if I belonged in a strange country, in an unusual restaurant, sitting across from Britt, smelling new odors, eating exotic food, and drinking odd drinks. If only there was some way to earn a living at it. Britt's face looked fuzzy in the smoky air. I brought the glass to my lips and sipped again.

Forget about filing papers for *Talmadge's Weekly* or being a journalist. What if I wrote about my travels, jotted down my experiences, and worked them into a collection of stories? *Tales of Distant Lands*, that's what I'd call it. The title had a nice ring. Travel stories sold well, didn't they? Marco Polo had done it and people still read his book.

I took another drink.

Never mind the idea of a travel book. I'd write magazine articles: "An Encounter with the Hottentots," "Scaling the Matterhorn," "By Dugout Down the Mighty Amazon." I'd sell them to *Harper's Weekly* or *Frank Leslie's Illustrated Newspaper.* Travel articles would be more fun to write than pieces about communism, emancipation, or Free Love. Well, maybe not Free Love.

But what if Britt left without me? What if he gave up patent medicine or whatever he did and hopped a ship to Egypt or someplace new—India or Africa or even Australia? Without Britt, I'd be forced to slink back to Pottsville hat in hand.

I couldn't bear the idea of him leaving without me. I slammed my glass on the table. Shen's liquor splashed. "Take me with you, Britt," I cried, voice cracking in desperation.

Britt stared at me, apparently shocked at my unexpected emotion. "What are you talking about?"

I reached across the table, grabbed his hand, and jerked it to me. "I want to travel. I want to see foreign lands."

A blurry Britt tugged back. "You're drunk."

I wouldn't let go and clutched his palm to my bosom. "No, truly, I want to go with you."

He worked his hand from my grip. "You've gone buggy."

"Listen to me, Britt. I want to travel. I want to see deserts and oceans and mountain ranges. I want to walk the streets of Paris and

Rome, London and St. Petersburg. I want to climb ancient pyramids and ruined temples. I want to discover cities lost in the jungle for a thousand years. I want to ride a camel. I want to catch a hippopotamus, a whale. I want to...."

The call of far-off countries overwhelmed me. They beckoned me, tugged me, heaved me up from my chair. I was standing now, swaying on my feet, arm drifting in lazy arcs through air, waving to all those distant peoples: the Chinese in pigtails, the Germans in lederhosen, the French in berets, the robed Bedouins, the naked Bushmen. I could see them, see them all standing on their respective shores calling to me, welcoming me....

Britt's big hands pushed me into my seat. He snapped his fingers under my nose. "Jenny, get hold of yourself. Our food is here."

My eyes focused. Shen had placed a bowl of white rice on the table next to a steaming platter. On a painted plate, a vegetable stew of some variety swam in thick sauce.

Britt was speaking again, sounding like my mother. "Jenny, eat your food, you'll feel better."

Feel better? How could I feel any better? I felt wonderful, delightful. I felt like I could conquer the world. Jenny Crispin, empress of the world, and all men were my slaves. "Bow before me, you silly man."

Britt frowned.

My stomach lurched and a wave of sobering nausea washed over me. I clamped my fingers over my mouth.

"You're not getting sick, are you?"

My stomach lurched again.

"Jenny?"

Nausea replaced my elation. My empire vanished. Britt was right; I needed to eat. I patted the table for my silverware. My fork, where was my fork?

Britt dangled a dab of meat from two sticks wedged between his fingers. He popped the morsel in his mouth and chewed. "Eat," he said, sucking at his lower lip. "It's good."

I picked up my bowl and looked underneath. No spoon, no fork, nothing but sticks. Were these Chinese savages? How was I supposed to eat with sticks?

Britt clicked his little sticks together demonstrating how they worked.

Concentrating as best I could, I jammed the preposterous pieces of wood into my fingers. It felt like some child's game. My stomach twisted again.

I dipped the sticks into my bowl and scooped up a bit of food. What was this stuff? Cabbage? Rutabaga? Halfway to my mouth, the food fell into the bowl. I tried again and again and... The whole thing was hopeless. I threw down the sticks and crossed my arms.

Like a patient parent, Britt slid his chair beside me. He plucked a sliver of meat from my bowl and dabbed it against my pouting lips. I snatched it up like a hungry nestling.

The food tasted fabulous, marvelous, the complete opposite of Shen's medicine. I opened my mouth for more. Britt fetched another bite and fed it to me—then another, and another, and another. After ten bites, he began to tease me. After a full minute of his torment, I started to throw food at him.

Our meal degenerated into a smeary faced, dribble-chinned, exercise in baby feeding. Our faces were sore from laughing. Tears rolled down our cheeks. The Chinese—most likely fearing they sat in the presence of demons—stilled to palpable silence.

I dabbed my eyes and wiped my face. I was smiling, sated and sober—well, almost sober—happy yet vulnerable. "Britt?"

He took his wallet from his jacket pocket. "You'll owe me a handsome sum for this fine repast."

My finger traced the empty bowl's rim. "Britt?" I asked, licking my finger.

He peeled a paper dollar from his wallet and laid it on the table. "Thirty-five cents, at least."

I touched his hand. "Britt, I'm beginning to like you."

Britt rose from his chair, ignoring my confession. He consulted his pocket watch. "I told the driver to return at 7:00PM. Let's go. We have another destination."

I slouched behind him, energy sapped.

Maybe some remnants of Shen's liquor remained in my blood, but I felt a powerful urge to grab Britt's arm and spin him around. I wanted to yell that I was a woman, that he was a man, and that I had special feelings for him.

But I didn't. I didn't say anything. I just followed him to the door and out into the street.

As I climbed inside the carriage, Shen hurried down the front steps. "Britt. What hell you do? I not take money."

Britt made an excuse. Shen responded with a chain of angry syllables. He stuffed the bill into Britt's pocket. "No. You save Shen's life. Khedive almost kill you. You never pay Shen, never."

Hands waving, muttering his alien tongue, Shen stalked back into his restaurant. Britt climbed inside and sat across from me. The carriage jerked forward and rattled south.

The curious incident made me forget my disappointment. "Have you saved all your friend's lives?"

"Most—or they, me."

"What did Shen mean?" I asked. "'Khedive almost kill you.'"

"Shen's crazy."

"Tell me what he meant, Britt."

"There are things you're better off not knowing."

"What things?" I pressed.

"Things that could get you into trouble."

"Britt, I'm already in trouble."

"More trouble."

I scooted into the corner and looked out the window. Why was Britt hiding his past? Why would he conceal something that had happened in Egypt? Had he lied when he'd said he was working for the Khedive? Maybe the Khedive's men were still after him. Maybe he'd killed someone. I'd seen him angry. He could certainly snap a man's neck with one hand.

"Will you tell me where we're going, then?"

"It's a secret."

"Am I being kidnapped?" I asked.

"A rajah would pay handsomely for you," Britt said.

"You wouldn't sell me to an old rajah, would you?"

"Into his harem, yes."

"How many wives does he have?"

"Hundreds."

"No, he's old and tired," I said in a bored voice. "I need a young rajah, possibly a sultan."

"What about a prince?"

"Yes," I said eagerly, "a young and virile prince—with large muscles."

Britt crooked his arm. "Like these?"

I crossed over and sat next to him. I squeezed his arm and my heartbeat quickened. "Yes, exactly like these."

The humor, however, belied my anxiety. My head fell against his chest, and Britt wrapped his arm around my side. It was little comfort; I was worried.

I slipped my hand inside his coat and onto his green shirt. My fingers spread across his stomach. If only I knew some way to keep him close, a way to hold tight to this Britt Salter, this contradiction, this mystery, this unknown man. Pursued by police, without money or home, this big reticent fellow was all I had in the world—and I really didn't even have him.

Chapter Twenty-One

Britt placed his hand over Jenny's fingers and strained to hear her breaths as she drifted into sleep. He pressed his face against her hair, light with an exquisite, natural scent unknown in his encounters with paid women. Who was this girl who held sway over him at the worst possible moment in his life? Why couldn't she and her damned wrist irons have jumped into his bed on some other day, during some other year? Why not before war, when he worked the mines, when he blasted coal from Satan's depths?

He knew the answer, of course. Because she wouldn't have had him. The drunken nights, the bar fights—what woman except the ones he bought would touch a man with drink fouled breath and skin so black with coal dust a wire brush wouldn't clean it. Certainly not a woman of Jenny's temperament: smart, independent, industrious. And why even bother to even consider their meeting in the past. Living in two different worlds, their paths would never have crossed.

But what if, perchance, they had? What would he have said to her? Girls like Jenny couldn't be ordered about like the paid variety. They had to be cajoled and sweet-talked. He'd watched the jaunts ply their trade with the art of an angler, baiting their hook with sweet compliments, keeping the little Nereid on the line with jokes and banter then reeling in a beauty.

Personally, he'd never developed the art beyond the most rudimentary elements, nor seen any need to. No cock-a-dandy he, strolling about the barnyard, plumage fluffed and preened. Dollar to dimes, he was many things, most of them bad, but glib-tongued, fancy-man he was not. If a girl would have him, then she would have him as he was—a plain-speaking, blunt-nosed ruffian.

Still, if he were to dream—and what harm could there be in doing so—then dreaming about the past was futile. Yesterday was gone, never to return. Tomorrow, though, contained many roads, all yet to be taken. And if the road yet taken were not preordained as some have said, then damn it, why could he and Jenny not meet a month from now in some far away city—Chicago, for instance—when this Khedive business was over. Why could he not be sitting at a table at the Albion enjoying a plate of blue points and pint of Diversey beer, look up, and see her dressed in stunning green, standing by the door, her hair twisted and curled beneath a flowered hat, her expression fretful, dismayed that some flop-eared escort had not arrived as promised?

Of course, gentleman that he was, he'd stand and bow. He'd offer a seat and, if she so desired, buy her dinner, two old friends who happened to meet again by chance. They'd talk, reminisce about their time in New York, and when the fool finally showed, she would dismiss him summarily. Later, a stroll in the park, a walk home and... Britt shook his head. Dime romance drivel. Was he losing his mind? Had he not learned his lesson with Penelope?

He clamped his teeth and glanced outside. The carriage was drawing closer to Chatham Square. Street lamps once again lined the sidewalk. A square of light drifted across Jenny's face. Lips curved to a smile, her pupils darted back and forth beneath her closed lids. Was she dreaming, he wondered? Of what? Something pleasant, he hoped. Foreign adventures. Egypt probably. The Nile at sunset, triangular sails beating the wind, pyramids rising in the distance. Those were enjoyable memories for him.

Or maybe she was shopping in the market below Citadel Prison, trying on baubles and bracelets from the silversmith's stall. Beware,

Jenny Crispin; thieves are watching you. Britt almost laughed out loud. If she thought New York City was dangerous, God forbid she should find out what truly barbarous cultures were like.

Or maybe, he thought, glancing once more out of the carriage, watching the rows of smutty tenement windows slide past, maybe she dreamt of more domestic affairs. Her family perhaps. Her father, the cobbler. She spoke lovingly of him. Killed in the war, she'd said. And her mother, gone mad, also passed beyond this veil. Pity, Jenny had no one now. A girl alone, an orphan, as are we both. Maybe that's why she latched onto me so strongly. I'm all she has. Like Jeffery, she's just a babe surrounded by hostiles. Or could it be she's dreaming of the family she will one day have, a daughter, a son, a husband? Jenny, poor Jenny, these dreams will never be if you don't leave the city tonight.

Britt cast his gaze once more upon her face, frustration and anger rising inside him. Wouldn't a sensible, intelligent girl take his advice and return home? No, of course not. Why should she do that? Better she stays close to McCauley, who will track her without mercy and throw her in the Tombs—or worse, perform some foul violation of decency upon her body. Why in heaven's name would she stay in the city when the danger was so great?

Why did you volunteer to dig that tunnel under the Rebel battlements at the Crater?

The question startled Britt even though it came from his own brain. Not to be made a fool, he answered himself. "That was different; the lives of hundreds of soldiers were at stake."

The lives of Jenny's friends are at stake.

"What friends? Mrs. Satan? Bah! The woman is no friend. She's a charlatan, an opportunist. Besides, the Talmadge woman can take care of herself."

But what of Cleo? She's a true friend.

"Yes, well, they're all misguided feminists, aren't they? They've gotten themselves in trouble with the law. Why should Jenny risk her life to set them free?"

You've never risked your life to help a friend?

"That's different. I'm a man. I can take care of myself."

Doesn't that make Jenny all the more brave?

"Foolhardy, if you ask me."

As if you were never foolhardy?"

"Not like her. Not like this."

No?

"Never."

Insulting the Khedive? To his face? Did you truthfully think that would get you anything less than eleven bullets in the heart?

Britt scowled. One should never argue with oneself. There were no secrets. "Insulting that tin-plated tyrant might have been foolhardy, but it felt damn good."

And who saved your neck?

Jenny squirmed against his side and brushed her hand across his chest. Britt said nothing. The argument was lost. What was he supposed to do then? Give up his revenge on the king? Put everything aside and save Jenny from herself—against her will? Would she even allow it? No, of course not. The only way to truly save her would be to carry her onto a Pullman car and strap her to a seat. That, he would not do. He would not save her against her will. He'd tried to save Penelope and look what it had gotten him.

Britt opened the panel and spoke to the driver. "Stop at the corner of Chatham."

The carriage parked at the intersection of Chatham and Worth. Britt extracted himself from Jenny, eased her gently to the seat leather and got out. He gave the driver some coins and promised to return in a few minutes.

Chatham Square News was a shanty, narrow and squat and made of unpainted wood. The owner, a balding gent in spectacles and a scarf, sat in a rectangular opening surrounded by newspapers. In the light of twin oil lamps, Britt glanced over the dailies and weeklies: *The Times, The Post, Age, The Daily Witness, The Evening Mail,* and *The Observer.* Magazines covered a slanted tray: *Frank Leslie's Illustrated Newspaper, Harper's Weekly, The Atlantic, Scientific American,* and *National Police Gazette* caught his eye.

Behind the proprietor, fire crackled in a miniature wood stove.

How the place kept from going up in flame, God only knew. Cool air and the smell of burning pine reminded him of the campfires around Appomattox the night of the surrender.

He approached the window. "Britt, old fellow," the man said, looking up from a sheath of papers and lifting his spectacles to his forehead. "Didn't expect to see you out this Hallows' Eve night."

"I didn't expect to be out, Newton."

Newton dropped the papers in his hand and held up a small book. "Something every sporting man needs: *The Gentleman's Companion.* Rates every bawdy house in Manhattan by price and quality." He slid his glasses back onto his nose, opened the cover, and read: "'Mrs. Mayrs at number 145. There are seven lady boarders who for loveliness and amiability compare favorably with the best.'"

"Not tonight, Newton."

Newton held up a finger and continued: "'The same may be said for number 147 which is kept by Miss Georgia. This house contains five beautiful girl boarders and every attention is paid to visitors.'"

"I've been to Miss Georgia's establishment, and I'll vouch one of the girls is not so beautiful. What I came for is a train ticket to Pottsville."

Newton closed the book and laid it aside. "Where the devil is Pottsville?"

"Pennsylvania. Near Harrisburg."

"Oh, Harrisburg," Newton said, nodding. "Why didn't you say so?" He pulled a ticket from a rack behind him and punched a hole in the corner. "You catch the 10:15 ferry at Slip Seventeen. When it docks in Jersey City, find the Philadelphia Railroad agent. He'll direct you to the train depot. Five dollars, twenty. Need some reading material for the trip? I've got an advance copy of an excellent book. *The Times of Paris* is carrying it next month in a serial. *Around the World in Eighty Days*, it's called."

Britt laughed as he counted out five dollars and twenty cents and took the ticket. "Circle the globe in eighty days? Preposterous."

Halfway back to the carriage, just as they'd arranged, he met Lockie leaning against a lamppost. The Kullberg chimed faintly in his open palm. "Where's the lass?"

"Asleep in the carriage."

Lockie slipped the timepiece into his pocket. "Did you get the nitro?"

"Not yet, but I believe Gideon will try and destroy the Manhattan bridge tower at 9:00PM."

"With only six bottles? You think the general has the skill to bring down the tower with so little?"

"You or I would have no problem dropping the tower with just six bottles, but whether Gideon can or can't isn't the question. We have to take his nitro away."

Lockie pushed off the lamppost. He looked toward the newspaper stand and then at Britt. "Assuming Gideon shows and assuming we stop him from blowing the bridge—and nae get killed doing it—we'll never be able to return the nitro to our shop by twelve."

"What are you saying?"

Lockie stepped closer. A halo of gaslight lit his face. "Life is short. Our time tonight is shorter—less than six hours. Britt, give up this revenge. Jenny is a fine lass. You can both leave town and make a life."

"I thought you wanted me to get rid of the girl."

"That was before you fell in love with her."

"Love?" Britt asked. "You're an expert now?"

"Five wives—good women all—if I've learned nothing from them, I've learned this: a heart filled with love has nae room for hate."

Britt flexed his back against the sting of ill-healed wounds. "A heart filled with hate must be purged before there is room for love."

"So you'll abandon the lass?"

"I bought her a train ticket home."

"Ach! Such a grand gentleman you are. You know she won't use it."

"I'll make her."

Lockie chuckled. "That I'd like to see. And if you fail?"

"It will be her choice."

"Her choice," Lockie mocked. "You'd throw away Jenny's life—and her love—just to satisfy your lust for vengeance?"

Britt focused on the night beyond Lockie's eyes. "I won't force my will on her."

"That old tired story? You're nae a child now. A man makes the decisions he must."

"And so I have."

Lockie lifted his hands to his hips. He stepped back and peered at Britt as if the two were strangers. "Then, if that is the case, Mister Brittan Salter, consider my debt paid in full. I wish you luck on Satan's night." Head down, he turned, jammed his hands in his pockets and walked away.

Jenny was still sleeping when Britt opened the carriage door. He lifted her carefully and slid in. Everyone makes choices. Jenny made hers, and Lockie made his. So be it. He'd finish the job himself. As the carriage jerked forward, Britt took the ticket from his pocket and held it to the light of the window.

Chapter Twenty-Two

Shen's medicine must have been stronger than I thought because I awoke still snuggled against Britt's chest. How long I'd been asleep or how far Britt and I had traveled I couldn't say.

I rubbed the moisture from the window with my sleeve. We'd reached a more prosperous part of town. Flickering street lamps passed us one by one. I pressed closer to the glass. A sign drifted by: Reade Street. That was near City Hall, wasn't it?

My ears perked. The cadence of drums echoed off brick. Music? Distant horns blared. Fifes blew, high and airy. Two people dressed as a cow hoofed down the sidewalk. A portly Poseidon strode past carrying a trident in his swinging hand. Beside him, a slender woman wore a crown of seaweed and a long gown decorated with fish. I slid across the carriage and dried the other window. A tall man in red tights and a horned skull-piece strolled casually south.

"Look," I cried, now fully awake, "there's Satan."

Britt leaned over and glanced. "Lately, he follows me everywhere."

I slapped his arm. "*You* are Satan."

"Some have told me that."

"Lady friends, I'll wager."

Music drew my ear. City Hall Park was coming into view. Limelight illuminated a newly constructed stage where bandsmen in red uniforms played beneath orange and black bunting. Kings and queens and gods and goddesses wandered through the audience while acrobats formed human towers that collapsed in rolling somersaults.

The hack lurched to a halt. Britt swung open the door. His hand enclosed mine, and we stepped into the cool air. Britt paid the driver then pulled me onto the grass to the park.

A man hawked strips of beef cooked on a pit of coals. Twenty feet beyond him, people crowded around a juggler in lace collar and cuffs. Balls flew about his head and he spoke a seamless stream of patter about his house, his children, and his wife. Further on, a bonfire roared. Lit red by the flames, ghoulish creatures roasted potatoes on long sticks. We passed a bell-ringing sailor who jingled a bucket of coins. A placard on his chest begged money for the Great Whaling Disaster. Dancing beside him, a woman in a pointed hat and long robe touched people with a star-tipped wand. As if late for an appointment, the Satan we'd seen earlier dodged her wand and rushed into the crowd. I tapped Britt's arm and pointed to the devil. He only nodded.

On stage, the music ended in a great finale and a man in a top hat appeared. Sweeping his gloved hands through the air, he shouted in grand theatrical tones, praising the New York to Brooklyn Bridge and the prosperity it would bring. Someone heckled him from the crowd. Others cheered.

Britt tugged my hand. "This way."

The shouting faded as we walked south of the courthouse. Here, a fire-eater blew giant balls of flame. In the orange glow, I saw a balding Nero shake his violin as he argued with a diminutive centurion. We passed a horse, a sheep, and a pig standing around a folding table. Two men, both in long capes, danced together over the brown grass. Close by, a gangly teenager sold masks, which he wore heaped on his head.

I tugged Britt's sleeve. "Let's buy some masks."

Before he could answer, an immense roar drowned out the music. Fifty feet above the crowd, a gigantic globe illuminated. Resembling a paper lantern from Shen's establishment, it had been hovering invisible over our heads until its fire ignited.

"Britt," I cried, pointing to it. "That's the balloon I saw this morning." The flame ceased, and I pulled his sleeve again. "Let's go see."

We arrived just as the balloon touched down. The wicker basket carried an array of tanks and brass pipes, at the top of which burned a small flame. Below the pipes stood a fierce looking creature, more bug than man. He wore a leather cap, goggles, and long leather gloves. Only his tweed coat and handlebar mustache gave any hint of humanity. My breath caught as he beckoned me closer.

I touched my breastbone.

"Yes, you," the balloonist said. "Don't be shy, step right up."

Mysteriously drawn to the strange man and his craft, I disengaged my fingers from Britt's and approached the balloon.

"That's good," the balloonist said. "A mite closer, now."

I took another step.

"Yes, there you are. A little closer."

I inched nearer and, without warning, the balloonist clapped a gloved hand around my shoulders and drew me right against the wicker. He bent low, peered sideways at me though his glass lenses, and whispered in my ear.

"My name is Professor Thaddeus Constantine Lowe, young lady, and if you will give me your assistance, I will gladly repay you with something worth more than gold."

Embarrassed by this confidence, I glanced at Britt then searched the gathering crowd. Surely this strange man had mistaken me for someone else.

"Young lady," the man again whispered, "tonight, you and I will write our names in the book of history. Destiny, my dear, has chosen *you* to be my assistant."

I touched my breast again. The balloonist looked furtively about to make sure no one was eavesdropping. "In a moment, I will address this rabble and you must assist me. Whenever I ask a question, you will respond in a very loud voice: '*No, Professor Lowe, tell us.*'"

As if certain that I would comply, he straightened up and pushed his goggles onto his leather-clad forehead. I shot Britt a questioning look and shrugged. Britt only shook his head.

Professor Lowe hoisted himself up by the netting until a knee-high lace-up boot rested on the lip of the basket. He raised a gloved palm. The murmuring crowd stilled, and all eyes fell upon him.

"Ladies and gentlemen," he shouted, voice booming above the music's din, "have you any idea what this magnificent device is?"

My stomach jumped into my throat. "Ah... No, Professor Lowe, tell us."

"I most certainly will, dear lady. My friends, you see above you the greatest miracle since the invention of the electrical telegraph. Professor Lowe's Aeronautical Engine is not a crude observation balloon of the kind used during our recent war. No, no, my friends, Professor Lowe's Aeronautical Engine does not fly by use of highly dangerous and explosive hy-dro-gen. Professor Lowe's Aeronautical Engine flies by means of an entirely unique method. Do you good people have any idea *what* that entirely unique method is?"

I was looking at Britt and almost missed my cue. I quickly spoke my lines. "No, Professor Lowe, tell us."

"Why, I'd be proud to, my dear girl. Professor Lowe's Aeronautical Engine is powered by the same energy that powers our United States Congress—hot air. Yes, friends, you heard me correctly, I said hot air. And do you know where this hot air comes from?"

"Your throat," someone shouted.

As the crowd erupted into chuckles and titters, I called out, "No, Professor Lowe, tell us."

The professor cleared his throat. "Thank you, madam, thank you. I'll tell you where the hot air comes from. It comes from fire, the very same fire that heats your good homes. This fire, however, is generated by the combustion of atomized spirits of coal. Yes, I said atomized spirits of coal, the worthless byproduct of coal tar manufacturing."

Murmurs shot through the audience while Lowe paused to survey the reaction. He slapped the balloon's surface. "Ladies and gentlemen, fire heats the air captured in this canvas envelope and, in accordance with the principles of buoyancy first set down by Archimedes over two thousand years ago, the craft rises into the sky, carrying me and my crew aloft."

The professor pulled a cord and a tremendous flame roared into the globe. A collective gasp broke from the crowd. Eyes opened and jaws dropped as each mesmerized face illuminated like a minor moon.

In the orange light, I saw Britt, a head above the rest, watching me instead of the balloon.

The flame stopped. The professor waited a moment then resumed his oration. "My friends, tomorrow morning, my crew and I will rise into the sky. Propelled by the trade winds, we will cross the Atlantic Ocean and alight somewhere on the continent of Europe. Ladies and gentlemen, have you any idea what this momentous event will mean?"

I stared at Britt.

"I said, ladies and gentlemen, have you any idea what this event will mean?"

His face, his eyes, somehow they looked different. I saw it on his lips and on his cheeks, in the set of his jaw and the bent of his brow.

"Ahem, ah, have you any notion what landing in Europe will mean?"

I reached out my hand. We were alone, just Britt and me, in the night.

"Well, good people, then, ah, I will tell you what it means myself."

Britt came toward me, floating over the grass, arm out, hand extended, fingers touching mine, squeezing them, running up my arm, around my waist, eyes probing, lips pressing, tongues touching.

"It means mankind will no longer be shackled to the earth. It means that, like the birds, we'll be free to roam the heavens. Yes, a new era is dawning, my friends, an era of cloud-borne transportation. In the near future, aerial schooners and steamers will ply the skies as easily as they sail the seven seas."

Britt's strong arms held me, enclosed me, protected me. I felt the warm, hard pressure of his body against mine. I felt his chest rise and fall, slow and sure, and, in the far, far distance, I heard cheers and applause.

Britt's lips parted from mine as the ovation faded. Professor Lowe called out a hearty thanks to his audience. Kings, queens, emperors, horses, sheep, and other Halloween curiosities wandered away to pursue further diversions as the beaming professor climbed down from the net and hopped into the basket. "Thank you, my dear, for that, ah, questionable assistance."

I offered the professor a sheepish look.

The professor glanced at Britt momentarily then faced me again. "As payment, ah—what did you say your name was?"

"Jenny Crispin."

"As payment, Miss Crispin, you are going for a ride. Put your foot here. That's right. Now climb up and over."

To my amazement, I stood in the balloon's basket right next to the professor. I took Britt's hand. "Come with me."

Britt tried to pull away, but I held his fingers tight.

Lowe leaned close. His eyebrows rose. "Your friend appears apprehensive about the ascent." He addressed Britt in a loud voice. "I assure you, sir, there's nothing to fear. The Aerial Engine is quite safe."

Britt hung back. "I'd rather not. You go, Jenny, I'll wait."

Lowe pulled on his goggles. "My good fellow, you'd let your lady fly away with a strange man while you wait behind? Really, sir, are you made of porridge? Show your stuff."

I wouldn't let go. "Please, Britt."

Britt climbed into the basket as Lowe pumped furiously on a long handle. After turning knobs and checking gauges, he nodded to us then pulled the cord. A column of fire as tall and big around as Britt himself burst from the maze of brass.

The flame's tremendous heat fired my excitement. My body trembled with anticipation. Ascending in a balloon was positively the most exhilarating thing I could ever imagine. I reached for Britt's waist. "Isn't this—"

The ground fell from beneath the basket. My stomach dropped. I grabbed a shroud line for support as the balloon broke free of the earth and began to rise.

I gulped in the experience. We were climbing higher and higher, rising as if we weighed nothing: a feather, a wisp of cloud, smoke. The ground shifted quickly in an unsettling but thrilling perspective. Soon, all I could see were the tops of people's heads. Then the courthouse roof and clock tower appeared along with the stage, the band, the bonfires, and the entire grounds of City Hall Park. I saw everything and everybody. Nothing escaped my view. I was Zeus gazing down from Olympus.

The roaring stilled and the balloon continued its ascent in silence. A mosaic of buildings spread beneath me. I could see the whole city now: street lamps dotting the roadways, windows lit yellow, fires burning red along the river. The smoke from a thousand chimneys surrounded us in a plateau of haze. We broke through and, above us, stars twinkled.

The basket wobbled as its tether jerked tight. I expected Lowe to spew more sideshow babble, but he remained silent. Whether he wished us to commune silently with the gods of the air or just wanted me to enjoy the experience of flight, I couldn't tell. But up there, hovering above Manhattan, looking down upon the world, I realized the troubles of one life were small and insignificant.

The basket's floor squeaked and flexed as I moved closer to Britt. I pressed my palm against his back. "Isn't the view beautiful?"

Britt stared at me, face pale in the full moon. "No, you are."

We kissed. For how long, I don't know. But when we finally parted, almost imperceptibly, the balloon began its descent. Rooftops moved closer, the park grew bigger, ants became people, and the music's volume changed from soft to loud.

The basket touched Earth with a bump. Britt gave me a boost over the wicker and then climbed out himself. Still inside the basket, Lowe touched his lips to my hand. "Young lady, I could use a brave girl like you in my crew. You're a natural aeronaut."

"I've read *Five Weeks in a Balloon*," I said with pride.

Lowe's brow wrinkled. "Jules Verne. Yes, I'm familiar with the book. Quite entertaining, but he got everything wrong. You know more about ballooning now than he does."

I eased my hand from his grasp and glanced toward Britt, now standing a few feet away.

Lowe continued. "Think of the publicity, the fame. Imagine the headlines: 'Jenny Crispin, first woman to cross the Atlantic by air.'"

"What exactly are you asking me?"

"To join me on my transatlantic flight."

My brain reeled. "You can't be serious."

"Completely serious, Miss Crispin."

"Fly across the Atlantic with you? How do you know I'm not a silly female who'll start crying after ten minutes and demand to return home?"

"Your courage and poise are quite evident."

"But what about your other crewmen?" I asked. "Would they want a woman on board?"

"Sideshow talk. I have no other crewmen, Miss Crispin."

"So you're asking me to fly with you alone across the Atlantic when I know nothing more about you than your name."

He snatched the leather cap and goggles from his head. "Miss Crispin, I am a gentleman, and I dare say you are a modern woman."

I glanced at Britt standing large against the costumed crowd then turned back to the professor. "I'm a thoroughly modern woman."

"Well, there you have it," he said. "Come with me and you'll not only be famous—you'll be the *most* famous woman on Earth. What shall it be?"

Chapter Twenty-Three

The most famous woman on Earth. The words sounded magical. I cocked a narrowed eye at Lowe. "More famous than Glorianna Talmadge?"

"More famous than even President Grant."

My resolve strengthened. "When are you leaving?"

He pointed a leather finger skyward. "Tomorrow morning. We lift off at five."

Lost in thought, picturing my name and likeness on the front page of the *New York Times*, I walked to Britt's side.

"Did the good professor proposition you?" he asked.

"In a way. He wants me to fly with him across the Atlantic."

"And will you?"

"He said I'd be the most famous woman on Earth."

"And fame is what you seek?"

Violet's voice returned to me. *"Young lady, fame is paramount."* I considered her words carefully. My name printed in twenty point Bookman boldface type had nearly gotten me arrested. Violet spoke again, louder. *"If you wish to change the world, my dear, fame is essential."*

"Yes," I said resolutely, giving Britt my attention once more. Fame is what I desire.

"Well," he said, eyebrows raised, "you wanted to see other lands

191

and civilizations."

I pictured myself in Professor Lowe's basket, the great Nile stretching into the horizon as the peak of the Great Pyramid passed below me. "And as a balloonist I could do both: travel the world and write about it, too."

"You could also escape McCauley."

"Yes," I said, gleeful at the thought, "of course." Aeronaut, as an occupation, was sounding better and better.

"And Cleo could join you."

"Cleo?"

"Certainly," Britt said, his voice almost giddy. "First, you'll rescue Cleo from the Tombs, then you'll both meet Professor Lowe at dawn. Everyone will jump into his balloon, float away into the sky, and live happily ever after."

My vision of the Great Pyramid dissolved like sugar in tea. "Are you making fun of me?"

His mood darkened. "Have you ever considered that Professor Lowe is a fraud just like these scalawags collecting money for the Great Whaling Disaster?"

"What do you mean?"

"The Great Whaling Disaster is a sham. No one died."

"That's not true. Thirty-three ships were crushed in the ice. Hundreds of sailors died. Their families were devastated."

Britt pulled out his watch by the chain and let it dangle. "I bought this timepiece off a sailor from the *Elizabeth Swift*, one of the ships lost. Twelve hundred and nineteen crew were aboard those vessels. All were rescued. Not a one died."

I watched the timepiece spin, mesmerized by his words. "How can that be true?"

He thumbed the watch into its pocket. "Lowe is no different. The man's a carnival barker, a mountebank. What if he's sweet-talked a hundred investors into giving him thousands of dollars, and tomorrow morning he'll simply float away with their funds and never be seen again?"

I gazed at the ground and shook my head. "Why must you always see the worst in people?"

"Because I don't want you hurt, that's why. Besides, what about Cleo? Are you just going to fly off and leave her?"

"No, of course not," I said, astonished at the suggestion. "You must help me rescue her. If Lockie was in trouble, wouldn't you risk everything to save him?"

Britt glanced toward Professor Lowe, now addressing another curious crowd. "I'm afraid that circumstance will never arise. Lockie has abandoned me."

I peered at him dismayed. "That cannot be true. You've known Lockie for years. He cannot just leave. You saved his life, and I suspect he has saved yours."

"We had a disagreement."

"A disagreement?" I asked, bewildered. "What could possibly be important enough to come between fast friends?" No sooner had I spoken the words than I read the answer on his face.

He took my hands and pulled me close. "It's not your fault. It's no one's fault. There's more to the events of tonight than you know."

What more was there to know? Lockie had apparently given Britt an ultimatum—him or me. I had torn apart two best friends, and whatever their big plan was, my presence had ruined it. Behind me, fire thundered in Lowe's balloon. Choking my emotion, I spoke over the roar. "Where is Lockie now?"

"Probably at Marm's packing his bag."

Instantly furious, I pushed Britt's chest hard with both hands. "You must go there now. You must find him. You must beg him to return."

Britt stood immobile. "Lockie has made his choice."

I pushed him again, harder. "Well, it's a stupid choice. Go. Now. You may still catch him. Lockie is your friend, your best friend. Think about your big sale. Whatever it is, you can't complete it without him."

Britt shook his head as the roar of the flame ceased, and the balloon began to rise. "I'll complete the sale with or without Lockie."

Tears brimmed in my eyes. "Are you sure of that? Are you quite sure? You planned this together."

"I don't need him."

His stubbornness appalled me. I wiped my eyes. "What about me? I can do his job. Then afterwards, we can find Lockie together and all of us can rescue—"

"No. It's too dangerous. You could be hurt or worse."

I felt my soul rip in two. Why would the man not listen to reason? Yes, he was big and headstrong and narrow-minded and sexist, and had we met under any other circumstances I would have dismissed him immediately as a bully and male supremacist. But now, forced by events, I had come to realize there was none with so great a heart. I would not allow myself to divide him and his dearest friend. I just wouldn't.

Inhaling a deep breath, I crossed my arms. "Mr. Salter, I see that my efforts to make you abandon your so-called big sale and help me have come to naught. I had harbored a small hope that I could persuade you to find and free Cleo, but now I understand you are too bull-headed and selfish to help anybody. Even my efforts to physically seduce you have failed to motivate you. In Molly de Ford's establishment, you complained I was a virgin. In your room, when I desired sexual congress, you pushed me away like I had the plague. Nothing I have done has caused you in any way to rise to my assistance. Heaven knows why I have wasted my time on you thus far. From here on, I will have nothing to do with you. I will seek out a more pliable man to fulfill my requests. Mr. Salter, I implore you to find Lockie immediately and explain to him that a callous siren lured you away from your friendship and that you humbly beg his forgiveness."

With that, I hurried away.

Ten paces into the crowd, Britt grabbed me and spun me around. He encircled my body with his arms and pressed his mouth to mine. Overwhelmed by passion, I opened his coat and thrust my hands inside. My arms wrapped around his waist and my head whirled beneath his lips.

After many minutes, he pulled back. "As an actress, you lack much."

"What are you talking about?"

"I saw right through your performance."

I looked up at him. "Every word I spoke was true."

"As were mine."

"Then," I said, peering into his eyes, "we're at an impasse."

Still embracing me with one arm, he took out his watch and snapped it open. "It's 8:40PM. I've got to—"

"8:40!" I broke free of his embrace. "I'm late for Glorianna's rally."

Britt closed the watch and slipped it into his vest pocket. "You're not going to that rally."

Dear Lord, was he still barking orders? Had we not made any progress at all? "Oh, yes I am. I've got to warn Glorianna about McCauley. And don't forget about Cleo. You promised to help."

"I told you I'd *try* to help Cleo, and I will, but Glorianna Talmadge needs nothing. She's a swindler who's only after publicity and money. She can't legally run for president and women in this country can't legally vote. What's more, McCauley would give up cigars forever to arrest her. If you go to her rally, you might as well take a hack to the Ludlow Street Jail and wait for the next wagon to the Tombs."

A dull ache settled into my brain. I was getting mad, at him and at myself.

Surely I hadn't expected him to react differently. Surely I hadn't thought ten minutes of conversation, a kiss, and a few minutes of passion would change anything. He'd been against everything I believed in from the very start. Universal suffrage, women's rights—to him it was so much silly twaddle. I was wrong. Only some misguided masculine nonsense about protecting the weaker sex had kept him from abandoning me hours ago. I could see that now.

My voice was cold and my soul numb with realization. "You can drop me at Apollo Hall."

"So you're going there anyway?"

"Yes."

Britt strode toward Broadway. I followed behind while drunken barn animals, royalty, and mythical creatures sang and laughed. A chain of carriages and their drivers lined the street. Britt walked to the nearest one. The driver, a lad in scuffed ankle boots and a fur cap, held the door as Britt and I climbed in.

Britt concentrated on the window. I studied his face, a gray outline

195

against the glass. I could guess what was going through his mind. He was counting the time until he was rid of me.

Ten minutes later, the carriage slowed to a crawl. A crowd of celebrants had spilled out of the park in a drunken stampede, running between the carriages, pulling at bridles, smashing bottles, and stopping traffic. The night was insane, a confusion of inebriates and madmen. Unable to bear it, I looked to Britt, hoping his mood had softened.

His face was stone.

My fists clenched. Without Britt's help, I'd have to do everything myself. That meant if I could stay out of jail long enough to warn Glorianna, maybe she could persuade Commodore Vanderbilt to get Cleo out of jail. He practically owned City Hall, didn't he?

And if everything collapsed, mountebank or not, there was always Professor Lowe. A balloon flight across the Atlantic? The idea was laughable. But then, with everything else in my life up in the air, why not my body as well?

The tide of drunks passed and the hack rolled to a standstill a block before Apollo Hall. The boy opened the slotted window. "Traffic's jammed all the way to the hall, sir. It'll take an hour to get through. Maybe the lady could walk from here."

"We'll both get out," Britt said brusquely, opening the door.

I stepped out behind him. Britt paid the driver then pushed some papers into my hand.

I unfolded them. "A train ticket and fifty dollars?"

He closed my hand around the ticket. "Go to your rally if you must, but, when it's over, take a hackney to Slip Seventeen. From there, a steam ferry will take you across the Hudson."

I shook my hand free. "Why are you abandoning me, Britt?"

"When you get to Jersey City, a Philadelphia Railroad agent will direct you to the depot."

"Why are you doing this?" I asked. "I know you care for me."

Britt looked away. "Tonight at midnight something very bad is going to happen. Use that ticket and never return. Swear you won't try to find me."

And then I knew. "Those scars on your back... The Khedive hurt you, didn't he? You helped Shen escape. The Khedive punished you for it. He had you whipped."

Britt took my hand again. "You'll be fine."

I jerked my fingers from his. "He put you in prison, didn't he?"

"Promise me you won't try to find me."

"How long were you in prison, Britt?"

"Go to your rally."

"How long, Britt?"

He stared at me for what seemed like minutes. "Too long."

Realization clicked together like a gears in a clock. "You're going to kill him, aren't you? You're going to kill the Khedive."

His eyes burned into mine, the eyes of a man discovered. He seized my shoulders and shook, then the fire in his face ebbed. What he said next had the quality of a vow.

"I'll make him pay for every stripe on my back and every hour I spent in that stinking cell."

A lump grew in my throat. I couldn't look at him any longer. My emotions were spent. I turned away and faced the traffic. "Do whatever makes you happy."

I dabbed my eyes. I could feel him standing behind me, feel his presence looming over me like a stone colossus. The clot of carriages trickled forward in the street. Two bumped. An angry driver shouted curses. The other driver yelled back.

Then something inside me snapped. I didn't care about women's rights anymore; I didn't care about universal suffrage. I didn't care about traveling in a balloon, fame, the Khedive, or even Cleo. I only cared about Britt. I wanted him to touch me, to take my arm, to spin me around, and crush me against his body.

"Britt," I cried, voice cracking. I swung towards him, ready to throw myself against his chest.

But he was gone, disappeared into the shadows of New York.

So that was that. He was out of my life as quickly as he'd come into it.

A shiver rippled down my spine, a strengthening tremor, a solidification of each bone, each vertebra. I didn't need him, not anymore. I'd survive without his help. No, I'd do more than survive; I'd come out on top.

What choice did I have? I jammed the train ticket and money into the pocket of my dress.

Chapter Twenty-Four

Head down, blowing hot breath into his cupped, cold hands, Britt walked east into the darkness of Walker Street. Madness, that's what it was, naked madness. He should have known better right from the start. Why had he allowed himself to be drawn into her misfortune? Was it hope? Some foolish, desperate desire that he might have what other men had: a home, a wife, a child, instead of a charade, a series of one act dramas, played out in flesh, bought and paid for with cash? He should have listened to Lockie. Now it was too late.

At Lafayette Street, Britt found a waiting hansom and gave the driver instructions for Fulton Street and the riverfront. When he arrived, except for a few merchants cleaning their stalls, Britt found the fish market deserted. He got out, paid the driver, then checked his pocket watch. 8:57PM. Gideon would be leaving for the bridge any minute.

He jogged north along South Street past the Khedive's ship, motionless in the filthy water. A short distance up the river, the Manhattan bridge tower, black against the stars, pointed toward the full moon. Further down, at the address listed on the paper he'd found at the stable, lights burned in a low house with gables and shutters. Britt waited in the shadows across the street. With luck, Gideon and

Maxwell were inside making their final plans.

Most likely only one sentry guarded the bridge tower, someone to deter the curious. Getting by a single watchman would be easy for Gideon, a man with a commanding presence, used to ordering people about. Once the guard was dispatched, the three would attach the nitro, light the fuse, and be gone. Five minutes and one-hell-of-an explosion later, if Gideon or one of his men had the skill, the bridge tower—or at least half of it—would be in the water. Britt couldn't take that chance: he needed that nitro intact.

He crept closer. At the clapboard wall, he flattened himself beside one of the windows and listened. He heard nothing. Curious, he peeked through the glass. Lit by two oil lamps side by side on a table, the main room appeared deserted. He walked around the house peering into windows. Damn it, he was too late. Gideon and his men had already left.

Night air stung Britt's face as he raced through a short maze of docks and shipyards along the riverfront until he reached a tall, wooden fence. Walking beside it, his fingers skipped across the rough-sawn planks. When he felt the wood move, he stopped and lit a Lucifer. The padlock on the gate was a Champion Six Lever, higher quality than the average but still an easy pick.

Once inside, Britt started down a series of catwalks. Spools of steel cable stood on either side of him like monstrous thread bobbins. Granite blocks as big as water wagons lay scattered here and there. At the river's edge, he stepped onto a pier and then down a ramp onto a barge.

The bridge tower rose over him, black and silent. He'd seen the pyramids—they were big but in a blunt, squat way; this structure, on the other hand, although built of stone, felt as if any moment it might take off starward like a skyrocket.

A powerful light suddenly blinded him and a voice called out, "Don't move if you value your life." Britt raised his arms in the air and the light grew brighter. "How did you get past the gate?" the voice asked.

"Are you the watchman?" Britt asked, careful not to lower his arms.

"You bet I am, and there's a pistol aimed at your belly."

"Turn the light aside. Put down your weapon. I'm Inspector McCauley of the New York Police." Britt lowered his arms. "The front gate was unlocked. I'll have to file a report. Who's responsible?"

After a moment, the beam moved away. Britt's eyes adjusted. A man of thirty pointed a pistol at him. "That would be the foreman." The man shoved the pistol into his belt. "I don't even have a key. You sure you have to file that report?"

Britt scrutinized the watchman's bullseye lantern, which appeared to be the latest focusing variety. "We had a tip someone might try and damage the bridge tower tonight. Will the beam of that light make it to the tower base?"

"You bet."

When they reached the edge of the barge, the watchman twisted the lens on the front of his lantern. A hundred feet away, an amber disc played over the granite. Water sloshed against the stone base. Nothing looked out of the ordinary. If General Gideon was planning an explosion, it wouldn't happen here, not tonight.

Britt shook the watchman's hand, thanked him for being a good citizen, and promised not to file a report. Climbing the catwalk, he wondered where Gideon was and what mischief he was up to. Blowing up the bridge tower was probably one of many options he'd considered and given up on. At the wooden fence, Britt stepped outside, hooked the padlock into the hasp, and locked it.

He walked west past darkened buildings. Lockie was gone. Jenny was gone. The nitro was gone. His planned revenge on the Khedive was gone. He had nothing, just like when he'd fled Madame Becker's. It was fate.

He believed in fate, believed in it strongly. Fate had given him every hardship—and seen him through. He should have died as a baby like most prostitute's spawn, aborted by some drunk of a doctor or side-alley midwife. Fate made him fall in love with Penelope and put him in that fight with her brother. If not for Jed's death, he'd never have been a coal miner or an explosives expert. During the war, he should have been killed in the battles he fought: The Crater, City Point, Shiloh…

201

The bar fights too, the shootouts, the mine accidents, and Egypt. Yes, Egypt. He'd never been as close to death as he'd been in Alexandria.

Yet he'd survived.

But of all his brushes with death, City Point had been the most terrifying. Worse than The Crater. In its way, even worse than Egypt. He could still see the fiery chaos in his mind. Still hear the thunder and shriek of 30,000 exploding artillery shells. Still feel the heat on his skin.

Fire and debris had rained down in a hellish blaze a half mile in circumference. As many as three hundred people had died—most never found. General Grant's headquarters had been dangerously close to the blast area. Britt had personally fought his way through the conflagration to escort the general to safety.

The reality of John Maxwell's mission in igniting the munitions had never been revealed to the public: that the whole operation had been an assassination attempt on Grant's life. Had Grant been killed, who knew what direction the war might have taken, or how many more years it might have dragged on?

The street lamps ended. Surrounded by moonlight and shadows, an odd thought occurred to Britt. What if Maxwell was out to finish the job he'd attempted eight years ago? What if he and General Gideon were again trying to assassinate General Grant, now President of the United States?

But that was impossible. Colonel Warder had said their action would send a message to the Union this very night. To do that, Grant would have to be in New York City, not Washington.

Of course! The King of Egypt was here, in Manhattan. It would only be fitting that the President of the United States should visit him, a meeting between two heads of state. An announcement hadn't been made because Grant's travel arrangements must be kept secret. Confederate sympathizers were abroad, men who would happily sacrifice their lives to kill the demon who'd destroyed their homeland and way of life. President Grant would come up from Washington, DC on the Philadelphia Railroad, which terminated in Jersey City. From there, he would board the ferry, cross the Hudson, and arrive at Slip Seventeen at 10:15. There, Gideon and his men would lie in wait, armed with six bottles of nitroglycerin.

Britt stopped in his tracks. The drawing of the bridge left on the stable floor, the six arrows, the lamps on the table in the vacant house— they had all been a distraction, a ruse, a battlefield subterfuge deployed by a wily general. But if Grant was in mortal danger at Slip Seventeen, then so was Jenny.

He broke into a run. At Water Street, he turned and sped south until he reached Fulton. A hansom waited at the curb. He leaped up the wheel and threw the startled driver from his seat. Lying on the sidewalk, the man shouted as Britt spun the reins from the brake, gave them a shake, and dashed away.

Unused to galloping, the horse stepped wildly. The wheels of the hansom skated over the cobblestones. Britt stood to keep his balance, cracking the whip, shouting and pulling at the reins as he steered the rig down Fulton Street, weaving between merrymakers and carriages. At Broadway, hackneys clogged the intersection. Britt barreled through at full speed. Pedestrians leaped. Drivers shouted. The hansom's wheels glanced off another rig. Steel rims clanged and sparks flew. Free of the obstructions, Britt flicked the whip and picked up speed.

At Greenwich Street, he jerked the reins left. The horse veered and the hansom skidded into the turn. Halfway around the corner, the animal lost its footing, its hooves beating a mad dance over the cobblestones. No sooner had the beast recovered than Britt jerked the reins right, guiding horse and hansom around another corner.

Cortlandt Street was deserted. Britt snapped the whip. Buildings sped past and the horse settled into a rhythm. Wheels clattered as a sour wind beat his face. Slip Seventeen lay straight ahead. The Hudson's stink hovered close, putrid and foul like the smell of death, his old friend from the war. And when it was over, the country cried for President Lincoln, lost to another mad Confederate. Britt couldn't let that happen again.

He had to reach the slip before Grant arrived. Gideon had set nitroglycerin traps, maybe an underwater mine or a clockwork bomb. They'd be set to go off the moment the ferry docked. Both wharf and ferry would be crowded. If a bomb exploded, chaos would follow. But what about Hinson? Why did Gideon need a sharpshooter? If shooting Grant was his plan, why did he need nitro?

The lights of the riverfront came into view. Britt pulled on the reins. The horse resisted, staggered to a trot then a walk. He hated to overwork an animal, but the president's life was in danger. By the time the slip was in sight, the animal's breathing had almost returned to normal.

Britt parked the hansom, tied off the brake, and climbed down. Conspicuous among a line of hackneys and carriages was a Viking ice wagon. He hurried to it. A bullet hole near the roof proved this was the ice wagon from the stable. It also proved Gideon was here. Britt opened the rear doors and peered inside. The case of nitro was empty and the ice had melted away. Gideon's plan was already in motion.

Built of weathered planks, the dockmaster's shack stood elevated above the south end of the slip. A series of brightly lit windows offered a good view of the river. Britt climbed the steps to a narrow platform and kicked open the door without knocking. The sleeping dockmaster, a bearded man of fifty, sprang upright at his desk. "Who the hell are you, busting in here?"

"President Grant is arriving on the Jersey City ferry."

"Damn it, man, who are you? One of his staff?"

"I'm with the Secret Service. There's going to be an attempt on Grant's life. You've got to divert the ferry."

The dockmaster consulted first the clock on the wall and then his pocket watch. "That's impossible," he said, looking up. The ferry has already left Jersey City."

Britt walked to the window and looked down on the wharf. In the light of the lampposts, a group of people in coats waited behind a gate for the ferry to dock. It was still early, though. The real crowd had yet to arrive. "Then we must contact the ferry before it docks and keep it from landing."

"Contact a ferry steaming across the river in the middle of the night?" the dockmaster asked. "You must be crazy."

Britt turned and faced the man. "We could row out and board the ferry."

The dockmaster stood and pointed. "Even in the moonlight, it's black as Satan's soul on the river. The ferry is making almost two knots. The pilot can't see ten feet in front of him. Besides, with the president on board, they'd shoot us out of the water as soon as we got close."

"You're saying, come heaven or hell, the president will arrive at precisely 10:15PM."

The dockmaster pointed to the wall clock. "I'm saying in thirty minutes the ferry will pull into that slip and there's nothing anyone can do to stop it."

Britt turned back to the window. Across the water, lights shimmered like fireflies in the liquid night. Most of the lights came from buildings in Jersey City. Some came from the docks and wharfs along the New Jersey shore. A few came from tugs and packets plying the Hudson north to Albany and south to the Atlantic. One of those lights, however, was the ferry that carried President Grant to his death.

Chapter Twenty-Five

Limelight blazed at Apollo Hall. Out front, several carriages disgorged latecomers. Women crowded the ticket window. More pushed to get inside. Revived by this display of feminine camaraderie, I blinked away my tears for Britt and walked toward the light. A hundred feet from the theater, I stopped dead beside an alley near the entrance and remembered his warning. "*You might as well take a hack to the Ludlow Street Jail.*"

Three chitchatting women passed me, each carrying a small bag. Excitement buzzed around them like bees. I nodded and half smiled, but they didn't notice. As the women entered the theater, a carriage arrived with even more women.

Curious, I thought. Where were all the policemen? I hadn't seen a single bluecoat, not in the street, not even directing traffic. That's why the carriages had been in a snarl.

I looked around. There *were* no police. Britt had been entirely wrong. The police didn't care about the rally. They hadn't even bothered to show up. They must all be at City Hall Park. Keeping order at the festivities was more important than nursing a gaggle of freethinking, emancipated women.

My fear evaporated. I felt wonderful, refreshed, like someone emerging from a smoke-filled tunnel. The whole notion of being arrested was a phantom. I wanted to laugh.

But then a glint of silver attracted my eye. Something or someone was moving in the alley. I flattened myself against the brick and peered into the shadows.

Silver flashed again: buttons, buckles, badges. Police. Four, six, ten, twenty, thirty, maybe sixty or more blue-coated policemen packed into the alley.

Horror-struck, I rolled my head against the brick and stared at the theater entrance, now deserted. That many police meant only one thing: at some point they were going to storm the building and arrest Glorianna.

The policemen were talking in hushed tones. One held his hand in the air. He was pointing in different directions, assigning duties no doubt. The man stepped into a wedge of light. Cigar. Yellow derby.

McCauley.

I sped toward the theater, boots clacking the wet pavement. I had to warn Glorianna. But how long did I have? Minutes? Seconds?

In front of the theater, I turned toward the door. An usher's red-capped face appeared behind the glass. He opened the door and reached out his hand.

"Ticket?"

Without slowing, I stiff-armed him in the chest. He tumbled backward and collapsed on the purple carpet.

I raced across the threshold and into the lobby. Near the curtained entrance to the auditorium, a carded easel bore Glorianna's likeness. Three smiling women stood in front, each swathed in a *Talmadge '72* banner, programs held in their outstretched hands.

I hit them at a run. Arms rose in horror. Programs exploded into the air. One lady screamed. She bumped the next, who bumped the next, and they all fell in succession onto their broad, bustled bottoms. The last woman kicked down the sign and easel. I danced over Glorianna's printed face and through a pair of velvet curtains into the immense blackness of the auditorium.

I lurched to a stop in the carpeted aisle. My vision adjusted. Placards and signs oscillated in the dark. Three thousands seats sloped down to a naked stage bearing a single brown podium. A woman wearing a white banner and a black gown stood beside it. She swung her arm dramatically. *"Ladies, I give you the next president of the United States: Glorianna Talmadge."*

Three thousand women—seamstresses, mill girls, housewives, servants, librarians, and prostitutes—rose en masse. Thunderous applause vibrated the air. Placards shook. Signs bobbed. Whistles, shouts, cheers. The very floor trembled beneath my feet.

A dazzling ring of limelight illuminated a single woman in a black suit and white shirt standing at the corner of the stage.

The deafening tumult increased. Foot stomping, hollering, screaming so loud I feared the roof itself might collapse. I squinted into the spotlight. Was that really Glorianna?

Basking in adoration, the woman in black raised her hands and strode confidently to the podium. Yes, that was Glorianna, no doubt. What other woman wore that confidence, that swagger, those scandalous *long pants*?

Glorianna waited beside the podium until the roar dimmed and faltered. As the last few shouts faded into coughs, the ladies took their seats and a restless quiet blanketed the hall. Glorianna observed the audience for a few seconds then lunged forward and shouted a single word.

"SATAN!"

A collective gasp broke from three thousand throats.

"WHORE!"

A crypt-like silence fell over the crowd. Glorianna bent over and glared into three thousand dumbstruck faces. I felt she was staring directly at me.

"DEVIL!"

Shocked murmurs rippled through the audience. Glorianna straightened up and rested her hands on her hips. "That's what men call me. That's what men call a woman who speaks out against male despotism."

Male despotism. I mouthed the phrase silently as the audience fidgeted. I'd certainly run into that several times today.

"The despots are after me," Glorianna shouted, pounding her chest with a white-gloved fist. "They're after me this very night. My crime? Printing an article about birth control."

Angry mutterings rumbled through the crowd.

"Somewhere in this city, detectives from the Society for the Suppression of Vice are conspiring with the police to arrest me. Ladies, I vow here and now that-will-not-happen."

Cheers erupted as the audience leaped to its feet. I glanced over my shoulder. *If you only knew how close the police really were, Glorianna.*

The seamstresses and mill girls, the housewives and servants quieted. Society ladies, librarians, and prostitutes sat back down.

Glorianna raised her hand. "Men scoff. They say I've no legitimacy. But the Woman's Suffrage party, the Temperance Party, and the Peace Party say I'm legitimate. Men say I have no right to run for president. But the Spiritualists, the Socialists, and the Liberal Christians say I have the right. Men say what I'm doing is illegal. Well, the Free Religionists, the Free-Thinkers, the Free Lovers, the Land Reformers, Communists, Positivists, and the Harmonialists say my campaign is legal."

Boisterous waves of applause swelled to a clamorous tumult then ebbed away like the surf.

"Women of America, it's time to shrug off the yoke of male despotism. Haven't we been treated like cattle long enough?"

Three thousand women shouted a single resounding answer. "YES!"

"The black man has been freed, but have women?"

The ladies were on their feet. Six thousand fists shook in the air. "NO!"

"An idiot or a mental defective may vote in this country if he has a certain appendage in his pants, but can a college-educated woman?"

"NO!" three thousand angry throats responded.

"Ladies, the shimmering temple of equality is within our sight. In five days, our long trek will be over. England has its queen and on November fifth, 1872, America will have its first woman president."

Riotous ovation thundered the hall.

"You've been squeezed by male society until you feel suffocated.

You're constricted, restricted, bound, and restrained by male domination."

Chaotic uproar seized the audience.

"Ladies, have you shrugged off the fetters of male control?"

"YES!" the seamstresses, mill girls, housewives, servants, society ladies, librarians, and prostitutes shouted.

"Have you sworn to never again be forced into the confines of male domination?"

The auditorium trembled a unanimous. "YES!"

"Ladies, have you brought with you the symbol of your repression?"

"YES," a single monumental voice shouted.

"Then give up your constraints. Give up your imprisonment. Give up the object of your enslavement."

Three thousand enraged women opened their purses and bags and withdrew three thousand gleaming white corsets, strings dangling, stays flopping, and shook them in the air.

Glorianna strode in front of the foot lights, arms high, fists clenched. "Men of America, listen to us. We demand freedom."

"FREEDOM, FREEDOM, FREEDOM," the women chanted, shaking their corsets like whitecaps on a storm tossed sea.

"We demand equality."

"EQUALITY, EQUALITY, EQUALITY," they intoned, girdles flapping in the air.

"We demand the vote."

"VOTE, VOTE, VOTE," a single voice resonated, white foundations quivering above their heads.

Glorianna strutted in front of the footlights, gloved hands high, arms wide, absorbing adulation like Caesar returned from Gaul.

Ecstatic jubilation erupted in every corner of the auditorium. Women jumped. They convulsed. They danced and hugged in a mad, religious frenzy of freedom as corsets flew through the air.

Feminine foundations fell around me as I descended the aisle to the stage, drawn by Glorianna the leader, Glorianna the prophet, Glorianna the enchantress.

I found myself shouting. I was jumping up and down, fists in the air, screaming, yelling, demanding my freedom, my equality, and my vote.

All at once, a sharp penetrating sound broke the magnetic pull and made me halt. The bewildering noise came from behind me and seemed at once both strange and yet familiar.

Whistles. Hundreds of them, it sounded like. Screeching, squealing, tweeting high above the noise of feminine euphoria. As the house lights brightened, I swung around to find the source.

Cheeks red, whistles blowing, a swarm of blue-coated policemen descended into the auditorium, clubs swinging.

Chapter Twenty-Six

Britt danced down the steps from the dockmaster's shack and back to the wharf. Gideon could have planted one immense clockwork bomb somewhere, or six smaller bombs in various places. Finding any or all of them would not be easy.

Carriages and broughams had joined the hansoms and hacks along the street. Men in Ulster capes and ladies in tweed waterproofs gathered behind the wooden fence under the corona of the street lamps. The plays and musicals in the city were over. The theater crowd from Jersey City had come to Slip Seventeen for the ferry home. He scanned the group looking for Jenny but saw only a blur of indistinct faces. Breath pluming in front of him, Britt pushed through the men and women. If Jenny was among these passengers, he could not see her. Lockie was right; the girl had probably chosen to stay in Manhattan. McCauley or Gideon: both were of equal danger.

He climbed over the fence and walked to the edge of the wharf. Waves broke against pilings with an ominous slap. Lit clearly by the gaslights, he could see beer bottles, bits of wood, and dead fish floating in the water. He knelt down and peered into the shadows under the wharf to look for anything unusual. Nothing seemed out of the ordinary.

And why should it? What would blowing up the entire wharf accomplish? How would that kill the president? Indeed, why have the nitro at all? Why not just wait until Grant stepped from the ferry and let Hinson fire a bullet into his skull?

Because Grant would be surrounded by Secret Service men, that's why. A clear shot would be impossible, and if the first shot missed, chaos would ensue. With people fleeing every which way, the Secret Service would drag Grant to safety, and General Gideon's grand statement would become a footnote.

"Stand up slowly, sir."

A gentleman in a leather-trimmed coat pointed a long-barreled revolver at Britt. A walrus mustache hung below his crooked nose, and a string bow tie drooped from his collar. Britt stood, arms held out from his sides. "Pinkerton?"

The man was as tall as Britt, older but not as muscular. "I'll ask the questions. What is your name?"

"Brittan Salter. There's going to be an attempt on the president's life."

"So the dockmaster told me. He also told me you were with the Secret Service, which is a lie."

"I had no time for lengthy explanations."

"Mr. Salter—if that is your name—how did you know President Grant would be arriving here tonight?"

Britt described the stolen nitro and General Gideon's grand statement, leaving out any incriminating details. "We must find the bombs before Grant arrives."

"How do I know you're not mad?"

Britt dropped his arms to his sides. "You don't have time to believe anything except that the president's life is in danger."

The man pushed the revolver inside his coat and offered Britt his hand. "Oliver Wells, Pinkerton Detective." They shook. "Mr. Salter, if I find out you are, in fact, mad, I will personally shoot you and toss your body in—"

A faint whistle blasted far out on the river, one long toot followed by three shorts. Britt gazed into the darkness. "Is that the ferry?"

"About fifteen minutes out. We've got to hurry. What do the bombs look like?"

"They look like clocks, Mr. Wells. We'll meet at the dockmaster's shack in ten minutes."

The Pinkerton took off down the left side of the wharf. Britt went right. Passengers whispered as he looked in empty crates, behind stacks of luggage, under coils of rope, and even through trash barrels like a vagabond in search of a meal. Pushcarts filled with cotton lined one side of the wharf. Britt forced his hand between the bales and felt for anything suspect. Coming up empty, he dug his fingers into the white batting, but the bales were too tightly bound to hide an object inside.

Just past the cotton, several sheep in wooden pens bleated mournfully. Britt gave their cages a quick look then moved on to stacks of lumber bound with ropes. A feeling of futility followed him. He could not grasp Gideon's plan. Where had he set the bombs? If indeed he'd set any at all.

The whistle blew again, louder: one long, three shorts. Britt gazed once more across the river. The ferry was closer, but he still could not see it. Time was running out.

Someone called his name from above. Wells, the Pinkerton, stood on the deck outside the dockmaster's window. He leaned against the rail and shouted down to him. Britt hurried up the steps to his side. "What did you find?"

Wells looked skeptical. "Not a damn thing. How about you?"

Britt scrutinized the passengers milling about on the wharf below. Beyond them, in the distance, he saw the ferry's lights reflecting off the water. Sparks flew from twin smokestacks. Above the sound of the breeze, thick with the smell of the river, he heard the faint drone of paddle wheels. "I found nothing."

Within minutes, the ferry emerged fully from the gloom, bell clanging above the chug of the steam engine. As the vessel drew within a hundred feet of the wharf, the engines reversed the paddle wheels, stopping the ship in its berth precisely on time.

"Are you sure you're not mad, Mr. Salter?"

Britt watched sailors jump from the ferry and tie off its lines. White steam hissed from the stacks while passengers shuffled about on the wharf. He had less than an hour left to find his nitro. "We'll know for certain in a few minutes, Mr. Wells."

A wide ramp lowered from the ferry's bow. Behind it on the deck, fifty or so passengers waited to disembark. Farther back, a dozen horses and two carriages lined up: the president's transportation, no doubt.

Just as the ramp hit the wharf, a thunderous boom heaved the bow of the ferry upwards. Water plumed into the air dousing passengers on both the wharf and the deck of the ship. As violently as the ship had risen, it plunged back into the water and rocked along its length.

The suddenness of the explosion stunned Britt but did not surprise him. The Confederate Navy had practically invented torpedo mines. Maxwell must have used those beer bottles in the water to suspend a clockwork nitro bomb beneath the surface set to explode a few minutes after nine.

Groaning like a dying beast, the ferry inched down into the water. Beside the wagons on the deck, the horses reared and fought their restraints. In front of them, passengers mobbed the ramp, joining the people on the wharf in a rush toward land.

Above their shouts and screams, Britt detected the unmistakable crack of a rifle high and to the left. On the wharf, the cotton bales exploded. Flaming meteors shot into the sky and floated down like a fiery, biblical plague.

Damn it! A bottle of nitro was concealed in those bales after all. How had he missed finding it? Only Hinson the sharpshooter could have hit a target so small. But what was Gideon trying to achieve? Holing the ship's bow and exploding the cotton bales did nothing.

Something moved behind the windows of a cargo crane at the next slip over. Britt pointed. "There's a sharpshooter in that crane. I'm not sure what he's up to, but we've got to stop him before he fires again."

Water spilled over the ferry's bow. The horses broke free and splashed across the deck to the ramp and safety. Wells was right. Britt finally understood the plan. Drive away the passengers. Sink the ferry. When Grant left the ship in desperation, Hinson would either shoot him or blow him up. If the president chose to stay on board, he'd drown.

On the ferry, a man with a pistol in his hand stepped from a side door and onto the deck. Britt recognized him immediately as Secret Service. He didn't take three steps before another rifle crack echoed, and the man collapsed. Gideon and Hinson didn't want anyone leaving the ferry until they were ready.

Britt started down the steps then stopped and turned. "Wait three minutes then fire on the sharpshooter. I'll try and get closer."

Wells unholstered his revolver. "In three minutes, we may all be blown to dust."

At the bottom of the ladder, Britt rushed toward the shore then across and onto the wharf beside the next slip. The crane was built on four tall, iron girders. Hinson hid at the top in a sheet metal enclosure, which housed the steam engine and the controls. A series of windows gave him an unobstructed view of the entire waterfront.

As a firing platform, it was ideal. At any appreciable distance, a pistol shot wasn't strong enough to breach the metal, nor accurate enough to strike Hinson even if one could see him. Right now, Hinson was concentrating on the ferry, but as soon as Wells opened fire, the dockmaster's shack would come under attack. If the Pinkerton was smart, he'd keep moving.

Wells' first shot snapped like a popgun. Britt was near enough to the crane to hear the bullet ping off the metal enclosure. Hoping Hinson was busy searching for the source of the bullet, Britt hastened across the wharf. When he reached a stack of wooden crates, he crouched and waited for Wells to fire again.

Wells' pistol snapped a second time. Britt jumped up, firing the Webley as he ran. Fifty yards from the crane, he ducked alongside a line of barrels and reloaded. Another flash and a snap came from the dockmaster's shack, then a rifle crack rang out. Hinson had found Wells' position. Wells scurried down the steps. He dove behind the lumber stacked on the wharf just as Hinson's Vetterli repeater barked twice more.

A great hissing sound drew Britt's attention to the ferry. Instead of black smoke, white clouds blasted from the smoke stacks. River water had reached the boiler room and quenched the coal fires. With no steam, the pumps could no longer empty some of the water rushing in from the leak. The ship was doomed. She'd sink fast. Grant and his entourage would have to crowd into the deckhouse to keep from drowning.

Wells popped up from behind the lumber and fired. Hinson shot back. Time was not on Grant's side. Everyone was stuck in a waiting game while the ferry sank. General Gideon had planned his strategy well.

Where *was* Gideon, anyway? Probably, like all generals, well away from the battle. And what about Maxwell? Where was he? Lying in wait? Was he in charge of the end game if all else failed? Was that where the last bottles of nitro were hidden—in his clockwork bombs? And how many bottles of nitro were left? They'd used at least two for the bow explosion and one for the cotton bales. Three bottles of nitroglycerin left.

The Vetterli cracked again. A lamppost in front of the ferry exploded. Nitroglycerin and gas ignited a fiery orb that boiled and churned as it rose into the night sky. Exhausting itself, the fireball dissolved into smoke leaving a twenty-foot high torch roaring from the broken lamppost. Its brilliant light flooded even the darkest corners of both wharves.

The huge flame also illuminated the windows of the crane enclosure, silhouetting the sharpshooter in red. Hinson had to be well armed up there: pistols, rifles… He might even have a few of Maxwell's gunpowder bombs. Britt didn't mind taking a chance, but the only way to get to Hinson appeared to be a metal ladder. Climbing that affair would make more noise than a cat on a keyboard. Announcing his own funeral did not seem like a good idea, nor did facing Hinson with only a revolver.

Britt spied his next position—a bench halfway to the crane. It wouldn't give much cover, but there was nothing else. With the next snap of Wells' pistol, he sprinted to the bench, sliding behind it just as Hinson's Vetterli returned fire to Wells.

The bench was sturdy but crude. Nailed together from rough-cut boards, it had most likely been built by dockworkers as a place to eat their lunch. Tied around one of the planks was a red bandanna. Britt probed the cloth with his finger. Something was inside. He worked his hand into the folds and closed his fist around the object. No sooner had he pulled it out than Hinson's rifle cracked and a bullet ripped through the bandanna. Britt opened his hand. The object was a bottle of nitroglycerin.

Chapter Twenty-Seven

I froze in the aisle of the theater, paralyzed by the discord of whistles, shouts and screams as a hundred policemen invaded the auditorium. Three abreast, they swarmed from the lobby entrances like water into a sinking ship.

Jubilation ceased. Corsets dropped to the floor. Women rushed from their seats and into the aisles. There, they collided with the policemen who struck them viciously with their clubs. Bloodied and beaten, the women collapsed in piles like so much cordwood.

A red-haired officer broke from his comrades. He barreled between the seats in my direction, twirling his club above his head. A lady wearing a Talmadge banner stood in his way. The officer swung. His club smashed her forehead. The woman's neck twisted. Her eyes rolled. She spun and slumped unconscious over her seat.

The woman beside her screamed. The red-haired officer lifted his club. She raised her VOTES FOR WOMEN sign. He pushed it aside and struck. She tumbled between the seats. He bent over her, his savage club striking again and again.

Sickened, I looked away and toward the stage. I had to get to Glorianna. Every exit was blocked, but maybe there was still a way out. With no exact plan in mind, I took off toward the aisle, but a hand seized my arm and pulled. It was the policeman with red hair, his face wild with rage.

Energy exploded through my body. I spun in a circle, swinging my handbag like David's sling. It whirled past the red-haired policeman's club and slammed his temple with a sickening crunch.

Feminine Virtue had saved me again.

I jerked to a stop. The officer lay unconscious at my feet. Dizzy from my spin, I took my bearings. Where was I? Where was Glorianna?

She came into focus on the stage, waving and shouting atop the overturned podium. "Ladies, arm yourselves. Defend your honor. Don't let these thugs overpower you. There are thousands of us. *We* are the stronger sex."

Illuminated by the footlights, a chorus of bannered women surrounded her three deep. They brandished umbrellas, handbags, chairs, and whatever they could muster as weapons to keep the policemen from storming the stage. Bluecoats, meanwhile, had massed around the orchestra pit but seemed unable to breach the women defending Glorianna.

I felt elated, giddy, alive with the fight. We were winning. We were driving them back. We were beating the police. Women were a force to be feared. No one could stop us, not even Badger McCauley.

Maniacal laughter shattered my joy. Standing near an auditorium fire exit was Badger McCauley, smiling and laughing. He opened the door.

A symphony of whistle blasts peaked my horror. Police reinforcements cascaded in from the open exit, hundreds of them filling the aisles like rats running straight toward the stage. Terrified, I rushed to the side of the theater and flattened myself against the velvet curtain to let them pass. Bluecoats streamed by. They joined the officers at the stage, shouting and pushing their way up the steps on either side.

More women moved to defend Glorianna. Policemen struck them with clubs while other officers attempted to boost their fellows onto the stage.

The tide of battle had turned. The feminists were overwhelmed. Hope was all but lost. In the aisles, manacled women sat in bunches, some sobbing, some cursing, some wearing their wounds like a crown.

Still flattened against the curtain, I clenched the fabric in white-knuckled fists. Damn it, McCauley wasn't arresting me, he just wasn't. I was getting out of here. I yanked the curtain in frustration.

The velvet opened.

Baffled, I lifted the cloth and peered beneath. Dingy plaster looked back at me.

Hope ignited in my mind. If I got behind the curtain and sneaked to the front of the auditorium, there might be a chance I could climb onto the stage, find Glorianna, and escape out the stage door entrance. What did I have to lose?

I slipped beneath the cloth. Back pressed to the wall, I shuffled toward the stage behind the thick material, listening to muffled shouts and cries and screams.

Ten steps along, someone slammed into me through the curtain. I grunted from the impact but kept going. Further on, two struggling bodies pinned me to the wall. I wiggled out from under them, scooted a few feet, then stopped.

How far had I gone? How far was the stage?

Arms out, hands spread, I felt along the plaster as I went. Hours seemed to have passed when my fingers finally touched something: a molding, a door and then a doorknob. I turned the knob, slipped through the opening, and pulled the door shut.

The sounds of the battle died to a buzz. I was in a dark, narrow passage. Dim light glowed somewhere in front of me.

Of course, theaters had all sorts of secret entrances and doors, places for actors and managers to slip in and out. I'd read there were even trapdoors in the stage floor. That's how magicians made assistants disappear and appear amid smoke and flash powder.

Muffled shouting reminded me that time was short. A loud thud shook the passageway. With my hands outstretched, touching opposite sides of the corridor, I felt along the rough walls until I found another door. On the other side, pounding feet vibrated and thumped the floor above me. I was under the stage. Feeling blindly through the darkness, my knee slammed into something—stairs.

I hadn't climbed very high before I encountered the ceiling. My fingers traced the outline of a trapdoor, then a latch. Head pounding from the rumble of feet, I threw the bolt and thrust my shoulder against the lid.

The trapdoor barely budged as if a great weight lay on the other side. I dropped down a step and collected my thoughts. Someone on the stage had to be standing on the door. I stepped up the stairs and pushed the door again.

The door rose an inch. Noise and light streamed in. Shoes, dresses, shuffling feet. Were those black pant legs? Cuban heel boots? It had to be. That was Glorianna, not five feet away. The door closed with a thud.

Determined, I pressed my shoulder to the door once more. Straining and groaning, I pushed with all the vigor my body could muster. The door suddenly opened and I found myself propelled halfway out of the stairway onto the stage.

Dresses and shoes danced madly around me. Voices called out, shouting and screaming. A woman stepped on my back. I pushed her off then searched the stage from the stairway.

Women gallantly fought a rising tide of blue. Clubs cut the air. Corsets littered the stage. Women lay in clumps, bleeding, passed out, wailing, moaning, sobbing. I was on the deck of a sinking ship with no lifeboats in sight.

My God, I thought, returning to my purpose, *the police are breaking through.* I had minutes, maybe seconds, left before all would be lost.

I stepped fully onto the stage. Where was Glorianna? Where had she gone?

A dazed woman collapsed in my arms and I eased her to the floor. Blood oozed from a gash in her scalp. My vision blurred as I covered my mouth and gagged.

"Jenny Crispin?"

I straightened and swiveled, hand still pressed to my mouth. Glorianna stood next to me, sweaty, bedraggled, shirttail out.

"Glorianna," I gasped, "thank God I found you."

An enraged woman shook her fist in Glorianna's face. "It's all your fault, you and your damned ideas. Don't you see they're killing us?"

The woman lunged, but Glorianna stepped aside and the woman fell to the stage. The candidate didn't blink. She gripped my arm and pulled me close. "How did you get here?"

I pointed to the trap door.

Glorianna hurried down the steps just as an army of blue stormed the stage. Fifty policemen breached the women's defenses and began clubbing everyone within reach. Someone seized my dress and pulled me to the stage. I looked down at him. McCauley!

From the stairs, Glorianna grabbed my arms and held me tight. I kicked my boots, digging my heels into McCauley's arms, but he only pulled my dress harder. Summoning my remaining strength, I gripped the edge of the trap door and together Glorianna and I gave a mighty tug. Caught between two irresistible forces, the buttons on my dress popped like a string of firecrackers. The garment ripped off my body, leaving me dressed in nothing but my neck-to-ankle blue chemise. Forcibly undressed for the second time in one day, I tumbled down the steps with Glorianna and fell in a heap on the floor. I heard the door slam and the latch lock.

I climbed to my feet and straightened my chemise. "What about the others?" I asked. "We have to save them."

The barest light illuminated Glorianna's face. She was panting hard. "Never mind them; how do we get out of here?"

I couldn't believe what I heard. "But the women on the stage are getting massacred."

"There's nothing we can do."

The stage above boomed and shook. Shouts and cries sifted through the floor. A muffled scream split the musty air.

Angry as hell, I made for the stairs. "I'm going up there. Someone's got to help them."

Glorianna grabbed my arm and jerked me back. "Damn it, there's nothing we can do. You open that door and we're dead. Now listen to me. How do we get out of here?"

I stared into the blackness, wishing I could see her face. No—wishing I could see her eyes, her callous eyes. Is this what presidents did, sacrifice their followers to the enemy?

I swallowed my anger. "This way."

We felt our way across the room, through the door and into the passage. But instead of turning right, to the door behind the curtain, we turned left. A few seconds later, we came to another door.

I pressed my ear to the wood. Except for a few bumps, I heard nothing.

"What do you hear?"

Glorianna's voice knotted my fists. I didn't answer. I just twisted the knob and peeked outside.

Ropes dangled beside bare brick walls. Several chairs lined up under a painted arrow. A small table stood in a corner.

Glorianna pushed me aside. "Let me see."

I stepped away, biting my lip.

Glorianna poked her head out the door. "We're backstage. I passed by here earlier. The door to the street is to the right."

She flung open the door. We rushed out, past the ropes, past the chairs, past a row of doors, and down some steps. A heavy beam barred the door.

Glorianna put her hands under the wood and lifted; I slammed it back down. "There could be a hundred policemen outside."

"We'll have to take that chance."

She lifted the beam and opened the door to a wall of blue uniforms.

Chapter Twenty-Eight

A second bullet ripped through the bandanna. Britt jumped and raced full speed toward the girder, left hand clutching the bottle of nitro, right hand wrapped around the Webley, clicking off rounds at Hinson's outline in the window.

Pistol empty, he slammed into the iron support, hugged it, and caught his breath. Directly beneath the sharpshooter, he was safe—for the moment. Hinson and Gideon were smart. They'd planted the nitro on the bench as insurance. If anyone tried to storm the crane, Hinson would shoot the nitro and blow them up. But they were probably thinking about a whole group of men, not one half-crazed lunatic with a gun. Either way, the plan was spoiled now.

Below the dockmaster's shack at the stack of lumber, Wells' pistol snapped. Hinson's Vetterli answered with a quick report and the Pinkerton spun to the ground, wounded or dead. Britt grit his teeth. This was no time for emotion.

He took out his knife, reached into his coat and cut the top strap of his suspenders. Shame to ruin a perfectly good pair of braces. Marm had given them to him when he'd first arrived in town. Nothing to be done about it now. He unbuttoned the bottom. With the bottle of nitro pressed tight to the iron girder, he wrapped and tied the suspender around it. Two could play "shoot the nitro."

Britt put away the knife and scrutinized the area around him. He had to find a safe firing position, one that offered good cover but wasn't too far away. The line of barrels he'd hid behind was the only place close that fit his needs. Fifty yards was a bit distant for an accurate pistol shot, but he didn't want to be killed by the blast either. As far as cover went, Hinson's Vetterli might penetrate one side of the inch-thick barrels, but not both.

Without further thought, he dashed from under the crane like a rabbit running from a wolf. The Vetterli cracked and bullets struck the wharf around his feet. He changed course after each shot to throw off Hinson's aim. Five feet from the barrels, he dove. Three bullets drilled into the oak staves as he hit the ground, then all was silent.

Britt's breath came deep and hard. His heart beat like a regimental drummer. Fingers shaking, he opened the side gate of the Webley, spun the cylinder, and pushed out the spent brass. He reached inside his coat for the cartridges in his shoulder holster. Only three bullets remained. Cursing his lack of foresight, he pushed them into the pistol one at a time then closed the gate and cocked the hammer. He needed to be perfectly calm to make the shot. With only three cartridges in the Webley, he couldn't afford to miss.

Jenny came to mind. Had she been down in the crowd when the first explosion occurred? Had she fled with the rest? Was she safe? Would he ever see her again?

He tried to picture her face but saw only Penelope's hate-filled eyes. He pushed them away. What was the last thing Jenny had said to him? "Do whatever makes you happy." Cowering as he was behind a row of barrels, heart thumping, chest heaving, the words seemed almost funny.

His thoughts drifted to Hinson up there in the crane, his all-seeing-eye affixed to his scope, rendering judgment and vengeance with the pull of the trigger. Britt had read that during the war, his two sons had been captured as bushwhackers by Union troops, that their heads had been cut off and placed on the gateposts of Hinson's farm. Little wonder Hinson's soul was filled with hate. He also lived for revenge.

Britt chanced a peek at the ferry. The wharf looked deserted. The passengers were gone. The horses had gathered under the dockmaster's shack. Wells' body lay nearby. At the end of the wharf, only the stern of the ferry was visible above the water. Several Secret Service agents had ventured out and were taking cover in companionways and hatches. They fired sporadically at Hinson, but their bullets hit the iron enclosure with no more than a useless clink. Britt heard glass shatter as one penetrated the window. Hinson still had the upper hand. The ferry would be submerged from stem to stern in less than a minute. Grant would either drown or die of a gunshot.

Britt's heart slowed to a steady rhythm. He stretched out his arm and took aim on the nitro. The Webley's sights moved ever so slightly on and off the target. When the tiny bottle was behind the blade of the front sight, Britt pulled the trigger. The pistol fired and kicked.

The bullet ricocheted off the girder with a ping. He looked over the top of the pistol. Bare metal glittered above the bottle. The shot had been high. He aimed again bringing the Webley's sights a hair's width lower.

Above him came a crack and a thud as one of Hinson's bullets penetrated a barrel. The metal hoop broke and sprung open. Britt knocked it away with the Webley. He moved down two barrels and took another bead on the nitro. Steady, steady... He squeezed the trigger.

Again, the bullet pinged harmlessly off the girder. Damn it, one shot left.

On the ferry, more Secret Service men had emerged. Some were on the deck, knee deep in water. As Britt watched, a bullet from Hinson's Vetterli hit an agent standing on top of the deckhouse. The Vetterli cracked again and another agent clutched his chest.

Britt aimed his last shot at the bottle of nitro. Above him, the Vetterli cracked. Further off, the ferry gurgled as the final bit of air drained from its hull. The breeze murmured and somewhere in the far distance, a bell rang.

Britt closed his mind to all of it. He heard nothing, saw nothing except a bottle of nitro and the two sights on his Webley. When all three aligned in front of his eye like a holy celestial conjunction, he squeezed the trigger.

Another metallic ping rang out for what seemed like minutes then dissipated into the night air. Britt again stared over the top of the Webley at the bottle of nitro mocking him on the girder. Three cartridges, three shots and he'd missed them all. What was he supposed to do now, throw a rock at the damn bottle?

"I told you to get rid of that pig iron and buy a decent sidearm."

Lockie squatted beside him. He took aim with his Smith & Wesson and squeezed the trigger. The girder disappeared in a ball of red and yellow. Fire roiled up the side of the crane and into the sky illuminating both wharfs and the black water between them like the noonday sun. A tornado of thunder sent the barrels tumbling. Britt and Lockie rolled with them, landing spread eagle on the wood some distance away.

When the hurricane passed, Britt looked, not comprehending what he saw. The crane still stood. That could not be. He knew the power of nitro. It should have at least buckled the iron.

Lockie crawled up beside him, pistol still in hand. "That damned leg is stronger than my fifth wife's left hook. What now?"

Vibrations shook the wharf. Britt climbed to his feet on shaky legs. Lockie too. "The crane's coming down," Britt said quietly. "We better run."

Lockie holstered his pistol. "After you, Mr. Salter."

A loud, low groan reverberated over the waterfront as the damaged girder bent inward like a lazy knee. High above, the crane leaned farther and farther toward the open water between the two wharfs.

Britt took the lead, jumping over boxes and barrels and crates as the crane fell, first slowly then faster and faster, its three good legs ripping enormous, jagged sections of wood from the wharf. Still clutching his Vetterli, Hinson, a tiny figure against the huge crane, climbed from a broken window and leaped. He hit the water, but the crane came down on top of him with an enormous splash and disappeared beneath the black water.

"The president," Britt yelled to Lockie as they ran. "We've got to get him out of the ferry before it sinks."

When they were below the dockmaster's shack, Britt slowed.

228

Carrying President Grant on their shoulders, Secret Service men were splashing across the partially submerged deck, arriving at the wharf just as the entire ferry sank beneath the water. The president was safe. As Grant smiled and chatted with his men, Britt knelt beside Wells' dead body.

Except for his enormous mustache, the Pinkerton's face looked like stone. Blood soaked his leather-trimmed coat. Britt arranged Wells' arms over his chest then stood.

"You knew him?" Lockie asked as they walked toward Grant.

"Oliver Wells, a Pinkerton detective. He thought I was mad when I told him Grant's life was in danger. I couldn't have tied that nitro to the girder without his help."

"You have a way of finding people to aid in your madness."

"Is that why you returned? To aid my madness?"

"If we're talking about the Khedive, without nitro that madness is over."

Britt stopped walking. "We're talking about what brought you to Slip Seventeen tonight."

Lockie faced him. "Someone had to save your ass."

"Maybe," Britt said, narrowing his eyes. "Or were you waiting to catch the ferry out of town?"

Lockie's lips bent to a broad smile. "Well then, Mr. Salter, you'll never quite know the answer to that question, will you?"

Not far from Grant, a chilling scream rent the night. Britt had heard the sound a thousand times during the war. It was a Rebel Yell, the maniacal Confederate war cry.

A man in Southern gray rushed toward Grant, his arm cocked, carrying something. Britt didn't have to look twice. John Maxwell was running toward the president and he carried a bomb.

Ten shots rang out from the Secret Service agents. Maxwell staggered and threw. Illuminated by the roaring flame from the broken lamppost, a small object glittered through the air toward Grant and his men. Britt ran. He leaped, hand open, arm outstretched. Something hit his palm. His fingers closed. As he fell into the crowd of agents surrounding the president, he turned and pushed the object into his pants. The agents pulled him to his feet. They stretched his arms out front and clamped him in wrist irons.

"Mr. President," Britt yelled as they dragged him by his elbows across the wharf. "President Grant. Ulysses," he shouted, twisting his body back and forth, throwing men to each side. "Hiram!" A dozen agents piled on top and dragged him to the wharf's wooden deck.

Smothered under the weight of the agents, Britt covered the bottle in his crotch with his manacled hands and prayed the nitro would not explode. After a long, hot minute, the agents peeled off one at a time. A circle opened up around him and a man with a close-cropped, gray beard and tired eyes appeared over him. "Britt?" the man asked. "Britt Salter, is that you?"

"Yes, Hiram," Britt said, "it's me."

The president's pants were soaked. He carried a large glass of brown liquid over ice. He looked at his men and gestured at Britt. "Unlock those wrist irons. Britt is a dear friend."

Agents scurried to unlock the manacles and help Britt to his feet. He rubbed his wrists.

"Thank you, Hiram."

The president wrapped his arm around Britt's shoulder, drew him close, and spoke. "Ah, Britt, not many people know my real name is Hiram. Better call me Mr. President while I'm around these fellows." He made an exaggerated wink.

Britt gazed at the puzzled Secret Service agents. "Yes, Mr. President."

The president nodded. Abruptly, his jaw set and his back straightened. "Report, officer. What the hell has been going on here?"

"Do you remember General Archer Gideon?"

"The man is infamous for the massacre of captured Negro soldiers at Fort Pillow."

"He headed a conspiracy on your life tonight."

Grant sipped his drink. "And the other conspirators?"

"Jack Hinson."

"That explains the sharpshooter in the crane. Hinson killed hundreds of Union officers during the war."

"And this man." Britt kicked over Maxwell's body.

Grant bent down and examined the man's face. "John Maxwell," he said, standing. "He tried to assassinate me at City Point." Grant's brow knit. "Britt, you've saved my life twice now."

"In return, I ask for only two favors."

Grant gazed at his men and then at Britt. "Anything."

"First—I need two fast horses. Second—give me that drink."

The Secret Service led in two horses. Once Britt and Lockie were mounted, Grant handed him the drink. "It's an honor to share my Old Crow with you."

Britt downed the rest of the drink. He placed the ice-filled glass carefully in his saddlebag then leaned down. "Hiram, I know you came to New York City to meet with the Khedive. The Astor House will not be safe tonight."

"Oh, why is that?"

Britt hesitated. "General Gideon, sir. He's still on the loose and may yet attempt to kill you. I cannot be there to save you a third time."

Grant slapped Britt's knee and grinned. "You've done enough for me, Britt. My men will be on alert."

Despite Grant's confidence, Britt hoped the president would reconsider and take his advice.

Lockie was on his horse, waiting at the end of the slip. A rifle with a long scope lay across his lap. Britt trotted up alongside. "Is that the Vetterli?"

Lockie patted the rifle stock. "I found it sticking out of the water. It'll make a nice souvenir."

"For your children?"

"Aye, if I ever find wife number six."

Britt wiggled the bottle of nitro from his pants, twisted sideways and placed it gingerly inside the glass of ice in the saddlebag. He turned to Lockie. "Just so we're clear, my friend, any debt you thought you owed me has long since been satisfied. You don't have to come along."

Lockie shook his head and smiled. "I'd nae miss this show for anything in the world."

"And Satan's night?"

"To Hell with him. Besides, this time, you owe *me*."

Chapter Twenty-Nine

In the alley behind the theater, silver buttons, badges, and clubs blurred in the light of oil lamps. Rough hands seized our arms and dragged us out the back door and into the night. Cold iron clamped around our wrists, and stiff hands thrust us into a circle of blue coats.

Glorianna balked. "Release me at once, you blackguards. Don't you know who I am?"

All movement stopped. The circle tightened around us. Clubs slapped palms. I shivered in my blue chemise. What would they do? Beat us? Kill us?

I searched the men's faces for any trace of humanity. Cleo had told me stories of corruption and bribery and beatings. At the time I'd scoffed, but after what I'd seen in the theater, I now believed every word. Glorianna and I could simply disappear, our bodies never to be seen again. I wouldn't put anything past the police.

Glorianna shook her wrist irons. "Get these manacles off me, you baboons."

The woman's arrogance, her gall. A bearded policeman jabbed Glorianna in the stomach with his stick. "Demanding, aren't we, Madame President."

She swatted the club away. "Your captain will hear about this brutality."

A grim chuckle rippled through the men. The bearded officer's lip curled. "We're counting on it."

Glorianna bared her teeth. "The whole city will read about your savagery when I'm through."

The officer stepped closer. His mouth straightened to a humorless line. "Your followers were no less savage than we. They injured a lot of our boys."

Glorianna sneered. "Big, strong policemen hurt by the weaker sex? You must be joking."

The officer pointed his club at Glorianna's face. "Mind your tongue, bitch."

Glorianna stepped closer bringing the club within an inch of her nose. "If you're going to beat me with that substitute for your inadequate penis, then do so."

The policeman's face reddened, his hand trembled, and his club shook. He swung the club away from her face and pointed up the street. "Get these witches out of here."

We were pushed forward again, hustled across the broken sidewalk over torn placards and ripped banners. One of my black practical boots hit the curb and I stumbled onto wet cobblestones. A mound of corsets smoldered in the gutter. Up ahead, black police wagons lined the street. Marias, Cleo had called them. Not far away, a hundred or so women waited against the theater wall while policemen dragged them one by one into the wagons. A group of drunks cheered from the doorway of a bar.

My eyes watered. Tears dripped down my cheeks. The running was over. Ludlow Street Jail was our next stop; I was sure of it.

Britt's face appeared in my mind, his big jaw, his golden eyes, his smile. If only I could see him once more, hug him, kiss him. I tried to wipe my eyes on my shoulder, but a policeman jerked me forward, pulling me by the chain of my wrist irons. I stepped over another curb. We were alongside the police wagons and still walking.

I looked behind us. A bleeding woman stared at me, seeming to ask: *Where are you going; why are you so special?* I turned forward. I didn't know.

Glorianna was a real catch, though. McCauley wanted her more than anything. Everyone wanted her. She'd stirred up a nest of hornets. She wanted to turn society upside down, and now she would pay.

The police led us into a trash-strewn alleyway. Glorianna cursed lowly, "Bastards."

Fear's hand gripped my throat. "What are they going to do to us?" I croaked.

Glorianna's eyes burned into me. "Use your imagination."

I didn't want to use my imagination. I wanted to squeeze my eyes shut and keep them shut forever. I wanted to cover my ears. I wanted to curl up in a ball. I wanted to be in Britt's bed. I wanted to feel his arms around me, feel his hands and his kisses. I wanted to be anywhere except here in New York City at 10:30PM walking down a dark alley surrounded by angry policemen.

The group jerked to a stop. My legs trembled. My arms shook and the wrist chains rattled. The police were doing something to me, something to my hands.

The manacles fell away. I clutched my palms to my breast. My nerves drew taut as wires. They were going to beat me, I knew it, beat me to a senseless, bloody lump. Tomorrow someone would find Glorianna and me lying in a heap. I could see the headlines: "Glorianna Talmadge Murdered." There'd be no mention of the unknown girl found with her.

I clamped my eyes even tighter. My body constricted to impossible rigidity. Any second the impacts would start, the bone breaking, flesh pounding blows.

Something touched my face.

I screamed.

I screamed a scream that chilled the bone and curdled the blood, a mirror-shattering scream, a scream that woke the dead, that raised hair and rendered small animals unconscious. I screamed until all attachment to my life left and I slumped over, spent.

"My Lord, young lady."

Life and breath rushed to me. I recognized the voice from

this morning and pulled myself upright. White curly hair, thick muttonchops, puffy face: Commodore Vanderbilt stood before me, cigar in one hand, a brick of greenbacks in the other.

"What lungs," he said, looking around to gauge other reactions. "Have you considered the stage?"

Not waiting for an answer, he wedged the cigar between his lips and began counting dollars into the policemen's outstretched palms. A few minutes later, the last hand withdrew. Vanderbilt looked up, smiling, and pulled the cigar from his mouth. "Have I missed anyone?"

Muttering happily amongst themselves, the policemen ambled away, leaving me, Glorianna, the Commodore, and his driver alone in the alley.

Vanderbilt looked my chemise up and down. "Interesting costume you're wearing." He lifted Glorianna's hand and turned her side to side. "And you, my dear, have suffered quite a mussing. But no permanent damage done. Shall we go?"

"Quickly," Glorianna said, "we've plans to make."

The Commodore tossed his cigar to the ground. "Not presidential, I hope."

Glorianna's face glowed in the carriage's sidelights. "The Khedive's money. We must make our offer before Bulwark Bank tries to sell him their Erie shares."

Hearing the Khedive's name jarred me back to my conversation with Britt. *Was he really planning to kill the reigning monarch of Egypt at midnight?*

Vanderbilt spoke. "Theobald de Greer. That weasel would sell his own mother for a fiver."

"Fisk sold him as much worthless Erie stock as he did you," Glorianna replied. "You can't blame him for wanting to recoup his money."

"Yes, but de Greer is a humorless box of lard, whereas I..."

"Whereas you," Glorianna said, tugging the Commodore's muttonchop, "are the epitome of charm and grace."

Vanderbilt beamed. "So I am, my plum."

I was dumbfounded. What were these two talking about? Hadn't

Glorianna and I just endured the ninth level of hell? We'd barely escaped with our lives. Three thousand feminists had been beaten and arrested, and here Glorianna was blathering on about selling Erie Railroad stock as if we were enjoying a cup of tea. Did the woman have a heart? Did she have a soul? A conscience?

Glorianna took the Commodore's hand. He helped her into the carriage then offered his hand as I climbed in behind. The Commodore seated himself next to Glorianna. He barked an order into the speaking tube then settled back against the white leather.

The carriage rattled down the alley and turned onto Chambers Street. Battered women floated past on the left, some crying, others limping, some clutching their heads. Policemen routed their prisoners like wagon traffic, blowing their whistles and motioning with their clubs to guide the women into waiting black wagons. Not far away, two men in white coats carried a sheet-covered stretcher toward an ambulance wagon.

My stomach lurched and I looked away from the window. Glorianna sat snug against the Commodore, who nodded reflectively as she whispered in his ear. My gaze dropped to the Commodore's finely made Moroccan slippers and Glorianna's Cuban heeled boots side by side on the carriage floor. Glorianna's boot had suffered a gash on the side. Looking closer, I saw that the footwear I'd once thought of as expensive were made only of cheap leatherette, dyed and textured to resemble calfskin.

"Yes," the Commodore said, pulling away from Glorianna, "de Greer is most certainly a crafty fellow. He'll do anything to keep us from the Khedive."

Glorianna grinned. "The king will be attending a masquerade at the Astor House. Bulwark Bank is holding the ball in his honor and I've obtained invitations. We could make our offer and cement the deal right under de Greer's nose—especially if we include a significant incentive."

"A sexual incentive?" the Commodore asked, glancing to me.

Glorianna turned the Commodore's face back to her with a finger on his cheek. "The Khedive's passion is well known."

"A little icing on the cake," he said, grinning.

"Precisely."

"Who do you have in mind?"

Glorianna examined her fingernails.

The Commodore's brow rose. He took a fresh cigar from a silver case and rolled it excitedly between his fingers. "Glorianna, you are a she-devil. I'd marry you right now, but I fear my wife would not allow it."

Glorianna pecked his cheek. "The wife who is forty-five years your junior? And you call *me* a devil?"

I had heard enough. My fury exploded like a powder charge. "What is wrong with you, Glorianna? Women have been beaten. They're lying in the street, injured, maimed, and dead. They're being herded into wagons and taken to jail, and all you care about is defrauding the Khedive. Have you no compassion?"

Glorianna trembled with anger. "Compassion? You question my compassion?"

"I believed in you, Glorianna. I followed you. I hung on your every word. Now I see what you really are: a power-mad, money-grubbing opportunist. You chat gaily about seducing the Khedive while Cleo—arrested because she fought for your beliefs—lies helpless in Ludlow Street Jail. If you possessed one iota of decency, you'd help me free her."

A confusion of emotion sped across Glorianna's face before she settled on a sugary smile. "Jenny, dearest," she said, "when we women bound ourselves together to fight for our rights, we knew the risks. We understood that some might fall in battle. Cleo accepted this."

"Which is more important to you, swindling the Khedive or helping a loyal comrade?"

"Make no mistake," Glorianna said, falling into her campaign voice, "the Khedive is a brutal dictator. His wealth derives from the oppression of his subjects, half of which are women. Taking his money is a defiance of tyranny and victory for womanhood."

Glorianna's high-sounding talk didn't fool me anymore. "You care nothing about victory for womanhood. You don't care about anything or anyone except Glorianna Talmadge, the greediest woman in America."

She exploded in outrage. "Yes, damn it, I'm greedy. I admit it. I've struggled my whole life. You've never known what it's like to be hungry, cold, and have nowhere to sleep. Well, listen to me, Jenny Crispin. Without money there *is* nothing. Freedom is good. Equality is good, but to implement those high ideals there must be money. Don't you see?" she said, leaning close, her voice softening. "Greed is what drives this country. It's the fuel that fires the great economic engine. The creator endowed humankind—men and women alike—with an unquenchable thirst for power and possessions. Without greed, the species would have died out eons ago. Only a fool can't see that."

"I see that you have no qualms about using others for your own gains," I said. "Power and wealth are all you want. Women's rights are secondary. Ambition, not altruism, is what drives you. You don't even care about the people who made you what you are—your own followers."

Glorianna's face curled in disbelief. "My followers? Let me tell you something. You think women like Cleo follow me because they're idealists, because they believe in some lofty goal called feminine equality? Make no mistake; they do it for greed. They're just as greedy as I am. They want the vote. They want jobs. They want money. They want the things men have controlled since time began. They're not noble soldiers in some high moral fight. They're as power-mad and money-hungry as I am. They're just not as smart."

My head shook in small rapid movements. I turned away, unable to look at her any more.

Glorianna spoke in my ear, low and sympathetic. "Jenny, dearest, I was once like you. I believed passionately in the rights of women, in universal suffrage and equality, but after beating my head against the wall for years I realized the truth. Only by pursuing our own selfish goals will the world become a better place."

I spun around. "Our own selfish goals?"

Glorianna slid next to me. She hugged me close and whispered. "I see now I underestimated you, Jenny. We're alike, you and I. We're above the mass of common fools. The unwashed crowd needs us to survive. Where would they be without people like us, people of power? They'd still be living in mud huts groveling to keep warm and stay fed. People like you and I and the Commodore have raised them up, given them houses, jobs, food to eat, even transportation. Let them fight for us. Cleo should consider it an honor to fall in battle. You don't think she could possibly rise to our level, do you? For women to be victorious we must stand on each other's shoulders. If the bottom few like Cleo get crushed, then so be it. And if we should make a little money in the process from books, speaking tours, or swindling a foreign dictator, what harm does it do?"

The Commodore bit the end from his cigar and spat it into the corner. "Young lady, the acquisition of wealth is a time-honored tradition. My father chased the dollar, as did his father before him. Without people like us, there'd be no railroads, no steamship lines, no bridges to Brooklyn."

I felt my body shrink, as if it had withered and desiccated to a shriveled hull, as if my soul had been sucked out and tossed away. Could they be right? Could the world really be such a sordid, self-serving place?

I shrugged off Glorianna's arm and shook my head violently. "No. You're wrong. You're both wrong. Everyone is equal. It says so in the Constitution. We're fighting for equality among the genders. No one has to use anyone, no one will stand on anyone's shoulders, and no one will get crushed. Everyone must work together in a grand co-operative, a great union, a wonderful singing collective of workers, male and female, united in achieving an advanced civilization where everyone works according to his abilities and receives according to his needs, a place where men and women will live together in peace and harmony and everlasting good will."

Glorianna and the Commodore stared at me dumbstruck. Slowly, the corner of the Commodore's mouth began to twitch then spasms gripped his face.

My passion vanished into concern. Was the old man well? Had the verbal exchange been too much? Was his heart giving out? Was he dying right here in front of me?

The Commodore's head reared back. His tongue protruded. Gasps or gags—I couldn't tell which—wracked his face. He was... laughing.

He bent over and grabbed his gut, belly shaking in a great guffaw. But Glorianna's features remained stern. She slid across the carriage and thrust her elbow into his ribs. "Shut up. Stop laughing. It's not funny."

But Vanderbilt only laughed harder and, infected with mirth, Glorianna's face cracked too. Laughter filled the carriage as Glorianna and the Commodore hugged each other in face-aching, knee-slapping merriment.

When the laughter died, I swallowed my humiliation and played my last card in as serious and solemn a voice as I could muster. "Please Commodore, you have friends in City Hall. Will you help me free Cleo?"

The Commodore wiped his eyes then took my hand in his. "Of course I'll help you free Cleo. First thing Monday morning I will go to the mayor's office and demand her release. I'm certain that in a week or so she'll be free."

"But by then," I said, "she'll be sent to the Tombs where some knife-wielding maniac will kill her."

The Commodore smiled sweetly. "The wheels of government grind slowly, my dear. Deals must be struck, favors granted, bribes paid: the mayor, the police commissioner, the warden, and so on and so forth."

What a fool I'd been. These two would never help Cleo. Britt was right. I slipped my hand from the Commodore's and stared out the window. Revelers still occupied City Hall Park. Near the fountain, the Transatlantic Balloon loomed above the crowds. I could see Professor Lowe standing on the basket's edge, addressing the masqueraders.

The clock on City Hall began to chime the hour, 11:00PM. Cleo's fate, sealed or not, faded to the background as Britt's vow returned to me. *"I'll make him pay for every stripe and every day I spent in that stinking prison."*

Barclay Street drifted past and, caught in the light from the street lamp, the window of Britt's store reflected bottle blue. Within the hour, Britt would kill the Khedive—but how?

My mind wandered to his shop. Questions floated through my head. Why was the floor covered in dirt? Why did it fill the room from floor to the ceiling?

Fifty yards across the street, a blaze of torchlight drew my gaze to the Astor House where the Khedive lodged. Two carriages parked by the curb. I watched partygoers in masquerade climb the steps. When the Astor House's two great bronze doors closed behind them, I looked again at Britt's shop. Slowly, the seed of an idea sprouted in my mind.

Britt had been a miner. During the war, he, Lockie, and others had dug a tunnel under the Confederate fortifications at Petersburg. They had planted so many explosives, and blown a hole so large, people referred to it as *The Battle of the Crater*.

Glorianna and the Commodore were still chuckling when the carriage stopped at the Astor House and a red-coated footman opened the door. Dabbing their eyes and sniffling, Vanderbilt and Glorianna exited the carriage, ascended the marble steps, and disappeared through the Astor's massive doors.

I stepped out behind them then froze in the carriage doorway, transfixed by a horrible thought.

Had Britt and Lockie dug a tunnel from his shop to the Astor House? Had they packed it with explosives? Was Britt's hatred for the Khedive so great that at precisely midnight he was willing to kill everyone at the ball to avenge his mistreatment?

"Madame?"

The footman offered his palm with practiced boredom. Brain churning with explosions and mutilation, I took his hand. As I descended to the sidewalk, I pictured the Astor House erupt into flame, bodies fly through the air, women scream—

"Madame?" The footman smiled vaguely. "My hand, Madame? Could you let go?"

Embarrassed, I relaxed my fingers. The man hurried to an arriving hackney. He opened the door and a man resembling Louis the Fourteenth appeared. Behind him exited a reluctant Maria Teresa wearing a lopsided white wig and feathered mask.

As she reached for the footman's outstretched hand, Louis jerked his queen out of the carriage. After a few steps, the queen stopped, defiantly yanking her hand from the sun king's grip. Her wig slipped sideways, but she caught the hairpiece before it fell. After yelling some obscenities, the king bit his thumb and vanished up the steps into the hotel. Clutching her hair with both hands, the queen hurried up behind him.

As if nothing unusual had happened, the footman closed the hackney's door and scurried off toward the next carriage. I stood alone beneath the light of a street lamp.

An object on the sidewalk attracted my notice. I picked it up. In her haste to catch her falling wig, the queen had dropped her mask. I called out to her, but the French monarch had already disappeared inside.

Someone coughed conspicuously. I turned around. Officer Quinn, the policeman from the Second Ward police station, stood in front of me, buttons and badge glinting in the gaslight.

Chapter Thirty

"Well," Quinn said much too friendly. "If it isn't Missy from this morning. Find your friend? Cleo was it?" His hand clamped around my wrist and his tone hardened. "You played me for a dunce at the precinct, didn't you, Missy. Well, I've seen your poster. There'll be no whoring on my beat, not in front of the Astor."

I winced as he dragged me down the sidewalk. Whoring? I wasn't whoring. I was penniless, cold, and dressed in my undergarments, but I wasn't whoring. And I wasn't about to get arrested, not now, not here, and certainly not before I warned everyone at the ball about the impending explosion. I had to escape, had to talk my way out. What would Glorianna do? It was then I found my voice.

"Unhand me, you idiot. Release me this instant. You've confused me with someone else."

"Fool me once, Missy..."

"See here," I bellowed, "I'm meeting my gentleman on the steps. We're going to the Banker's Masquerade."

"And I'm the King of Madison Square," Quinn said. "I know a codhopper when I see one."

I remembered Mavis' brother in law. "Don't make me report you to Commissioner Westerfield. Even a fool like you must have heard of

243

him. He'll have you dismissed."

The officer's grip slackened. His eyebrows rose. "Police Commissioner *Simon* Westerfield?"

I pushed the performance. "His sister-in-law, Mavis, is an old family friend—the mayor too."

Quinn's fingers closed hard on my arm and jerked me up against his chest. "Save your air, Missy. Your picture's in every police station on Manhattan."

Pain shot up my arm. My teeth clenched and my thoughts boiled. *Words, words, they're all you've got. Think fast, keep up the game, talk louder, bolder.*

"You barbarian, you've seen my picture on the Times society page. Unhand me. I'll have your badge. You've no right. I'll—"

"My dear, where have you been? I've been looking all over for you."

A familiar elderly man in colonial garb, bifocals, and buckle shoes appeared from the darkness. He carried a kite and an oversize key. Finger by finger, he pried Officer Quinn's hand from my wrist.

"Haste makes waste, officer. I believe there's been a mistake; the lady's with me. I only stepped away for a moment to relieve myself." He leaned close to the policeman. "It's an old man's affliction. You'll have it soon enough."

Quinn huffed.

Ignoring him, the old man took my arm and draped it over his. "Come, my dear. We may delay, but time will not."

He escorted me to the top of the stairs and, as the doormen swung open the bronze doors, I looked back and smiled. Officer Quinn glared at me from the sidewalk, club twirling ominously on his finger.

The elderly gentleman tugged me through the doors and then, as if in a fairy tale, warmth and light enclosed me. Blue carpet lifted my weary feet; soft music soothed my nerves. Marble, gold, velvet—the trappings of wealth leaped from every corner of the expansive lobby. Patterned draperies covered the walls. Leather settees and Morris chairs lounged beside gilded tables. Tuxedoed musicians played harp and violin from a cast iron stage. Bellmen crisscrossed the lobby.

The old man led me to a floor-to-ceiling mirror. "That officer seemed quite determined to arrest you, young lady."

"You saved my life, Mr..." I suddenly remembered his face. "Aren't you the teller from Bulwark Bank?"

"And you're the young lady who socked old de Greer in the head. Well, I'm glad someone did it. The way he demoted me... I used to be head accountant. But all that's behind us now. Tonight, I am Ben Franklin." He bowed as far as his belly would allow.

I curtsied. "A pleasure to meet you, Mr. Franklin."

"The pleasure is mine, dear girl. I feared this masquerade would be a complete bore, devoid as I am of female companionship. But now, in the company of beauty, the night may yet prove pleasurable."

The word pleasure caused me dismay. "Mr. Franklin, you're not expecting any—"

"Favors? No, of course not. I expect to pay full price as I'm sure all your clients do. What's the usual fee? Three dollars? Five?"

My anger peaked—first the policeman, now this Franklin fellow. Why did all men assume an unescorted woman dressed in her undergarments to be a prostitute? My face tightened and I shook my fist.

Franklin hid behind his kite. "No need to get violent. I was only jesting. You're worth much more. Here, is this sufficient?"

He pushed a fold of money into my hand.

Fuming, I opened the bills. My wrath became astonishment. He'd given me a full ten dollars. My God, no wonder Hilda had turned to prostitution. A girl could get rich.

I eyed the grinning Franklin. Short, with thinning hair, pendulous belly, and spindly legs, he looked more the kindly uncle than a lewd old man. His clothes evaporated in my mind and the kindly uncle became a vulgar gnome.

I blinked the disturbing picture away and glanced again at the money. Ten dollars seemed an enormous sum for thirty minutes work. I tucked the bills in my purse, looked up, and forced a smile.

The key shook visibly in Franklin's hand. "Wonderful," he stammered. "Won't my colleagues be surprised when I show you off? You know, a man without a woman is but half a man."

He took my arm and, chest out, led me down a hallway wallpapered in floral gold. We stopped in a line of guests at the ballroom entrance and waited to be announced.

Orchestra music drifted in, and with it came thoughts of Britt. The man infuriated me, but I worried for his life—and also for mine. "Benjamin, what time is it."

Franklin fished a silver octagon watch from his pocket by a long chain, the other end of which bore a penknife. "11:15PM. If you're Cinderella, you have forty-five minutes left."

If he only knew. "I'm definitely not Cinderella."

The hall ended in an arched opening. Beside it, a white wigged servant balanced a silver platter on his hand. Franklin searched his pocket and extracted a card and pencil. He stepped back to examine my blue chemise. "Your costume, my dear. If you're not Cinderella, who are you?"

Yes, who was I? My fingers dropped to the blue silk of my chemise. Wasn't it apparent to every man? I was a prostitute. Anger renewed, I felt determined to set the old man straight.

"Wait," Franklin interrupted, "let me guess."

He tapped the key pensively to his lips and examined me over his spectacles. "You're something allegorical. *Spring Eternal*, possibly. No, no, *Youth Everlasting*."

He frowned and shook his head. Abruptly, his face illuminated with inspiration. "I have it. You're the *Spirit of Womanhood*."

My anger vanished, dissipated by Franklin's whimsical guesses. I laughed out loud then slipped the mask over my face and curtsied. "Close, but wrong on all counts, Mr. Franklin. I'm *Feminine Virtue*."

"Ah," he said wisely, adjusting the glasses on his nose. "Of course, I see it perfectly now."

Franklin scribbled something on the card, placed it on the valet's silver tray, and a haughty voice preceded us: "Doctor Benjamin Franklin and his consort, Miss Feminine Virtue."

Three steps beyond the arched opening, I was stunned: the music, the decorations—no, the costumes. Far from the homespun disguises of the mob in City Hall Park, these were elaborate theater wardrobes:

Cupid, Pan, Athena, sceptered kings, medieval queens, a jester in bells, an elephant, a lion. There was even a knight in full armor.

Pity to blow everyone up, I thought. But how does one empty a two-hundred-guest party? Approach the management and tell them a fiend has burrowed under the building and planted a bomb? Why, they'd haul me directly to Bellevue Asylum.

On my left, an Amazonian woman in leopard skins and tights flirted with a sword-wielding gladiator. Next to them, a horned rhinoceros conversed with a minuteman leaning on his musket. By the wall, three Spanish conquistadors posed for a photograph. I pictured them all flying through the air, propelled by a fiery explosion.

I edged closer to Franklin. "Mr. Franklin, may I confide in you?"

"Anything, Miss Virtue."

"Would you believe me if I told you there is a bomb planted under the Astor House?"

"I'm not sure," he said. "Is it a large bomb?"

"Very large."

"Is it *your* bomb?"

"Heaven's no," I said. "A madman wants to assassinate the Khedive." I explained the situation in the briefest terms.

After a moment of thought, he spoke. "We might need help."

I followed Franklin through the crowd until we came to red fox holding his tail.

"Miss Virtue," Franklin said, "may I introduce Horace Maymeade, Bulwark Bank's attorney."

I curtsied again. This was getting to be a habit.

"Horace," Franklin said, "we have a problem. There is a bomb planted under the Astor House set to go off at twelve midnight."

"That seems a dubious statement," Maymeade said, stroking his tail. "Why should I believe you?"

Franklin peered over his spectacles. "I have it on very good authority."

"And whose authority is that?"

"Miss Virtue's authority."

Horace looked me up and down then turned to Franklin. "Has she witnessed the bomb in question?"

"No, but she knows the gentleman who planted it."

"She is his accomplice then?"

"No, of course not."

"Accessory?"

"No."

"Associate?"

"Acquaintance," Franklin offered.

Horace nodded. "Well, did she try to stop this alleged bomber or warn the authorities?"

"She didn't know he was going to set the bomb until minutes ago."

"How did she find out?"

"Deduction."

Horace stroked the whiskers of his fox chin. "Interesting. But we have no direct proof of a bomb."

"None except her word," Franklin said.

"How long have you known Miss Virtue?" Maymeade asked.

"We just met tonight."

"I see," Maymeade said. "And why, pray tell, would this alleged bomber want to disrupt a perfectly good party by blowing up the Astor House?"

"He desires to kill the Khedive."

"An anarchist then?"

Franklin shrugged. "His motivation is unknown."

"But he wants the Khedive dead."

"Apparently," Franklin said.

"How long do we have before the alleged bomb explodes?"

Franklin consulted his silver watch. "It's 11:20PM now, that means—"

"The bomb will go off in approximately forty minutes," I said, impatient with Maymeade's line of questioning.

"The alleged bomb," Maymeade corrected.

I was starting to doubt the bomb myself.

"So," Maymeade continued, "we have an unreliable witness who claims there is a bomb which she has never seen nor has she any physical evidence thereof."

Franklin and I looked at each other.

"In light of these facts," Maymeade continued, "I motion we recess to take the matter under advisement."

"How long a recess?" Franklin asked.

Maymeade dipped a paw into his pocket and pulled out a gold watch. "Forty-one minutes."

"Done," Franklin said, taking note of the time on his octagon watch as well. "We'll re-adjourn at one minute after midnight."

Franklin turned to me as Maymeade hurried away. "That was easy, wasn't it?"

I snatched the octagon watch from his hand and disappeared into the crowd.

Chapter Thirty-One

Just past the Astor house at Barclay Street, Lockie waved goodbye and turned his horse toward their shop while Britt continued north.

After a lifetime of working into the late hours, lights still burned in Madame Becker's brownstone. Britt tied off the horse then climbed the steps and knocked on the door. Curtains parted in a side window and an aged face appeared, hair swaddled in a cloth.

The door opened, spilling light onto the steps. "Brittan," the old woman said, holding a lamp aloft, "it's 11:30. Is something wrong?"

Britt could not remember when he'd last seen the grand lady without her makeup and finery. Her eyes seemed small and filmy, her face wrinkled. "Nothing is wrong; I came to see Jeffery."

Britt entered the house and followed Madame Becker through the arched foyer, down a narrow hallway into a small bedroom hung with framed needlepoint. Jeffery, cheeks rosy and arms splayed, lay on his back asleep. Rolled quilts surrounded him in a bed much too large for his tiny body.

Britt rubbed his finger across the boy's palm. "You've found a home for him?"

"A childless couple," Madame Becker whispered, smiling down at Jeffery as if he were her own grandchild. "They have a small farm in

Brooklyn. You've made them very happy. And me, as well. They said I could visit any time."

"When will they arrive?"

"Tomorrow afternoon. You'll be here, I hope."

Britt stroked Jeffery's hair. "No, I've been called away on business. I leave tonight."

"My Brittan, always traveling. And your virgin? Will you leave her, too?"

"She has left me."

"Maybe there is still time to find her?"

Britt smiled. "I take no stock in miracles."

"You're looking at one."

"Jeffery?"

"Where would he be if you hadn't found him?"

"Placed with the Children's Aid Society probably. Sent on one of the orphan trains to a loving family out west."

Madame Becker cast him a wary eye. "Grown up an indentured servant in someone's business, you mean."

"As I was?"

Britt was sorry the moment he said it. Jeffery stirred and Madame Becker hurried into the hall. Britt kissed the boy on the forehead then joined her. Facing away from him, she sniffed and wiped her eyes. "I never claimed to be your mother, Brittan. I did the best I knew how."

He folded his arms around her and rocked the old madam's shriveled body. She seemed to melt against him. "You will always be my one true love," he whispered.

She turned in his arms, smiled, and kissed him on the cheek. "Go find your virgin."

Outside, Britt opened the saddlebag and checked the bottle of nitro before mounting the horse and riding south. The boy would have a good life, better than he'd had, certainly better than if he had stayed with Billy. For that, Britt was glad.

Pigs, devils, and other merrymakers from City Hall Park wandered the streets, shouting and drinking. There seemed to be more masqueraders than ever. A woman dressed as a ballerina tried to grab his horse's bridle as he turned on Barclay Street. He kicked his heels and galloped past her.

In front of his shop, Britt dismounted, opened the saddlebags, and took out the glass the president had given him. He held it to the light of the street lamp. The ice was gone. He'd have to be very careful from here on out. Good thing he only had a short distance left to travel. He placed the nitro in his inside coat pocket then returned the glass to the saddlebag. With a smack on the rump, he sent the horse running down the street. When the animal was a good distance away, he unlocked the door to the shop.

Inside, their gear was laid out on a table: two miner's safety lamps, a small pick, a shovel, a canvas bucket, crow bars, gloves, wedges, sledge hammer, chisels, two boxes of cartridges, and one Smith & Wesson Model 3 revolver. Lockie picked up the pistol and handed it to Britt by the barrel. "I bought you a new sidearm."

Britt laid his Webley on the table. He took the Smith & Wesson from Lockie and hefted it. "Doesn't feel quite right in my hand."

Lockie dropped the tools into a sack one at a time. "My first wife used to say the same."

Britt pushed the Smith into his holster. "The one who left you for the cobbler?"

"Aye, poor man. I should have warned him the woman was losing her mind. He was an excellent craftsman, though." Lockie turned up his heel. "Made these boots—very practical."

Lockie handed Britt one box of ammunition and stuffed the other in his pocket. He tied the sack shut with a rope then threw it over his shoulder with a grunt. Britt followed him through the doorway. The next room was filled with dirt from floor to ceiling. A stairway led down to the basement.

At the bottom of the stairs, Lockie struck a lucifer and lit their safety lamps. Britt shined his light down a black hole in the center of the room. "I'll go first. Hand me the sack."

Lockie obliged. Britt dropped the sack into the hole. When he heard a clang, he climbed down the ladder after it.

The area at the bottom was only big enough for one man. Britt tied a loop in the rope on the sack and slipped his arm through it. Down on all fours, he forced himself into a hole no bigger in diameter than a beer barrel. He crawled forward a few feet and waited for Lockie. A minute later, light flickered behind him. Lockie's hand tapped his boot and the long journey on shins and forearms began, dragging the sack of tools behind him.

In the lamp's dim light, smidgens and atoms floated in the hot air, dank with the smell of things long dead. Soil fell where his shoulders brushed the walls. His hair dragged the low ceiling. He heard nothing save limbs scuffing dirt, his breathing, and the rising squish of blood in his ears.

A hundred feet into the tunnel, the air became thick and fetid as swamp water. The walls pressed inwards and the light from his lamp seemed useless against the blackness stretching forever in front of him. For the first time in his life, panic crept into his heart. He'd spent half his years crawling through holes beneath the earth, but this one seemed different: a grave more than a tunnel.

Rumbling filled his head. At first he thought it was a train passing over him, but there were no trains in Manhattan this far south. Maybe it was a wagon, or a whole parade of them. It had to be—what else could make a sound as loud as the furnaces of hell. His limbs began to tremble and the fear of a cave-in rose to the point of explosion.

Why in damnation was he fifty feet below the Manhattan streets creeping like a corpse through wormy muck? What was he trying to accomplish? To heal the wounds on his back? The wounds to his pride? To his soul? Was he trying to prove he was the better man? And at what price? Losing the woman he loved? Losing his freedom? His life?

And then, without fanfare or announcement, the rumbling stopped. Calm swept over him like a Nile breeze. He'd known the answer to his questions all along. It was fate. There was nothing to do but keep crawling. Whether king or peasant, fate guided your life. The tunnel was too narrow to turn around. Life was like that, a one-way proposition. You couldn't go back.

The shaft opened into a small chamber. Britt took hold of the next ladder and pulled himself upright. Lockie came out behind him, stood, and stretched. "I feel like a blasted turd."

Britt chuckled. He lifted his watch from its pocket and flipped the cover. "Damned hands have stopped."

"Ach! In all this excitement you forgot to wind it." Lockie pulled his Kullberg chronometer out by the chain. "11:45, nae a moment too early."

Britt watched the moon and sun circle Lockie's timepiece as it chimed the quarter hour. "And nae a moment too late," he said, mocking the Scotsman's accent. He climbed the ladder. At the top, he rested his shoulder against the underside of the floor stones and called down, "I warned the president that Gideon still wanted to kill him."

Lockie untied the sack and tossed him up the pick. "You think the general will try again?"

Britt caught the tool by the handle. "I'm certain of it."

"Tonight?"

"At the masquerade."

Lockie's teeth glowed in the lamplight. "They'll be in for a surprise, then."

"A big surprise," Britt said, touching the nitro in his coat pocket. He reared back and buried the point of the pick into the floor stones.

Chapter Thirty-Two

Somewhere past the orchestra I stopped running and slid the mask over my face. Fifty or so guests were dancing with abandon. In their midst I saw Moses—complete with stone tablets—dancing with a she-devil. Hercules waltzed with a woman in a white gown: Hera, I assumed. Louis the Fourteenth twirled his queen while she clutched her wig with one hand. It pleased me to see the two monarchs reconciled. A few couples behind them, Commodore Vanderbilt twirled Glorianna. They wore long cloaks and masks, but Glorianna's pants and the Commodore's muttonchops were unmistakable. As the music ended, the two embraced. Hand in hand they wandered into the crowd, past Diana with her bow and Medusa with her snakes.

In contrast to these excellent costumes, I then saw what had to be the worst disguise of the night. A man had come dressed as Ulysses S. Grant except the beard and the hair were all wrong. I had seen numerous engravings of the president, and this gentleman looked nothing like him. To make matters worse, the impostor had hired a cadre of men in black suits to closely follow him, posing as Secret Service Agents.

I checked Ben's pocket watch. 11:47PM. Thirteen minutes left. My only option now was to cry fire. How long it would take to clear a party this big, I didn't know. Some people would be crushed. But hadn't

Glorianna said that getting crushed didn't matter as long as the overall goal was achieved? Besides, time was less than short.

As I weaved among the partiers, searching left and right for a table on which to stand and shout, I smacked headlong into a wall of dark, bare-chested men. Gold armbands and purple fezes: they were the very same men I'd seen earlier on Molly de Ford's porch, the Khedive's personal bodyguards. Before I could flee, two of them reached out and pulled me within their circle. Once inside, they closed ranks to form an impenetrable wall and I found myself facing Ramses reincarnated.

He sat on a paper mâché throne surrounded by crepe paper palms. His head bore a blue-and-gold-striped headdress. Black lines enhanced his eyes. A tubular beard sprang from his chin. A golden mantle covered his shoulders and breast. One hand held a hooked scepter and a white garment hung beneath his armpits.

Seized with fear, I beat his bodyguards with my fists. They absorbed my blows as if I were air. Exhausted, I pressed my back against the Khedive's men and faced the monarch.

The Khedive's eyebrow lifted in amusement, as if I, the party, New York, and the entire world had been created solely for his pleasure. He motioned me closer with his scepter. When I complied, the royal mouth parted to reveal even white teeth, the grin of a cat or a wolf. The king leaned forward in his throne, imposing and formidable, a man of noble bearing, darkly handsome, the omnipotent ruler of the oldest nation on Earth. Slowly, the sovereign rose to full height and stepped down from his throne.

He stood all of four foot nine.

"Praise, Allah," he said, arms spread, accent thick but with a hint of Oxford. "You have finally arrived. I can scarcely control my person. Where have you been? No matter. Let me gaze on you. It is good you are beautiful, or I would have the responsible human beheaded. Please, come closer."

Not knowing what else to do, I inched toward him. Should I kneel? Curtsy? Kiss the little man's ring?

I dropped to one knee and stared into the stripes on his mantle. The king lifted my chin and slid up my mask. "Please, this is America.

Stand girl. Show me your dazzling womanhood."

I stood. The king admired me and sighed. "How wonderful is America. Its women are magnificent: so beautiful, so tall, so…"

"Your Highness," I said, "you must let me leave."

"…so bold, so audacious. Why do you keep me waiting, girl? You will return with me to Alexandria, of course."

"Your Highness, I beg you to listen. As we speak, evil is plotted against you and everyone at the masquerade."

He touched the fabric over my thigh. "You shall have camels, horses, the finest clothes, the finest food, a golden carriage to drive you through the city. You shall have servants, slaves, a thousand goats. Your every wish will be fulfilled, your hungers satisfied, your desires met." His dark fingers stroked my leg.

I batted away his hand. "Your Highness, listen to me. There is a bomb planted under this building."

Eyes focused in the far distance, he took hold of my fingers and pointed his scepter toward imaginary vistas. "The desert sands will part before you. Wealth beyond all fantasy will be yours. Streets will be named your honor, villages, cities. Anything you desire will be given. My body cannot wait; I crave your fleshiness."

"Your Highness," I cried, "everyone must evacuate the building."

A sudden urgency overwhelmed him. He grabbed my hips and pulled me against his groin. "Your beauty ravishes me. Come. Now. I must possess you. Let us go. I have a private suite upstairs."

Without waiting for an answer, the Khedive lunged forward and thrust his face between my breasts.

"Your Highness, please," I shouted, thrown off balance.

The little man dropped his scepter and slid to his knees. He dragged his hands down my spine, dug his fingers into my buttocks, and pressed his face into my crotch.

"Your Highness, I've come to warn—"

His head thrust deeper into the blue silk of my chemise. His headdress clanged to the floor. Free now of its golden encumbrance, his head shook violently as he uttered a stream of unintelligible grunts.

Trapped by his embrace, arms spread, torso twisting, I searched for help in all directions, but the wall of men in fezes answered with indifference.

The Khedive began humping, thrusting his hips against my knees like a wire-haired terrier on a houseguest's leg. I tried to work my fingers under his hands and untangle his arms, but the little man seemed possessed of extraordinary strength.

Wavering from his impacts, legs constricted by his grip, I lost my balance and tipped backward. My feet made tiny steps. My arms fanned the air, but it was futile. Eyes shut tight, I plunged downward toward the floor with the Khedive humping feverishly.

The impact never came.

Someone caught my armpits. I opened my eyes. A knight in shining armor bent over me, supporting my body with his gauntlets. How did he get past the bodyguards?

Britt! Who else could it be? He'd decided not to kill his old boss and negotiate instead. "Britt," I whispered, "is that you?"

Rattling like a tinker's wagon, the knight lifted me upright. With deft strokes, he pried the Khedive from my legs then scooped the golden headdress from the carpet. A metallic voice rang behind his grated visor, "Excuse me, Your Highness, I believe you dropped this."

That voice—was it Britt's? I couldn't tell. The words were distorted, tinny. "Britt?" I whispered again, "tell me it's you."

Annoyed, the Khedive jammed the damaged triangle on his head. "What do *you* want?" he asked the knight, as if they were acquainted. "Can't you see I'm mating?"

The knight could be no one other than Britt. He'd decided to postpone blowing up the Khedive. "Britt? Damn you, say something."

The knight touched a metal finger to his visor and shushed me. He bowed toward the king, every joint squeaking. "Please forgive the interruption, Your Highness."

The Khedive dropped into his throne. "I have been sitting at this party for hours. My liquids are boiling. If I do not make consummation, I will explode."

The knight reached beneath his cuirass and extracted a folder. "Your Highness, this may interest you more than your liquids. If you sign tonight, Bulwark Bank will offer a ten percent discount."

I saw the words *Erie Railroad* on the cover. This wasn't Britt. "Dorian?"

As Dorian came forward to present his offering to the Khedive, a wild haired blond girl wearing dark mascara and a Zebra skin dress stepped from behind him.

I couldn't believe it. Hilda? Here?

The Khedive saw her too. Grinning, he jumped from his throne, past Dorian's offering, and straight to Hilda. His hands caressed her body.

"You shall have camels," the Khedive announced, "horses, the finest clothes, the finest food, a golden carriage to drive you through the city."

Hilda giggled.

Dorian lifted his visor. "Hilda, what are you doing?"

The Khedive rambled on. "You shall have servants, slaves, a thousand goats."

Dorian tried to wedge his armored hand between the two but the Khedive slipped to Hilda's other side. "Your every wish will be fulfilled, your hungers satisfied, your desires met."

Hilda held tight to the little man as he gazed in the distance, his palm tracing a vast circle. "The desert sands will part before you. Wealth beyond imagination shall be yours."

Dorian tugged at Hilda. "Get away from this maniac. I brought you here. You shall leave with me."

Hilda pushed him hard. "Go away, Dorian. As of this moment I am an emancipated woman. I can do whatever I want."

I cried out as the Khedive caught me by the waist. "I will have both of you. Pleasure me and streets will be named after you, villages, cities. Anything you desire, my twin New York beauties. I cannot wait; my flesh craves your bodiness."

As I struggled against the king's grip, Dorian bent close to Hilda. "Damn it, Hilda, you must leave with me. For God's sake, I bailed you out of jail."

Hilda licked the Khedive's cheek.

Dorian turned to the Khedive. "Your Highness, please, the lady is mine."

"Nonsense," the Khedive said dismissively, "I am Khedive. My will is law. Now go, or I'll have you beheaded and your tongue removed—but leave your Erie Stock."

Dorian glowed. "Then you'll sign?"

"Possibly—in the morning."

Dorian bowed. "Your power is legend, Sire."

Seizing the moment, I jerked away from the Khedive. "Where are you going?" he shouted.

"In this country," I said, "women must consent to sexual congress."

The king's face twisted in rage, and he rose in height at least an inch. "Disgraceful. Outrageous. My kingdom would die if we had such laws. Besides, the hour is too late to return to Madame de Ford's. My fluids are overflowing. One woman is not enough." He pressed his palm into his temple.

"Possibly I can help, Your Highness."

I knew that voice.

Caped but unmasked, Glorianna and the Commodore stood side by side.

The Commodore sniffed a cigar as Glorianna embraced the Khedive. "Your highness," she cooed, "I had no idea you were so handsome."

I suppressed a gag.

The Khedive's anger melted to a curious grin. "Who is this lovely creature?"

"Call me Glorianna."

"Are you emancipated?"

"Emancipated?" she asked.

"Can you do whatever you wish?" the Khedive asked.

Vanderbilt stifled a chuckle. "Yes, Glorianna, tell his Highness. Are you emancipated?"

Glorianna flipped the Commodore a poison smile as she rubbed a soothing hand across the Khedive's chest. "Of course I am, Your Highness. Let's go somewhere quiet and talk."

I hardly heard what Glorianna said. Beyond the bodyguards, the party was becoming impossibly loud and the noise was getting closer.

The Khedive kissed Glorianna's neck. "But, dear lady, my fleshiness requires more than talk."

The knight rattled forward, interrupting their tryst. "Your Highness, this woman will deceive you and take your money."

The Commodore puffed out his chest. "Who the hell are you?"

Dorian removed his helmet and shook his hair. Teeth sparkled beneath his aquiline nose. His skin glowed. "My name is Dorian de Greer, of Bulwark Bank."

The commotion was now just outside the circle of bodyguards.

Dorian pointed a silver finger at Glorianna. "Don't trust this woman, Your Highness. She is coarse, perverse, and intemperate. She's a common cheat who wishes only to sell you worthless railroad stock."

Directly in front of me, a bodyguard struggled with someone trying to get into our circle, one of the Khedive's admirers most likely.

Glorianna reacted with outrage. "Cheap? I'm not cheap. I'm worth a hundred times the average man."

Dorian glared at her. "And gotten that wealth by fraud."

I bent over and looked between the bodyguard's legs. Checkered pants. Raggedy shoes. McCauley! Good heavens, did the man ever stop? I'd escaped him at the theater by the thinnest margins, and here he was again.

"What meaning is *fraud*?" the Khedive asked, searching the faces around him.

Glorianna stroked the monarch's ear; her voice was low and husky. "It means let's go to your room."

Smiling, the Khedive shouted an order in Egyptian. Then he, Glorianna, the Commodore, and Hilda disappeared into the crowd surrounded by a circle of bare chests and purple fezes. Dorian clanged off after them shouting and waving his gauntlets.

I found myself facing a black-eyed, cigar chewing McCauley—and Benjamin Franklin too, kite and key in hand.

"There she is, detective," Franklin shouted. "She's the one who stole my pocket watch."

His pocket watch. My God. What time was it? I popped open the lid. 11:51. Nine minutes before the explosion.

McCauley grabbed for my arm but I was ready. I swung my purse hard catching him in the head. A dull whack thudded off his skull as *Feminine Virtue* connected with bone. His jaw deformed sideways knocking the cigar from his lips. Like a penny skyrocket, the cheap stogie arced through the air on a tail of sparks and landed on the seat of the Khedive's paper mâché throne.

Chapter Thirty-Three

The throne exploded in flame like a kerosene soaked rag. Fire raced up the crepe paper palms faster than a burning fuse races toward dynamite. From the palms it leaped to the spider's web of overhead streamers, and from there to the drapes.

Women shrieked. Men shouted. The music ceased, replaced by the sound of four hundred shoes thundering toward the bronze doors.

McCauley lay on the floor, unconscious. Dumbstruck, Franklin stared at the flames spreading rapidly overhead. I grabbed his arm. "Hurry, Ben, let's go."

In the lobby, people jammed against the front wall. Behind them, Moses swatted flames with his tablets. Hercules climbed on top of the crowd and was crawling from shoulder to shoulder toward the bronze doors. The sham Secret Service agents gathered around their sham president. In one corner, a bear and a tiger threw buckets of sand at the fire while Cupid, Pan, and Athena raced back and forth looking for other ways out.

I dragged Franklin to a side window. Together, we lifted a Morris chair, heaved it through the glass, then climbed out into the night. At City Hall Fountain, we joined a hundred or so other escapees from the party. Nearby, a thousand revelers congregated around Professor Lowe's

Transatlantic Balloon to watch the Astor House burn.

More furniture flew through the Astor House's windows. A storybook of characters—mythical, historical, and literary—climbed out and fled for their lives. Others rushed from the bronze doors. Like sound effects from a comic opera, police whistles blew, fire bells clanged, and the clock on City Hall began to chime.

Twelve, eleven, ten...

Pan, Athena, and Cupid jumped from an Astor House window.

Nine, eight, seven...

Moses, his tablets on fire, rambled from the front door.

Six, five, four...

The counterfeit Grant and his agents fought each other to get out the door and into the street.

Three, two...

The last person staggered out holding his head—McCauley.

Damn!

One...

I hugged Franklin tight, closed my eyes, and braced myself for the explosion.

Seconds ticked by.

Minutes, it seemed.

Hours.

I opened my eyes and looked.

Nothing.

"Maymeade was right," Franklin said meekly. "There is no bomb."

As the word *bomb* left his lips, a deafening concussion shook City Hall Park. People swayed and fell. Front doors vanished. Windows disintegrated and blew into the air. But the explosion hadn't come from the Astor House.

It came from Bulwark Bank directly opposite the Astor House on Barclay Street.

I struggled to my feet. Smoke boiled from the roof of the bank. Soot charred the brick above each shattered window. Where the front doors had been, I saw a small fire burning in the lobby.

I helped Franklin to his feet and he dusted off his kite. "Right bomb, wrong building."

I stared at the ruined structure. Why had Britt blown up the bank? The Khedive was still alive in his Astor House suite boiling off his liquids with Glorianna and Hilda. Nothing had changed.

A piece of paper landed in my hair. I plucked it out. A ten dollar bill. A sprinkle of money fluttered down. The sprinkle became a drizzle, the drizzle a shower, and the shower a torrent.

Cheering, Franklin snatched money from the air and stuffed it into his vest. "God helps those who help themselves. I don't have a job anymore, but maybe I won't need one."

I gathered up twenty-three dollars and put it in my purse. I didn't need more than that—didn't want it either. Around us people were singing, shouting, rejoicing, and gathering up money in their hats and pockets and shirts.

Gunshots split the celebration. Two men holding bags dashed from the bank. Police fired at them. The robbers shot back. Revelers ducked. They screamed. They fled. Others continued to harvest money. One thief looked familiar, large, wide, and tall. Could it be Britt? And Lockie? Is that what they wanted? To rob the bank? Of course, that's exactly what they wanted. The Khedive's funds were on deposit. Lockie had said so. "*Make him pay!*" Britt had said. Who knew he meant that literally?

Britt and Lockie had made it to the crowd. Now the police couldn't shoot without hitting an innocent. They holstered their guns and ran in pursuit. Britt and Lockie slammed into the mass of celebrants and pushed their way through. They seemed to have planned everything except their escape.

A mighty roar erupted behind me. Orange light illuminated the fountain and I turned to see flames leap into Professor Lowe's balloon.

With the police thirty yards behind them, Britt and Lockie, each carrying a leather satchel over his shoulder, were almost to the balloon. Finally understanding their heist, I sped toward the balloon too. "Britt," I shouted, "wait, don't leave me."

But they couldn't hear me over the rumble of flame and the tumult of the crowd cheering for them like spectators at a horse race.

Lowe cut the tethers with a knife. The balloon's basket tipped and shook, straining to break free. As Lowe bent to cut the final tether, Britt and Lockie reached the balloon.

"Wait," I shouted, still fifty feet away. "Wait, Britt, I'm coming with you."

Lockie threw in his satchel then heaved himself over the basket's edge. Lowe cut the last rope as Britt scrambled up the wicker and fell inside.

I reached them too late. "Britt," I screamed into the air, standing alone on the matted grass where the basket once rested. "Britt, don't leave me."

Thirty feet above, Britt's face appeared at the wicker's edge. Instantly, he disappeared then returned. A coil of rope dropped at my feet with a thump.

I stared at the uncoiling rope ascending silently into the blackness. What did Britt expect me to do? Haul the balloon back down to Earth? Scamper up like the boy in the Indian Rope Trick?

People gathered around me, thrilled by the prospect of aerial escape. A short distance into the crowd, a man pushed toward me, throwing the bystanders aside. He wore a yellow derby.

Driven by images of mad inmates and shivs, I snatched up the rope. Using my best shoelace knot, I tied the line around my waist and waited for the inevitable jerk. But the jerk never came. Instead, I was plucked gently off my feet.

And then I was flying.

Fearless I flew, wind in my hair, my face, my eyelashes. Below, people pointed. They waved. They shouted. I saw Athena, Pan, Hercules. Franklin cheered and shook his kite over his head. Men chased after the rope as it dragged along the grass. One of them was McCauley.

I looked above. Beneath balloon and flame, Britt leaned out of the basket. Hand over hand he hauled in the rope, and me with it. I was saved.

The line jerked. Thirty feet below, McCauley had caught the rope's end. Feet dangling, he was hoisting himself inch by inch into the sky toward me. His derby fell off and floated onto the cheering crowds below.

I panicked. The balloon was drifting northward toward City Hall, its cupola and clock growing ever bigger. McCauley's weight had slowed the balloon's ascent and, with me hanging only slightly above the treetops, I feared I would smash right into the clock tower.

Terror gripped me as the cupola's clock grew larger and larger—until I collided with it.

Upended by the impact, I seized the giant hour hand for support. McCauley hung under me six feet above the roof. The dozen or so police officers assembled there grabbed his shoes and pulled him into their midst. The effort ripped me from the hour hand and I too began to descend.

In the basket, Lockie joined Britt in the effort to reach me before the police. "Hold tight," Britt shouted, "we've almost got you."

There was nothing to say. I shook and twisted in an effort to break the rope free of the officers' grip. My purse, along with *Feminine Virtue*, dropped from my shoulder and struck a policeman on the head. He fell to the roof, unconscious. I relished the small victory, but now, only ten feet from their grasp, a sense of doom pervaded me.

Britt would never give me up. Somehow I knew that. But the fact remained that the police were winning the tug of war. In less than a minute, they'd have me. And even after they had me, they'd keep pulling until the balloon's basket was within their reach. Then they'd climb onto the basket and drag Britt and Lockie and Lowe from it. Worst of all, Britt would allow them to do so. He'd welcome it. He'd fight for me. I was sure of that too.

Five feet from their grasp, I knew what had to be done. I took Franklin's watch from my pocket and opened the penknife on the end of the chain. As I put the blade to the rope, I looked up at Britt one last time.

Knife in hand, he was sawing the last cut on the rope.

I fell on top of the officers. Above me, silhouetted by the moon as large and bright as my father's face smiling over me in my bed, Professor Lowe's Transatlantic Balloon shot into the starry sky with Britt and Lockie and Lowe leaning helplessly over the wicker as I was led away in manacles.

Chapter Thirty-Four

Violet Obermyer sat upright on her bench as the double cellblock doors clanged open and I was led into Ludlow Street Jail, Woman's Section. Bedraggled, still spattered with egg, the famous writer looked much the same as when I'd seen her in the office of *Talmadge's Weekly* early this morning.

"Jenny, darling, is that you?"

What does one say to the prime source of one's misery? "Yes, Violet, it's me."

She shook the girl beside her, slumped over against the wall. "Cleo, wake up, it's Jenny."

The officer opened their cell and pushed me inside. Violet and Cleo rose to meet me. We hugged.

"Regular homecoming in here," the guard wisecracked before locking the door and leaving.

Violet sat. "Cleo told me of Laura's death."

My fists clenched. "McCauley will pay for his crime, I swear. Did he arrest you too?"

She nodded. "Not five minutes after leaving the newspaper this morning. I never did meet John."

"The crapper salesman?"

"Sanitary appliances," Cleo said, sniffing.

Violet sighed forlornly. "He'll never marry me now."

"Goodbye baking pies and making beds," I said.

"And producing offspring," Cleo added.

Violet kissed Cleo on the cheek. "Yes, but there's still Free Love."

Cleo winced. She wiped her cheek with a sleeve then turned to me. "Have you heard anything about Abigail?"

"She returned to Brooklyn with her father."

"Abigail was always a smart girl," Violet said. "When did McCauley arrest you?"

"Thirty minutes ago," I said.

"What happened to Glorianna?" Cleo asked. "Is she safe?"

"She's with the Khedive."

Violet pressed a palm to her forehead. "White slavery?"

"She went willingly," I said

Cleo gasped. "Merciful heavens."

I rubbed my waist where the balloon's rope had made it tender. "It's a long story."

Shouts and curses turned our gaze toward the cellblock doors, which rattled and shook then opened with a bang. Four guards entered, struggling to control a gentleman in a dark suit who flailed about like a trout on a hook. As the guards pushed the man along, one of his Cuban heel boots caught beneath a guard's leg and all five men tumbled forward onto the floor.

Cuban heel boots?

I looked again. Frock coat, bow tie, long pants—*Glorianna?*

Before the guards could rise, Glorianna was on her feet in a boxing stance, fists circling like a professional.

"You reprobates have violated my rights."

One of the guards lunged at her from a crouch, but she stepped aside and punched the man's cheek. Flattened by the blow, he crawled to his fellows on hands and knees.

Knuckles up, Glorianna danced from foot to foot. "Who wants a broken nose?"

The guards huddled together, unsure what to do.

"Have you imbeciles learned your lesson? Release me this instant. I'm a presidential candidate."

Three more guards appeared at the doorway. Bolstered by fresh troops, all seven spread in a line and prepared to rush Glorianna.

Shouting some dubious war cry, they lunged forward. Glorianna sidestepped through the door of an open cell and shut it behind her. The guards slammed into the iron bars with a sickening clang. Two fell to the floor unconscious. The others pitched and faltered, nursing contusions and scrapes. Having accomplished their goal, however, the survivors picked up the injured and retreated through the cellblock doors.

Glorianna sat on the bench in the cell and fanned her face with her hands.

"Are you injured?" Cleo asked.

"They got the worst of it," she said, panting.

"I thought you were with the Khedive," I said.

"I was, and poised to unload twenty thousand shares of worthless Erie Railroad stock on the fool, but your Romeo ruined everything."

Cleo perked up. "Jenny has a Romeo who ruined everything?"

"He blew up Bulwark Bank," Glorianna said.

"Who would blow up a bank?" Violet asked.

"He's not my Romeo," I said, "just a scoundrel I met."

"Do you always tie yourself to scoundrels' aerial balloons?" Glorianna asked.

Cleo stood. "Your Romeo has an aerial balloon and you tied yourself to it?"

"He's not my Romeo, and I was only trying to escape from McCauley."

Cleo sat down. "Damnation, I've missed everything."

"So," Glorianna said, ticking off each point on her fingers. "Mister just-a-scoundrel-you-met blew up the bank, stole the Khedive's money, ruined my stock sale, fled in a balloon—which you tied yourself to— then cut the rope and abandoned you to the police. Does that sum it up?"

"Apparently, you saw everything," I said.

Glorianna dragged her hand through the air. "Everyone in City Hall Park saw everything."

"Poor Jenny," Cleo said, shaking her head. "Dumped by her Romeo."

"He's not my Romeo. And I was cutting the rope—he just cut it first."

Violet patted my shoulder. "Men are pigs, darling."

"No," I insisted, "I had the knife in my hand. I was cutting the rope."

"Of course, you were," Violet said. "We don't need men anyway."

I crossed my arms over my chest. "Never mind, what happened to Hilda?"

"Shrewd girl," Glorianna said. "Quite a business sense."

Shrewd girl? Business sense? Was she talking about the *gute* girl from Pottsville?

Glorianna continued. "She's conducting business with the Commodore."

"You mean the Commodore ran off with Hilda?"

"He didn't *run* off. I told you, it's a professional arrangement."

"The oldest professional arrangement," I said.

Glorianna rubbed her forehead. "From time to time the Commodore makes a temporary business liaison."

"With younger, prettier women," Violet offered.

"Isn't his wife forty-five years his junior?" Cleo asked.

Glorianna cleared her throat. "You'll see, the Commodore will bail me out within the hour."

"And what about Dorian?" I asked.

"You won't be seeing him for a while," Glorianna said. "When the Khedive's ship sails tomorrow, Dorian will be on it. He's Egypt's new finance minister."

"Wait a minute," I said. "If you were safe with the Khedive, how did McCauley arrest you?"

"The Commodore sent me downstairs to retrieve the Erie Stock portfolio from the Astor House safe. The portfolio turned out to be a treatise on birth control. McCauley bribed someone on the hotel staff to set me up then pinched me in the lobby for holding illicit material."

The cellblock doors clanged open. Checkered pants, black eyes, cigar, derby, bloody bandage where *Feminine Virtue* had kissed his cheek: McCauley stepped inside. "Well, what have we here? Miss Duncan, Miss Obermyer, Miss Crispin—I haven't kept you ladies waiting, have I?"

"I'll see you hang for Laura's death," I hissed.

"The view won't be that good from your cell at the Tombs." He turned to Glorianna, smiled, and tipped his hat. "Mrs. Satan, my pleasure."

Glorianna sneered. "I wouldn't smile too long, McCauley; the Commodore will be here to bail me out any minute."

McCauley laughed. "Don't count on it. The Commodore is the one who set you up by having the stocks in the portfolio switched for birth control material." He swung to Violet and Cleo and me. "As for you three, your indictments are right here. Fifteen counts of disseminating information on birth control and contraception through the mail."

Glorianna's chin rose. "*Talmadge's Weekly* has published at least thirty articles on birth control and contraception."

McCauley's ironed lips spread to a grin. "Thanks, but I already have enough to put these ladies away for ten years."

He motioned with his hand and two guards entered the cellblock, one holding a shotgun, the other keys. The one with the keys opened our cell then locked manacles around each of our wrists.

"I'll return for you shortly," McCauley said to Glorianna, alone in her cell.

Violet left the cell first, followed by Cleo. As I exited behind them, a familiar voice came from the hall beyond the cellblock.

"Darlink, you look so good in dat shirt. Vat color is it?"

A second later, rouged and wigged, Marm appeared in the doorway with guards front and rear. "Look," she said, seeing me, "is skinny *shiksa*. Vat you doink here?"

"Get her in a cell," McCauley barked. "I'm trying to transfer these prisoners to the Tombs."

When she got close, Marm threw her arm around McCauley.

"Darlink, vat is big hurry. Party is just starting."

McCauley tried to squirm free but Marm pinched his shirt. "Who sell you such ugly shirt? Tell me, darlink, vat color is dis?"

"Get this bitch off of me," McCauley yelled, trying to wriggle from Marm's grip.

As the guards attempted to grab her, Marm reached into McCauley's coat and pulled out his pistol. She slammed the barrel into one guard's head and elbowed the other in the face. They dropped to the floor.

Stunned, McCauley staggered backward. The guard with the shotgun pointed it at Marm and pulled the trigger. She slapped the barrel aside and both charges blew into the wall near McCauley's head. Marm wrenched the gun from the guard's hands. He lunged at her but she swung the shotgun hard, and the butt caught him in the temple. The last guard, seeing his fellows unconscious, dropped his keys and dove through the double cellblock doors. Marm shoved the spent shotgun through the door handles, making it impossible for anyone else to enter.

"You won't get out of here alive," McCauley said, picking a stray shotgun pellet from his face.

Marm leveled the pistol at his belly. "Your reign of terror is over, McCauley."

McCauley leaned toward her. "Who the hell are you?"

Marm swept the wig from her head.

"Britt!" I shouted.

Britt stepped closer to McCauley. "I should have killed you years ago for raping those two girls."

"You're as good as dead, Salter. There's no way out."

Britt punched him in the face. McCauley's head snapped back and hit the wall. Before he could fall, Britt caught him by the waist. He pointed at Violet and Cleo. "You ladies get into the corner. Pull that bench over top of you. Jenny, come here."

I rushed to his side. As Cleo and Violet huddled in the corner and Glorianna followed their lead, Britt pushed me into the opposite corner. He settled over me and held McCauley on top of him like a shield.

"Hang on," he whispered. "*Fifty-eight, fifty-nine—*"

A colossal boom of smoke and dust filled the cellblock. My ears rang and my eyes burned. Before the smoke cleared, Britt stood and threw McCauley's lifeless body to the floor. He lifted me to my feet. I wiped the dust from my eyes to find a six-by-six-foot hole gaped in the wall. Cold wind swept through it, clearing the dusty air in seconds.

Violet and Cleo climbed from under the bench as Britt and I stood at the hole. We were three stories above the street. "What now?" I asked.

Britt pointed up. The basket of Lowe's balloon hovered just out of reach. Britt seized a line and dragged it down.

Gloves and helmet, goggles and mustache, Lowe saluted as he came into view. Beside him, Lockie handed Britt a rope who tied it to the bars of a cell.

Britt picked the keys off the floor and unlocked our manacles. Cleo scrambled into the basket with Lowe's help. Lockie took Violet's hands and pulled while Britt pushed her posterior over the basket's edge. With the others safe, Britt lifted me by my waist and placed me gently into the basket.

As he prepared to climb into the basket, Glorianna called out from her cell. "What about me? You're not leaving me here, are you?"

Britt tossed her the key ring. "I heard somewhere that only by pursuing our own selfish goals will the world become a better place."

He turned and vaulted into the basket. Lockie cut the rope that held the balloon in place. Lowe triggered the burner, and Britt released a dozen sandbags.

My stomach dropped to my knees as the balloon ascended into the night sky. Below us, torches and lanterns massed in the street.

Chapter Thirty-Five

The last thing I saw of Ludlow Street Jail was Glorianna leaning out the jagged hole shaking her fist skyward. Soon after, lit by a brilliant moon, New York City shrank smaller and smaller until it became a craftsman's miniature surrounded by sparkling waters.

Gentle winds swept the balloon northeast. The East River passed beneath us like a shimmering snake and the twin towers of Roebling's bridge to Brooklyn moved like the hands of a great clock as we drifted toward Long Island. What destination lie ahead I could not tell, but so unique and wonderful was the journey that had I died just then, I would have considered my life well spent.

Britt placed his arm around me and I realized that, despite the flame burning not ten feet above me, I was shivering from the cold. He handed me a coat, a pair of pants, and a bright red shirt.

"I borrowed them from Lockie. It's the best I could do on short notice."

I took the clothes and, as Lockie, Cleo, Lowe and Violet turned away, I stripped off my blue silk chemise and stood naked to the moon and stars and Britt. He stared at me fully. Far from shame, I savored his gaze. But the chill was strong and I pulled on the clothes. They felt wonderful and we laughed at each other, Britt in a dress and me in pants.

We floated many hours above dark land and moonlit water. Eventually, at 6:00AM, the sun pierced the horizon like a diamond ring. In the morning's light, I rubbed the paint from Britt's cheeks and the rouge from his lips. He pulled the dress over his head to reveal a blue shirt and brown pants. At noon, Lowe cut the flame and we began to descend. The balloon landed near a barn in a pasture overlooking an ocean glistening like hobnails.

"Where are we?" I asked.

"Lloyd's Harbor, Long Island. About thirty miles east of the city."

Lockie tied off the ropes and Britt gave each man a satchel. From the barn, Lowe led a team of horses hitched to a wagon with brass tanks and gauges. Letters painted on the side of the wagon read: *Professor Lowe's Antarctic Ice Machine*. He walked the team to the balloon and stopped the wagon beside Violet and me.

"Antarctic Ice Machine?" I asked.

Lowe struck a pose, his forefinger thrust skyward. "Young lady, Professor Lowe's Antarctic Ice Machine operates on the principle of expansion and contraction of gases first set down in 1824 by Nicholas Carnot. My dear girl, have you any idea what people in the southern climes will pay to enjoy an ice cold mint julep on a hot day, not to mention preserve perishable foods for weeks, possibly months?"

"No, Professor Lowe," I said, grinning, "tell us."

As the professor took a deep breath, Violet clamped her hand over his mouth. "Thaddeus. It's time to go."

Lowe helped Violet onto the wagon seat. "Have fun making beds and baking pies," I called out.

"And producing offspring," Violet shouted as the wagon trundled off.

Cleo walked over and took my hands. "I owe you my life. Thank you, Jenny."

"Where will you go?" I asked.

"Lockie has arranged a boat to carry us across the sound to Bridgeport, Connecticut. From there we'll take the train to San Francisco. And then, who knows?"

We hugged. Astride the saddle of his horse, Lockie came up next to her. "Six has always been my lucky number," he said, eyes sparkling. He took Cleo's arm and swung her up behind him.

As they galloped away, I returned to Britt. He poured the last drops of coal spirits into the balloon's fuel tanks and set the empty can on the ground. I kissed him. "What now?"

Hands on my waist, he lifted me into the basket of the balloon and climbed in beside me. From a canvas bag he withdrew a leather helmet and goggles and placed them in my hand. "Remember all those exotic people and lands you wanted to see?"

As I pulled the helmet over my hair, a voice behind us spoke in a velvety Southern accent. "Mr. Salter, you deprived me of my vengeance on President Grant. Now, sir, I will take my vengeance on you."

Britt and I turned together. A tall, thin man with a haggard face and narrow beard stood beside the basket. His bony fingers held a revolver, hammer cocked.

Britt pushed me behind him. "How did you find us?"

"It's not hard to follow a large balloon in bright moonlight, sir. I rode all night."

Mouth firm, Britt nodded. "You never wanted to make a grand statement or change the president's policies toward the South. You just wanted Grant dead."

The man burned. "Grant thwarted me at Fort Donelson in West Tennessee, and at Vicksburg. If not for him, those would have been *my* victories and Jefferson Davis would have promoted me to replace Lee. As commander of the Army of the Confederacy, I would have led the South to victory."

It took a minute, but by sight and word I recognized the southerner as the Confederate General Archer Gideon. Enraged, I stepped from behind Britt. "Even Jefferson Davis had more sense than to promote a butcher who allowed men under his command to slaughter three hundred Negro Union soldiers after they surrendered."

Gideon's gaunt face reddened. "In the South, Madame, ladies do not address men with such disrespect."

"Southern ladies," I quipped, "have been slaves far too long. They also need emancipation."

Gideon glared at me a moment then tipped his hat and smiled as a gentleman might do when passing a lady on the sidewalk. "I had planned to kill only Mr. Salter. Now, it will be my pleasure to kill the both of y'all."

To have come this far and conquered so many obstacles only to be murdered by a lunatic general out to avenge his personal defeat seemed a terrible waste. As General Gideon raised his pistol, and I braced myself for the inevitable, his head gave an unexpected jerk. An instant later, a distinct crack sounded in the distance.

The general wavered on his feet, body limp, hanging in the air like a thrown ball having reached the apex of its flight. First, the pistol fell from his hand, then his arm collapsed, and finally, like that thrown ball, he dropped to the ground. Blood pumped from holes on either side of his head.

Confronted with such horror, I buried my face in Britt's chest. His warm hand on my neck comforted me. After a minute passed, he turned my chin and bid me to look at something. On a distant knoll, standing next to Cleo and the horse, Lockie waved what appeared to be a very long rifle above his head. I waved back.

Britt donned his helmet. We kissed again then he jerked the cord, and atomized coal spirits ignited in the burner. When the balloon strained against its tether like a wild horse against its bridle, Britt severed the rope and we shot into the air. Below us, General Gideon's body grew smaller and smaller until it blended into the vegetation and terrain. Long Island too eventually disappeared, and soon the only thing I could see anywhere around us was the deep, deep blue of the Atlantic Ocean.

A week later, physically exhausted and out of food, water, and coal spirits, we landed near Fort William, Scotland. The next day, Edinburgh received us with bagpipes and full military honors. Four days after that, in London, we met the queen. Across the channel, a train carried our deflated balloon to a champagne celebration in Paris after which we toured Berlin in a blitz of beer and waltzes. Rome, still giddy with national unification, honored us with wine and opera. In Naples, we sold the balloon and bought a yacht.

The Cobbler's Daughter

The sun dips low on the sea as I sit on the afterdeck. Stromboli smokes in the distance. I rest my bare feet on the rail and close my eyes. Above the wind, I hear the ping and tap of the rigging and the slap of canvas. Seabirds cry their reedy songs. Amid the rattle of plates and pans, the smell of green onions and shrimp wafts through the open companionway.

Britt bellows orders from the ship's wheel. Ignoring him, the crew chants as they hoist the topsail. I feel the ship catch wind and heel, rising from the water as she picks up speed. Tonight, we pass through the Straits of Messina. Once in the open Mediterranean, there will be no stopping until we reach the Holy Land.

All the major newspapers and magazines want my articles. I still have the black, practical boots my father made for me but I seldom wear them, preferring on land to wear my riding pants and knee boots. Britt has taught me to shoot and fight, and I have convinced him that a woman's intellect is every bit as sharp as a man's.

Well, almost convinced him.

Author's Note

My first goal in writing *The Cobbler's Daughter* was to tell a good story. My second goal was historical accuracy. To that end, the astute reader will notice many similarities between the character, Glorianna Talmadge, and the real life feminist, Victoria Woodhull, the first woman to run for president. The reader will also notice similarities between General Archer Gideon and the notorious Confederate General, Nathan Bedford Forrest. Thaddeus Lowe, President Grant, the Egyptian Khedive, Molly de Ford, Marm Mandelbaum, Cornelius Vanderbilt, and others play themselves. I encourage those interested in the actual lives of these real life figures to read more about them. Except for the story's main plot, such things as the Great Whaling Disaster, Black Friday, the first woman to run for president in 1872, Professor Lowe's attempt to cross the Atlantic, the Society for the Suppression of Vice's reign of terror, the explosion at City Point, and the Battle of the Crater, to name a few, were all real events.

G. S. Singer

About the Author

G. S. Singer grew up in South Florida's Redland district where he camped, hiked, and devoured every science fiction novel he could find. At the University of Florida, he studied creative writing under authors, Harry Crews and Smith Kirkpatrick. After graduation, Singer co-founded a small-town newspaper filling the roles of reporter, copy writer, editor, and even cartoonist. Praised for his wry humor, intricate plotting, and unforgettable characters, Singer's fiction has been honored in both the Daphne du Maurier, Kiss of Death competition and the Amazon Breakout Novel Award. When he isn't plunging unsuspecting heroes into impossible situations, Singer enjoys the tranquility of the North Georgia Mountains, where he lives with his wife and children.

Enjoy Other titles from Fireship Press

Last Dance in Kabul
Ken Czech

The Ultimate Dance Between Love and War

When his superiors ignore his warnings of an impending Afghan insurrection in 1841, British army captain Reeve Waterton vows never to return to Kabul. But then he rescues strong-willed Sarah Kane from an ambush and his plans for civilian life and self-preservation unravel around him

"Reeve Waterton, a dashing rogue, is a true hero who stands among the most valiant officers of British fiction. Sarah Kane is an assertive woman assured of her own mind yet vulnerable in her heart. Together they spark the blaze that energizes *Last Dance in Kabul.*"

—**Rex Griffin,** historical writer.

Straight Uphill: A Tale of Love and Chocolate
Jess Wells

In a hilltop Italian village, women chocolatiers work the improbable magic of love and chocolate…

After tragedy strikes, brokenhearted Gretchen takes a holiday in a hilltop Italian village to seek peace and solitude. Through chance, she meets Bettina, an elderly woman estranged from her legacy as a chocolatier. Gretchen soon finds herself wrapped in the aromas of chocolate and caramel and butter and wine, as villagers past and present, question all aspects of love that send her on a journey of self-discovery and healing. But will Gretchen truly be able to leave the past behind and open her heart again to life and love, or will she be content to drown her sorrows in chocolate?

"This book is a gem. It is delightful proof that a literary novel can be a deeply satisfying page-turner!" —**Mark Wiederanders**, author of *Stevenson's Treasure.*

For the Finest in Nautical and Historical Fiction and Non-Fiction
www.FireshipPress.com

Interesting • Informative • Authoritative

All Fireship Press books are available through leading bookstores and wholesalers worldwide.

CPSIA information can be obtained
at www.ICGtesting.com
Printed in the USA
FSHW021401260719
60370FS